PLEASE RETURN

TO

RKO STUDIO

LIBRARY

A - 4065

Books by Robert Shaplen

A FOREST OF TIGERS

[*1956*]

FREE LOVE AND HEAVENLY SINNERS

[*1954*]

A CORNER OF THE WORLD

[*1949*]

THESE ARE *Borzoi Books, published in New York by*
ALFRED A. KNOPF

A Forest of Tigers

A Forest of Tigers

by Robert Shaplen

New York

ALFRED·A·KNOPF

1956

L. C. catalog card number: 55-9269

© Robert Shaplen, 1955

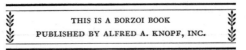

THIS IS A BORZOI BOOK
PUBLISHED BY ALFRED A. KNOPF, INC.

Copyright 1955 by Robert Shaplen. All rights reserved. No part of this book may be reproduced in any form without permission in writing from the publisher, except by a reviewer who may quote brief passages in a review to be printed in a magazine or newspaper. Manufactured in the United States of America. Published simultaneously in Canada by McClelland and Stewart Limited.

FIRST EDITION

This book is dedicated

to my mother,

and to the memory

of my father,

who fought for freedom

against tyranny everywhere. . . .

THE ACTION *of the novel takes place midway in the decade between 1945 and 1955. The* MAIN CHARACTERS *are:*

ADAM PATCH, an American official with consular status at the Legation in Saigon.

MR. SMYTHE, the American Minister.

ROBERT GOODENOUGH, a Vice-Consul.

NELL FINCH, Mr. Smythe's secretary.

TRAN PHAN DANG, a Vietnamese doctor.

GENEVIEVE BROUILLARD, a Eurasian resident of Saigon.

CAU MINH THIEN, a cadre (officer) of the Committee of the South and the head of several terror squads, all part of the Communist-dominated Vietminh, the revolutionary front engaged in a war against the French in Indo-China and seeking ultimately to create a Communist state. Opposing the Vietminh are the French colonial administration, the French and French-directed forces, and the French-sponsored government of Vietnamese, headed by the Emperor Bao Dai.

THE POLITICAL OFFICER, a northern Vietminh cadre.

LI KWAN-SEN, a Chinese gambling king and night-club owner with convenient political connections.

JACQUES LACASSE, an opportunistic Corsican, a hotel manager and night-club operator.

PAUL REMY, a prominent French official in the High Commissioner's colonial administration.

IRVING LOCKMAN, a director of the United States Economic Cooperation Administration.

The term Vietnam *is used by all partisans as the proper name of the country, embracing what used to be the French colony of Cochin-*

◇◇

China in the south, of which Saigon is the capital; the protectorate of Annam in the center; and the protectorate of Tonkin in the north, where Hanoi is the capital. Vietnamese *applies to the people of Vietnam, whether they be pro-Vietminh, pro-Bao Dai, or neutral.*

A Forest of Tigers

Chapter I

THE grenade was thrown shortly before noon. It was the third one in ten days and Adam knew what it was as soon as he heard it, a low, flat burst, like the cracking of a whip across the hot sky. He was two blocks away, walking up rue Catinat toward the cathedral, and he had stopped momentarily at the window of a silver-shop. The air was very still, with a quality that was both motionless and limp. The leaves of the plane trees hung limply in the void, and in the layers of light the motes were scarcely turning. In the seats of their *cyclos*, their straw hats pulled across their faces, the *cycloists* slumbered.

Adam had bent down to examine a bracelet, the red stone of its dragon's eye regarding him like evil. The heat swabbed his face, making him sneeze. His whole chest shook, and the stone eye, a blood-red ball, spun in its silver socket. Just then the explosion sounded. He straightened and whirled, and his first thought was: "Which café is it?" A month ago two Vietnamese had been blown up at the table where, fifteen minutes before, he had been having coffee and cakes. Yet one continued to sit in the cafés. . . .

He began walking rapidly and could smell the smoke before he saw it, twisting like a small tornado under the café's low roof, wreathing the gold-leafed, red-tongued serpents on the ceiling and wafting out into the street. Death lay in the doorway, in two solitary heaps, the bodies of a Vietnamese and a French sergeant, a member of the Foreign Legion, Adam noted, from the green V on his blood-soaked blouse. It was a café he knew well, where the cakes were

◇◇◇

always excellent. A crowd had gathered, and the flies had begun to circle the bodies, that of the soldier drawing more, possibly because of the larger pool of blood around it. The blood was already flowing, thickly and crookedly, into the gutter, where someone had thrown part of the grenade's broken core. Someone else, a waiter, now closed the iron shutters.

The crowd was strangely quiet, more curious than aroused, but less awed than that other one, Adam thought, which might have seen him stretched out on the ground the way this Frenchman was. He remembered those faces, having run back, and the feeling of wondering if, with a white man dead, they would have looked any different, staring. Now he knew they would have been the same. The expressions were as fixed as the voices were silent, though the eyes were concentrating on the figure of the legionnaire, whose size, while average, seemed overlong next to the smaller native body.

From the police station up the block a man in civilian clothes emerged and came walking down the middle of the street. He carried a blanket on each arm. When he reached the front of the café, he covered the two corpses, without touching them. Then he walked slowly away. The blankets were darkly stained. They had been used before, apparently, for a similar purpose.

There was a voice at Adam's side. "Three were injured as well," it said. "They have been taken to a hospital."

Adam looked down at an Annamite in a Western suit.

"The police were very prompt about furnishing a car," the voice murmured.

The Annamite paused, still staring at the covered dead. "The grenade was thrown by a boy on a bicycle. He was riding extremely fast." He pointed with a finger to the edge of the square and slowly shook his head. "There," he said, "he vanished. I saw him throw the thing, and go. He was very young. It was surprising how young he actually was. It was possible to see."

The man now looked up at Adam. A drop of perspiration hovering near his ear ran quickly down his cheek.

◇◇

"Younger than—" he said, and suddenly stopped.

Adam nodded and began to walk slowly toward the opening of the square. He felt the need of a swim more than ever. The Anna-mite was following, a foot or so behind. "The terrorists are becom-ing more bold," he was saying. It was evident that he wanted to talk to someone. "I suppose there will be many such occurrences—they are bound to take place." The voice fell off as the space between the two men widened. "Nevertheless, the use of the children remains quite astonishing. . . ."

The moment of violence was over. A calm had settled, like a curtain quickly dropped; but in place of the stillness there was a flow of activity, as if the grenade had set back the siesta clocks. Death, Adam thought, had become at once so casual and abrupt that one had to accept it, deal with it as a matter of course, weigh its schedule and gauge its next assault. Its vagaries reminded him of a game of Russian roulette: now the pistol had spun, the bullet had entered the wild friend's head, the chamber lay smoking and empty; the act of tempting fate became part of a grim statistic, a talisman of all their lives, which seemed perpetually threatened here. What he had just witnessed, of course, was the war itself, this kind of war that could go on endlessly, for thirty or a hundred years, of which the throwing of a grenade by a boy was as much a part as the brutal fighting in the north; as a napalm bomb hurled blindly on the jungle, as the poisoning of a plate of food, or as the hemor-rhage induced by mixing tiger whiskers in a bowl of rice. Ulti-mately, by accident or whim, they might all be destroyed, animals as well as men, and life in the interim would be the survival of the luckiest. . . .

The straw chairs were being reoccupied on the sidewalks, and the youngsters with their shoeshine boxes and their trays of shelled peanuts were scampering back and forth, shouting imprecations. The flower-market unfurled. Adam regarded the slim Annamite women who floated by like petals in their softly jouncing, silken trousers. It was hard to believe the flare of violence, harder even to consider its source. Yet one had a vision of the young bicycle-rider on the edge of town, squatting in a mud hut over his rice-bowl. At dusk he would be dispatched again, with another grenade wrapped in a handkerchief in his pocket. . . . .

The Annamite had come back to his side. "Do you mind if I walk with you?" he asked. "We seem to be going in the same direction."

He was small, Adam saw, even for his race, but the steps he took were surprisingly long, as if he were a boy meditating about bigness. His suit was brown, and he wore a white tie with etched figures. A pair of faded horn-rimmed glasses fitted him snugly. There was a look of cheap newness about his black leather shoes. He looked like a professional man, a French civil servant; but there was something else, a sense of wonder.

The keening of the midday sirens made them jointly quicken their step. One could see as well as feel the heat, rolling toward them as it rubbed its way into the buildings. Now the stores had begun to close, though a few of them, those run by the Hindu merchants still willing to exchange money in the face of French warnings, stayed open, the owners poised in velvet slippers behind the counters, their faces impassively innocent, yet darkly eager underneath their turbans.

Two trucks filled with French soldiers sputtered across the square and halted near the center. The soldiers debouched and fell into formation. Then they marched off in separate files toward the sides. As if by a silent signal, all other movement ceased. Everyone waited for the inspection. Self-consciously, a few felt for bulges in their pockets.

"It is a strange thing, even when one has dealt with death, to see it take place so directly, so—uncontrollably," the Annamite murmured. He spoke without turning his head, keeping it lowered. They were beyond the area of search.

For the first time Adam replied, his question provoked as much by some delicate attribute in the man's manner as by the remark. "You are a doctor?"

The Annamite nodded.

"Your practice is here, in Saigon?"

There was a shrug, and a Western gesture, a slight lifting of both hands and an extending of the short fingers, with the palms inward. Adam said nothing more. They were heading toward the river, into a sudden whiff of salt breeze quickly submerged in the smell of food that rose from pots off the side streets, where the soldiers had not reached. The dry, burnt odor of the charcoal blended with the pungent mixture of fish and rice and vegetables and floated, almost visibly, toward the great hot grill of the sky. Along the curbs and in the doorways, squatting on their haunches, the people laughed and chattered as they ate.

"One would say," the Annamite explained, "that I am in search of a practice, or of something else—a cure."

"A cure for uncontrollable death?" Adam smiled, in spite of himself.

The doctor did not return the smile. "I do not mean to be mysterious," he said. His voice caught, so that he had to clear his throat. "But I am more interested in what can be avoided."

"There's a need for preventives," Adam said, "for antidotes."

The Annamite grinned. A large sedan with white-walled tires and flying an American flag passed up the street and swung toward the Hotel Continental. When it came to a halt, two officers in suntans climbed out. The empty car slid off, past the children's garden. He watched it go.

"And you?" he asked, finally. "You are an American?"

Adam said: "Yes."

"One could tell," the doctor said. "One could tell it was not French."

"We are easily spotted."

"I have not seen many Americans. In the north there are not

many." There was a pause. "In Hanoi, that is," the doctor added, hastily.

"Your practice is in Hanoi, then?"

"You see—" the doctor began, and stopped, uncertainly. There was more than shyness, more than diffidence.

"We are increasingly on display, everywhere," Adam said.

"It is a proper thing," the Annamite replied, with enthusiasm.

"A view not universally accepted." Adam laughed.

The doctor looked up. "But of course!" he said. "It is the truth. I have seen, myself . . ."

"It will take a long time, just the same, to be everywhere so true," Adam said.

"Ah, a long time, yes," the doctor replied, suddenly sighing, "to make up for the hundred years of neglect." He paused again. From off on the right they could now see the soldiers, pushing the suspects into the trucks. The doctor glanced twice, then quickly looked away. "It will be different, however," he said. "For the Americans, it will be different."

"One must still consider the French."

"I do not think so," the doctor said flatly. After a moment's reflection he added: "It should no longer be a matter of considering or of not considering."

"If there's time enough, and patience—" Adam began. He found himself unable to finish the sentence.

The Annamite appeared to be deliberating. "There is a contest here, you understand, between the patient and the impatient." He spoke with sudden though modulated forcefulness.

Adam waited.

"It is more than that, of course," the doctor continued. "There are various contests, and many complications. Each season they multiply."

"Yes," Adam said.

"There was ignorance alone at first." The doctor had grown

quite solemn, and for a moment he seemed hardly aware of Adam's presence. "After the long war the complications began, and also the impatience. It was not to be avoided, perhaps."

"No," said Adam.

"Now it is more difficult than before."

"To stop the impatience?"

"To determine which of it is justified." He hesitated, then opened his mouth, but quickly closed it. All he finally said was: "It will depend—"

"Yes," Adam said. "There will be luck involved, naturally."

So softly that Adam scarcely heard, the Annamite said: "There are those who would kill the patient"—he was unaware of the play on words—"but there remains a cure. . . ." Again the voice dropped off. They had reached the far side of the square, and Adam halted abruptly.

"You'll have to excuse me," he said. "I've come too far."

"Oh, I am sorry." In the glare of sunlight the doctor seemed dazzlingly white and tinier, like a tumbling stone.

Adam stood in the street, half-turned. "A grenade is reason enough for forgetting." He lifted his hand in a gesture of salute. "Well, then," he said, and waved once more.

Behind him, in the glare, he heard the Annamite murmuring: "Yes, good-by."

There was the awkwardness of a sudden break, the embarrassment after a moment too quickly captured, now too suddenly dispersed. Adam walked quickly and cut diagonally across the north end of the square. He had left the Legation at noon and it was almost one o'clock. The Cercle Sportif would already be crowded. A feeling of enervation came over him, and a sense of grotesquerie, which the huge face of His Majesty Bao Dai, looking down from the top of the Assembly building, enhanced. The Emperor was back on the Riviera, where he was bound to stay as long as the weather lasted, or at least until he wrested another small concession from the

French. The negotiations had dragged into months. The everlasting battle of face and pride was slowly sapping the energies of them all; each week's fresh imponderable, like a drug, was creating a tolerance to crisis. The very atmosphere had grown redundant, the claims and counterclaims, the rumors. More than anywhere he had been, time and space seemed to Adam foreshortened here, to be caught as in an amber-locked void. Yesterday's fallen fort became the object of today's crusade. "Crusade" was a word that had come more and more to be used in the communiqués.

The artillery sounded from across the river. At dawn and at dusk, and once or twice a day between, the shells came, as if by rote. Occasionally they struck near the waterfront, but they seldom reached the shore. One got used to the sound, as to everything else. Drinking and debate continued unimpeded. From their river rooms the Americans made bets where the splashes would occur, while the veterinarian from the Economic Co-operation Administration strummed his ukulele the louder and sang his lewdest songs in counterpoint.

The grenades were something else, Adam reflected. In the last two months the number thrown in the city, or in the two cities, Saigon and the adjacent Chinese city of Cholon, had more than doubled. The increase had coincided with the Communists' seizure of the northern forts, which would broaden the area along the border where the Chinese could funnel supplies to the Vietminh. If the terror here was in concert, there was also a peculiar combination of premeditated and unpremeditated attack. For the first time, it seemed to him, the Vietminh was boldly determined to show its hand. By hurling grenades into crowded theaters as well as into private homes, killing Vietnamese at random as well as by design, the terrorists had apparently decided to frighten the people of the two cities into acceptance of their program; or at least into mute neutrality. And whether or not it was true, as the French now claimed, that Americans were also on the assassination lists, it was

◇◇

a fact that the Vietminh broadcasts had become equally vituperative toward them both. It was possible, Adam thought, that the intelligence reports were correct. More likely, the French were bluffing. To create the appearance of a solid front, it was proper tactics to make one's benefactors nervous by embrace.

There had, as a matter of fact, been no open attempts on Americans as yet; at any rate—Adam smiled to himself—none that could be determined. He had begun to walk faster and now reconstructed again, as he had found himself doing at odd moments ever since the event, the scene in that earlier café where he had been sitting. It had been late in the afternoon, about six. He had chosen a table halfway in, by a pillar near the counter of chocolates. A mistake, of course, to select the same area regularly, to indulge in even so slight an open habit; but there had been a fan overhead that had seemed to gyrate—it may only have been his imagination—a little faster than the others. So minor a benison became a basis for decision.

Was it also merely his imagination that for five days previous he had seen, on the opposite side of the café, a man he knew casually as one of the information officials, a *fonctionnaire* whose duties had seemed to him rather vaguely defined, who had come to him once, months ago, for routine knowledge readily available, and had lingered, with an odd mixture of ingratiating politeness and scorn, to discuss some abstruse point of colonial economic philosophy? Adam had hardly seen him since. But then in the café, for those successive days, or at least for most of that prior week, the same man had silently sipped his coffee, seeming, Adam recollected, to glance over now and then, but making no effort to start a conversation. Once they had nodded. On the afternoon of the explosion the man had not appeared.

A sudden nausea in his throat made Adam stop walking. He took out a handkerchief and wiped his tongue, then mopped his hands and wrists. Could the incident have been planned that way? Was

◇◇

it, after all, so inconceivable? If he had suggested this to the Minister, the Minister would have laughed outright, in that thin, unmirthful way of his. Or, his face tightening, he would have said: "Come now, Patch, we're not all of us worth killing. . . ." Had Adam tried to explain that from the standpoint of some, not excluding certain elements among the French, it would be an ingenious and relatively simple solution, Smythe would have been insulted. Adam could hear him saying: "There are easier ways, short of murder, you realize, of conducting diplomacy. When *persona* is *non grata*, there are always channels . . ."

Adam had, in fact, said nothing; nor could he. There was no point to conjecture, especially where the lines were so narrowly drawn. If the Minister had a proper sense of humor, or were at least sardonic, the ludicrous aspects might be shared. A little uneasy laughter might do all of them some good, Adam reflected. But this way, dwelling upon the possibilities, the more he thought about them the more they made a kind of perverse sense, as a vivid dream or a nightmare becomes more real than reality. It would be all of a piece, somehow, down to the use of an American grenade that had wended its way from a Manchurian arsenal, a trophy captured by the Chinese Communists from the decapitated armies of Chiang Kaishek. To have the pin pulled here, in this city of anonymous death, by one of the boys on bicycles who, *pour le sport*, or for a few piasters, hurled explosives through open windows at faceless strangers in white suits, was somehow fitting. The final note of irony would lie in the attempt to mask the child killer, to hire him, as it were, in someone else's swaddling clothes. When one thought of the history of assassination in the West, of the secret plottings, the elaborate preparations, the everlasting waiting for the day on which the open-top limousine would turn the appropriate corner at the approximate time, with the prince alongside the foreign minister, this way of killing was, by contrast, refreshing in its nonchalance.

It seemed impossible to Adam that the Minister would not be aware of the existence of danger, whether he was able to fathom a personal application or not. The degree to which he continued to deny it, even subconsciously, accounted perhaps for his inability to cope, for Smythe's insulation. The Minister had served most recently in Europe, among the satellites. He had been in arctic isolation for so long that the process of thawing out, where the burden of the thaw was on him, was painful to watch. Adam had been watching it for almost a year. At first he had been sorry for him. But as it had become apparent that the differences between them were fundamental, involving not so much a specific policy as an attitude, Adam had reduced sympathy to silence; or at least, he thought, remembering the morning's conversation, to less frequent if more frustrating attempts at reconciliation, which were in fact a queer process of ultimate reconcilement for himself. It was clear by now that he would never succeed Smythe; or the men like Smythe. For him, as for others, it was a time of cocoon.

He looked up at the sun and sneezed, with purposeful violence, as if by shaking his body he could unshackle himself. There was a moment's darkness, and then the sun again, white-hot. He felt that he had been walking at it for hours, as through a quarry of soft stone. There was a permanence to the yellow palaces, vestigial, a universality of stucco that matched the deadlock of minds. He laughed aloud. One had to dramatize.

He hurried on. His trousers clung stickily to his thighs. The chimes in the cathedral sounded. Ahead of him, like penguins, the Vietnamese nuns went in to pray. They had emerged in their black robes, softly, in single file by the line of trees, themselves a distillation of time. The red cathedral took them at its narrow vestry door. The chimes stopped, and there was only the bark of a *motorpousse* scuttling nastily up the block.

Chapter II

HE WENT past the iron grille gates of the Commissioner's palace. The French guard in front of the sentry box yawned, then looked away, abashed at having caught his eye. In a few moments he had reached the Cercle Sportif. He went below immediately to change, without first sitting, as he generally did, on the terrace for a gin and bitters. The damp mustiness was a relief after his time in the sun, but when he had undressed and got into his trunks, the warmth outside felt good again and he climbed eagerly back into it, up to where the pool lay like a pale-green stone set in a white-gold glare. The water had been changed the day before, and now the clean and barely rippled surface caught the sun's rays and balanced them, to and fro, in gentle titillation. Adam lay on his side by the deep-end railing and let their warmth run through him on the way to the water, in which his own reflection glistened. He could smell the chlorine faintly; at the start of the week it was always a little medicinal, and he had come to prefer the softer, sweeter, musklike odor the pool sometimes had after several days of especially humid weather. He turned over on his stomach and felt the sun in his sinews. He stretched his feet and heard the small, pleasurable snap of tendons. From below, from the tennis courts, rose the pop of balls that told him two good players had begun to volley. The sound, as sharp and as clear as a girl's voice, had its own quality of excitement, a denial of heat and somnolence. He sat up and lit a cigarette.

A sense of peace, like a cool wave, swept over him. There was a tonic quality to being here after the morning's events, which, partly out of his own morbid curiosity, had delayed him. Would he, six months ago, he wondered, have gone down the street to the front of the smashed café? Or even more recently, one month ago, before his own experience?

There was more to it than that, he decided, blowing smoke out across the emerald water, watching its curled reflection grow darkly dim. Veering from involvement on one level, the formal level of dealing with the Minister and the business of the Legation, he felt freer to experiment on this new one, to be foolhardy even. He was no longer so responsible for success or failure; nor, therefore, for his own official skin. It was a rationalization, yet valid, though the Minister would scarcely agree. By exposing himself, standing idly in the street, talking to strangers, he had, if there was any truth to his own theory, acted irresponsibly in the Minister's eyes. If in his own eyes it was simply a matter of non-responsibility, Smythe, even in disbelief, would consider it tantamount to taking to the bush.

He raised himself on an elbow. Sun and air and water, he reflected, were proper palliatives. He watched a Eurasian girl in a bikini suit and a yellow cap climb to the top platform of the diving tower. She stood there, trim and taut, balanced on her toes, symmetrical against the sky. Adam had seen her before around the pool. In a moment, in a thin curve, she arched into the water.

He ordered the gin and bitters after all, sipping it as he let his legs dangle, re-creating the conversation in the Minister's office. It had been his own doing, he realized, and he had held the options. Having allowed it to start, he could either have stopped it or, with relative ease, have seized the opportunity, have said the things that would have brought the whole relationship to a head. It had been only a postponement, and a partial one at that. Sooner or later he would have to follow through, as inevitably as he had followed the grenade's roar down rue Catinat from the silver-shop to examine the bodies on the pavement. What he still wanted, however, was time, before he left Indo-China. It was too soon to go home. . . .

Even had he wished this morning to go further with Smythe, the

◇◇

moment had hardly been propitious. The presence of the others, Jackson and Goodenough, the political-section men, had made it embarrassing enough. Yet in spite of the fact that it had been an un-comfortable meeting, he had profited by it. Goodenough particularly, with his supercilious, collegiate manner, underlining by vague smirk the Minister's pronouncements, had created a tension on Smythe's part that had been a revelation. The Minister had been overly conscious of his audience. It had been worth discovering his need.

They had started talking of the stalemate, of the manner in which patience and impatience had peculiarly crossed lines, with a growing number of French critics of colonial policy, chiefly the Socialists and their friends, beginning to show a disposition to be done with Indo-China, or at least to pretend they would like to be done with it so as to pass the burden on, without prerogatives; while the Vietnamese, led by the Emperor himself, were now waiting, with the properly inscrutable mixture of hope and despair, for procrasti-nation to run out. It was a dangerous game all around, with the Americans in the middle as usual, tilting fitfully at windmills.

"We can't indefinitely prop up a vacuum," Adam had said. "It's what the French would like, but it'll only make things worse in the long run. We've got to make our own position clear, if only in terms of letting it be known that we stand firmly for a timetable—that at such and such a date control of the river should pass to the Viet-namese, or internal security, or even so small a thing as giving the Emperor his own palace to live in."

The Minister had simply grunted. Adam had gone on to mention the current negotiations in Paris, now in their fourth month, hung up as they had been before on exactly such specific surrenders of colonial power, some of them symbols, most of them more impor-tant and concrete aspects of the economic hold the French (those whose names one heard least) maintained and insisted on maintain-ing under the old guise of *mission civilisatrice*.

"These delays, the longer they last," Adam had added, "make our own position more untenable."

◇◇◇

The Minister had responded to this with a quick look and an odd resultant expression that was close to injured pride.

"Untenable?" he had echoed, softly.

Adam sipped his drink again, frowning, recollectively, at the prick of correction. The position was untenable in various ways, of course—most dangerously, as far as he was concerned, in the effect it had of frittering away the vestiges of prestige and almost divine good will the Americans had enjoyed when the war had ended in Asia. If one looked far enough ahead, one could already see the possibility of complete Communist victory, and the loss of considerably more than prestige alone. But tenability at this point became ambiguous. To the Minister, it obviously meant being on the side of those who retained, momentarily, the advantage of the biggest arsenal.

Adam had finally murmured, in compromise: "More difficult, at any rate."

It was then that the Minister's thin smile had been so surely reflected on Goodenough's face. Jackson had stared out the window, tapping, as he always did when he had nothing to contribute, on the desk-top with the rubber end of his pencil.

"At this juncture," Adam remembered the Minister saying—it was a favorite phrase of Smythe's, seeming always to leap nimbly over a multitude of sins, of omission and commission alike—"at this juncture we can't afford to prod. The French are doing all they can."

It was precisely the point on which their disagreement hinged. Far from doing all they could, Adam was convinced more than ever that the French, the significant elements behind the policy-makers here and in Paris, were malingering. The politicians as a group, even more than the military, did as they were told. Their hearts were perforce in their mouths. Only the unaffected, those with a remnant conscience, such as the ghostlike Léon Blum himself, could speak freely, but with scant influence.

There was another involvement, however, of a personal sort, as all of them in the room had been aware, one that went beyond what the French did or did not do in this still half-forgotten war. It concerned the element of risk, the no longer inviolate privilege to recommend, or even safely to broach, an unpopular solution, especially one that could be readily misconstrued back home in the United States. There was more at stake here than the slow, attritive search for policy itself. What was incapacitated was the very quality of boldness, of imagination. It did not seem to matter, for instance, what the intelligence reports might show about the now unconcealed strength of the Communist extremists in the Vietminh, or about the disillusioning effect this was having on many of the old independent nationalists, the non-party intellectuals and professional men who had joined the movement as much out of zeal as innocence back in 1945 and 1946, and whose brains had been properly picked ever since without being washed. Here might lie a true chink in the Vietminh armor. The Communists had made the earlier gamble of admitting these "non-political personages," as they were always called, into the structure of their jungle government, of giving them jobs at the advisory and even the ministerial level, and the gamble had paid off handsomely, not only in point of specific achievement but in stimulating popular appeal and further establishing Ho Chi Minh in his supra-party, benevolent father image. But now time and world events had caught up. In the moment of their weakening and doubt, however, when the chink might be widened, to suggest that these apostates and potential apostates could become part of a real opposition in place of some of the puppets the French were using would be considered "soft." They were automatically tainted or traitorous, and, besides, one was out to save not personalities but positions. Fire was not to be fought with fire, but steel with steel. And the stalemate would continue, supported by American weapons kept in dusty warehouses for contingencies that might or might nor arise after the monsoon died.

This lack of imagination in the midst of crisis affected other aspects of the problem too. Adam had at length gone so far as to restate, more bluntly, something he had said before. He had felt, while he was saying it, that it would be for the last time; but he had often felt that way.

"The one thing we can still do is disassociate ourselves as much as possible from the French," he had suggested, staring over the top of the Minister's head. "We have our own social-welfare and economic experts. They should be welded together into effective working parties and be allowed to make their own contribution in the villages. Immediately." The formal word was "bilateralism," but, as someone had said, there had always been three parties to bilateral agreements in Indo-China.

"This is one facet, at least, we can insist be ours to deal with, the fight against dependence," Adam had continued, sensing Goodenough's eyes on him as the Minister had kept his lowered. "We're footing the bill. What we do to help the people of Vietnam has nothing to do with the French. It comes from us, it goes to the Vietnamese. Into their stomachs and into their blood-streams."

"And the French still say into their heads," Goodenough had interjected, laughing.

"If it were made clear that any additional military support would depend on our supervising our own non-military aid programs, then the French would have to back down," Adam had replied, not looking at Goodenough. "Are we to give up giving simply because it hasn't got a French label on it, matching ours?"

The Minister had coughed, and poured himself a glass of water from the chromium pitcher. When he spoke, his tone had been avuncular, but Adam had recognized the touch of pique. "You must remember, Patch," he had said, and his eyes had suddenly twinkled, "that some of you folks who have been out here for a year or so have, shall we say, a different sense of urgency from those who come in fresh from other battlefronts."

Goodenough had smiled again at that, as if he had been put in charge of the admonition. This time Adam had stared back. "I don't see how or why urgency elsewhere precludes winning friends and influencing people here," he had said, abruptly. "It's a slow, laborious, and maybe thankless task. But it's just as important as all the planes and political pronunciamentos. We're still regarded with less suspicion than the French, and can make Vietnamese friends and keep them, some of them, if the worst does happen. . . ."

Goodenough's smile had lingered. Adam had suspected for some time that Goodenough felt he was losing his grip. It was a supposition that would have to be corrected. No matter what was lost, his grip would not be, he told himself. Under certain circumstances, however, the Goodenoughs could be more upsetting, in their educated righteousness, than the Smythes, and perhaps more damaging as well. It was at this moment that he had resolved to avoid being inveigled again into any such spectator discussion.

Smythe had spun the empty glass on the desk-top. "The French have their own pride, and, granted, their own sources of jealousy," he had said. "And it's their bailiwick. How would it have been if they had told us what to do in the Philippines?"

Adam had permitted himself a smile. "There are undoubtedly aspects of our own colonial unburdening that can be questioned. But we kept our political promises," he had answered. "And there's a big difference between retaining an economic advantage for profit and practicing a policy of economic exclusion when life and death are concerned. Between a sawbuck and a serum, let's say."

The Minister had nodded in vague acknowledgment. "Very true," he had said. "Clausewitz would be touched."

It was the first time Smythe had indulged in sarcasm, and Adam had flushed, which he never did. He thought of it now, knocking his heels gently against the concrete wall of the pool as he set down the empty glass. Until he had come to Saigon, everything had been neat and precise, in proper layers. There had been no such crises of

personality and faith. Respected in the Department for his ability
to write concise and lucid appraisals of situations without resorting
to academic phrases or innuendo, he had been an easy rover, moving
gracefully, urbanely, from one continent to another. Promotions
had come regularly, or perhaps a bit ahead of the others in his grade,
until, at thirty-eight, he had achieved Consular status. It was true
that nothing had ever much mattered; that no chips had been down.
In South and Central America the revolutions he had seen had been
stifled by mass lethargy and mute acceptance which even the Communists had found hard to combat. Here it was different, unpredictable yet undeniable, impossible to muffle, ready to explode at any
moment and at any place, as the grenades blew up the cafés of the
city. When that happened it had nothing to do with what they
endlessly talked about, with the sad arguments and vertigris of
politics and the stalemate that so inevitably follows a missed opportunity. What was solely concerned then was the color of the
skin, the smolder in the eye. There were times when Adam felt
naked in his whiteness, and the pool, more than oasis, became a
sanctuary.

He felt a pall and, looking up, found himself searching for the
girl in the bikini suit and the yellow bathing-cap. Just as he saw
her, at the far end, he heard the voice of a man above him saying:
"*Ah, Monsieur le Consul, comment allez-vous aujourd'hui?*" Adam
turned, suppressing his annoyance, and saw above him the round,
liver-pale face of M. Remy, of the High Commissioner's political
staff.

Remy was just out of the hospital. Sooner or later all the French
went there for varying periods, usually from two to five weeks. It
was always the liver, but to that had now been added a diagnosis
of another disease that was secretly described by the *fonctionnaires*
as *le mal de minuit*, the result of repeated summons to the High
Commissioner's palace at all hours, especially between midnight
and three in the morning.

"I'm fine, thank you," Adam said. "Enjoying the scenery, as always."

"The scenery is always very pretty here," said M. Remy. He was looking out across the city. "It's a fact, don't you think," he went on, "that we French at least had the good sense to put trees in our cities?" He coughed politely. "Consider what our neighbors, the British and Dutch, have done."

"The Americans as well," Adam suggested. "Or don't you think of us any longer in our imperial splendor?"

M. Remy laughed, showing yellow teeth. "Yes, you are right," he said. "Manila was a lovely city before the war, in some respects, but it did not have sufficient trees. Now, of course, it is still despoiled."

In view of the distance he customarily kept, Adam was surprised that M. Remy had spoken to him at all. For several weeks he had not even been able to reach Remy on the phone. He had wanted information on some of the southern Vietnamese landowners, lawyers, and doctors who were the backbone of the Emperor's Saigon government, which the French had virtually selected. Remy would know at once, of course, what Adam's purpose was, to promote a proportionate northern influence in the cabinet, to put forward, in permanent balance, some of the anti-Vietminh Tonkinese leaders who had burrowed down in Hanoi after the Communists had taken their troops and government into the jungle. These were no renegades, these northerners; even though some of them had belonged to the amorphous wartime popular front the Vietminh had so quickly come to dominate, they had remained ardent nationalists afterward. They included, for example, members of the Dai Viet, a party of mandarin and bureaucratic influence, and some members of the old Kuomintang groups from across the Chinese border, whom the Communists had rapidly outmaneuvered and eliminated from the Vietminh by 1947. There were also some capable professional men who had never even flirted with the Vietminh, and who now stood ready to enter the Emperor's govern-

✧✧

ment if its purely French coloration were removed and it was constituted along truly nationalist lines. This was an issue the French had done their utmost to duck. And as for Adam's curiosity, Remy's reasoning, logically, would be that the less that was known about the current Saigon cabinet, about its members' double citizenship, wealth, and possessions, and the reluctance of some of the ministers to serve, the less likely it would be for any more recommendations to be forthcoming from the Americans. There had already been some suggestions unofficially behind the scenes in Washington, Adam knew, and it was to bolster them that he had sought more facts to report. Now the Frenchman had something of his own on his mind, Adam suspected, and he resolved to let the fatuous poolside discussion continue just so long as M. Remy desired.

"You are perhaps being unfair to the attractions of Singapore," he said, offering Remy a cigarette.

Remy popped his lips in disdain and dismissed Singapore with a wave of his hand. "A city without a soul," he said. "Or a soul of rubber only."

They sat for a few moments in silence and Adam looked around again for the Eurasian girl. He couldn't find her, and was newly annoyed with M. Remy. "Would you care for a drink?" he asked.

Remy's retort was another question. "Have you been in the water yet?" Adam said no.

Remy was pursing his lips and scratching his white face. "This matter of Vietminh disaffections," he said. "Have you given any particular thought to it?"

So that was it, Adam thought. He wondered if the Minister had talked to Remy since eleven o'clock.

"They're increasing, aren't they?" Adam said, as ingenuously as he could, thinking that here Remy was on safer ground, since one could say anything about deserters.

"Five in the last fortnight," Remy replied. "Not all important, of course."

"I know of three," Adam said, waiting.

"That is it exactly!" Remy said forcibly, though he actually dropped his voice. "It is the other two that puzzle me. The three we know. They are old friends of Ho Chi Minh, from the time of Hong Kong and Kunming. It is not strange for them to go. It is the other two we do not know."

Adam was now aware that Remy was fishing, not for information, which he must know Adam would not have or assuredly would not offer as free bait, but for even a slight reaction, a nuance of opinion. He said nothing again.

"It is perfectly possible they are spies," Remy continued, with what seemed to Adam somewhat purposeful abstractedness. He was looking away once more. "We have no proof, of course. Nevertheless, it is entirely possible, don't you think?"

Adam shrugged. "I have no opinion," he said. "It is possible that everyone is a spy—everybody here, for example," and he motioned toward the pool.

Remy laughed. "That is so," he said, "but I do not believe it. It would be too much like an American film, yes?"

"Yes," Adam said.

"You are very brown from the sun," M. Remy commented.

"You'll excuse me if I take a dip," Adam said, and he jumped off and away. Just before his head struck the water, he heard the murmured "But of course," of M. Remy behind him, in another world.

Adam below water was a man released, a man set free from the calculated chatter of M. Remy and the chin-chucking logic of Smythe. The longer he stayed in Saigon, the more he came to welcome the particular moment when he felt this first coolness and measured the liquid lunge of his body. As far back as he remembered, he had known how to swim. Living on a New England shore had soon put him in touch with the surf. At six he had been at home on the mile-off sandbar; at ten he had sailed out a storm. At college he had built his own boat, and his first love-affair had been consum-

◇◇

mated in its tiny home-made cabin. Wherever he had been, in Tangier, Rome, Rio, Stockholm, and Mexico City, he had always somehow managed to find time to swim.

He let himself float lazily on his back, and caught a glimpse of M. Remy, alone at a table. Remy seemed to be waiting for him. The Frenchman looked transparent in the sun, his body tubular and frail. More surely than ever, he had a purpose in mind; what he had said had been too precisely vague. It was typical, under the circumstances, for him to act in this fashion, with sudden nonchalant sociability and an air of sharing a confidence that pretended to excuse all past fencing. Remy had the true grace of the informer.

Above, the sky had become a robin's-egg blue. There was something at once gentle and foreboding in these pale Oriental skies, or perhaps it was simply that the cloud-wisps he saw resembled the puffs of artillery. Now, once more, he thought he heard the sound, a far-away and hollow roar that rose from below the horizon and echoed along the circumference of the sky like a rock falling in a canyon or the sound of the sea in a shell. But when he lifted his head, he found that it was only laughter on the pool's bright edge. He could see, through the watery film, the Eurasian girl, sitting with two companions on the white tiles. He hadn't noticed how far he had drifted.

The three women were smiling at him.

With a few long, encompassing strokes, he was quickly up beneath them. Blinking to stop the chlorine's smarting, he hoisted himself alongside, letting the water drip down and away, feeling it dry and dissolve in the quick-parching heat.

"It was the fish," he explained. "They were tickling."

They laughed at that, as only three pretty women can laugh at a man they have suddenly in their midst, an American above all.

"You are the Consul, yes?" one of the Frenchwomen asked.

"That's right," Adam said.

"You are a very good swimmer," said the other.

Adam said: "Thank you."

"You come very often to the pool. One sees you here often."

"Yes," Adam said. "I come every day. It's my one recreation."

"The Americans work very hard. There are so many now," the Eurasian girl said.

She spoke lightly with what seemed to him only mild mockery, polite and meant to be shared. The suit she wore, he suddenly thought, was wrong for her. It was not extravagant in its cut, but its colors enveloped her too dramatically. She was thin, but well formed; a single pastel would have served her better. Her dark hair, the cap now off, fell easily away along the sides of her head. Her mouth was red without lipstick, wide without coarseness. Her eyes were black.

"There are more coming," he said. "Many more."

"The Americans have always experts," the first Frenchwoman murmured.

"We are a nation of experts," Adam said.

"In some things only," she replied.

There was a pause.

"The experts are very dull," the Eurasian girl said. "That is always the trouble with experts, of all nations. They are very dull."

"They make the wheels go round," Adam said.

They introduced themselves. The two Frenchwomen were the wives of colonial officials and they had long names that Adam didn't hear clearly. The name of the other girl was Genevieve Brouillard.

"Adam Patch?" she repeated. "That is an American name?"

"My ancestors were English," he said.

He beckoned for the waiter and they moved to the tables on the other side of the pool. The club was still filling, and the air was wet. Adam loved the sight of so many bodies in the sun. They cast an aura that blended with the lushness of the foliage and the silent yet kinetic street beyond. The sense of vegetation and flesh, of the overclad trees and the underclad bodies, heightened desire

◇◇

and made him think of primitive paintings and love-making in a canopied forest.

"Have you been living here long?" he asked Mlle Brouillard.

"Since the war—the other war, with the Japanese."

"And you like it?"

She tossed her head. "Sometimes," she said, "but not so much as before."

"Then why do you stay?"

She smiled, a smile that was like opening a door on white linen. "There is nowhere to go," she said. "Here I have my home, so here I stay."

The sun grew hotter. The two Frenchwomen, after a gay burst of protestation, withdrew. Around the pool the other voices mounted off the water like a hum of low-flying birds.

Mlle Brouillard regarded the veranda. "It is like an aviary," she said. "So many feathers."

"And you do not belong to the aviary?"

"Perhaps," she said. "You do not know me." She smiled again, and Adam stirred. He squinted at the sun.

"The heat at its zenith, the wrong hour for sentiment," he said. He hesitated a moment. "There is a restaurant near by that is cool. Would it be presumptuous—?"

Mlle Brouillard replied, softly, that it would not.

They dived in, side by side, and came up together by the tiled steps. Twenty minutes later, newly immaculate, they emerged from the dressing-rooms. By the parapet, as they left, M. Remy watched. He followed them with his eyes, until they went out the front gate beyond the lawn and turned along the outer hedge. When they had disappeared he walked quickly down the splayed flight of the stone entrance and went away from the club in the opposite direction.

Chapter III

THE fly settled, hovered, and settled again, inching in a streak of light down the man's spine. When he stirred, it stirred with him, but remained on the moist vertebra. The light filtered through the porous shade and spilled across the bed.

In the street, the soldiers passed, stepping soundlessly through the dust, sleepy-faced and sullen. They were the Vietnamese of the Emperor, going to the towers along the road to the sea. In the young light they looked earthbound, their legs, in the baggy uniforms, like open roots, transgressing. A whistle blew from somewhere up ahead, and the column increased its speed. Another whistle followed, and the men began trotting. They jogged ludicrously, the old French guns slapping their shoulders. When they had gone the pye-dogs re-emerged, circling in the deserted street, pointing their noses through the affected air.

In the upstairs room the Annamite reached out behind him as he lay with his face to the wall, and brushed away the persistent fly. . . .

There was a hollow at the end of the tunnel of trees, and the ground was wet with rain. They had been walking out of the ricelands, back into the jungle where the camp would be. At the joining up there would be jubilation, but also grief and pain. The fighting had been costly, but they had driven the French twenty miles off, farther north again, shortening the perimeter where it needed to be shortened, so that the people would be able to get the rice crop out before the colonial soldiers returned. Once the French took the rice from the villages and fields, as they had done elsewhere, they brought it to the city and then on to Haiphong, where it was put aboard ships and sent abroad, according to the political officer, to get more money for the imperialist war. . . .

The political officer was a small man with a chicken-pocked face and a bemused smile, and for some reason he had been walking with Tran all through the night. Tran had listened to him in silence, partly because he was extremely tired but also because he knew it was what the political officer expected. It was a convenient kind of penance, if only a postponement, and it would make the political officer believe, for the time being, that he was aware of his short-comings. He was chiefly aware, however, of the shortage of medi-cines and of the promises that had been made, but not fulfilled, of more supplies to come; "from the north," was what they had told him. But nothing had arrived and the wounds were more numerous and of a greater variety as a result of the greater variety of weapons that had come to be used; especially the bombs that were made of jelly and were dropped from the sky in what appeared to be metal baskets, bursting with such awful fury and burning the clothes and skin off men's bodies in a matter of seconds. There was little that could be done about them. . . .

Tran was aware, too, of the change that was taking place among the troops because of the bitter and the longer fighting, of the battles that now endured for days instead of hours, and sometimes for weeks. There was a greater variety of troops now also, of trained and untrained, of young and old, and they had many kinds of guns and pieces of guns, which made it difficult to keep the weapons clean and to obtain the proper bullets. And, above all, he was aware of the Chinese, the newcomers from the camps in the north who had come among them. . . .

The political officer was part Chinese, Tran thought. He had a Chinese way of speaking in tight parables and phrases, and he seemed to chew his words. There was nothing loose and free about him, but only a kind of hardness and a certainty, but at the same time a dispassion amid conviction, as if he were a tight ball of twine the knotted ends of which were held by a fist hidden deep inside himself, or by a metal spring somewhere in his hard, cropped head. They had been walking since dusk, into the rain and then out of it, then back into it again, a dripping if not a pouring, as if the canopy overhead were a soft green sponge through which the drops were squeezed and drained by an invisible hand. The words kept coming the way the water came, in a slow, steady stream against his ears and against his comprehension, dulling the senses so that it made no difference after a time whether the water or the words ceased or flowed; the feeling was the same, in and out, a numbness, and all he could do was continue walking across the soggy ground, stepping carefully to avoid the holes and the snares and the possibility of snakes whose poison would kill quickly, with no serum available, often in a matter of minutes, a swelling, a bursting, a hot fright, and the sky shut off with the breath. . . .

The political officer used to speak about the meaning of the war. He had a way of summing things up pragmatically. "It will take us longer than we had expected, in view of the American warmongers' aid and the improvement of the French," he would say. "But it will make no difference in the outcome. It will be necessary simply to maintain the utmost discipline in all the ranks, from the new soldiers who are the peasants in the fields by day and who fight in the jungle at night to the cadres of the trained and educated, who have special abilities and tasks. It is important that all of us understand the true nature of the forces with which we are engaged and of our inevitable and glorious triumph, which will finally spread . . . through several stages . . . the mobilization of peasants and workers together . . . progressive culture of the Soviet Union and New China . . . to beat the French colonists and the American interventionists to their knees . . . the counteroffensive . . ."

At one point in the night they had come upon the animals quite suddenly. He couldn't tell what animals they were; they seemed all colors and shapes, and they had gone around them so as not to disturb them. Afterward Tran had turned back to look at the animals and had seen them staring at the soldiers in the forest and at the political officer and himself especially with great soft eyes that appeared at once to be full of tears. "The animals are weeping," Tran had said to the political officer, but the political officer had not answered and had only regarded him at first with dismay and then with a peculiar compassion that was like an iron pity, dutiful and stern, resuming thereupon his discourse as if the animals had not existed and Tran had not looked back to see them. And what he talked about was the peace that was to come and the good things to come with it, long words in widening circles that Tran knew he could not share the meaning of. It was soon thereafter that he discovered his hands were fastened, but without cord, and the ends of his fingers had become stubs without feeling, which made it impossible to take hold of the surgeon's tools which the political officer for some reason kept thrusting at him, laughing as they fell to the floor of the jungle, where they wriggled away like snakes.

They came into the camp before dawn and he had lain on the ground where it was not quite so wet beside a tree that was full of sleeping birds. The birds had beaks that were twisted into smiles as frozen and bemused as that of the political officer, but more inscrutable in the silence of sleep, full of secret, silent mockery. But when he opened his eyes the birds were moving, flicking through the branches with a wild, persistent chirping; and among them, wearing the tallest plume, was the political officer himself, all green and gold and splendid. When he tried to stand up, Tran found he couldn't move, his legs unfunctioning and his arms now shriveled; and it was then that he saw the animals once more, a solemn jury on the forest's edge. The trial began, with the political officer acting as the prosecutor, flourishing and ruffling his feathers, which made the animals clap with human hands, and stamp the ground beneath the log with animals' paws. The trial was very short, in the fashion of the

◇◇◇

day, with no witnesses, but simply a series of questions to which the jury of the animals responded with additional stamping and clapping, and the birds in the branches echoed a shrill affirmation. The political officer asked such questions as "What should we do with him whose hands are covered with the enemy's germs?" and when he added: "Has he not proved himself unworthy of his task?" the animals agreed and the birds agreed, rending the forest with their din of agreement, clapping and twittering louder and louder as only Tran lay fixed and silent beneath the cacophonous tree by the log where the animals sat and roared, no longer soft-eyed and weeping.

He had gone into Hué early in the morning to forage for drugs, and he had said at the camp that it might be the next night before he returned, that it would depend on what he found. The faces of the wounded had brightened, but the political officer had merely nodded, saying nothing. He had not discussed the matter with any-one, for he had made no friends in the jungle other than the young Moi courier from the hills whose life he had saved in the campaign of the winter before, but who hardly spoke any Annamese beyond what little Tran had taught him.

He could not tell if the political officer suspected. Or, beyond that, if it mattered. There had been, Tran knew, a difference of opinion. Some of those in the party were in favor of allowing all malcontents to go unmolested, to vanish, as it were, into the jungle and to make their way out across the mountains as best they could, into the limbo of the cities. Others were vehemently opposed to such carefree withdrawals, to such easy loppings-off. If the political officer belonged among the latter, as Tran suspected, he was not yet able to act independently. All that had ever been said between them, as a simple intimation but enough to tell Tran that his un-tenable position was clearly accepted, was a suggestion that, if the doctor desired, the political officer might arrange his participation in one of the coming cultural expeditions to the north, to Peking.

It was a convenient way of not having to make a decision on the spot. Such journeys usually lasted from three to six months. On occasion, if one had been cleansed and purified and had undergone "the sweepings of the closets of the mind," one might be permitted to return, most often to a strange place, where the old and the new dispensations could be accepted without scars of embarrassment. It was, Tran reflected, not unlike taking what the French called the waters, where one also went to rid oneself of bile and wrong-doing. Except one came home. . . .

He could not afford to temporize, he had decided. The personal factor might be a matter of accident and whim, of the attitude of a particular political officer; but what had become significant was the party itself, and the new order that had followed the re-emergence of the Communists and the elimination of the old "Marxist study-groups." "In the interests of consistency and to create a solid wall against the imperialists and the interventionists," the manifesto had boldly declared. One heard the name of Ho Chi Minh less and less. The names one listened to now were those of the young men who had come back from the north, and even from Moscow. When one pointed out, as Tran had once foolishly done, that "Uncle Ho" had sprung from the same school, that he had spent his life serving the cause of revolution throughout Asia, the response was likely to be a bland smile and a polite acknowledgment of Ho's efforts. They knew, all of them, the young men included, that they could not do without him—not yet at any rate—that the tubercular old man with the driving, feverish eyes and the wispy chin was an indispensable symbol. It had been three years since Tran had seen him. There were those who said he was dead. Tran did not believe it. But as much as anything else this growing feeling that the old man would soon die, and perhaps be enshrined in the jungle, the way Lenin was kept in a crypt in Russia for all to see, served to burgeon Tran's doubts with shoots of fear. It worked both ways: so long as Ho was alive, he felt it unlikely these newcomers would disturb the disciples. But if the status remained, the sense of loneliness deepened with the increase of the jungle and the time one spent in it, until, whether it was true or not, Tran had come to feel that the breath in his own body depended solely on how much there still was in that thin, hollow chest a few hundred miles away. There had been days and nights when, walking through the tunnels of the forest, he had half expected to hear a sonorous gong.

For three nights he had lain awake. The time, he had told himself, was ripe and logical in view of the recurrent need for drugs and the nearness of the city. The penultimate silence of the political officer had worried him, and the way in which some of the others had looked at him, though it may only have been his imagination and the knowledge that he would not be seeing them again. Nothing, at any rate, had happened.

He had simply walked away. He had taken the path that led out of the jungle onto the fields and across the paddies over the narrow raised strips of earth that divided them, moving by successive right angles to the road beyond, in the white dust of which he could see others like himself going toward the town.

On the first afternoon, inevitably, as he went among the small stores and through the market-place where the drugs were sold, carrying out the ritual of his mission, he had the feeling that he was being followed. The shopkeepers had answered briefly and politely when he asked about prices, but their faces had been blank. He knew the ones who had suspected all along what his purpose had been, and he in turn knew those who had been the principal funnels of the swelling black-market trade that was conducted between the two sides; and that included more and more Frenchmen as well as Vietnamese. It was a conspiracy of silence they had all carried on together, a kind of thieves' market, but now, for the first time, Tran felt the effects of it. The awareness of how much he was irretrievably party to frightened him. Even the sunlight itself had grown artificial. The hum at dusk had sounded like thunder.

On the second day, at the height of the sun, he had turned south at the market's edge and had gone down the road, beyond where the shops ended, toward the mountains. By the fall of night he had reached the slope of the tallest range. He had sat on the floor of a farmer's hut, eating the generous farmer's food, and he had offered to pay for it; but the man would have none of it, seeming, by the firm shaking of his head, to be hurt, they being unable to understand each other's language. But in the silence of the evening, in the company of the farmer and his wife, Tran had felt the beginning of peace.

He had walked all the next day, and for a week thereafter, skirting the mountains and using the paths that cut through them and were pointed out to him; and then he had come one day onto the downward slopes where there were strange tribes whose members laughed as he went by and sometimes gave him looks that were curious and hostile. But he went unhindered, and when he reached the plains he found the Annamites again, in the villages of new valleys. And it was here, in this land between, where the soldiers of one side and the other had come and gone, that Tran's image had begun to form.

. . . This was the indefinite country. To the north and to the south, through the delta-lands of the great rivers, the Red and the Black and the Mekong, the fighting ebbed and flowed with the seasons, but the war went on endlessly; by night when the peasants left their huts and met secretly with the Vietminh, and in the paddies by day under the eyes of the Emperor's troops and the white lieutenants. But here, where the people of the lowlands and the highlands lived in proximity but seldom saw each other, there were few battles, though from time to time the Vietminh came in search of fresh food and young soldiers. There were no sentries, and no meetings. . . .

Tran came at noon into a small village that lay by the side of a dome-shaped mountain. There was a fountain in the square, and a dragon from whose stone eyes streams of water spun thinly onto a group of women and children cooling their sores below. The eyes of the people were encrusted with trachoma and their mouths spread wide with ulcers. The malevolent face of the dragon threw mocking shadows in the dust. . . .

Tran stopped at the fountain's edge and an old woman looked up from the bathing and said: "If you are one of those who have come for the men again, there are none to go." Tran smiled and said: "No, I am not one of those, although I, too, have come from the north." And then they told him that some of the men in the village were in the hills to hunt, but that those who were not had seen him on the road and had fled to avoid argument. "There are not men enough to work and to fight in the north as well," another of the women said. "I do not understand such a fight that goes on forever." And Tran told them of the increase of the fighting and of how the armies grew. When he spoke of the Chinese the women asked if they would return to the valley, for the Chinese had occupied the northern part of the country after the end of the long war and before the new war had begun. "Perhaps," Tran replied, "but they are not the same, for there have been changes among the Chinese as well." But the old woman who had spoken first said: "It will be the same, nevertheless, if they come, for of whatever spirit themselves, with us the Chinese are cruel in treatment, and sometimes even more so than the French." And there was nothing for Tran to reply, but he put out his hand and touched the face of a boy who had come alongside. "I am a doctor," he said, and the woman who was the boy's mother regarded him with anxiety but permitted him to examine the boy's face, which was covered with sores. The other children now gathered around, leaving the fountain and wishing to be seen by the stranger, and the women clustered behind them as he looked at all the children's faces, which were the worst he had seen. A helplessness that was the worst he had felt, greater than that caused by the bombs of jelly in the jungle, came over him, but all he said, after many moments, was: "The water will not help. . . ."

They told him then of a miracle that was said to have befallen a
valley beyond, where a metal bird had dropped from the sky and
men who were white but not French, carrying ointments and long
needles, had administered a great healing, which the healers had
not themselves witnessed, having left and never since returned.
Tran listened carefully, and when the women had finished he nodded
and said: "Yes, it was so, I believe, for such things are possible
and have occurred in other valleys, and I have heard of them happening." He did not tell them the quick thought in his heart, and the
great beating because of it, but allowed himself to rest and eat the
rice and broth of vegetables the women gave him before he took
the path they showed him that went south into the hills beyond.
And as he left the village and the fountain of the dragon, he thanked
them and looked back once more at the stricken children, speaking
the words he had been afraid to speak but could not swallow, "There
will come a miracle here. . . ."

2

HE reached out, feeling the fly again on his back, and when he
turned over he saw it on the ceiling. He lay there for some time,
regarding the enemy, his eyes opening and closing, still half-asleep
and otherworldly. Then he put his feet on the floor and sat up,
lifting the curtain alongside, and watched the fly buzz out into the
sun. He got up and went to the sink in the corner, where he threw
water on his face and washed his mouth. He dressed, taking care
with the new suit, and went downstairs, where he had his tea and
cakes in the small dining-room. The heat had not begun yet, but the
curtains in the windows hung motionless as shrouds, and the smells
released from the incubation of the night were rising. The hotel
manager, a Chinese, loomed in the doorway.

"Good morning," he said.

Tran said good-morning.

"It will be hot again."

"Yes, it will be hot."

◇◇

"You will stay for a long time?"

"Perhaps."

"Your room is quite comfortable?"

"Yes, quite comfortable. Perhaps a little too noisy in the night."

"Ah, yes, one gets used to it. But the bed is clean, and the room as well. Such things are important."

"Oh, yes, extremely important. It is clean."

"That is good. Well, good day."

"Yes, thank you. Good day, then."

Tran sat and smoked a cigarette in the empty hall. A sense of inertia suggested itself. Would it be wiser, he wondered, to wait another day or two? Or, on the contrary, should he not act immediately, to forestall distrust? The problem remained—where to start?

A small boy selling papers stuck his head through the curtains. Abstractedly, Tran shook him off. He sat drumming his fingers on the table until the manager glanced in again, then rose and went out the side entrance of the dining-hall. There was a haze, and the air was heavy. He walked a block, to where the street was less crowded, and hailed a *cyclo*. When he got to within half a mile of the square, he climbed out and began to walk once more. After three days he was beginning to recognize the streets and shops. He walked for more than an hour, listening to the buying and selling, to the clicking and clacking of wood against wood and china, and to the sounds of wheels. A steady whisper seemed to come from the atmosphere itself. Once he passed along a street where he had not been before and saw an American flag flying from a window. He looked up at it. Tomorrow, perhaps, he would return. It would be a place to begin. . . .

When he reached the center of the city, where the fine cafés and shops were, it was almost noon. A quiet had descended as the heat bore down, and the air had no motion. It was a quiet that was akin to the jungle's, when one knew that life still abounded. Instinctively, as he had searched the trees for a movement or for a sign of the sky, Tran looked up and saw the boy on the bicycle. He was pedaling furiously down the block, and in front of the café he suddenly swerved as his arm flew out. Then he sped around the corner, his small, lithe body high in the saddle and his bare feet pumping.

The roar shattered the senses. Tran stood, immobile, directly across the street as the smoke billowed. From inside the café the people began to emerge as through a gray gauze among the broken chairs and tables. It was only a moment later that the outlines of the two bodies on the pavement became clear and Tran crossed over. . . .

3

When the American had gone, Tran stood in the square and watched until he reached the far side. His white suit glistened in the sun and he moved gracefully, with a long and even step, as if, Tran thought, he consumed the ground as he went. At first Tran had felt like a ghost at his side. Death, he knew, did different things to different persons, making some talk feverishly out of a desperate striving to reassert their own aliveness, while others, more willing to accept it as a sign of their own mortality, remained subdued and silent. Undoubtedly the American had been among the latter.

The sight of death, so indiscriminately administered, had served to make his own life immediately precarious again. Yet the conversation had helped. On his part, it had been the effort he had needed to make, the approach of the laboratory worker, the small tentative probing at X, the unknown. But it annoyed him that he had not said more. It had ended too abruptly. . . .

He continued slowly along the edge of the square toward the gardens of the palace, where from behind the iron picket fence he watched the soldiers drill along the curve of the lawn. They were obviously newcomers, and extremely young as well. Probably they had arrived on the ship that had come in last week, the one the newspaper said had been removed from the *tourisme* in order to

◇◇

bring additional troops from Algiers to Saigon. It was difficult to imagine these young boys, most of whom must still be in their teens, manning the forts on the colonial highways or going out on patrol into the jungle. The heavy automatic rifles they carried, which could make such a fearful sound and could kill with such awful devastation, spoiling so much of the body, seemed so harmless over the thin shoulders of these adolescents, whose faces were white and pimpled and had expressions that bespoke fright, not so much of soldiering and war as of life itself. Yet they fascinated him; he could stand almost endlessly, watching them turn right, then left, drop and lift their guns, and he would wait with them for the guttural command of the lieutenant.

He turned away, back toward the river. He would have to do something more than this morbid staring. The grenade itself, even before the conversation, had restored his sense of reality. There was, chiefly, the question of money. He had only enough for another few days, though he might stretch it a bit farther by finding a smaller room and buying food in the market. He had chosen the native hotel in the Chinese city so as to be inconspicuous; yet he kept wandering about. The noise at night, after the long time in the jungle, had been difficult to get used to; he had not slept well under the impact of human voices and human-made sounds, the clang of cymbals and the whine of reeds from the dance-hall across the street and the click of the croupiers' chips and the mah-jongg counters from the next-door gaming parlor. It was only a different kind of jungle, more immediate and pressing than that of the bird-cries and the nocturnal howl of beasts, and the occasional flat crash of rifle-fire in the hills or underbrush, which had always seemed to Tran to be more the animals fighting than men, the natural, snarling consequence of the violation of a lair; but he hadn't convinced himself. There was something specially nervous about the noise in the city, and it had kept him awake until early each morning, when it became surprisingly still and he would drop off, finally, under a descending blanket of the utmost loneliness.

He had almost reached the river now, and the boats of the up-country fishermen and traders, gathered in a bobbing maze along the shore and held together, in a single floating consonance, by a skein of wooden boards and planks and swirling feet, and also perhaps by the smells in the river air and the attentive swoopings of the gulls. He stood across from the great new hotel that was almost wholly occupied, he had heard, by the Americans. For a moment he thought of entering. Perhaps in the stone lobby, or in the bar, where the Americans liked to gather, there would be someone else; or the stranger in the white suit might reappear. But he decided the hour was too early. Besides, it was a difficult thing to do. One would have to be extremely fortunate.

A boat from up the river glided by, and Tran turned and watched the boatman, a gnarled but lithe old man, shout at a young boy in the prow of a junk alongside and then throw him a rope, which the boy lazily grabbed just before it fell back into the water and fastened in the network of cords. The new vessel settled at once into the floating company; it might already have been there for days, or even weeks. Tran strolled onto the dock, through the dust on the soft, sagging wood of the planks. He walked exploratively among the debris and the sprawled mass of the boatmen and their families, toward the boat that had just arrived, and when he reached it he stood alongside and appraised it. From how far upriver had it traveled, he wondered, from how deep in the interior? He felt a sudden kinship with the old man—it was hard to tell his age, but Tran guessed it to be fifty—who had gone beneath the center covering but now re-emerged and regarded Tran with smoky eyes that flickered between hostility and fear.

"What is it you want?" the old man said.

"There is nothing that I want," Tran replied. "Except to bid you welcome and ask from where you have just now come."

The old man spat into the dirty water. "That is not at all what you want," he said. "And you might as well get it over with and tell me. One does not come here, dressed like you, in Western clothes, to inquire of such things."

The loud and querulous manner in which the old man spoke had led others, from the surrounding boats, to congregate. The movement took place very quickly, and beneath the universal impassivity were mistrust and slow-gathering anger.

"If I have done anything for you to arrest me, arrest me, then," the old man rambled on, his voice mounting. "You can ask me all you want at the police station."

He was almost shouting now, aware of the friendly audience around him. Overhead, the gulls shrieked with sharp disdain.

Tran started to turn, then swung back again, looking fixedly at the old man, who stood muttering in the hatchway. "But what is it you are afraid of?" he began. "I am no spy, or policeman. I am a stranger here, from the north myself—"

The crowd on the boats and dock laughed derisively. It seemed to Tran that it was moving in around him. Alongside he saw the face of a youth with one eye, full of menace. A second youth approached and stood on his other side. There was a moment of dead silence; then, slowly, Tran moved away, back over the narrow connecting planks to the dock, stepping carefully among the clusters of the river-burnt boatmen and their women, who seemed of the same tough integument, as if they had sprung, like dark Eves, from the bone and fiber of their men. Just before he reached the shore he nearly tripped over a small boy, naked, with a protruding belly, and he placed his hand on the youngster's cropped, sore-festered head. A woman snatched the boy away and slapped his bare behind until he cried fiercely. On the dock, as Tran started to walk off, the one-eyed youth came quickly up behind him. "We are not eager for visitors here," the youth whispered. "And if you are not a member of the Sûreté, so much the worse for you." Tran didn't answer. He continued across the dusty street to the tree-shaded sidewalk. Through the hotel windows he could see the Americans in the white lobby. He started to walk rapidly back toward the square. He wanted to get away from the river and the brooding fury he had caused.

The touching of the boy had been the climax, more than the hostility his mere presence seemed to have aroused. He thought of the village he had come through, and of the children there, of the mother whose anxiety he had overcome. Why were the cities so filled with suspicion and fear?

So involved was he in the sadness of thought that he scarcely noticed the tap on his shoulder. It was only when he felt his two arms held that he looked up.

"You will come with us, please," said the man on his left, a Vietnamese in the brown uniform of the auxiliary police. The other, who had taken his right arm, wore the loose and shiny thin suit of an ordinary coolie, and said nothing.

"What has happened?" Tran asked.

"You will find out shortly," the policeman said. He took a firmer grip on the arm, and Tran winced.

"You need not hold me so tight," Tran told him.

The policeman gave him a violent shove. "Never mind your telling me what to do," he said.

They were back among the flower-stalls and the market-stands, where the soldiers had searched before, after the grenade had been thrown. On the sidewalk the people hardly took notice of the procession of three, though the shopkeepers grinned at the sight of so well-dressed a man being under arrest. Tran saw a boy snatch a piece of cloth from a counter when the proprietor glanced up at the wrong time.

The walk took ten minutes and came to an end at the top of rue Catinat, by the cathedral square. Tran was ushered into the courtyard of a rectangular stucco building. The yard was filled with official French cars and jeeps. At the far end was a narrow door, through which he was taken upstairs to a small room on the third floor, where there was a bench and two chairs and a table. The two men who had brought him left with a word; Tran heard the door being locked from the outside. He sat on the bench and observed the wall opposite, where the plaster in one spot had begun to chip off; a small flake, jarred by the door's closing, now floated choppingly to the floor. He watched it come to rest by the table; then everything was still again.

The room was toward the back of the building, away from the noise of the courtyard. The single small window looked out on the rears of houses on the adjacent street, and farther off, among the low roofs, Tran recognized the red sloping one of the hotel where he had once stayed, years ago, during a physicians' conference soon after his graduation. The thought of that long-ago visit made him suddenly nostalgic, and for the first time since he had started out across the mountain paths away from the jungle, he acutely missed his wife and child. They were still in Hanoi, where they had stayed all during the time he had worked with the Vietminh. He had seen them only twice in three years. But simply having them nearby had kept them close. Now they seemed in another country. Just before he had left, he had sent them a message with the Moi courier. As soon as he was able he would get in touch with them, he had said.

His wife would wonder why he had gone to Saigon. Perhaps, after all, it had been a mistake. At the moment, surely, it would seem so. But the thought of going to Hanoi had never seriously crossed his mind. His mere presence would have endangered his family. And it would have represented a surrender, of the sort he was not ready to make.

He thought back again. What was lacking, of course, what had always been lacking and what had brought him here now after his error in approaching the boatmen, was the fact that he had no sense of conspiracy. He had never had one, not even when he had made his first decision to go into the jungle. He had admired Ho Chi Minh, but he had not been driven by any revolutionary or even political impulses. He had simply responded in a moment of crisis because he had felt he was needed to relieve pain. It was the trouble with being a scientist. Yet the crisis he had recognized—no one could possibly have avoided that. It had occurred during the incidents, what was only several but seemed so many years ago, at Hanoi and Haiphong, when the brutal killing had begun; and the terror. Whether the French or the Communists had been more to blame had been unimportant. It was actually the Vietminh that had destroyed his house, which was itself a travesty. His father, long years ago, had been imprisoned by the French, his death hastened, because he had belonged to one of the early nationalist groups. They had got nowhere, those first few cultural associations, with their vague and foolish attempts at assassination and appeal; but they had created proper martyrs. Tran's mother had fostered the compromise. It was she who had seen that he was brought up and educated in the French tradition; the physician's certificate he held had come from a French school, one of the few such that had been built in colonial times. He had, on rare occasions, even treated French patients.

At first, just after the war had started, when the Ho government had set up its northern capital in Hanoi and occupied Saigon as well, Tran had been disturbed at his own dispassion, his neuterness. He had kept to himself and not even talked to his wife about it, until he had suddenly decided. He remembered telling her, and the look of agreement, almost of relief that had passed across her quiet face.

There had been, of course, the considerable difference between his father and Ho Chi Minh, between the confined dream and the unconfined reality, and the need to make one's own effort at involvement. Perhaps he, Tran, had gone out into the jungle to discover himself. Under certain circumstances he might even have done as much for the French. Had it been inevitable, without any irony, that those who had caused him his greatest personal loss, the gutting of his home, happened also to be of the greatest need? And it was undeniable that Ho was a man who burned with a flame. One looked into his eyes, one listened. Tran had proved it for himself in half an hour's conversation. He would never forget the image of the taut, thin old man, on the edge of the cot, his finger leveled, crying: "They cannot defeat, the French, what I know to be true. We cannot lose, they cannot win." No matter what was said now, no matter what happened, Tran was certain that no one, neither the French nor the tyrannical young men from the north, would extinguish that flame. And it was the reason, he knew now, staring across the roofs toward the old familiar hotel, that he was here and not in Hanoi. His effort having failed, the cure he sought still lay somewhere between the dream and the reality.

He realized he had had nothing to eat since his morning tea and cakes. Now he might not eat at all, certainly not until they chose to let him. He was forced to laugh at himself. He would never before have worried about food, and he was amused at this new juxtaposition of dedication and need. Food had now suddenly assumed a different value. He was peremptorily faced, in this still-queer effort to come to terms with himself, by the absolute necessity of going on "living" for a purpose far beyond the old ordinary need to protect his existence out of force of habit or fear of dying.

He must have fallen into a doze, for he looked up, all at once, into the faces of two strangers, a Frenchman and a Vietnamese. They were standing by the table, like two contrasting statues, light and dark. Tran shuddered at the image of two pillars of a guillotine, with the blade, a sunbeam, suspended across the top. The Frenchman, for some reason, smiled, but the Vietnamese spoke.

"You are a Communist." It was said bluntly, and declaratively.

"No, that is not so." Then, almost to himself, Tran added: "I am here because, on the contrary, I am not a Communist."

"What is your name?"

"Tran Phan Dang."

"What is your correct name?"

"That is my only name."

"What do you do?" The Frenchman had sat down, but the Vietnamese, the questioner, remained standing. He was a small man, with a bullet-shaped head and a body that, even in its loose white suit, seemed composed of tight, hard muscles.

"I am a doctor."

"Where is your practice, then?"

Tran hesitated before he replied. "My practice is in Hanoi. But for the past three years I have attended the Vietminh soldiers in the jungle."

The Frenchman took out a gray handkerchief and mopped his face. Beyond the sunbeam, his skin now seemed even paler. Tran could tell, by looking at him, that he was sick.

"And yet you say you are not a Communist?" the Frenchman repeated, slowly. He had a peculiarly dried-out voice.

"Yes, that is what I said. It is the truth."

"You are very well dressed for a Vietminh doctor," the Vietnamese said, sharply. He grinned. "That is no doubt your jungle costume?" He pointed.

Tran saw no reply to make.

"What are you doing in Saigon?" the Frenchman asked, after a pause.

This was the question for which Tran had sought to prepare himself, and he gave his answer promptly, and with brevity.

"I left the Vietminh because of certain political events," he said. "Because I refused to join the new party, it became impossible for me to continue in my work."

"Doctors are scarce with the Communists," the Vietnamese shot back. "They would set no such compulsion. You are lying."

"No," Tran replied. "That is not so. It is especially those, such as myself, who have been engaged in separate and independent work who have been invited"—he smiled at his own choice of word—"to join."

"You have not answered my question," the Frenchman said. "I should like to know—what are you doing here, in Saigon, if your practice is in Hanoi?"

Tran knew he could not afford to hesitate. "I have come here first," he said, "to determine if I wish to resume my earlier work in the south rather than in the north."

"You have not been to Hanoi?"

"I came directly, across the mountains."

"And you have been here—?"

"Four days."

The Vietnamese turned his almost completely round head toward the Frenchman. When the latter said nothing more, he resumed the questioning himself. "If you will pardon me a moment, Monsieur Remy," he prefaced his next remark, "I should like to ask our friend, the physician, about his activities of the day. Now, in order to determine the place of this practice you wish to resume, you have come here to Saigon?"

"That is so," Tran said. He knew what was implied and once more he tried to anticipate the question.

"Did you have in mind a practice on the river, for the fish? Are you perhaps a fish doctor?"

The Frenchman laughed, but the face of the Vietnamese achieved a sudden and remarkable cruelty, as if a scar had come across it.

"I was walking about—" Tran began, but the Vietnamese interrupted.

"Obviously," he said. "We were aware of that. Yes, you were walking. And you paid a visit to some friends in the boats. Did you give them the message you wished?"

Tran sighed. "There is no message," he said. He was getting more and more tired, and he could feel his stomach tighten with the nervous ache of hunger and also with the bile of his own frustrated anger. It was hard for him to think, and impossible to tell if they had already prepared a formal accusation against him, having followed him to the river, or if they were only seeking a clue. He tried to recall having seen either the policeman or the man in the coolie suit. The former, he was certain, had not been on the dock; but the other might have been anyone, anywhere in the crowd.

After a few moments of silence, during which the three men in the room seemed transfixed as by some painter's exterior hand in the frame of their own reference, the Frenchman stood up, nodded at the Vietnamese, and together they went out. Again Tran heard the key turn in the door, and the lock snap. He closed his eyes as before and let himself drift back into half-consciousness, where all he could hear was the soughing of the evening breeze and somewhere, far off, the imagined slap of water against rock. He wondered what it would be like actually to starve. There had been times in the jungle when he had eaten very little for days at a time, but always enough to keep off the kind of griping hunger he now began to feel, which could give rise, he knew, to a state wherein one stopped remembering or caring, looking back or ahead, and the present evolved into a set of light images, sun-dried poppy-seeds that flickered in the broken bulb of the brain. . . .

He rallied himself. He had not done too badly, despite the fatigue. Whatever it was they obviously thought him guilty of, he had seemed to shake them in his bland denials, or at least to force them into the retreat of sarcasm. Nevertheless, he hadn't bargained for so much so soon. What had happened today had surely ended the dreamlike incubation of his initial act, of the euphoria of flight. Here he was abruptly confronted, in the market-place of his destination, with the hatched enormity of how far he had come and why.

The door opened and Tran opened his eyes to a yellow glare from the bulb that hung in the hall. He heard voices, but no one appeared. The dangling spines of light became fangs, and the empty space loomed like an animal's mouth. He wondered if he might be fainting, but then he saw the squat figure of the Vietnamese inspector emerge and heard the little man say, hollowly: "Well, then, you may go. But leave your address. We shall have another conversation. . . ."

It seemed quite unbelievable until he was out on the street. He found a small restaurant and ate ravenously, drinking many cups of tea, and when he emerged, the sky was a cloth of gray, as if a storm were brewing. The food had restored him, and although he was tired, he did not want to go back to the hotel. He began to walk again, along rue Catinat. Despite the change in the weather, there was a crowd out, strolling past the silver-shops and the cafés. The morning's ugly incident seemed to have had scant effect, for the cafés were packed, though Tran noticed that the tables in front were empty. He went past the place where the grenade had been thrown. Inside was broken wood and plaster, and there was a dark stain on the pavement. Had he noticed, in the doorway of the tobacco shop across the street, the dark-suit coolie loitering, he would not have stood so long staring at the patch of blood.

Chapter IV

M. Remy would be elated. He had seen them leave the club, she knew. By five he would expect the message; could they have tea at six? They understood each other well, in most respects, though he had lately taken to patting her hand like a lascivious uncle and telling her she ought to work harder.

◇◇◇

They were like actors in a bad play, all of them, she reflected. Remy himself made no pretense any longer. He had adopted the American system of mass production. Genevieve now knew of at least eight others like herself, most if not all of whom, she was sure, were equally aware of her. A few days ago she had witnessed an exchange, arch yet sheepish, between two of these girls on the street and had suddenly found herself joking and chattering volubly, the three of them standing like magpies in front of the Hotel Continental.

She would let Remy wait, this time. It would be the penalty he would pay for his impatience and for his condescension. Besides, she would have to be careful with the Consul. She knew he had been watching her, that he had watched her before. It was something that had to have happened casually. She had scarcely known the two Frenchwomen at the pool. They had started to talk, and the Consul had suddenly popped up alongside. It had been quite fortuitous, except that in one sense she wished Remy had not been there to see it.

He had chosen the restaurant well. Undoubtedly he wanted to be as *intime* as possible. She found herself vaguely wondering what the official attitude toward Eurasians was among the Americans. Was there, somewhere in the infinity of those steel cabinets, a directive, neatly typed, forbidding above or below certain ranks any "indiscriminate" comingling? For a moment Genevieve's imagination played her tricks; she thought she had actually seen the order. When she looked up, the Consul was smiling at her.

"And you will remain here, by yourself?" he was asking.

Genevieve smiled back and gave a small shrug. "I have been alone before, you see. I do not mind," she said.

A streak of sunlight, as sharp and thin as a needle, shot through the trellis and stitched his face. He was quite handsome, she thought, alongside the green vines. His smooth features, almost Oriental in the way they blended, with their yet completely American expres-

◇◇◇

sion, provocative and boyish, made for a peculiar attractiveness, more one of poise and confidence in himself than of actual good looks. The sealed sidewalk cage in which they sat, with its padlock gate, which had become the grim fashion in the city, seemed scarcely to discomfit him as it did others. The owner, with the key tied to his wine-chain, who was hovering now by the curtain that led to the kitchen in the rear, had managed well, Genevieve reflected, in his camouflage. The vines and flowers covered the trellis and still offered a fragrant, leafy glimpse, but less prison-pent than most, of the street outside. The meshed screen to ward off the grenades was carefully hidden.

The bottle of wine was nearly empty, the coffee served. There was a glow without as yet a drowsiness. The conversation had veered to themselves.

"It is better in Paris," he said. "In Paris there is a better loneliness. There is the sympathy of the streets, a softness of color and sound, and always those to be sad with you."

Genevieve laughed. "You are very poetic for an American," she said.

"We aren't all of us cash registers." He pretended to be hurt.

"But you are so preoccupied," she said. "There is no time for poets."

"It's not quite so bad," he said. "Now and then we manage."

When he smiled he looked his best, she thought. "Perhaps with us," she murmured, "there are too many. Too much is written, especially, of love."

"It is a way out of loneliness." He was regarding her closely.

"Or a way in, of self-pity. . . ."

She let herself think of Paris. For the first time in months she was reminded of the soft shades he spoke of, of the shimmering river-light and the cheap hotel where she had lived with her parents in the last season of the war, of the cot in the closet they had brought out at night for her to sleep on behind the Oriental screen. She thought of the imprisoning streets and of the German soldiers who stared, leaving her naked, and of the cold pursuing click of their boots on the parallel pavement. And then, inevitably, she thought of Pierre.

She sipped her wine, and drew slowly on the American cigarette, turning it between her fingers. There was, after all, no reason why he shouldn't know. To mention it now, having told the untruth earlier, could be turned to advantage.

"Actually," she said, "I was married, you know. But for a short time only."

He scarcely altered his glance, and Genevieve felt newly embarrassed. He must, after all, have suspected, she thought.

"Oh, to whom?" he asked.

"To a Frenchman. A soldier."

"Here in Indo-China?"

"He was," she said. "He is back in Paris. His family did not approve, you see."

"Because you are Eurasian?"

She paused. "Yes, because of that," she said quickly. "And because he did not tell them at once." She felt more on the defensive. "It was his father who objected," she explained. "His father was a famous soldier. Of the faculty of Saint-Cyr."

"It is not unusual, such things," Adam said. "Not even in America."

"It is finished, at any rate," Genevieve replied.

Through the trellis the pungent smell of a peddler's cooking-cart wafted toward them. She saw the cart's shadow in the dust, and then the cart and the old man pushing it. The world outside and the world within, the street and the café and herself between, affected her as though the shutter of a camera had stopped halfway between the flick of light and dark, the complicated mechanism locked, and she exposed. She followed the slow creak of the cart after it had disappeared, with only a faint cloud of dust where the shadow and the wheels had been.

◇◇

"I am sorry," the Consul was saying. "Perhaps I shouldn't have reminded you—"

"It is not that," she replied, still staring out. "When one eats and drinks, the sun is full of sleep. . . ."

Soon, she felt, whenever the opening presented itself, he would say: "But of course everyone knows it's *comme il faut* to spy in Saigon." It was more than a gambit by now. The Americans, too, had taken to playing the game, leaving spurious papers half-concealed in corners of their rooms. A floor-boy at the Continental, she had heard, had got his fingers caught in a mousetrap secreted at the bottom of a briefcase. The best way perhaps was to admit it, to let others think at the outset that one spied, to encourage the belief even, so that, feeling it was done foolishly, they would come to think it could not possibly be done well.

For the moment, however, the Consul remained merely inquisitive.

"It was your mother who was Vietnamese?"

"My mother was French," she said.

"But that's unusual, I think?"

"What do you mean?" She confronted his glance again.

"Only that in such marriages, isn't it most often the woman who is Asian?"

"My mother was the daughter of a rubber-planter," Genevieve explained. "My father, you see, came often to the plantation. He was an agronomist in the French service."

"Afterward you lived there?"

"We lived in Hanoi. Occasionally we would return, my mother and myself, to the place of my grandfather in Cambodia."

There was another silence, and then the Consul suddenly asked: "Your father had no politics?"

Genevieve was taken aback. "You are very curious," she said. "We did not discuss these matters. I do not know what he believed."

"And you?"

He was coming close, she thought, to the inevitable question.

She regarded him with a look of amusement. "I do not know," she said. "I do not know what I believe either, or whether it is even good to believe—"

"Nothing?" His eyes were twinkling.

She shrugged. "When one is uncertain, when so much of life is uncertain, it is better perhaps to believe surely in nothing." She allowed her glance to drop. "It has become too large a subject, this matter of believing. It is true of politics, and of other things as well."

"There are still individuals—"

"If there is opportunity," she said—"and luck." She paused once more, seeing a way out, or a postponement. "My mother provided a belief, but of a different variety."

"Because she was French?"

"Perhaps because it was, as you have said, 'unusual.' My mother was a woman without fear. She was also proud. She believed in my father, and she was always pleased with him."

He smiled at the phrase. "She must have been a good woman," he said.

Genevieve felt her color deepen. "My father was very kind," she went on. "He was good, and he was wise. With the French he was a great success. But, you see"—she hesitated—"I did not understand as my mother did. Without companions, living as we did, I grew frightened. I did not appreciate the advantages—of being as I was. Afterward I was ashamed. It was foolish, but the feeling was there, nevertheless." With a touch of gentle crossness, she added: "I do not know why I should tell you. . . ."

By confiding, she would gain his sympathy. He would suspect what he wished to suspect anyway, but less strenuously if she managed to disarm him now. Frankness and nostalgia were points in her favor. Besides, it had been a long time since she had spoken about herself to anyone. The sense of rediscovery made her seem suddenly alive within and to herself. The challenge of the Consul took on an added dimension.

She pursued the theme. "It was my own difficulty," she said, "my own fault that I felt as I did. But there is a loneliness of combined blood that is difficult to cure."

"It's something that's hard to comprehend," he said, "for others." He was tapping a finger against the tablecloth. "And with your husband—?" he asked. "If his family had known, if he had told them?"

"If my mother had lived, perhaps Pierre and I might have returned to France," she replied. "My mother would have helped."

"If there was another opportunity?"

She gave him a mischievous grin. "I would like to go to America," she said, "but it is too far away. Besides, I do not speak English very well, or understand the Americans."

"In many ways they are like the Vietnamese," he said, now laughing.

"I shall observe them more closely, then," Genevieve said, "but the view from here is limited."

"It is strange we haven't met before," he murmured. "At the pool, that is. . . ."

"I am there late in the afternoon most often," she said, "so that I can have the sun for myself."

The restaurant had emptied and the Chinese boy hovered near by, tall and willowy. The owner, the pudgy Frenchman, stood behind a curtain of transparent silk, fidgeting. In a joint burst of awareness that spanned embarrassment and led them each to look once more at the carefully cut flowers suspended from pots and vases on the shelves around the room and at the balloons above, Genevieve and Adam returned to regard each other across the table and to laugh at their tardy perception. The boy disappeared with a doe-like look over his shoulder, and they heard him a moment later softly singing as he crept up the stairs.

"The identity of anyone, you see, is hard to discover," Adam said. "It's more than a matter of blood alone."

Genevieve waited, and then he looked sharply at her. "Tell me—

the rest of the time, what do you do with it, with yourself?" he asked.

She shrugged lightly as before. "It is astonishing how it vanishes," she said. "One sleeps, one eats, one drinks wine with a few friends, and one goes to the pool. For the most part, one waits."

"For what?"

"For the war to end, I imagine," she said, "so that it will become possible to know whether it will be permitted any of us to continue such things."

His eyes, she noticed again, were darkly limpid. They seemed now to be sparkling at her.

"But, of course," he said, with a small wave of a hand, "you must also report to the Sûreté."

Genevieve was prepared. "Of course!" she said gaily. "But it becomes a matter of routine."

"And what do you think you will tell them about me?"

"Oh, that you are handsome and charming, and also very polite," she replied.

"And that is all?"

"That is all I know so far," she said. "I have done all the talking, you see."

"A good spy is a good listener."

"I am not a very good one, it is apparent," Genevieve said.

"The best way," Adam said, "is to find an angry man."

"An angry man?" she repeated, her brow wrinkled.

"A malcontent," Adam said. "A good malcontent is worth a dozen file clerks, or six room-boys."

Genevieve cried out: "Very well, then, tell me where to find such a one!"

Adam poured fresh coffee from the pot. "They're a native Indo-China product," he said.

"It is the monsoon, you know. It depresses some, while others grow mad," Genevieve suggested.

"No," Adam said. "It's more than that, but the monsoon helps."

"What is it more than that?"

"That's better," Adam said. "Now you're doing it better."

Genevieve blushed and burst out laughing.

"Well, then," she said, "are you one of them? Are you an angry man?"

"I'm an official identity," Adam replied. "Consul accoutered. A walking diplomatic pouch."

"You are very lucky," she said. "It is simpler to be one thing, in its entirety."

"On the contrary," Adam said. "There are various parts, and it's complicated. I'll tell you an unclassified secret, Genevieve. There are things sometimes one regrets doing, and things one always regrets that one cannot do."

"The Americans can do everything," she insisted. "It is their *raison d'être.*"

"It's not as easy as that either," he replied, with a smile.

"But you are the Consul!" she cried.

"There are others concerned, from Hanoi to Washington."

"That is the trouble with a war such as this." She shook her head sadly. "Especially one that lasts so many seasons."

"It becomes hard to give assistance for war and at the same time assistance for peace," Adam said.

Genevieve took this in and considered it. If he suspected, or simply assumed, that she was casually in touch with the Sûreté, then now he was wearing his discretion in a martyr's cloak, the way the Americans liked to do. It was the pose they pretended, of nobody understanding, of being maligned.

He was regarding her bemusedly.

"The human comedy, you see," he said. "But it happens all the time. You send guns, and then you send drugs to heal the wounds from the guns."

"Only it is not such a comedy."

"No," Adam said. "It's not."

"The Americans, with their good intentions, are responsible for much death."

"I wouldn't put it as harshly as that," Adam said.

"The Americans are always rushing in when it is too late, or insisting on reform when it is too soon," she said.

"Our timing's bad," Adam said flatly. "We're always one revolution or a war or two behind, aren't we?" He waited a moment before continuing. "Tell me, Genevieve," he said then, "why is it always 'the Americans' with us and never an American, Monsieur A or Monsieur B, the Premier, the High Commissioner or his political adviser, as it is with you?"

Genevieve decided to be careful. "I do not know about such things," she said. "Only that others, with more experience in such matters than the Americans, are apt to be wiser."

"The dictatorship of the *fonctionnaires*, yes?" He laughed.

"But of course!" she said, with pretended solemnity. "The French have not been here a hundred years for nothing."

"No," Adam said. "No one will ever accuse them of that."

He rose to pay the bill. The rotund little Frenchman swayed forward from behind his curtain, a soft white smile on his face.

Genevieve turned and peered once more through the vines that invaded the apertures among the blossoms of white flowers. The sun lay waiting, a tiger in the streets. She had a vision of the Cambodian plantation, an image of coolies returning to their huts, and she could even hear their voices as they headed for their mats of straw.

Suddenly she saw the shadow approaching. It spread in the dust like a stain, seeming to come to the very edge of the trellis, and Genevieve drew back. She knew, in that same camera-flick moment she had sensed before, that this time she had been seen; and, with a prescience that was frightening, that set her heart fluttering, she knew who it was who had recognized her.

The stain emerged, embodied, and stood ten feet away.

Through the glare she could see the familiar birthmark, the spreading scar, like a red spray covering the side of his cheek. Was it the suggestion of the shadow mounting that had let her know? Or had it been something else?

The man, a Vietnamese, was wearing the nondescript clothes of a common laborer, a brown shirt and a pair of baggy trousers. The skin of his mottled face seemed to shine.

Genevieve sat immobile. From the rear of the restaurant she heard the Consul's not quite perfect French expressing thanks and begging perfunctory pardon for being the last to leave. The Frenchman murmured, and then, incongruously, she heard the Consul's whispered request to be directed to the lavatory.

The shadow of vines flecking her face with light and dark, she now moved with a slight shake of her head. Outside, the man gazed up at the sun. Then he looked down again, at his wrist, where by a quick thrust of light from above she knew he was wearing a watch. He brushed at the dust with his feet, and with a final glance in her direction walked away.

She watched him carefully until he vanished, and then she swung around and almost lost her balance. The plump Frenchman in the corner crooked a finger to his left and Genevieve nodded, noting with vague distaste his half-open, pinkish mouth.

Lifting her eyes, she looked gingerly beyond the trellis. She saw the street as through a fragrant gauze. He would be amused when she told him with whom she had been dining. She remembered what he had said the last time: "We are gossips, all of us. . . ."

He would be coming tonight, she was sure of that. But what was he doing in the city by day?

She heard the Consul's voice, above her, saying: "Shall we go, my dear?" It was a first note of familiarity, properly struck.

Genevieve stood up. He had his hand on her arm, and she turned to him, her head tilted. "The lunch was excellent," she said. "It is a pity to leave the gilded cage. . . ."

◇◆◇

2

THE owner unlocked the gate, his small, obsequious smile substituting briefly for his pinched impatience, and before they had walked away they heard him trudging up the stairs. The sun reached down at them like a hot breath, and they went quickly for the cover of trees. Silently they went along the street, and Adam reached for her hand. Her fingers yielded, tenuously at first and damply, then discovered their own grasp of his. At the entrance to her house she asked him in for more coffee.

It was a small house, beyond the orange stucco hospital of the Sisters, set back from the road by an oblong garden that had a touch of wildness beyond neglect, as if, Adam thought, she had purposely allowed it to grow as it intended, with a modicum of care. The grass in a corner was knee-high, and then came gradually down until it lay greenly subdued at the edge of the path. A small willow stood over the roof, politely bowing.

Adam sat on the couch under the slow-turning fan and heard her stirring in the kitchen. He knew he would want to hold her, that it was no longer too soon, that their conversation in the restaurant, the long, leisurely lunch, had made it possible; that she would even expect it now, of an American. He liked, above all, the way she had countered, the manner that was both Gallic and Asian. She was a true Eurasian, a proper product, not simply the uncalculated, half-accepted, half-rejected child of the frequent marriage of convenience. Whatever rejection had come in her own marriage must have been a matter of pride.

He felt a sudden enervation. Since the moment at the pool when he had touched the water, leaving the pale, taut face of M. Remy behind him on the tiles, the episodes of the morning had fallen away. Now, when he least expected them, they were back, confronting him like wax blocks, cornices of guilt in the front of his mind. He had the quick conviction that the Minister, this particular afternoon, must have asked for him. Smythe accepted, reluctantly, the ways of

◇◇

the tropics, and among his crotchets there was at least no insistence that senior officers keep stringent hours. Yet this time, Adam was certain, Smythe would be annoyed by the absence.

She was still moving about. Adam smelled the coffee, the peculiar French blend they used, made from beans as black as tar, whose aftertaste lingered and made one's mouth bitter and dry. His mouth was like that now, and what he wanted most was a glass of ice-cold water.

"In a moment," she cried from the kitchen. "It will soon be finished."

He got up without answering and walked twice around the couch, slowly, then sat down again and lit a cigarette. His legs were set squarely on the floor, apart, and he placed his elbows on his knees. The ash of the cigarette fell, and he moved his shoe to erase it on the rug.

He could feel the blood in his head, flowing through his temples with its itch of life. Its liquid, interior whisper sounded like a taunt in his ears. What was he doing here, after all? Genevieve, inside, seemed far away, on the other side of the pool again in a haze of bikini suits.

How long, actually, could he manage this balancing act of himself? All the various layers of time and choice, the decisions rationalized or postponed, the issues he hadn't faced and the girls he hadn't married—above all, the confrontations of himself he had altered or avoided—were now suddenly impinging. It was bound to have happened, somewhere, he thought; but to have it occur here, in this particular place, where the running options were themselves so complicated, where drift and indecision alternated with quick, belated thrusts of action, bitter and romantic, wrathful and righteous, bumbling and brave, was a final irony for him, who had always managed to find a new horizon, a fresh compensation, simply by turning his back. What was it one did when one could not change a situation—one changed one's relationship to it? Philosophy, in these circumstances, was useless. Here one could change nothing, because nothing was permanent. . . .

He put the cigarette out against the sole of his shoe and flicked the butt out the window. He was frightening himself, setting unnecessary traps. If his old ability to sublimate, his special gift that had accounted for so many things, was jeopardized, he would find another way. He would not shift his ground, but simply hold this time, statically, like the French forts on the colonial highways. Even in non-responsibility there would be accountings.

Genevieve came in, carrying the small pot on a tray, and after she had filled his cup she walked to the cabinet for a bottle of cognac, bringing it back and removing the cap, bending over, until, without a word, he put his arm around her waist, which seemed smaller than ever, and brought her gently down. He kissed her quietly, and she let him, saying nothing, the smallest last-second smile on her lips and the cognac bottle still in one hand. The fan spun on, making a slight ticking sound as it filled the room with its hush of warm air.

It was better now. There was a peace again, and the logic of time. She rested against his shoulder and neither of them spoke, even yet. Knowing what he should be doing, where he should be instead, no longer rankled without meaning. But he thought sadly of the sad Southern girl who was his secretary and who must already be cursing him with the knowledge that he would be keeping her late again, past dusk, sitting across from him in the darkening room, where the shuffle of bare feet on the street below seemed always to Adam to counterpoint the running sound of her pencil across the pad, the footfalls filling the room with their whisper, the pencil the mechanical echo of his own official voice, which hung out there in the void, dealing, or trying to deal, with the shuffle outside, translating into cold and impractical sentences the untranslatable language that bare feet speak. . . .

Gently once more, Adam kissed Genevieve's brow. . . .

"You are thinking of something," she said. "Of something far away."

He laughed. "Perhaps I, too, have a conscience."

"You are the first American that I have ever kissed."

"It's a sign of the times," he said.

"You are cynical, as well as romantic."

"It's the American grain. It's necessary sometimes."

"But there must be a proper sorrow."

"Ennui is not enough?"

"No," she said, "it is not the same. One gets bored, as I do, it is true, but with a man there must be more."

"In my own case," Adam said, "it gets more complicated, but you're right."

"Perhaps you will tell me—"

He took her hand. "Perhaps," he said, "but not now."

He got up to go, and finished the cognac in his glass.

"I'll see you tomorrow, at the club?" he asked.

Genevieve thought a moment. "I will try to be there," she said. "I think it will be possible."

She came with him to the wooden gate of the garden and he took her hand once more and held it before he went out. Then he walked quickly away.

The heat seemed less oppressive, but the air was thick and moist, as if it were finally about to rain. Far above the treetops, shimmering, the light of the sun was like a translucent, yellow blanket laid out to dry.

The refraction was queer, as if the atmosphere were undergoing a violent change, the violence of which was unseen and unheard. It was neither light nor dark but somewhere between, like a phenomenon created off-stage. A herald of the monsoon, Adam thought, walking faster, breathing hard.

He imagined Genevieve, by now having cleared away the coffee cups, lying beneath the gauze of her mosquito net, incarnate of herself, meshed in blood and tone in the uncertain glow. He thought of the smile that had flitted across her mouth before he had kissed her, recalling responses that were both Eastern and Western. The allurement was not alone in the exhilarating mixture. There was something else, a purposefully fostered dichotomy of herself. It was as if she wanted to hover willfully between two worlds.

She had been at ease with him, however. Only once, in the café as they were about to leave, had she seemed nervous. It was when he had left her alone at the table. Moving through the transparent curtain, he had turned and seen her, with her head down, fidgety. Then she had looked out into the street.

Adam smiled. Perhaps she had simply seen someone, the very person or persons they had been joking about, someone who might have startled her by suddenly appearing outside the trellis just as she had been thinking of him. It was quite foolish, the game they played. What could there possibly be, on the surface, that the Sûreté did not already know about the luncheon chatter of the American Consul?

He was nevertheless puzzled at himself, at the contradictions of the day. The brief flagging had seemed the foretaste of an illness. It had been more than enervation, more than the result of the walk and the explosion following the talk in the Minister's office. The pool's assuagement had been anodyne enough for that. This was something different, something uncertain, like the atmosphere that hung miasmally above. He thought he could smell the monsoon's approach.

A flurry of jeeps broke the stillness. Sputtering, they bore down from the corner, and in a moment the street was full of soldiers. They were both white and native, and they deployed quickly among the houses, their guns at bayonet point, covering an area approximately a hundred yards square. Adam stood on the pavement and watched. There was a sudden shot, and the sound of glass shattering, then the angry voice of a French officer. Alongside Adam, two young Vietnamese privates laughed sheepishly.

A lone jeep drove up, protected by canvas, and Adam was surprised to see M. Remy leap out. The Frenchman was obviously flustered. He wiped his brow and, grinning embarrassedly, looked more liverish than ever.

"A coincidence to find you here, *Monsieur le Consul*," he said. "So soon after—" He grinned again, more widely. "We are conducting a small mixed exercise, which I have been invited to observe."

"A political exercise?" Adam said.

M. Remy snorted. "Everything in war is political," he said.

"Your bird-dogs have spotted a quarry," Adam said. "But one of them unfortunately has just barked."

Remy frowned. "They are young, as you can see," he said. "And the training is not yet complete. It will take a little time—I am told."

The young officer who had shouted at the shot strode up. He saluted Remy haltingly and was shaken off with a quick glance.

"There is no one in the house, sir," the lieutenant said.

"What are you telling me for? I am not your superior officer," Remy snapped. The lieutenant turned away with a look of perplexity.

The Frenchman saw the smile on Adam's face, and saw that he could not dissemble. He signed, long and audibly, and then, too easily, he yawned. "There was a report, you see, in connection with the throwing of the grenade this morning—" he began. He was interrupted by a scuffle at the far end of the adjacent driveway, and presently three soldiers appeared, dragging a boy of no more than fourteen.

One of the three stood aside. "We found him in a hut behind the house," he said, and pointed. "He was hiding."

Remy stared at the boy. "So," he said, and his eyes were like black spiders. "And where is his bicycle?"

"There appears to be none," the Vietnamese soldier reported.

"It will make no difference," Remy said. "We will find it later." He waved for the boy to be taken away.

Adam waited a moment and then he asked: "How do you know he's the one?"

Remy shrugged. "We do not know, of course," he said. "We suspect. It is simply customary, such cases. The Vietminh will hire such boys for a small sum. When they are caught, they know very little. It is never the same person who arranges the hiring. The Communists, naturally, offer no protection. It is expensive work, and dangerous, eh?" Remy laughed. His volubility was in sharp contrast with his initial discomposure. He shook his head. "It is a pity," he said. "Nevertheless, the boy will have to suffer so that others will not do the same. It is necessary, you agree, Monsieur Patch?"

Adam shrugged.

"But they are not members of the party, with voting rights," Remy added by way of explanation. There was a note of sarcasm Adam scarcely missed.

The soldiers returned to their jeeps. In a moment they sputtered off again.

"Can I offer you a ride?" Remy asked. "Back to work?" He stood smiling.

Adam shook his head. "No, thanks," he said. "I prefer to walk. It's not far."

Remy hovered a moment at the side of the covered jeep. "By the way," he said. "The ones we were talking about, before." He stopped, and laughed shortly. "The representatives of the people's republic—the emissaries. I think we will discover them, soon."

Adam nodded.

Remy gave up waiting. "Well, then," he said. "I hope you have enjoyed your siesta." He climbed back into his car and Adam saw him through the isinglass like a sea-horse under water. The street was emptied. The stillness settled back, the houses so silent that they seemed forsaken; but Adam knew a hundred pairs of eyes were watching him. He hurried away.

◇◇◇

At the Legation he found some cables in his desk. He glanced over them quickly. Near the bottom of the pile was one he read and re-read carefully. "Quai d'Orsay denies any reorganization of Saigon Vietnamese cabinet would purposely seek to exclude northern leaders," it said. "Further pressure this matter extremely delicate. Reinvestigate." It was signed by "The Secretary." There was a note clipped beneath, from Smythe, a single typed line: "Pls. see me tomorrow."

After staring at it for some moments, Adam put the cable back in the desk drawer and locked it in. The hand of Remy was again apparent. The Minister had probably mentioned the matter in passing, and Remy had alerted Paris. In the midst of negotiations, the last thing the French wanted was to have new members in the Saigon cabinet pressing for concessions.

His girl had left. There was another note, telling him she felt ill. He was sorry for her again, for all the girls like her. If he had known, however, he would not have come back. It was too late now. It would also have meant, as he would have wished, that he would not have seen Remy a second time, or witnessed the arrest. He did not relish being so privy to Remy's multifarious activities.

He put his feet up on the desk and swung around in the chair. The stillness endured. He closed his eyes and tilted himself back, his head catching the thin breeze now rising off the river, and he would have fallen asleep had it not been for the sound, distant yet clear, of artillery. It came from upriver, where the legionnaires were said to be mopping up. There was something elusive about the noise of the firing, week after week, like a doctor snapping his fingers from different corners of a darkened room to test a patient's hearing.

It grew quite dark, and the breeze died. He stood up and locked the papers back in the drawer, and was halfway down the hall when he heard the night phone in the Minister's office ringing. He debated whether to answer it or not. It could be anyone—the code clerk, someone from the High Commissioner's office; or, as was most likely, a mistake, something that happened regularly with the patched-up Japanese phone system jointly operated by the Vietnamese and the French. He decided to answer and ran back. Smythe's door was kept closed but never locked. Adam reached across the desk and got hold of the receiver in the middle of a ring. There was a pause, and then the flat, nasal "Hello, hello—is that you, Patch?"

It was the Minister.

"I thought you might have returned," Smythe said, after Adam had replied: "Yes, sir."

"Did you find those cables?" the Minister asked. "I gave them to your secretary."

The connection was bad and Smythe sounded far away, as if he were in a tunnel.

"I read them," Adam said. He must have spoken too loudly, for he thought the Minister grunted with more than acknowledgment, as if he had backed away from the phone at his end of the line.

"There's something more serious," Smythe said. He hesitated. Adam sensed a rebuke for his late return to the Legation. He quickly asked: "What's happened, sir?"

"The government in Paris is out again," Smythe said. "The IC appropriation was a reason, of course. The peacemakers are apt to take over."

"Do they have the votes?" Adam asked.

"With enough help from the center they could do it," Smythe said. "At any rate, even if it doesn't happen we've got to go slow."

Adam knew the Minister referred to the cable from the Secretary. It was not something to mention on the phone.

"I want to see you early, as soon as you get in," Smythe said. He hesitated again, but all he added was: "I'll be there at eight forty-five."

"Very well, Mr. Smythe," Adam said. He heard the clipped "Good night," and the receiver's click.

He went downstairs, past the Marine guard at the desk, a youngster he couldn't recall having seen before. The air had cleared, and even the wetness had diminished. The monsoon seemed to have veered, but he knew it would not be long now. The Vietnamese driver sat in the car in the ill-fitting uniform, waiting to take him home. Adam had almost forgotten the Navy party he had promised to attend. He took the wheel and let the driver go.

Chapter V

THE cathedral bulked in the upper square, a purple mass against the sky. It was like one of the hills in the north, Tran thought, where the jungle lowlands ended. The cathedral was like the conical shape of the hill, massive yet graceful in its ascent.

He had been walking since he had left the teashop, and now it was quite dark. The storm threat had passed, but the stillness was pervasive. Not even a *cyclo's* lamp could be seen, nor the whisper of its wheels heard. The tightness at the bottom of his stomach was gone, and only the bitter taste of the tea still lingered, pleasantly, in his mouth. He had walked around the cathedral twice, and now he stood and regarded it from the park with a sudden quietude. Then he turned back toward the square below. As he passed the police station, Tran smiled. For the first time in the city, he did not feel like a total stranger. The events of the day, even though adverse, had returned him his identity.

Rue Catinat had become filled with a hum, as though a rumor had been floated. The men and women on the sidewalks moved more deliberately than before. Tran passed a large restaurant where the tables were already re-distributed to the curb. A guard of soldiers stood nearby, but as Tran looked up he saw that they were not for the guests in the café but for those above, on the second floor, where there were Europeans. The men in their white suits and the women in flowing, light-colored dresses moved along the veranda, from where the tinkle of glasses wafted down. Presently a man came to the stone balustrade and leaned on it as he blew the smoke of a cigarette out into the night. Tran recognized, with a start, the American he had been next to at noon when the explosion had occurred, and with whom he had afterward briefly walked. He took a sudden step forward and bowed slightly. But a woman came quickly out and took the man's arm, and a moment later they were both leaning with their backs against the stone rail. Each of them held a glass, and Tran could tell, by the way their heads bobbed, that they were talking animatedly.

He stepped back into the shadows of the boarded-up flower-stalls, beyond the refracted light, and then he stumbled. A figure he had not seen was behind him. A voice grunted, and Tran, as he turned, muttered an apology. The stranger, like himself, had been watching the party. He was Tran's height, though more stockily built, and across his face, running down his cheek, was a dark patch that was like an ingrained stain of blood.

"You should have eyes at the back, when you stare at such lights," the stranger said. He spoke gutturally, and his tone, while contemptuous, was neither crude nor angry, the remark seeming to be directed upward, to the balcony, rather than at Tran for having stepped on his toes.

"Nevertheless, it is a pretty picture," Tran said.

"Do you think so?" The stranger scrutinized him. "It will not last," he added.

"The balconies will endure."

"Perhaps," the man said. "At any rate, the complexions of those up there will soon change."

The veranda above was now empty, but from the rooms a woman's single laugh broke like a cry across the square. The soldiers of the guard stirred, and one of them, a few feet from where Tran stood, dropped his rifle and softly cursed.

"What will happen to them?" Tran asked, curiously.

Without meeting his look, and moving his head so that a shaft of light made his skin seem the color of parchment, the stranger replied, with odd gentleness: "They will go. In one way, or in another way—"

"It will be necessary, still, to have friends," Tran said. He examined the stranger more carefully. There was a way about him that was familiar, an air of combined hardness and suppleness. Tran felt himself transfixed, as he had been outside the café in the morning, feeling he should go, that he was being imprudent, that somewhere close at hand was danger; but having to stay and engage himself as he had remained to look at the bodies in the sun, and had crossed the planks of the dock in the morning to address the old man in the boat. His doctor's self now cautioned him against further carelessness, but there was also this new curious self of his with which he had crossed the mountains.

He had already said too much, it seemed, for now the stranger's voice, so close that Tran felt the breath in his ear, was asking: "Do you call yourself, then, a nationalist?" There was a hollow quality that seemed to mock, Tran thought, yet he could not quite be sure.

He felt his heart pound as the adrenaline surge dissipated the calm he had felt in front of the cathedral. He waited a moment before answering.

"Yes, I am a nationalist," he said at length. "I am for the independence of Vietnam, of course."

"Then you should know we will assist ourselves," the stranger replied. "It is the fault of those such as yourself, who live in the cities, that you deem it necessary to seek help, when those who would ever extend it would only defeat you."

Tran could not help smiling, nor asking: "The Americans as well as the French?"

There was a pause on the stranger's part, and Tran could sense his stare. "The Americans above all. If you believe otherwise, you are the worst of many fools."

Tran looked back to the veranda. He could hear a single voice, declaiming, and then another, followed by a phrenetic laughter. A vagrant breeze lifted the sound and carried it, so that its echo hovered, fluttering, like a beating of wings against the wind around the square.

When he turned, the stranger was gone.

He started at once for the hotel, a mile away. The idea of a *cyclo* was appealing, but the walk, he thought, might do him good, might settle his nerves again. It took him thirty minutes, and he went upstairs immediately to his room, where he undressed and lay down on the bed. He felt hollowed out, more than physically excavated, as if the fatigue had at length welled over like a flood to fill the caverns of his body. For a long time he lay still, not wanting to move, with the recurrent image of the subcutaneous blood-patch on the stranger's face.

2

EXCEPT where the block of light was and the guard of soldiers still stood, the square lay dark and silent, far away to those in Irving Lockman's apartment on the second floor of Saigon's best apartment-house. Nearly fifty persons were present when the cap ceremony took place. It had been a badly kept secret, but if the commander knew it, he was covering up extremely well. "Skippy" Jones was the assistant naval attaché, and he had just received his third full stripe. Lucille, who was the secretary to Lockman, the economic-aid adviser, had sent to Hong Kong for the gold-braid cap. It had arrived just in time, on the weekly plane courier this morning, and Lucille has rewrapped her surprise in dry seaweed, for which she had made a special trip to a spot on the river, and her amah had fetched a hat-box from the cellar luggage-bin of the girls' compound. Irving's cook-boy had furnished a pair of chopsticks, with which Irving was now beating the top of the box like a drum major while rendering a South Sea tribal chant. Kelly, his chief assistant—he and Lockman were always joking with each other about the Irish and the Jews— had made a skullcap out of his old army handkerchief and put it on top of Irving's head. "A regular one-man wailing wall," Kelly shouted, and leaped away as Lockman aimed one of the chopsticks between his legs. Everyone laughed. Kelly was relatively new in Saigon, and his tireless enthusiasm, so far uncurbed by heat or dysentery, was widely cherished. He was a momentary lion, not yet at bay.

Lucille clapped her chubby hands, looking flushed. The couples were slowly drifting in. It was like a senior prom, she thought, all white and summerish, and as she looked over at Skip, his face red from drinking but handsome and still wonderfully boyish, she had a brief ache as she remembered, and for a moment it was ridiculous and sad. But then her palms were striking together again, and she managed to forget that in two more months their time was up— there was no longer any doubt about it—and he would be going back to his wife and family in Nebraska.

Outside on the veranda Adam and Nell Finch, who was one of Mr. Smythe's secretaries, had just clinked empty glasses. "We'll forget it, darling," she said. "But don't do it again, not ever. You made my poor little table all uneven." Nell called everyone "darling," though for Adam she reserved a special note, a subdued lingering over the first syllable, mellifluous and almost indecent. Adam gave her hand a light, perfunctory squeeze. What had happened earlier, on a sudden week-end in Manila, had been a mistake; it had seemed safe enough then, without any of the daily complications of office life.

"I'm really sorry," he murmured. "You know I couldn't help it."

He could, of course, have helped it, but after a difficult day he had been unable to face the prefabricated charm of the girls' apartment, a sorority-like affair near the center of the city that had only recently been built to handle the growing number of arrivals.

"That's all right, darling," Nell drawled. "We'll make up for it, won't we?"

Adam nodded. When she looked at you, he thought, her eyes shone with sad, rather canine wanderlust, a far-away and misplaced yearning. It was as if she had strayed into the whole world that was a pound for the unclaimed. She was approaching forty, and this was her fifth post. As with so many of them, she had left a small town out of boredom and a vague desire to travel to distant places, which, he knew, was in effect the desire to cast a wider net. But the places were always a gamble, and the people in them, the eligible ones, even greater gambles. It became something more than impermanent, more than tentative, Adam thought, a constant battle against time, a war of nerves that did different things to different girls, immobilizing some in fear and self-absorption and phreneticizing others into spurious gaiety. In all the time he had been abroad, he had yet to know a State Department girl who had been able to escape the strange, dragging anchor of home. They lived in compounds, often behind barbed wire, and they moved back and forth from their desks to a few cafés and their little Americas—the screened porch, the record-cabinet, the icebox stacked with beer and stateside rations. What went on in the streets outside remained a travelogue. . . .

"Let's go in," Adam said, taking her arm.

In a corner, holding a drink, Goodenough was observing the surroundings with scarcely concealed distaste. Goodenough's expression was always the gauge of the number of drinks he had had. It was only after the third or fourth that he began to relax, and the tautness disappeared and the tendency to flush too easily. He was obviously on his first of the evening. Spotting Adam, he now made his way along the edge of the room, like a well-bred pointer.

"The peasants and the Navy have taken over, I see," he said, nodding cursorily at Nell, but smiling at Adam. Goodenough always referred to those who worked for ECA as "the peasants."

"It's their show," Adam said.

"Oh, sure," Goodenough said, with casual restraint. "No objection raised. Just requires a little extra nourishment." He shook his glass and took a long swallow. For a moment he studied the amber liquid and jangled the pieces of ice.

"You were right noble today, I thought," he said. "Sort of took the old man by surprise."

"Thanks," Adam said. "I wasn't aware of the nobility. Just felt like talking, I suppose. Dangerous habit, sometimes."

"Oh, I don't know," said Goodenough. "Depends on what you really think."

"No," said Adam. "That's what it doesn't depend on."

Goodenough held his glass to one eye and squinted through it. "Doesn't, or shouldn't?" he said.

"It's a little late for improvisation," Adam said.

"You were listing alternatives like mad," Goodenough replied.

"Theoretical exercise," Adam said. "A little fun, at my own expense."

"You know," Goodenough said, slowly, "I think you're quite right. We ought to be pushing things more."

He seemed intent on continuing. "I doubt if we can pluck any of Ho's malcontents away, though," he added. "Be hard to find them, and even harder to get them to co-operate, right now. They'd be scared to death."

Adam nodded. "Hmmm," he murmured. In the circle, Lockman's chant was growing louder as his audience clapped and shouted in approval. Nell frowned at the distraction Goodenough was creating and put her arm around Adam's.

"Anyway, we ought to have these talks with the Minister more often," Goodenough was saying. "Good to lay the collective soul bare every now and then."

Goodenough's glass was finally empty and he drifted back to the bar. Adam and Nell joined the widening rim around Lockman, who had begun to perspire from the incessant pounding of the hatbox. He interspersed his mock chant with snorts of laughter as Kelly threw piaster notes, folded into miniature planes, at him. Several of the others standing around took part in this performance and now demanded a belly dance. Lockman's rendition of this had become a main attraction at American parties, and if enough drinking had been done he would combine it with a strip-tease, accompanied on Doc Gardner's mandolin, if the doc, who was public health officer, was around. The dance usually ended in Lockman's removing everything except his shorts, and he would then glide, like a hairy-chested sylph, around the room, collecting change. But, as Adam knew, he could be extremely serious as well. Adam had envied him his job, which permitted him to go freely about the country supervising the distribution of aid, the handing out of the cloth, the digging of the wells, and the movements of the mobile anti-malaria and anti-trachoma units. A month ago Adam had managed to take several days off and go with Irving, the excuse being a visit to the Hanoi Consulate. They had traveled by jeep and on foot around the rice-delta perimeter, the critical area south of Hanoi, and it had seemed to Adam that he had learned more in those few days than in all the months of writing reports.

Lucille had stopped clapping and was looking around anxiously, as if she were waiting for some final clue. Presently it came, as a whispered "Psst!" from Kelly, who disappeared into the adjacent coatroom. Lucille giggled and ran over, lifting a finger, a plea for all to remain as they were a moment longer.

Kelly was swearing softly. "Here, pin the God-damn thing on," he said, huskily. "I'm stuck."

Lucille helped him readjust the robe and the beard, as well as the scepter and crown—the last Kelly had purposely put on backward. "Hey!" he said as she righted it. "What'ya doin'?"

"Never mind, Father Neptune," Lucille whispered. "Get on out there!"

She pushed him into the main room, where Kelly promptly faded into a swan-dive and fell flat, barely supporting himself above the floor with his outstretched hands. "Now hear this," he gasped, in an Irish brogue.

"That's no Neptune, that's the Loch Ness monster," someone boomed, and a roll of laughter filled the room. Somewhere in the back a glass broke, the drink splashing.

"That's it!" Kelly cried. "I knew I forgot the liquid props."

Then suddenly he became sentimental. "Skip," he said, "I mean, Commander Jones, sir, we have here a tiny tribute from the deep, a little something from the topside fished up out of Davey Jones's locker."

"A cousin," someone murmured.

"It's not very much," Kelly went on, taking no notice, "but Lucille here," and he bowed to her, waving the scepter, "had to pay a special diving visit to me to arrange it. We hope you like it." He handed the hatbox to the commander, who fumbled with the string. One of the girls standing alongside undid it for him. When he lifted the cap out, with the seaweed dangling, another roar went up, and when he put it on, with two strands dangling around his ears, there was general clapping, and a flash-bulb suddenly went off. Then they had to pose for more pictures, he and Lucille—the young photographer, a storekeeper, had come by specially for the occasion —and the last one taken was of the two of them kissing under a piece of seaweed that had been tacked to the molding of the wall.

"That's one negative Skip better censor, isn't it, darling?" Nell Finch said, running a finger along the back of Adam's hand.

◇◇

3

LACASSE was way ahead when the Americans joined the game. He had been winning quite regularly lately and he had been waiting, with the fatalism that was part of his Corsican nature, for his luck to turn. He had determined, this time, to stop when the pendulum swung and to keep intact the bulk of his current streak's profit, which he would turn into francs at the official telegraphic rate, more than doubling his ultimate margin of gain and adding handsomely to his Paris bank account.

The wheel spun and came to a stop, with the ball again on number twenty-six, where he had piled a thousand piasters' worth of chips. The Chinese croupier doled out the calculated winnings, shoveling them nimbly toward the already sizable mound in front of Lacasse, who, with nicotine-stained fingers, embraced them tenderly and divided them into serried rows, diminishing in size, like the steps in the terraced rock-garden back home in Corsica, which had recently been on his mind. If he went to France this summer, he would go back to the island; it had been twelve long years and his mother was dead, and so was his brother, killed in the war, and there were probably squatters on the place, letting it run down, and he would throw them out and put it, after he had fixed it up, into the hands of someone he could trust, perhaps even of the Church. If the new war really came, the ultimate one, he might even go there and wait. He would dig a cave, deep in the stone at the garden's edge, against the bombs. Lacasse was so immersed in his thoughts of Corsica (there were canned goods that should probably be buried, and maybe also some of the money) that he forgot to put more chips down on the board and missed the next spinning, a sign, he had always believed, of impending losses.

He looked up and saw the Americans approaching. There were only two he recognized, the Consul, Patch, and the economics man, the Jew, Lockman. Lacasse felt something sharp, a prick of excitement that brought his mouth to a quick and cunning crease, which he turned at once into a benevolent smile, his best host's look for important patrons at his own riverfront club.

"*Monsieur le Consul, et Monsieur Lockman, bon soir,*" he said, and reached out to shake the five hands in turn, starting with the two he knew, and moving around to the two girls and the new man, the Irishman.

"You will come try your luck with me, yes?" he went on. "It is a good table, for myself at least," and he waved at the chips by his place. "That is bad luck, to boast, but I am very successful these days, you see. The wheel of fortune, yes, yes, it spins, it spins, all the time." He took Adam by the arm. "Come, you will play alongside me, and I shall bring you luck as well. . . ."

The little red ball danced and the eyes of Jacques Lacasse narrowed through the smoke as they watched the whirling and whipping luring of fate, shining like an elusive fish in the silver shoals of the revolving bowl. He loved the noise the big wheel made, a kind of hiss, sibilant and full of things he felt himself, secret things. Lacasse loved all mysterious and hidden sounds; water being poured in a dark room, the whisper of frightened, surreptitious lovers, and the muffled, fruitless stir of uncomfortable old women who prayed in the dim naves of cathedrals. He loved the night; the day left him dry, exhausted, and incomplete. It was only when the darkness came that he sensed the fulfillment of his private energy and power, the elixir on which he thrived and that had made him, in the quick postwar years, a figure in Saigon.

In the space of these few years Lacasse had built a hotel, two night clubs, and two expensive houses of prostitution, the one with Oriental girls from all the regions of China and the southeast islands, and the other with half-breeds, the Eurasians. He maintained, further, a certain influence on the docks, where he could get things both done and not done, depending on what suited his needs. But what pleased him most was that the attitude of the French officials toward him seemed, in the last few months, to have undergone a change. On several occasions lately this had gone so far as to include visits from certain persons Lacasse knew, quite surely, were working for the Sûreté. What is more, they had come to see him not for specific information, which he might have or might not have, or want to give, but simply to discuss what was happening in the city in broad and general terms. It was evident his advice had been wanted, and that he was no longer regarded as a pariah. There had even been a batch of invitations to semiofficial parties, and one to a rather select dinner-party at the home of M. Remy, who, Lacasse had ascertained, was one of the frequent nocturnal visitors to the High Commissioner's palace.

The gambling-hall was filling with the late, after-brandy arrivals. As they crowded around the tables and boards, the hall took on a luster. The green velvet surfaces seemed to glow with added attention, the chandeliers reflected the figures below in strange distorted patterns, flashes of color and bare skin. Voices rose, a babble of Chinese, French, and English that became a gamblers' Esperanto. The croupiers doled out fresh chips and waited for the bets.

Adam had begun to distribute his over the board, and Lacasse noticed with contempt the way the Consul played, dividing and covering himself, until, having already spread himself too thin, he dropped three blue markers at the last moment on square twenty-six. Lacasse was taken aback; he had been about to do the same. His hand now hovered, uncertainly, over the table. Just before the wheel started to move, he flung two hundred piasters on the zero. The wheel spun fiercely, and as it slowed, the ball skipped crazily along the rim, darting from blurred funnel to funnel, and bounced, finally, like a spent toy, into the zero groove. Lacasse sighed. He experienced a special throb of joy. The Consul having, as he chose to look at it, usurped the other number, Lacasse decided to consider the incident an omen, a private vengeance vouchsafed him. But while someone else, in relish, might have mentioned it, if only jokingly, he did not; to say nothing was part of the secret, masturbatory life Lacasse led. Only the croupier spoiled it. Raking the chips in, and handing him, as the sole winner, his new earnings, the Chinese said unctuously: "Monsieur has the ball at his command tonight." Lacasse grunted. Two spins later, he played the twenty-six and won again.

The cigarette smoke hung over the gamblers like a low bank of tropic clouds. The five Americans at the table were all playing now, but the two girls, one of whom was Nell Finch, were using chips dealt out to them, a few at a time, by Adam and by Kelly. Irving Lockman had crossed to the opposite side, where, in mesmeric absorption, and wrapped in the haze of his cigar, he pursued what he insisted was an infallible new system.

Lacasse was contemptuous of them all. The Jew at least seemed to take his gambling seriously, as befitted him; but it was obvious he knew little about it. The Consul, on the other hand, revealed in his random profligacy what Lacasse sought to discover in all Americans, their quality of nervous immaturity. The Corsican believed in the gaming table as a test of man's mettle. The newcomer, the Irishman, was a child, and played with his chips as he might play with marbles. The women were scarcely decorative. Among them here, Lacasse felt secure; this was his domain. At his two clubs, where he was constrained to treat the Americans as special guests who came more often and paid more generously than the French, he was too easily set off by their air of social superiority, or simply by their lack of curiosity and appreciation (had he not, after all, imported entertainers from all over Asia and even from Paris?). And at the new hotel, when they talked to him at all, it was to complain about their rooms. Lacasse could not attempt to weigh, dispassionately, the benefits the Americans were bringing to Indo-China, which cut too subtly across his own fortunes. Quite apparently, their guns were needed. But as for the rest, he was not so sure. Even what business they had created for him, he now reflected, carried with it a threat. That they had investigated him, he believed. He was aware they disapproved of the things he did, that in particular they objected to the influence he commanded among the coolies of the waterfront. Lacasse had suspected that some of the earlier antipathy of the French had been the result of representations, or at least of carefully dropped remarks made by certain Americans, perhaps by the very man now standing next to him (who was so foolishly expending his chips). It would have been one way, logical enough, for the Americans to assert themselves; and as for the French, they would not then have been averse to using him as a scapegoat. His position now suddenly and fortuitously stronger, Lacasse felt he could afford to be bold.

He addressed the Consul. "If you will pardon my saying so, Monsieur Patch, you are wagering too little on too much."

Adam regarded the formidable pile of chips in front of the Corsican. "You should teach me how, Jacques," he said. "In diplomacy, unfortunately, we learn to hedge our bets. We rarely gamble."

"Hedge?" Lacasse repeated.

Adam laughed. "Cover up," he explained. "Be prepared to withdraw, recoil."

Lacasse was perplexed. He looked across at Lockman, who for the first time had lifted his head from the board and was grinning at the Consul. But what Lockman said was merely further confusing: "Tallyho for Talleyrand. The Rover Boys in Indo-China, or Operation Stalemate." Then Lockman whistled, two notes, the first a little higher than the second.

Lacasse was never able to comprehend what the Americans were talking about. They spoke a language of their own, the words of which he understood, but whose combined meaning was always a jumble.

Adam, for his part, was not amused. He did not approve of Irving's cryptic, hit-or-miss humor and his friend's frequent lack of circumspection. Lockman could afford to quip; Adam envied him the privilege. As a non-career officer, Irving had true diplomatic immunity.

Lacasse sought to recover his point. "What I mean to say"—he turned again to Adam and spoke deliberately—"it is better at roulette to concentrate one's attention on a few selected numbers. Sometimes one wins, and perhaps one loses. But it is better not to try too many numbers at once, or the parts of numbers."

"As a boy, I played too much hopscotch," Kelly interposed. "That's my trouble."

Lacasse gave up. That was something else about the Americans: they didn't want to learn. They pretended to, but they really didn't want to. They were always there, however, with their money and their jokes, and they knew all the answers. If they didn't know them, they made them up, and then they made them sound authoritative. They knew how to do that too. They had a way, a quiet way, of imposing their authority, especially when they were together, and—it was something he had always noticed—they were seldom alone. There were always two or three of them, as there were now, acting as each other's foils and bodyguards. It was a fine system. There was no doubt about it, it was an excellent system. . . .

He played a few more games in silence, and then, cashing in his chips, excused himself. Without turning his head as he walked, but thrusting it slightly forward so that his torso seemed to be in natural tow, Lacasse made his way through the crowded hall, like a fish climbing through a clouded bowl. In the far corner he paused and, briefly resurveying his route, saw that the Americans were laughing, he felt sure at him. "*Les idiots,*" he muttered, and, turning back, approached a door by the vestibule. His hand on the knob, Lacasse knocked once and entered.

The room was empty, but there was a lighted lamp on the desk and a smell of incense, newly burned. He let himself sink into the sponge-like chair and, crossing his legs, sneezed three times. Then he spat into his handkerchief. The incense bothered him. He found it distasteful; it impinged on, rather than soothed, his senses, and he associated it vaguely with flesh and graves. He looked around for the stick and finally saw it, on a tray by the window, the red point glowing dimly, like a winking, wounded eye. He was about to get up and put it out when the door opened and Li came in. The Chinese greeted him with a perfunctory grin, the casualness of which did not quite hide the twinge of annoyance at finding him there.

"Ah, good evening," Li said. "So, you have won tonight some more, ha? You will put me into bankruptcy, soon, yes?" The short, jerky sentences, interlarded with rhetorical expletives, were something of a nervous affectation whenever Li spoke English or French. His native Cantonese he would speak swiftly, with guttural authority, neither hesitant nor questioning, but certain and cruel. Once, from behind the thin partition of a restaurant, Jacques had accidentally overheard him, and the sound had spoiled his appetite.

"You do not like the Americans, ha?" Li said. "That is an excuse, perhaps, for taking your winnings away." He laughed. "Well, there are other tables, you know. That is the advantage of my place. If you are successful with one wheel, too successful, you will lose with another, ha. My friend, you should have roulette at your club, as I have told you."

Li's jocose familiarity was, as always, neither friendly nor unfriendly. It was a curiously incomplete relationship they had, founded, at the outset, on mutual distrust, having blossomed into guarded interludes of conversational fencing, and developing, more recently, into a broader contest in which both men bartered as well as bantered facts about each other. In these exchanges Li had been the consistent victor. With indirection and a peculiarly offhand air, the Chinese would manage to surprise Lacasse by revealing himself privy to some detail of the Corsican's activities which Lacasse was always sure had been unknown. Li took obvious if mild sadistic de-

◇◇

light in passing these tidbits back, as if he intended indefinitely to keep Lacasse supplied. Lacasse remained patient. At some point, he felt, the barriers between them would be broken and understanding would arise; the parrying would cease. He was willing to wait until the Chinese made the first declaration. There had been little in the interim he had been able to find out about his adversary.

"The Americans do not know how to play," Lacasse said. "Their money is a toy."

"They have many toys, then," Li said.

"But they are children."

"Toys are for children, yes. Perhaps it is we who take our toys too seriously."

Lacasse sensed a barb, and again Li surprised him. "Come," he said. "We will go for a drink, ha." Li owned a night club across the street, the most expensive in Cholon. Lacasse got up from the chair, pleased at the invitation, glad to escape the joss-stick on the sill, and silently followed Li out, weaving through the still-crowded hall to the garishly emblazoned door, where all customers, European and Asian alike, were searched for weapons before they were permitted to enter. The Chinese paused and the harsh Cantonese dialect leaped out of his throat at a small man with an egg-shaped head that glistened, one of Li's assistants whom Lacasse recognized as having seen on the streets downtown.

When they were outside, Li reverted to French. "That man is a fool," he said. "He has too big a mouth."

Lacasse said nothing as they waited for some cars and a bouncing, antiquated bus, packed with soldiers, to pass in the dust, the motes dancing wildly in the glare of the headlights, and settling, afterward, through the kaleidoscope of shadows.

"For a Chinese," Li repeated, when they had crossed, "he has a mouth that is too big, that one. Perhaps because he was born in this country."

Lacasse was astonished. He had not expected such a disclosure, even indirectly, about Li himself. There were various stories he had heard. Some said the man known as Li Kwan-sen had been born in Cholon and had gone back to China during the war, and had then returned to Indo-China in 1945. Others claimed he was a native of Canton or Foochow and had come to Indo-China for the first time only three years ago. Still others were as certain he had been born in Hanoi and had lived almost all his life in Indo-China, making periodic trips to Canton and Hong Kong, where he had "interests."

Lacasse, at any rate, had no intention of losing his opening.

"But you have been here many years yourself," he said.

Li withdrew. "Yes, ha. Some years. Come, I am tired this evening. Let us go in."

They sat at a table in the corner, away from the five-piece Filipino band that played Hawaiian music against the backdrop of a Chinese landscape. Both men were silent. Lacasse pondered how he might pursue the advantage.

He tried a different method. "It is astonishing the amount of new business here," he said.

"Here? How?" Li echoed, absently.

"In Cholon," the Corsican said. "In the last year in particular."

"The French do not like it, ha?" Li asked, laughing.

Lacasse sniggered. "They are probably afraid of the Communists' using the merchants as a shield," he said. He was not aware of having said "they" rather than "we." In the dim light the face of the Chinese had grown impassive.

"Ha, but that is foolish," Li said. He sounded momentarily more friendly, despite the contradiction. "We are a business people, and we are citizens of China, but we have no politics overseas." Lacasse believed Li at least gave him enough credit to recognize the understatement.

"And if Mao comes?" It was a boldly naïve question, but Lacasse was determined to be as artless as Li mocked him to be.

◇◇

Li smiled. He was obviously enjoying himself. The barrier was tentatively down, even though Lacasse knew it would go up again. "Communist soldiers will dance the *Yangko* in your clubs as well as mine."

"And that is all?"

Li shrugged. The smile hovered. "The Americans will have to go," he said. "On this we are agreed, yes?" And now he laughed, raucously. "Roulette will become a profit-sharing game, ha? The wheels will belong to the people."

"As for the French?" Lacasse inquired, his voice curiously off-tone.

Li gave him an amused glance. He seemed, quite suddenly, an altogether different person to Lacasse; these unexpected changes were bewildering. "But you are always so far ahead, Jacques," the Chinese said. He had never before, Lacasse realized with some abashment and a touch of resentment, called him by his first name. "And why is it you believe Mao Tze-tung wishes to come here? He has troubles enough at home, ha?"

"It is altogether possible, at some time—"

"There are many things possible. Perhaps the Americans will come." Li raised his head. "There are two coming now," he said, and he crooked a finger in the direction of the shredded-bamboo door, through which Adam Patch and Nell Finch were entering. "We shall invite them over to join our discussion." There was a fresh note of sarcasm.

He got up from the table and went forward. Lacasse could not help noticing the calm host's manner, so much more adept and unselfconscious than his own. When the three came back, he squirmed and gave a slight twisting bow, still half in his seat, his stomach caught against the table, and shook hands for the second time in the evening with the two Americans. He wondered, at once, how much the Consul had lost.

"We are discussing the future," Li said. "Very informally, ha.

You will favor us by having a drink?" He beckoned to the waiter, who came running. "Don't run, you fool," Li muttered in Cantonese, under his breath. Lacasse heard him, without understanding, and shivered.

Adam and the girl slid onto the bench alongside Li, whom Adam knew only casually as the owner of both the club and the gaming parlor. He had no desire to become involved. Had it not been for wanting to make amends to Nell, he would have taken her home when they stopped playing. Now, when the Chinese turned to him, smiling too broadly, and said: "And when do the Americans believe Mao Tze-tung will come to Indo-China, *Monsieur le Consul?*" Adam felt a sense of despair.

The question might have been ignored, or politely laughed off, had not Nell made some response imperative. "Tell them, darling, what's the latest poop," she said. She reached for his hand. "Decode a cable for the people."

Adam was forced to play up. "We have it on high authority that he is already here," he said. "Right here in Cholon, not more than a mile away."

The Chinese roared at the joke, and Adam thought he was well out of it, until Lacasse turned to him, poker-faced, and said: "That is entirely possible. It is what I have been telling Mr. Li, but he will not believe me. It is a pity, don't you think?"

"Our Corsican friend is worried about all the gold he has buried, ha," Li said. "He does not think they will give him time to dig it up."

"Yours is the buried gold," Lacasse parried weakly. He resented as a wounded child the identification of himself as an island outlander. Turning to Adam, he sublimated by blurting: "And how much more gold did you lose to him this evening, Monsieur Patch?"

"I managed to break even," Adam said, "after you left." He was determined not to give Lacasse the satisfaction.

"A remarkable recovery," Lacasse murmured, dejectedly.

"I won," Nell Finch said, gilding the lily. "Well, I mean I was ahead until the last two spins."

"You should learn when to stop, mademoiselle," Lacasse said, with slight recaptured enthusiasm.

"You can say that again," the girl replied.

There was an embarrassing silence as they all sipped their drinks. What could one do with such people, Lacasse mused. His life seemed compounded of small hollow victories. . . .

"There was a grenade in a café, on Catinat, this morning," he said, at length. "Did you hear?"

"Yes," Adam said. "I was nearby when it happened. Only a block away."

"How fortunate you were not there!" the Corsican said. "How fortunate none of us were there! It might so easily have been the case."

"It is much safer in Cholon, you see," Li said.

"The Vietminh grows bolder," Lacasse went on. "Soon it will be impossible to travel in the city, as well as on the roads beyond."

"Then you will have to go home to Corsica, ha?" Li said. Lacasse ignored the taunt, but it was apparent the defenses were back up. "Are there *banditi* in Corsica, Monsieur Lacasse?"

"There are *banditi* everywhere," Lacasse replied. "Everyone calls the enemy of the moment *banditi*. In your country"—he emphasized the possessive, with an accompanying smirk—"first the Kuomintang called the Communists *banditi*, and now it is the other way around."

"There is no longer any room for the true *banditi*," Li said. "It is a shame." He turned to Adam. "And in America, *Monsieur le Consul*, are there still *banditi* there as well? Or have the Americans solved the *banditi* problem too?"

"There are crimes," Adam said. "But very few bandits. Perhaps in the West, occasionally."

"That is a pity," Li remarked. "It cannot be very exciting in

America. A country with no *banditi* must be very commonplace."

"We have other forms of excitement," Nell Finch said, as Adam reached for her hand, but not for the reason she thought.

"There is the atom bomb, of course," the Chinese said. "But that is an unsatisfactory excitement."

"Extremely unsatisfactory," Adam said.

"Then why do you practice it?" Li looked back at him.

It was the old story, the old resentment, Adam knew. Sooner or later it always came out, and there was no use explaining why the bombs had ever been dropped, even on Japanese soil. The fact that they might have been justified, on military if not on moral grounds, had nothing to do with it any longer; if it ever had. It was undoubtedly the greatest victory the Japanese had won in Asia, even though it had come too late, after their own vision of empire had been mutilated, cuckoo-like, in the blood and broken bones of the hundreds of thousands of fellow Asians they had destroyed with such compulsive fury at the old imperial dusk.

"We are willing, you know, to sign an agreement," Adam said.

Li shook his head. "If you wish to win friends in this part of the world," he said, sententiously, "a declaration must come first."

Adam refused to allow the argument to develop. "Perhaps there is still some hope," he suggested. "It may be—" he stopped. It would be wiser not to mention the Russians.

He looked down at Nell and said they would be going. It was three o'clock. "Well, I am sorry," Li said. "We will finish our talk some other time, yes, ha?" He came with them to the door, leaving Lacasse on the bench, and when he returned he stood across the table and breathed cigarette smoke out of his nose. "He is an attractive man, the Consul," he said, slowly. "Unlike other of his countrymen, he does not talk too much."

He stood waiting for Lacasse to move, until finally he stepped back and declared: "So, my Corsican, we must go home too."

"I am going," Lacasse said, extricating himself. "And if you do not mind, I am a citizen of France."

"What are you ashamed of, to be a Corsican?" Li asked.

"I am ashamed of nothing, but I am a Frenchman," Lacasse said, testily.

"I beg your pardon," Li said. "I thought you were a *banditi*, like me." And at this he put his arm around Lacasse as he guided him to the door, laughing. "Your car is across the street, yes? Good. When you come next time, you will lose some money to me, ha?" As the door shut, Lacasse could hear the laughter float away, shrilly, like the cry of a nocturnal bird.

The air was unexpectedly cool as he walked across the compound alongside the gambling-hall. The hall was still lit, and for a moment he thought of re-entering. He went to the side and urinated. The car, when he decided to find it, was at the end of the compound. The driver was asleep, his head against the wheel, and Lacasse opened the door and jabbed him sharply in the ribs. The Vietnamese jumped, and then grinned in sleepy recognition.

"Back to the hotel," Lacasse ordered.

The machine lurched, and as it went out the driveway, bounced Lacasse on the springs. The driver swung around and headed toward the European city. In the rear Lacasse belched, and closed his eyes. He felt buffeted. It had been a strange evening, yet one of some progress, he thought. His mouth fell into wet repose. By the time they reached the hotel, he was dozing, and in front of him the cave in Corsica loomed. . . .

4

THE girl had put her head on Adam's shoulder as he drove. She was waiting to see where he would turn, saying nothing, though she sensed his annoyance. Finally she could stand the silence no longer. "I'm sorry, darling, if I said something I shouldn't have."

"It's not as if one were talking with Americans," he said, but not too crossly, she thought. "The wise remark doesn't really work, even if it's well meant."

"But I only said we had other kinds of excitement," Nell said. There was a pout in her voice. "I wasn't thinking of the atom bomb at all." She moved a little closer to him.

"I know," Adam said. "But that's how it always is. It's easier to wait, to let them do the talking."

"Where are we going?" she asked now.

"Home," he said.

"Yours or mine?"

He looked at her. "Which do you want?" he asked.

"You know which, darling," she said.

It made no difference for the moment, he thought, despite his previous resolve. Perhaps, in the long run, it would be easier. Earlier, much earlier in the evening, there had been the possibility, as the ceremony in Lockman's apartment was ending, of leaving quietly and driving past the house of Genevieve Brouillard, to explore. It was Lockman himself who had suggested the gambling, and Nell had overheard, so that it had been quickly decided.

The streets were black. Adam went two blocks out ot the way. The small house with the gate at first seemed totally dark, but then he saw a faint glow as if from an all-night kerosene lamp. And as the car swept by, he thought he saw the dim outlines of two heads, a man's and a woman's.

Nell lifted her head from his shoulder. "What's the matter, darling?" she said. "You're not still mad, are you?"

Adam managed a smile. "No," he said. "You're forgiven." He was wishing he had driven straight home.

Nell stirred by his side and suddenly flung herself back against the seat. "Oh, Adam," she said, sighing. "Hurry. . . ."

At the corner he gave the wheel a sharp twist and the brakes screeched. Asleep in the gutter over the bars of his *cyclo*, an old man twitched and, leaping up in fright, stood hunched as the car vanished down the block. He coughed and lay down again between the shafts. . . .

Chapter VI

T<small>HE</small> clock in the tower of the cathedral struck twice. The sound sifted through the stillness and the white gauze of the mosquito net, until it seemed to Genevieve Brouillard to come into the bed with her, a distillation of tone, as if she herself had sounded beneath the sexton's bell. She shivered with the melancholy echo and turned over on her back. The sheet was hot and damp and clung to her skin like a shroud. A paleness invaded the room in the wake of a cloud and threw a mottled shadow, the reflection of the moon's haze on the tracery of leaves.

Why hadn't he come, she wondered. Outside the restaurant his behavior, the ritual of recognition, had seemed certain enough. The whole night had been strange, the weather shifting back and forth. The monsoon was capricious. Whatever was in the air, the tension had built up, until sleep was far gone. She awoke too often in the night now, and had taken to listening to the cats cry and to wait for the cocks to crow before dawn. Sometimes there was the far-away thud of the big guns, like a hollow beat from the depth of the swamp, and once there had been shots nearby and the noise of cars and men's voices; but she had remained quite still, with no desire to get up. In the morning she had heard that a neighbor had been murdered, the Vietnamese editor of a pro-French newspaper, whom she had remembered as a small figure always walking with a stoop of sadness. A week later, during one of Cau Minh Thien's visits, he had inquired if she had seen what happened, and had seemed relieved when she had not, exclaiming, as if in apology: "It was unfortunate to have it happen so close by."

It was hard to realize that she had known him only six months. He had appeared at the foot of her garden one evening at dusk. She recollected how he had taken her unawares. She had looked up at his scar, and it had frightened her. She had instinctively thought it was a wound, and that he was seeking help.

He had introduced himself as having come lately from Hanoi, where he had been a student at the university. There had been a letter, he explained, from her father, in Paris, to his father, an old friend in the north, a suggestion that he visit her. He never again referred to the letter, yet he had made it sound so real—even quoting her father—that Genevieve had never doubted it.

They had sat in the garden until the mosquitoes had driven them inside. He had described his life at the university to her, the classes, and the meetings outside the classrooms, where some of the same men who had taught innocuous lessons by day had given "the truth" about Indo-China by night. . . . "I led two separate lives," he had said, smiling across at her. "We all lead various lives, but two are better than many or none, and one is better still." And he had kept on oddly smiling.

That opening conversation had been a talisman. He had automatically assumed the role of an oracle, of a prophet who was determined to treat her like a disciple. For the first time, listening to him speak about his father and hers, Genevieve had comprehended her father's involvement. It had been a peculiar experience, listening to a stranger invest her father with a life she had only dimly suspected, with life itself. "They accomplished nothing, those old ones, with their meetings and manifestoes and their tea-drinking," she remembered him saying, "but they created a conscience. . . ."

It was not until the third or fourth visit that he had even mentioned the name of the Vietminh. And one night—it had been after the shooting nearby—he had spoken of the secret order, the *Tu Ve*. Thereafter he had left her each time like an austere lover who knows he must be patient.

What was it that, almost from the start, had made him necessary to her? Certainly he had played upon the special condition of her loneliness and had quickly created the idea of reality, an image of an identity that she might seize. There had been something truly prophetic about it, as she thought back, and something eerie. There were times when she felt that he had come to her like death, with prior knowledge. Softly, like death, he had dealt with her. She had been afraid. Today, in the restaurant, she had felt his shadow stalking her like a prescience of death.

She had tried, on occasion, to comprehend it, to examine as much of herself as lay exposed. Was it, she asked, the alternate life she had led and was leading, the pool and the promenades, the house secure, secretly paid for each month by Pierre's father through a Saigon bank? Or was it Pierre himself, and his old officer friends who still smiled slyly at her on the sidewalks? She had never forgotten what she had overheard one of them say, after Pierre had begun to rejoin them in the cafés: "Brouillard is with us again. He is tired of his mestiza. . . ."

None of them had ever approached her, or even said a word beyond a greeting. They were afraid, perhaps, not of involvement itself but of having it get back to the old man, Pierre's father, retired, but still a power in Army circles. Or was that, too, a rationalization? Did Pierre stand as a kind of symbol to them, half fool, half pioneer—a monument to the error of his ways? When she saw them now, she both pitied and hated them. They were not soldiers, but boys in uniform, full of the smugness of boarding-school cadets.

The Consul, inadvertently, had touched upon it, had made her aware how suspectible she had been. His solicitude, his other-country, almost non-white approach, his outsider's air of benevolence, were what she might earlier have wanted, in recompense even, from one of the others, whose ways she had been reared in, whose blood lay split within her. But she had been relegated to strangerhood. And what Cau had then provided was a secret vengeance, in return for which he had demanded his own brand of fealty. In the six months, he had not asked her for anything except on occasion some food, but he had made her listen to him talk. He had not so much as touched her hand, and if he had, she would probably have told him not to come again. But he had seemed satisfied to deal in something altogether different, metaphysical and sexless, something that in time, he intimated, might be accorded her more completely. It was part of the fear he inspired that she had waited instead of asking. In the world of Cau there were no easy volunteers; but she had sensed a clandestine violence.

The contrast with Paul Remy's world was sharp. At dusk, after the Consul had gone, Genevieve had sat in the garden, half expecting to see Remy drive up, uninvited, out of that uncontrolled curiosity of his that had seemed to increase since his illness. He had to be indulged, to be treated as a child and encouraged in his game. At the beginning, when she had met him at the Cercle Sportif, he had been far cleverer, she thought, and more amusing. Alone among the French, he had been solicitous. "It was not your fault with Pierre, you must always know that," he once had said. "In that world of theirs, Saint-Cyr, there is only guilt and pride."

She had dined with him several times after that and he had spoken casually about himself, though she knew, as it was generally known, that as a political counselor his standing was extremely good with the High Commissioner. He had come out to Indo-China with the earliest French contingent, dropping into Saigon by parachute when the Vietminh were being driven from the city by the British soldiers, the original occupiers. After the illness, when he had come out of the hospital, he could have returned to France. He had insisted on staying. Within him, beyond the malady that had made him querulous and didactic, that had led him to self-dramatize, remained a hard core, his own brand of dedication. The sickness, while it had affected his personality, had served more to split than riddle him. One could see him daily fighting it.

Eventually he had asked her for a "favor." He had put it very formally, as if he were embarrassed. It had been a strange request: to purchase books for him at a certain shop and to observe the shop-owner and his Vietnamese customers. Genevieve had laughed at the role, but she had done it to please him. She had performed well as an eavesdropper. A week later the shop had been boarded up. He had thanked her profusely. She had refrained from asking what had happened to the owner.

Their relations had remained proper and informal, the tea-drinking ritual becoming part of the small contest they played, the implication that she was somehow being "protected" remaining unstated. Lately he had said to her: "You should meet some of the Americans, you know. They are attractive, and they will take you to dinner at Le Vieux Moulin. It will be good for both of us, for your stomach to go, for my liver to stay home." And he had laughed, trying to hide his now discolored teeth. On another occasion he had suddenly asked: "Don't you consider the Consul handsome?"

Sitting in the garden as it had grown dark, Genevieve had thought about Remy's advice and about the Consul's kiss, what it had been like to have another white man's arms around her again, someone's mouth against hers. Had he at that moment touched her breasts, had he quickly undressed her, she would have allowed him. The moment of consent had come in the restaurant, when he had returned to her side after she had seen Cau in the sun.

She was thankful that Remy had not appeared. She had remained in the garden, becoming slowly conscious of the night's breathing, of its separate, immaculate existence, the round, danger-ous warmth of its prowl. The sibilance of *cyclo* tires had seemed like an improper whisper. Finally she had had her supper inside, and at midnight she had gone upstairs to bed. She had lain awake for an hour, and then she must have fallen asleep. Since two she had been awake again, and now, as the clock struck three, she heard the simultaneous howl of a cat just outside her window. She twisted on her stomach, with her face to the pillow. The old, full loneliness was back, and neither the gray light nor the cats helped, nor the three chimes' tolling. She closed her eyes and reached desperately for sleep; and then, quickly, she sat bolt-upright.

The gate whined. A rat scurried through the garden grass. She leaped up and went to the door before she heard the triple knock, three slow and single raps. When she opened it he entered swiftly, the moonlight pursuing him. He stood in silence as she searched for the lamp, and she could hear his heavy breathing. When she brushed up against him, holding the match, his arm was damp and his scar shone like a phosphorescent gash. As she touched the match to the wick, he walked over to the couch and sat down heavily. She waited for him to speak, but he remained silent, and after several moments she said finally: "It is light tonight, the brightest it has been for many nights."

For the first time, Cau looked at her. "It is their luck, to have the searchlights of the moon." His voice was tired and low, and even gruff.

"Are you hungry?" she asked.

"Some tea, perhaps. And some cakes or fish, if there are any."

"I will see," Genevieve said. She went to the kitchen and returned almost immediately with a platter of prawns and several pieces of thick brown bread.

"The tea is on the fire," she said.

He reached for one of the prawns with his fingers. "You were sleeping?" he asked.

"I was expecting you," she said, "but not so late."

"You should have known," he said. "It was the reason, at three o'clock, I looked at the sun and the watch."

"I saw that," she said, "but I did not understand the meaning of both."

Cau said nothing, biting into the bread. Genevieve fetched the tea and poured them each a cup. Then she sat alongside him on the couch.

A car engine sounded from far down the street, coming closer.

◇◇◇

The headlights threw a bright shaft that illuminated the garden and a corner of the room. Genevieve started, then turned her back, sitting sideways. "What is it?" she whispered, but the car, with a burst of light and sound, was gone. The stillness seemed even greater, broken only by the crunch of Cau's teeth against crusts.

"They are all about the city tonight," he said at length. "It is becoming more difficult each time."

"Has something happened?"

Cau bit on the bread again and shrugged. "Whenever there is activity on one side, there is activity on the other as well."

"There were two killed this morning," she said. "A Frenchman and a Vietnamese."

"Yes," he said. "I know."

"And that is the reason for the movement?"

Again he shrugged. "Perhaps," he said. "There are various reasons."

She waited, listening to the stirring of another rat, or the same one crossing back. Cau had finished eating, and she poured more tea. There was a breath of dampness.

"When there are strangers in the city, there is also more activity," he said. He had taken a folded pack of cigarettes from his shirt pocket.

"Who are these strangers?" she asked.

Cau's eyes looked grayly into hers. As if it caused him pain, he smiled.

"The lost ones," he said, "who have no home, whom all suspect."

"There are many such," Genevieve said. "Perhaps we have all become too suspicious."

"It is a way to be," Cau said. "A proper way."

Still emboldened, she asked, "Are these strangers from the north, then?"

He nodded. "They are northerners, yes. That is, they have come from the north now." He drew on his cigarette and blew the smoke out, staring up. "They are like moths, who come close to the light but will die without reaching it."

She hesitated. "Perhaps the Emperor's police will protect them."

"There are not police enough. And such strangers are expendable."

"Do you know who they are?"

"We know."

"Have you seen them?"

"The pattern of wandering is always the same, the way of the lost ones."

A silence followed, during which Cau ate more prawns and drank more tea. Genevieve waited until he was finished.

"Since it has become more difficult, is it not also more dangerous for you to go about the city when the sun shines?"

"Perhaps," he murmured. "But one cannot live continuously in the dark."

"Was it for them you were seeking?"

Cau's smile was like a glow within a glow. "You have grown more curious," he said. "That is a change."

Genevieve glanced down at him.

"You have made it so," she replied. "Is it not what you wished?"

He did not answer her, but, reflecting a moment, said: "It was not for the strangers I was searching. I had an appointment in the market-place with someone, but I did not find him."

He poured the remainder of the tea and sat with the cup in both hands. For several moments he stared at her over the rim. She waited, as she had waited before when she knew he expected her to.

"Was he solicitous, your American? Did he buy you a satisfactory lunch?"

Genevieve showed her surprise with a frown. "How did you know there was an American?"

Cau laughed. "There are advantages, you see, to walking in the sun."

Genevieve re-created the shadow at the trellis. She wondered if Cau had followed them all the way from the pool. "He was very polite," she said.

"It is the function of a consul," he said, dryly. Again she was silent. "I did not know there were Americans among your friends."

"I am not so solitary, after all," she replied.

Cau ignored the answer. "What did you talk about?" he asked. His tone was blunt.

"We talked about Paris," she said.

"Only Paris?"

"No, not Paris only."

"Did he say, as they all say, that he wanted to go home?"

Genevieve watched as Cau got up abruptly and walked to the shuttered window in the rear.

"The Americans are eager now to remain," he said. "Their words mean nothing. They have acquired the fever of saviors."

"There were things he would wish to do that he could not, he said."

She heard Cau's snort. "That much is true for us all."

He turned and looked at her impassively. She let her eyes drop, feeling disturbed.

"It is curious you should have selected the Consul," he said, slowly. "I am acquainted with him."

"He comes often to the pool. Today we met," she said.

Cau moved sharply away from the window as the lights of another car bore down the street and with a white sweep shot past. Then he came back to the center of the room. She remained still, so still that the breath in her body seemed stopped, her blood not coursing. He sat down again, with his hands in his lap.

"There will be help needed now," he said. His voice was flat, without emotion. "A general strike has been called. It has been decided that the campaign of action is justified, even though it has meant the death of some of our own people."

He had never before spoken to her so directly. By letting her understand what he believed, and why or, more importantly, how, he had begun by provoking the questions he sought, stirring, if only vicariously, her beginning attachment through the mystery and excitement of his own existence. She had been her own witness, standing aside from herself as a spectator to the process of persuasion. There was evil in it. The way he had done it was evil. He had made it infallible. And now, even worse, he was making her feel that he was commencing to trust her.

She waited once more, her lips dry with the taste of the tea. Cau's eyes seemed fixed on some object below. He struck another match, cupping it, and its shadow seemed to enlarge his face. "It is the Americans who have the endurance. Therefore it is the Americans who have become the second enemy," he said.

"Therefore . . ." Genevieve repeated, softly.

If Cau heard her, he was not yet ready to pick it up. "The activity of the revolution throughout the country, in the south as well as in the north, must be brought into focus," he said. She might hardly have been in the room, he seemed so detached, so bloodless, with that quality of withdrawal, of near-disembodiment, he could put on like a cloak. "We are in the stage of attrition. The work of those fighting in the field must be tightly co-ordinated with guerilla work and sabotage in the rear. This is true of the cities in particular, and of Saigon above all. Here the enemy is entrenched."

In the world Cau described, the battles in the north had always been made to sound like some distant hostility. From time to time he had referred to them as if he were issuing communiqués on a conflict that took place in another country, between two parties with whom he was scarcely concerned. What counted with him was the war waged here, night after night, in the two cities. The wider the sphere of the greater war, the more particular did his become, until his clenched fist seemed to contain all the fury that was necessary for the destruction of the enemy, if not for the destruction of them all.

She could no longer wait. "The help you spoke of," she whispered. "What is to be done?"

Cau crushed the cigarette out and smiled. When he spoke again, he was still grinding the butt. "One must act to avoid, as well as to correct," he said. "As the war continues, it becomes more important."

Genevieve said nothing.

"It is the Americans who have created the complication," he went on.

She forced a smile. "The Americans only? They are blamed for so much, the poor Americans." She thought of what the Consul had said. She had never before dared tease Cau, and now it had its effect as he looked at her queerly.

"The Americans have become the dangerous strangers," he said. "It is partly because they are so naïve."

"It is a virtue sometimes," she said. "Whether open or in disguise."

"It is not a virtue, but it can become a weapon," Cau replied, more tersely. "By themselves, the Americans are fools. Nevertheless, their foolishness is dangerous when encouraged by others. That is when they come to believe themselves saviors."

"The French do not encourage it. The Americans are suffered by them."

"As a sick man suffers his doctor," Cau said. "It is not the French, in this case, one must guard against."

"The Vietnamese here are their prisoners."

Cau looked patronizingly at her. "You, too, are naïve," he said. "That is a charm, however, and also a weapon."

She sighed and thought suddenly of Remy's tired provocations. She had never mentioned Remy's name to Cau. Once or twice, when she had felt herself on the verge of it, the incident of the bookshop had stopped her. That had been more than naïve, more than a game. Cau Minh Thien would surely remember the affair; to reveal her part in it would anger him. Perhaps he already knew that too and was waiting for her to confess. That was the trouble, the unspoken knowledge they all harbored, the masks of suspicion they wore. By keeping her counsel on Remy, she retained part of her mask. One should not drop one's masks too lightly. It was impossible to guess the number anyone wore. Probably they were all working for at least two sides, and it was only the third or fourth that counted.

"There are others, beyond the sycophants and the kept ones," Cau said. "We would not be so close to victory, if this were not so. But there are also the waiting ones, and the lost ones. Like the Americans, they are of little consequence by themselves. But there is a fresh danger when they come together. They are like harmless single substances that burn destructively when combined."

"If it is a natural chemistry, perhaps it is unavoidable," Genevieve said.

"Nothing is unavoidable," Cau said, shortly. "It is what I meant by acting to avoid."

Genevieve felt herself shiver with a nervous start. Cau noticed it and stopped speaking. Once more he laughed, but cruelly. "No," he said, "you need not be frightened, Genevieve. You will not be asked to throw the grenade."

He coughed and went to the window once more to spit. His voice continued from there hollowly, stagelike, out of the circle of the moon's refraction. "It is a matter of correct timing, you see." And then, like a patient schoolteacher: "Consider your experience today. You lunched, at a certain time and place. It could be arranged again, similarly. A small restaurant away from the center of activity, always an excellent site."

Genevieve's eyes ached with staring at him, and now she brushed a hand across her face. Cau's gaze fixed itself on her. With an odd, almost anticlimatic tenderness, he added: "Do not be upset. It is an example only. But you will understand that you must be careful. If you are ready to help—"

For several moments they were both silent. Cau finished the last bit of tea from the pot. Genevieve's mind was whirling. The thought that he was not altogether serious, that he had simply been fitting the Consul into a diagram of action, was hardly assuaging. What was important, she knew, was the reality of what he had been out-lining, the fact that anything, as he had said, could "be arranged." Death most easily of all. The Consul, in his cream suit, hovered in front of her, his dark face static.

She shivered again. The shape of Cau, compact and gray against the blackness of the wall, came closer. "It will of course be proper for you to see your American. It will actually be advisable," he was saying.

Genevieve stirred herself. She took the teapot and the empty plate of prawn shells back to the kitchen. When she returned, Cau was standing at the door.

"I will tell my friends," he said. "This evening we will speak together. In Cholon there is a Chinese club, on the avenue, across from the parlor of the gamblers. At one o'clock . . ."

The first thin light hovered in the garden. Suddenly she felt the tips of Cau's fingers brush hers, and then the grip of his whole hand. She heard him whisper something incomprehensible.

A shadow in the quarter-light flitted across his mouth, which seemed fuller than before. The loneliness of dawn surrounded them and they stood at the threshold and regarded it as if it were some immense and inarticulate animal, huge but gentle, encroaching out of the jungle on soft and ancient feet.

The shutters on the street were still drawn and dark, and the tiled roofs shone dully. Except for the aching of a branch across the way, there was a total silence. She heard him murmur: "Your American, after all, is more fortunate than myself. . . ."

He stepped forward as she removed her hand. "It is growing light," he said, "I will go quickly."

He pulled up the collar of his shirt and walked down the path, without turning. Genevieve closed the door and watched him through the latticed window. When he had disappeared she went into her bedroom and took her clothes off. She lay down on her back, drawing the net around her, pulling the sheet up across her naked body. Her arms were crossed behind her head.

All of it, she thought, was a contradiction, including the fact that she now felt so calm. There was awe, no longer fear. The incomprehension was of herself, not of anyone nor any thing. She did not feel herself in rebellion. There was no anger; only some new, strange quality in her soul, something hard and inflexible that had dimly begun to suggest flagellation and sacrifice.

Involvement to the point of non-recoil. . . . Was it, after all, what all of them sought, not Cau Minh Thien alone? Even the knowledge that with him, and with those like him, there was no game, that none would be possible, no longer disturbed her. Fanaticism must have its own core of conscience in denial of guilt, in denial of love as well. What Cau had said about the luck of the Consul would be as close as he would come to unmasking himself.

There was a new chill in the air, off the river. Genevieve turned on her side and closed her eyes, discovering them wet. There remained a reason to seek, a reason to want. The true conflict lay between loneliness and despair. For the first time in as long as she could remember, she wished she had a child.

She slept. In the dream she soon had, Cau stood menacingly at her side, wearing, for one awful moment, the Consul's cool, unblemished face.

She awoke to a vendor's cry that rolled up the street, piercing the unsatisfactory shutters.

Chapter VII

SLOWLY, hesitantly, the dawn slid across the rice paddies, il-luminating the covered water, stirring the blanket of flowing grass. In the bivouac to the north of the city, the French sentry unslung his rifle and handed the guard over to the young German legionnaire. *"Eh b'en,"* he said. *"Ça va."* The blond German said *"Gut,"* and added, politely: *"Gut schlafen."* Less than a mile away, where the jungle began, the Vietminh boy high on the branch observed the shift through an old pair of Japanese glasses. He scribbled the time down on a slip of paper and stuffed it into his pocket, then sat in the crotch of the tree and ate the bowl of rice an Annamite girl had handed up to him on a forked pole. In the city, the shutters of the small frame houses opened, while those of the larger homes stayed closed, the servants moving stealthily, squatting in the wet stone kitchens. The stalls in the markets opened like crude wood fans, and the produce appeared on top of them through a maze of hands and baskets. Surely, more permanently, the padding of feet came to the pavements. On the palace lawn the soldiers reappeared, and the young lieutenant. The cathedral clock struck, and the Annamite nuns went to pray. In her flat, where he had brought her two hours ago, Nell Finch twisted on the bed and turned off the alarm. She felt that she might sleep for days, but it would be a pity not to savor the response of her limbs to her stretching. Smiling as she yawned, she moved aside the mosquito net.

2

AT HALF PAST six the black-suit coolie had come out of the teashop where he had been dozing, and had resumed his vigil opposite the

Chinese hotel by the gaming parlor. An hour later, in the dining-room, Tran was finishing his tea. The pale figure of the Chinese manager hovered at the inner doorway and went by with a nodding glance.

Shortly thereafter, imbued with a sense of mission as he had not been before, Tran was riding downtown in a *cyclo*. The young *cycloist* stood high in his seat and pedaled hard. The very tempo of the morning city seemed heightened. Several blocks before they reached rue Catinat, Tran shouted to the boy to stop. He did not want to make himself conspicuous by debarking directly in front of the European hotel.

The lobby was dark and blinding after the sun. When his vision had cleared he saw the two Vietnamese and the elderly French-woman behind the desk. He recognized her at once. There was no mistaking it—the jutting jaw, the pince-nez, the powder-laden face, the faded yellow hair cast in the wide-holed net. Exultantly, he walked up to the desk and bowed.

"How are you, madame?" he said. "It has been a long time, many years, in fact, since I have seen you."

"Yes?" she replied, looking up at him blankly.

"And you remember me as well?"

Her pale-blue eyes regarded him out of the humid past, and she shook her head, a little sadly. Then her thin lips broke into a tired and slightly cynical smile. "But no—I am afraid I do not make the recognition. Your face—but we have so many—"

"Ah, but of course, it was many years ago. I am a doctor, you see. There was a meeting here."

"A meeting? Let me see. Ah, yes, I remember such a meeting, a gathering of the physicians. They were mostly French. That is to say, that is why, perhaps— But they came from everywhere, that I remember."

Tran laughed nervously. "Yes, yes, that is right. You have it now. It was indeed long ago. Well, you see, I was one of the native doctors."

The old lady sighed and reached into her pocketbook for a flowered handkerchief. "Well, well, and that was, let me see—" She paused, reflectively, and then she straightened up. "But we have no rooms, unfortunately, if that is what you wish," she added, shaking her head.

"No, no, madame, I do not wish a room," he said. "I will spare you the embarrassment of a refusal." And he laughed, tapping the counter-top. "However, there is a small matter about which you may be able, perhaps, to inform me."

"Monsieur?" She examined him again, with a degree of puzzlement, over the top of her strange glasses.

The two Vietnamese boys were listening. The younger one, barefooted and naked to the waist, was dangling a duster between his legs. For a moment, except for the liquid whisper of the three overhead fans, the lobby was soundless.

"I am searching for—one of the American journalists," Tran said. He stopped a moment and looked around, then added, hurriedly: "I have forgotten his name, but I was told he was staying here, at this hotel."

The woman lowered her head and ran a waxlike finger over a list tacked on the blotter in front of her. Then she turned around and looked at the wall behind her, where the names of guests were also posted beneath the key-hooks.

"But there is only one at present," she said at length, "and that is Monsieur Perkins. He has gone yesterday, to Hanoi."

Tran stood in silence. He stared past her head at the small white name-cards written in a flourished script.

"And you do not know if he returns, tonight perhaps?"

She shook her head. "No, I am sorry, monsieur, but there is no way of telling, of course. There are inquiries all the time." She shrugged. "Sometimes it is only for a few days. Perhaps it is for weeks. It will depend upon the fighting."

Tran thanked her. He walked back into the sun and crossed

over into the children's garden, where he sat on a bench in the speckled shade. Two Eurasian youngsters, a boy and a girl, chased a ball beneath his feet and he bent down to pick it up. The little girl stood before him, laughing shyly, and then, putting her arms around him, climbed onto his lap. Tran stroked her hair until the Chinese amah ran up, apologizing, and lifted her down. The nurse scarcely understood his counter-protestations as she dragged the youngsters off. Reproachfully, the little girl stared back at him.

He crossed the gardens and went through the center of the square in the white blaze. At the bottom of rue Catinat, where he had approached the boats and accosted the old man, he stood gazing at the new unfinished hotel, which the French and the American officials had already taken over. From the lobby the hammering and chipping of the workmen finishing the interior reverberated hollowly. Tran looked up and saw, standing on the third-floor parapet, an elderly American man with an extraordinarily pale skin. Steel-rimmed spectacles high on the bridge of his prominent nose glimmered whitely in the sunlight. He had his hands in the pockets of his pressed khaki trousers, and as Tran watched, he reached inside and brought out a khaki cap, which he jammed fiercely on his head, pulling the brim down. Now bent over the stucco ledge, the old man saw Tran below and grinned, foolishly. There was a sadness in the grin and something lonely and dispersed as he stood there. The man had an air of having arrived for the first time in the Orient.

From the hotel entrance a Frenchman in white shorts and shirt emerged onto the sidewalk and scowled into the brilliance. He was pudgy, and his stomach bulged; he had an unhealthy pallor, which the yellow light enhanced. Square against the dark patch of the doorway, his hands on his hips and his fingers extended, the Frenchman was like a block of soft, decaying stone. From his manner Tran guessed he was the manager. Had not the elderly American just then appeared down the wide circular staircase inside, stopping to drop his keys on the glass-top desk and continuing out, Tran would have asked.

The American stood blinking in the doorway. Then he pointed up the street and inquired, in French so bad that Tran hardly understood it, if the American Legation lay in that direction.

The Frenchman lifted his hand off his hip like a semaphore and motioned silently the opposite way. The American grunted, and took a khaki handkerchief from a pocket of his trousers, mopping the perspiration off his wrinkled neck. "It is very hot here," he murmured. "They told me it would be hot. But not like this."

The Frenchman still said nothing. A car came quietly to the curb, an American-made car driven by a Vietnamese in white, who sat motionless at the wheel without looking at the hotel. Against the shiny blackness his small figure looked like a stick of chalk. Presently the American walked over and spoke to him, and he nodded unconcernedly. The American climbed in as the Frenchman watched, his eyes alone moving as the car went around the corner. Then he softly grunted.

Edging closer to the hotel doorway, a foot or so from where the Frenchman was standing, and without directly addressing him but staring down the street, Tran said: "The American autos are beautiful. Also, they are extremely well constructed."

Lacasse grunted once more, a little louder.

"For the roads of Indo-China, however, they are not so suitable," Tran went on. He had not yet met the Frenchman's eye. "They are too large, I imagine. It will be especially difficult when it rains."

For the first time Lacasse looked down at him, then away again, across the river, and belched. "The Americans require such things," he said. His vehemence took Tran by surprise. "It is simple," he muttered. "With the cars comes cement, for the roads to be made wider."

"But with the increase of the fighting, how is that possible?" Tran asked, ingenuously.

Lacasse jerked his head back and snorted. "The cement has ar-

rived, you see, so it is settled." He motioned vaguely at the piers,
where the ships were being unloaded. "There it is," he said, spitting.

Tran wondered if this was a joke. He did not pursue the subject.

"And are there many ships that have come?" he inquired,
politely.

"Many, yes," the Frenchman replied, with a bored air. "They
arriving each week now." He snorted again. "They are full of
things the likes of which you have never seen before."

"What sort of things?" Tran asked.

"All sizes and shapes," the Frenchman replied, and he gave Tran
a sly look.

Tran stared out across the river. "The Americans are very
rich," he said. "It is both proper and good that they should extend
themselves."

Lacasse ran his tongue around his mouth. "It remains a question,"
he said.

Tran hesitated. "You are the manager of the hotel?" he asked.
Lacasse nodded vaguely.

"The Americans will live here, I imagine?"

"Yes."

"Others as well?"

"If there is room enough."

"It will be very expensive, no doubt."

"Oh, extremely expensive." Lacasse sniggered. "But our American friends do not mind."

"Are there many already arrived?"

"There are some," Lacasse said. "There will be more this week."

Tran debated with himself. He might, he thought, under the
circumstances of the conversation, inquire of the manager if there
was any objection to his going inside; or he might be bolder about
it and simply walk in, through the lobby and the lounge. Perhaps
there would be someone, another man in a white suit, such as the
one he had talked to in front of the café.

A jeep bounded down rue Catinat and swung sharply onto the hard dirt alongside the hotel wall. Before Tran was aware of it, he found himself looking into the eyes of the Frenchman who had been at the police station. Liverish as before, the face was even more impassive; without a flicker of recognition the man looked past him to the manager.

"Well, Jacques," he said, "have the Americans not yet cashiered you?"

Tran moved away. Behind him he heard the deferential reply: "No, not yet, Monsieur Remy, not yet. But soon perhaps."

"It is because you are not *sympathique*," Remy said.

"I shall let you know," Lacasse said. "I shall come to you for a job, or protection."

Remy was laughing as Tran moved another few steps. "Ah, well, Jacques," he said, "there are many things you can do, I am certain of that. As many, no doubt, as you have already done."

"Worse . . ." Lacasse said.

Tran felt the blood mount to his head. The laughter of the two men disintegrated. He found himself at the corner and, without looking back, went around it. With exasperation, he kicked at the dust.

The market drew him back. Here he could immerse himself. He wandered as before among the stalls, the impromptu counters and benches strewn with cloth, the pots of food and baskets of flowers, the voices praising and complaining. They held to a common level, like the hum of bees in a summer hive. The divines squatted over their coins and cards, and the old women sat crosslegged on the sidewalk, murmuring their bargains at the sun.

At the corner he bought an ice on a stick and stood sucking it by the pilot's quay at the end of the street. The perspiration was coursing over his face. There was a gleam of bodies in the unguarded sun of the riverfront, where the coolies were chanting as they worked, their straw hats bobbing. In the street the *cycloists* moved through the haze and heat and dust, bouncing like wet balls. All of it spun, vertiginous and bright, and for a moment he thought he was going to be sick. He shivered; and then his eyes focused, and the dizziness stopped. His heart seemed to stop beating, but he turned and ran down the adjacent block. In front of a teashop he came to an abrupt halt and, glancing back, darted in. His body was drenched. Quickly he drank several cups of tea, sitting with his back to the door so he could watch the street through a piece of broken mirror on the wall. There was still an awful throbbing where his temples pulsed, and his mouth stayed dry and sour.

He wondered if he had imagined what he had seen, if the two figures in the market had not obtruded, perhaps, on his subconscious. Such things could happen. He was sounder than that; besides, he had not been thinking of them, together or separately, but now he remembered the impression the one had made, in front of the European apartment. He had felt, even then, that he had seen the man before; or someone like him.

He could no longer do nothing. He had to reclaim himself. Fear belonged in the jungle. He did not believe the man had seen him; nor, he thought, could he be certain the political officer had. But the option of indecision no longer existed.

His eyes fastened on the rusted mirror. Its images were distorted, faces and bodies passing by were severed and foreshortened. But neither of the two men emerged from the lunatic glass. The round head of the Tamil shopkeeper hovered, proffering more tea. Tran shook him off and threw some piaster notes on the table. Outside, he headed for the marble building on the parallel street, where he remembered the flag on the tarnished staff.

3

REMY and Lacasse sat in the unfinished bar, where the workmen were hanging the huge mirror that had just arrived from Paris.

"You will be looking at yourself too much, with something as large as that," Remy said.

◇◇

"Perhaps I shall walk backwards to avoid it," Lacasse replied, testily.

"Never mind," Remy said. "None of us looks very pretty these days."

"You are feeling better?" Lacasse asked.

Remy smirked. "Sometimes," he said, "it feels better, then it becomes worse again. The liver is unpredictable, like everything here. This country, this war."

"There is a resemblance," Lacasse agreed. "A same quality of corrosion."

"The condition is chronic," Remy said.

They watched the mirror being adjusted by the half-dozen laborers, who suddenly, in weird, unordered unison, put down their tools and left.

"I am sorry I cannot offer you something to drink," Lacasse said. "We will be open for business next week."

"It does not matter," Remy said. "*Perrier* is a poor substitute for wine."

Lacasse was thoughtful. "I have been considering making a trip home this summer," he began. "To Corsica. It is many years since I have been there."

Remy nodded vaguely and Lacasse wondered if he had heard. "Do you think," he went on, "that there is any likelihood of a decisive battle before the autumn?"

Remy smiled, his yellow teeth showing. "You are better informed than I about such matters, Jacques," he said.

Lacasse blanched, then felt the blood rush to his face. He would not know what Remy implied.

"I hear gossip only," he murmured. "All of us hear gossip, but it is of no significance."

Remy was still smiling, like a cat. "There are those who live by gossip," he replied. "The making of it, and the dispensing of it, the believing or not believing of it."

"It does not win battles," Lacasse suggested.

Remy shrugged. "It is a form of skirmishing," he said.

Lacasse tried again. "It would be pleasant to see my family," he said. "However—"

"I am more fortunate, perhaps, in that I have no family," Remy interrupted. "It would have been better if I had, I imagine. I might have left this place last year."

There was another pause as Lacasse waited hopefully. Finally Remy looked up. "What do your Chinese friends say?" he asked.

Lacasse was surprised. "About what?" he asked, suppressing another eruption from his rebellious stomach.

"About what you have just asked," Remy said. "The decisive battle."

"We do not discuss such things," Lacasse replied, gingerly. He was not sure what Remy meant again. The fact that he had acquaintances in Cholon, that they included Li Kwan-sen, the gambler, was no special secret. What Remy might suspect of Li, on the other hand, was something else. Lacasse considered his own puzzlement. Probably Remy knew far more than he himself did about Li.

Remy must have been reading his mind, for he said: "Your friend Li, in Cholon. What is his estimate?"

Lacasse was sorry he had brought the subject up. He snorted, simulating derision while trying to compose an answer. Remy, he felt, was watching him. Why, he asked himself, self-commiseratingly, must he always get into these foolish conversational boxes? Why, like Li Kwan-sen, couldn't he maintain a better composure?

"I do not believe it concerns him," he replied at length. "At least he does not speak of the war. I do not know his politics either." He wondered, even if this was partly true, if he should have said it.

Remy sneezed and wiped his nose with a faded handkerchief. "It concerns him the way it concerns us all. That much is certain," he said. "Except," he added, slowly, staring across the table at Lacasse, "his concern is perhaps more evenly distributed."

◇◇◇

"It is the way of the Chinese," Lacasse said, weakly.

"One cannot blame them," Remy replied, agreeably. Lacasse breathed more easily, but for a moment only. "One cannot blame anyone, I suppose," he said, still gazing across the table and over the top of Lacasse's head.

There was an awkward silence. Remy then stood up. "I must go, Jacques," he said. "There is a matter I wish to discuss with you, but it will wait." The smile hung like a wax impression on the tight mold of his face. . . . "There is no expert advice I can give you," he added, leaning on one foot. "But if the mirror can hang on the wall by itself, and if you can trust your servants, go home to Corsica, Jacques. It will do you good. This war, you know, it is only a beginning."

4

WALKING along rue Catinat, Remy was chuckling to himself. He was amused by the vast uncertainty of everything. There was no promise of decision, no intimation even. The vistas were as limitless as they were complicated. One did not talk about it; but alone one could laugh.

He thought about Lacasse with amusement. The fellow was so transparent. Yet beneath the bumbling, the maladroitness, lay that native Corsican shrewdness. Lacasse possessed a kind of active, propulsive amorality, Remy thought. He was like some animal that never slept except with one eye open, sniffing the interminable unknown. Under the circumstances, he would yet be useful.

Remy quickened his step. He was panting again, and his skin felt cold against his shirt. He had a pain in his side, beneath the liver, and he could almost feel the draining of his strength. It was worse today.

Approaching the veranda of the Continental, he saw her waiting, sitting where he had told her to sit, at the table in the far corner of the bar. She was trying to shake off one of the youngsters with the peanut trays, who were as deliberate as flies. Remy saw her smile as he went up the steps, and he waited while she handed down a piaster and the boy scampered away.

"You are too soft," he said, walking up.

"It is easier," Genevieve said. "Good day."

Remy inclined his head and they shook hands. Then he sat down and ordered a *perrier*. Genevieve was drinking citronade.

He came to the point quickly. "And so," he said, "how is he, *Monsieur le Consul*?"

Genevieve returned his smile. "He is extremely pleasant," she said. "For an American, he is especially so."

"You must not disparage our allies," Remy said softly.

"On the contrary," Genevieve said, "I am praising them."

"One," Remy said, "but not them."

"He is the only one recently I have come to know."

"He is, in many ways, an exception," Remy said reflectively.

Genevieve sipped her citronade and waited. Remy was wetting his lips and frowning. "The Consul is a man of principles," he went on. "That is to say—" He paused again and looked away from the table. Genevieve watched his eyes rove. "Monsieur Patch is an idealist, do you not agree?" he finally added.

"An idealist?" Genevieve repeated. "An idealist perhaps, but he is also a fatalist. Oh, yes, he is a fatalist as well, and sometimes quite cynical."

"They go together, all three," Remy said. He debated how direct to be. "It makes for a spirit of independence," he said. "It is commendable, of course, but it is not always productive, such a combination of qualities."

Once more he hesitated, allowing his voice to drop. ". . . In a time of crisis, it is on occasion a matter of some embarrassment."

Remy looked around carefully and leaned forward. "In your estimation, is he actually against the position we have taken?" he asked. There was a note of pleading in his voice.

Genevieve shook her head. "No," she said. "I do not think, how-ever, that he approves of the way the war is conducted."

"I should not imagine so," Remy said, flatly.

He sat with the glass in his hand, holding it against his damp, hot cheek, feeling his skin and the edge of the glass become one and a pleasant numbness set in. He continued the rotating motion as he said: "Your lunch appears to have been a fruitful one. I told you, you see, it is a project worth pursuing." He had set the glass down and was smiling at her as before. "When will you see him again?"

Genevieve shrugged. "Today, perhaps. He comes to the pool every day, I believe, only earlier than myself."

"An early swim will be good for you," Remy said.

"Then I have nothing to do in the afternoon," Genevieve replied.

"A long lunch is an excellent solution, and a siesta perhaps," Remy suggested.

"Not every day," she replied. "One grows fat and lazy."

"It can be done moderately," Remy said. "As with most things, the reward will lie in moderation."

Genevieve looked across the table at him and smiled broadly. "I will maintain the friendship," she said, "but perhaps I will fall in love with him. Then what will you say?"

"I would prefer it the other way," Remy said, "that monsieur Patch should become intrigued. Nevertheless, even falling in love has its advantages."

"If done in moderation?" Genevieve mocked.

Remy laughed back at her. "By all means," he said, "in modera-tion. Otherwise one sleeps too much and there is no time for talk-ing."

"I will give you an accounting," Genevieve said as she got up.

"You are extremely thoughtful," Remy said. He stood up and shook her hand again.

"It will be a pleasure," said Genevieve. "*Au revoir, cher Remy*."

Remy remained standing until she had vanished around the parapet. Then, with a weary sigh, he sat down again. A dizziness made him close his eyes and he swayed slightly in his chair. He dipped an edge of his handkerchief into the *perrier* and mopped his brow. Glancing at his watch, he saw that it was almost time for his daily conference with the Vietnamese. There would be more news, perhaps, of the renegades. It was only then, with a start and a wave of anger over his diminishing acuteness, that he realized who the man loitering in front of the new hotel had been.

Chapter VIII

SINCE nine o'clock the thermometer on the ground floor of the American Legation had stood at ninety-five. The Marine sergeant got up from the desk and walked to the washroom, where he soaked his handkerchief at the spigot, already running warm, and mopped his face. Through the bars of the window he could see the bronze doors of the bank across the street swing open and the first customer, a Frenchman wearing shorts, appear with several bundles of paper money. A Vietnamese in a white suit rode by in a government car. A peddler passed, and two toylike slender women. In the gutter a group of naked urchins played with stones.

The sergeant stood by the window and blew the smoke of his cigarette out savoringly. He had a young face, but at the moment it seemed older, fretful with tedium and the early heat. He ground the butt fiercely on the sandstone sill and tossed it onto the sidewalk, where an old man bent over and picked it up, trying, with unnimble,

◇◇

crooked fingers, to separate the unburnt shreds of tobacco. The sergeant dipped into his shirt and gave him the remains of a pack. The old man stared at the cigarettes in the palm of his hand. He had a cataract in one eye, and the sergeant looked away. The old man's head was bobbing as he moved along.

The sergeant went back into the vestibule and sat down at the desk. Nell Finch came through the entrance and walked to the rear of the floor, and the sergeant said, glancing at her: "Elevator's out of order." He spoke as if it made no difference to him whether she heard him or not, but as she sighed and began the climb up the four flights, he added: "The gooks are coming to fix it, so maybe you can ride down." Nell didn't bother to answer.

When the Minister arrived, the sergeant stood up and made the announcement about the elevator at once, beginning formally with "Sir." The Minister frowned as he made for the stairs, which he mounted slowly, as if he were trying to roll with the waves of heat. Mr. Smythe had not even said good-morning. Some days he did and other days he didn't, and the sergeant played a little game with himself, betting what the Minister would do. This morning he had guessed wrong. The Minister, he noted, was late.

Upstairs, in the unfinished corridors of the building, the plasterers and carpenters had been at work since six. Two of the floors were being re-done. There were women working with the men, carrying pails of water and mixing the plaster. Mingling with the artisan sounds was a childlike hubbub of native voices, a gentle throb of merriment that imparted it was all a pleasant joke that suited the Americans. A young Vice-Consul passed, and one of the plasterers grinned happily at him as he pointed to the newly finished ceiling. "*Bon*, very good, yes?" he said. The young man nodded vaguely as he went on down the hall. The plasterer looked after him and gaily laughed.

Where the work of refurbishing was done, there was a strangely antiseptic atmosphere, accentuated by the smell of walls that were still damp and by the bareness of the rooms, which were as yet sparsely furnished. They seemed more like operating-rooms or decontamination chambers, and the men and women, dressed mostly in white, like slightly ruffled interns and preoccupied nurses. The hospital silence was broken only by the muffled clacking of type-writers at the far end of the corridor.

At her desk outside of Mr. Smythe's office, Nell turned her face to the moist breeze from the fan set temporarily on the floor and looked grimly back at the pile of papers before her. They had come over only this morning from the old building, and now she would have to re-sort them and file them under the new headings designated by the administrative officer, who had cleared the scheme with the Minister, who in turn had received the general directive from Washington. The increase in the amount of paperwork was astonishing, Nell thought. There had never been so much. Everyone's time seemed to be taken up in reading, copying, re-reading, digesting, writing, and re-writing reports. It had got so that the tiny red check-marks, which told her who had passed and who had yet to be shown the pieces of paper that flew in and out of her hands, had become the running signals of her life.

She glanced across the hall to Adam's office. He had not yet arrived, and the Minister was waiting. She kept looking at her watch and thought of going down the hall to one of the empty offices and telephoning him. She wondered if Mr. Smythe suspected anything. As she had left his desk a few moments ago, he had looked at her with the trace of a smile. Perhaps her sense of well-being shone through the fatigue. Adam's tardiness didn't help.

When he came down the hall a few moments later, Nell was vastly relieved. He waved casually at her as he walked into his office and took his jacket off, laying it on the polished wood table where the bulletins and magazines were piled. She waited a bit and then got up and went after him. "Mr. Smythe wishes to see you, Mr. Patch," she said, and then she quickly bunched her lips in the gesture of a kiss.

◇◇◇

"Thank you, Miss Finch," he said. He put his jacket on and followed her across.

The Minister looked up as Adam entered. "Oh, yes, Patch, come in," he said, laying down the letter he was reading. Smythe swung himself back in his leather chair as Adam sat down across from him. Then the Minister got up and closed the door.

"You said you had seen the cables?" he asked, when he was seated again. He took a monogrammed handkerchief from his breast pocket and wiped his lips.

"Yes," Adam said.

The Minister nodded.

Adam waited. Smythe seemed to be debating how to continue.

"Those are some of the points we were discussing," he declared, finally.

Adam was silent.

"Obviously," the Minister went on, speaking as much for his own benefit as for Adam's, "we would like some of these northern leaders you've mentioned brought into the Emperor's cabinet. Including the Dai Viet people, or their allies. Naturally we favor as broad a base as possible. But it remains an internal matter."

Adam paused. "Have you spoken to the High Commissioner about it lately?"

Smythe smiled. "The general is extremely busy with the campaign," he said. "*En principe*—he is all in favor, of course. It will take time, he says. I talked on the phone with the political section, and with the Overseas Ministry delegation from Paris. They all in effect shrug their shoulders and say it's a matter for the Vietnamese to decide." The Minister let a moment go by. "The fact that we suspect the French of being satisfied with the *status quo* hardly alters the circumstances. We can throw out feelers and hints. But I have no responsibility to do more."

The Minister sounded strangely defensive. It was Adam's turn to smile. "From your way of looking at it, I'm sure you're right," he said.

◇◇

"But you don't approve?" the Minister said, quietly.

"No," Adam said. "I agree it's extremely complicated. Nothing is more intransigent than French stubbornness. Especially when it pretends to be in compliance with a mysterious native will."

The Minister coughed. "All right, then, what can we do about it?"

"The composition of the local government is just part of it," Adam said. "Sooner or later the liberal Catholics and some of these northern politicians are going to have to be brought into the cabinet if there's to be any popular belief in its honest ability to stand up to the Vietminh. The French are simply trying to stave off action as long as possible. Touchy or not, it's got to be done while we've a chance to gain real ground."

"I think Washington's aware of that as an ideal formula," Smythe interjected. "Your reports, by the way, have been extremely thorough."

He wondered if Smythe was implying that no further search for proliferations of puppetry among the Emperor's ministers was welcome. He had not seen Smythe's last summary, which had ostensibly embraced his own, but he also wondered if the Minister had passed on his recommendation that economic ties between certain Vietnamese in the government and certain Frenchmen be cited in Washington and Paris. The Secretary's word "Re-investigate" could, in this connotation, mean anything. The Department either doubted the facts that had been sent, or wanted further guidance. It was only in the last two months that the Minister had not shown all the reports, both incoming and outgoing, to the top personnel. Adam had surmised there had been instructions from home.

"There are other ways of attacking the question," he said. "If the French refuse to press ahead on the cabinet now, we should concentrate on the calling up of a national assembly. Even if it's partly or mostly hand-picked, there'll be more Vietnamese voices encouraged to speak out. That's one way of moving matters."

"I've already asked for data from the field on how much enthuiasm there is in the villages for that," Smythe replied. "And I've asked Hanoi for more background on the geographic strength of the minority parties, whether or not their influence extends below the city. I would appreciate it, by the way, if you'd recorrellate the answers when they come in and bring them up to date with what we already know of the political situation in Saigon. You may feel free to add your own opinion."

"Thank you," Adam said. He was more curious than ever. "Might I ask—are my own recommendations, as I submit them, likely to be forwarded?"

"That depends," the Minister said. He was suddenly stiff again. "Naturally, your opinions are always weighed. But in the present context it would seem advisable—I'm sure you realize—"

"I realize," Adam said.

"I see no wisdom, as an instance, in relaying any speculation or material that may only confuse our policy-makers with a false picture of the chances of forcing the French hand."

"I was not aware that there had been any such report," Adam said, reddening.

"You were speaking yesterday of certain possibilities."

"I was simply appraising a variety of courses that confront us, in both the political and the economic spheres."

"On the ground?"

"Quite naturally, on the ground."

"Without consideration of the critical demands in Europe, with what the reaction of the French would be, psychologically and politically, toward security problems there and in Africa, and with no reference to the climate of opinion at home in America?"

"I wasn't overlooking any of that," Adam said. He had dropped his voice, to ward off the tenseness he felt rising in his throat. "As a matter of fact, sir, it was precisely those considerations, with respect to the problem of security here, that led me to speak." He looked sharply at the Minister, who was swaying gently in his chair.

◇◇

"I was simply trying to make clear that there's no security to be won by condoning a shadow of colonialism." He waited, briefly. "If you object, I'll not bring it up again."

"Oh, not at all," the Minister said. "I believe in the fullest and freest discussion."

"It seems to me that we know enough already, without having to conduct any fresh surveys, to be certain that hundreds of thousands in Saigon and in the villages would eagerly support any assembly, even a hedged-in one. There are enough Frenchmen around, editors and others, who would like to see that much done. If we made it clear where we stood, they'd speak up with less fear of being silenced."

At least, Adam thought, as he took a deep breath, he was alone with the Minister this time.

Smythe was looking at him curiously, almost archly. "And yet you spoke of by-passing the French and making our own approach," he said. "I don't see how you can have it both ways."

"I think I spoke of alternatives," Adam said. "Actually, and ideally, we ought to have it, as you say, 'both ways.' The chance to influence political decisions that affect us all, and the right to act on our own also, in the social sense, in giving aid. If we're blocked on one level, as we appear to be right now, then the need for freedom of action on the other becomes doubly important."

The Minister was dallying with an envelope-opener, prodding it against a blotter.

"We've still got the freedom to make our own appeals, in simple human terms," Adam added. "And the Vietnamese have the right to choose how they wish to be helped, when, and by whom."

"You're quite aware of the nature of the agreements," Smythe answered brusquely. "The French won't agree to change them, and you know that as well as I do. Wherever possible, they'll insist on the prior use of their own technicians."

"Where are they all?" Adam demanded. "That's the nub of it—

their whole attitude, this sense and theme of the French *présence*. The *présence* is something ethereal, a blank check written by the past on the future." He stopped, with a conscious effort, and then continued more softly: "It's a denial of opportunity for the rest of us, if you will, but chiefly for the people themselves." He quickly lit another cigarette. "Everything still depends on how firm we want to be. I've suggested that we've got our bargaining points."

"And you wish me still to look at it from here alone, from this tiny segment. Beyond the absolute necessity of holding a general line, particularly in Europe."

Adam breathed deeply once more. "I recognize the uses of caution," he said, "and the interplay. It's still a fact that if the French are at all serious about fostering the *dynamisme* they're so fond of talking about, then something, some measure, some compelling gesture even, is essential to give the Vietnamese a sense of what it is to act on their own, the right to mull and choose and make mistakes. There's a by-play too, between the French and us. It's mostly the result of our never having made up our minds what intervention really means in this kind of situation."

The Minister was suddenly smiling. "The danger of Communism isn't reason and cause enough to rally people?"

"There are millions out here who interpret it differently or who don't bother to make any interpretation at all, who remain subject to any blandishment," Adam said. "Which is where diplomacy ought to come in, and outright propaganda, too. Skepticism and mistrust operate against us in a vacuum. The threat and attraction of Communism mesh. All over Asia, they're asking what's worse than what they've got. How can we expect them to know that the worst of all is staring them in the face? Not by aligning ourselves with outworn postures."

"We've made it clear where we stand," the Minister said. "Haven't we?"

"The rush of events is what counts," Adam replied, "not what we say. Ideally, there lots of colonial areas where it would be better all around if freedom could be granted by degrees. But the timetable of history pushes all of us along at its own pace. Obviously it's Moscow's perfect dish of tea, but, even so, most of what's happening now has been brewed right here, in Asia itself. The Japanese had a hand in it, and so did we, for that matter, as the maker of promises men lived by from 1941 to 1945. It's an anachronism—that where change has always permeated slowly, over centuries, all of a sudden there's only a narrow inch of time left."

The Minister sat back with the smile's trace on his lips. "And so you still say we're being too timid?" he said, at length. He didn't wait to be answered. "You want me to recommend to Washington that the Quai d'Orsay be told that unless such and such is done, the cabinet increased or the black market in piasters eliminated, there will be no more irrigation wells, no more malaria serum, maybe even no more guns. That's not for me to suggest, under any circumstances. It's Washington's idea even to throw out."

"It isn't necessarily a matter of ultimatum," Adam replied.

The Minister hunched himself. "You cannot issue semi-ultimatums," he said. "Not when your own well-being as a nation is concerned."

There was a new brief silence as he swung his chair around. "And where, as you know, everything we do out here is being increasingly scrutinized back home . . ."

It was the final note Adam had sensed and, if only subconsciously, had been waiting for. He sighed. Smythe seemed vaguely disconcerted, and Adam let him be. This was something they had never talked about, or even alluded to, the Minister and himself or any of them, even though they had all obviously felt the impact. It was not only the disemboweling, in today's context, of yesterday's sins of judgment, things said and done, or not said and not done, but the whole inhibiting effect of having the aspect and process of diplomacy harangued and displayed like low gossip across the country.

The Minister was still staring at the wall, brandishing a cigarette absently. Adam waited a moment more, and then he said: "We can at least try to emphasize, keep emphasizing, that it's unwise to be perpetually six months too late in giving an inch, six months of bitterness, of fatigue and emasculation. If we're bargaining for time alone, it doesn't much matter. But if we still seek solvency—"

"We have tried. You may think we haven't tried enough. But if we try much harder, in point of threats, the French might be only too happy, as you can surmise, to see the malaria caravans removed, and the rest of the welfare program. And if we threaten to hold back on military aid, Paris might simply pull out and leave us holding the bag, with all the responsibility and blame on our backs."

"We've got to be gamblers," Adam replied. "It's been true all along, and it's still true. It goes for our dealings with the French, as well as with the Russians. The edge held by a monolithic state is great, but we needn't forfeit all parry and thrust. And I don't think the French would pull out, not in face of their own pressures. If anyone's gambling for time, a year even, it's the Bank of Indo-China and the whole catacomb wrapped up in it. I find it difficult to believe that diplomacy's come to be a matter of simply granting or withholding a favor, or that we're just messenger boys out here. We're still in a position to persuade as well as propose, and to do it effectively—if we believe in something ourselves. It's hard to think the worst—that we don't really believe."

"Believe what?"

"In the efficacy of our own revolutionary appeal, I imagine," Adam said slowly. "In taking the same risks we ourselves took, which means riding the unalterable principle of anti-colonialism, as we did, and looking for the way-stations afterward."

The Minister was gazing at him searchingly again.

"We've got to decide, once and for all, that we actually do believe in the kind of independence for these people we've so nicely professed. It may not be a polished product at the outset, and it may run into all sorts of fresh trouble. But it's that or—the other. There isn't any third choice, don't you see? No way of postponement. The sad thing is, they've looked to us for so long, are past looking in many cases, and yet somehow they keep looking back over their shoulders in our direction."

The Minister grunted.

"This matter of broadening the cabinet may be a minor episode," Adam concluded, "yet for the people in the north it could prove a way of final rejection, something that may make them no longer look back."

"We'll see," the Minister said. It was obvious he wanted the discussion closed. Adam got up.

"Just one thing more," Smythe said. "There's this question of local Chinese activity. The reporting seems rather scanty. Do you have any ideas?"

Adam thought a moment. "I've some old contacts in Cholon," he replied. "I'll look into it myself."

"Very well," the Minister said, formally. "Thank you very much."

Adam left the door open as he went out. The Minister, he saw, had stood up and was peering out the window. Nell Finch winked as he passed her desk, but Adam didn't respond.

Back in his office, his own door closed, he sat on the top of the desk and watched the dust-motes whirl in the sun. They gyrated like tiny sealed bubbles, suspended in the moisture as in an emulsion, whole and self-contained. He was glad, in the first momentary reconstruction, that he had said what he had. The Minister had been rather purposefully disputatious, but he supposed he had himself; essentially their differences had been soundly declared. There would be no further need for fencing. Amenities became fruitless. Diplomacy was up against enough as it was without befuddling itself further by moods and inhibitions. . . .

What the Minister could do, of course, if he chose, was ask Adam if he preferred to be shifted ahead of his time—such action was not uncommon when an overriding conflict arose between a top-ranking officer and the head of mission. The question, naturally, would be tantamount to a request; but the semblance of politeness would conveniently be kept. It seemed more likely, however, that under the circumstances Smythe would simply forget the quarrel, or at least lay it aside, treat Adam as a known but unserviceable quantity, make an occasional reference to his point of view in a summary report, and allow events to take their course without further ado. Adam smiled, permitting himself the momentary exaltation of a minor martyrdom, the self-righteousness of imagined oblivion. It was a classic condition, the brotherhood of the neglected. Old Litvinov, on the other side, waiting in vain in his latter-day seclusion to be trotted out again, living like a bourgeois trusty in his Moscow *dacha*. It was not like that in his own case, of course; yet it was reverse, sort of counterrevolutionary Walter Mitty, and just ludicrous enough to make Adam laugh out loud.

He stood up and glanced through the papers his secretary had placed on the desk. They concerned routine administrative matters, the sort of stuff that made up nine tenths of the work and that anyone could handle. He pressed the buzzer, and she came in, pad in hand, looking hot and wan. She was a small blonde with a pale and nondescript skin that had the perpetual look of the cradle about it. Although she came from Georgia, she was a chief complainer of the Saigon heat. It made her dizzy, she said, and she couldn't breathe. Adam suspected that she had begun to drink too much, alone or with the other girls. She apologized now for leaving early the evening before. "My head was just jumpin', up an' down," she said, her voice somewhat husky. "I just slep' an' slep'."

"That's all right," Adam said. "There wasn't much to do, anyway."

He gave her two letters, one in reply to some misinformation in an article about Cambodia in the *Monthly Bulletin*, and the other a

◇◇◇

routine answer to a visa query from the new Vice-Consul in Pnom-Penh. When they had finished, she sat waiting, pad on knee, her faded cotton dress wrinkled above her shin-bone, which, he noticed, was badly bruised. She brought the skirt's edge back down and, blushing, said: "Those new floors in the apartment-house, Mr. Patch—they're so slippery! Other night, in the kitchen, I just slip 'n' fell. Like to burned myself with some jasmine tea."

"You want to be careful," Adam said. "I've taken tumbles out here myself. They take a long time to heal." There was the night, he remembered, with Nell, when, dancing, they had suddenly fallen and nearly remained . . .

He twisted his head around, shaking away a tickling in his ear. "I guess that's all for now," he said. "Don't wait for me after six. I may go to Cholon after lunch."

"Oh, I'll wait, Mr. Patch, if you want me to," she said. "I'm all right today." Like all the others, she wanted to please him. "I'll wait till half past six, anyway. . . ."

She closed the door on the side of the room as she went out, and Adam sat back a moment. Then he got up and put his jacket back on and followed her through the same door and out to the corridor through the adjacent offices, avoiding thereby the area in front of the Minister's office and Nell's desk. The bottom of the concrete stairs still smelled damp. An Annamite was bending over, watching as the sergeant filled out a pass. The sergeant looked up and said brightly: "Good afternoon, Mr. Patch," and Adam wiggled his fingers. The Annamite turned in time to catch the back of the white suit, vanishing.

Chapter IX

THE sergeant removed his watch and scratched his wrist where the strap had irritated. It was almost noon. He wrote the time on the small pad in front of him and asked the Vietnamese to write his name on a separate slip. "How d'you say it?" he asked, copying it.

"Dang. Tran Phan Dang."

"And you want some information?"

"Yes. That is—to discuss it. . . ."

"Are you looking for work?"

"I do not know. Perhaps."

"What do you do?"

"I am a doctor . . ."

The sergeant frowned and picked up the phone. The voice of the Vietnamese receptionist answered. The sergeant always liked the sound of it and now he cupped his hand over his free ear, as if this helped his savoring. "There's a man down here, a Viet—namese," he said, almost forgetting. "A doctor, he says. I think he wants a job. Where'll I send him?"

When he had hung up, he finished preparing the pass. "You'll have to walk up," he said. "It's the fourth floor. There's a girl there. She'll talk to you. Anyway, I think you came to the wrong place. . . ."

Tran thanked him. He started for the stairs, stopped, and returned a step toward the desk, where the sergeant had already gone back to the adventure book. "If you will pardon me—" he began. "I wonder, could you tell me the name of the man, that one who went out a moment ago?" Tran motioned toward the door.

The sergeant lifted his head briefly, his brow wrinkled and his expression fretful. "Oh, him," he said, after a moment. "That's the Consul." His eyes fled back to his book.

"Will he return soon?" Tran asked. The sergeant kept his head down as he murmured: "This afternoon, yeah."

Tran stood awkwardly. He wished the sergeant would look at him. "Do you know, perhaps, where he is—at this moment?" he asked.

Now the sergeant raised his head once more, with a combination of annoyance and incredulity. "Look," he said, "what the hell are you bothering me for? You're supposed to go upstairs. How the hell do I know when he'll be back? He goes swimming."

Tran murmured his apologies. He climbed the four flights slowly, and at the top he saw the Vietnamese girl behind a mahogany desk. Alongside her was a temporary, cut-open switchboard. She was no more than twenty, Tran thought, and she was pretty. She had on a European dress. "Good morning," she said, in English.

"I am Tran Phan Dang." He handed her the piece of paper.

"Oh, yes. What is it you wish to have an interview about?"

"It is a personal matter," Tran said.

"If you wish to be employed—" the girl began.

"It is not that," Tran interrupted her. "The question will come later, of employment. I wish to speak with one of the American officials."

"But we must know what you want," she persisted.

"It is a matter of importance, although personal."

"We do not hire doctors here," the girl said, sharply.

"I understand," Tran said. "As I have explained—"

"But if you do not tell me what it is you wish to speak about, it is impossible to arrange. We are extremely busy, it is—"

Tran looked about him. One of the laborers carrying a pan of wet plaster-mix came padding barefoot down the hall. The man was singing softly in a high, lilting voice. Tran listened to him as he went by. The plasterer was absorbed in the happiness of his moment.

"It is a political matter," Tran said, turning back to the girl. "It is also of particular importance to myself, to—" he hesitated. Then he sighed. "If it is impossible, I will go," he said, and he started to move off. He stopped when he saw the girl put one of the phone keys into the board and press a lever. From the other end, from somewhere within, he could hear a woman's voice answering. The Vietnamese girl reported what he had said, and when the voice on the line had spoken, she looked up at him again. "You are from Saigon?" she inquired.

Tran shook his head negatively.

"No," the girl said into the small curved mouthpiece. "He is not from Saigon."

In a moment she had hung up. She told him to wait, switching suddenly to Annamese. Then an American girl came walking down the corridor with long, slow steps.

"You are Mr. Tran?" she said as she approached. She was a tall girl, and very thin; and looking at her eyes, Tran thought she was suffering from fever or from dysentery.

"Mr. Dang," he said, and bowed.

"You were sent by someone?"

"No, I have come myself." He paused and added: "From the north, across the mountains."

The girl said: "Oh," and went back down the hall. In a few minutes she returned. "Mr. Goodenough will talk with you," she said. Her smile flickered and vanished. Tran followed her.

"Mr. Goodenough?" he repeated.

"He is one of our vice-consuls," the girl said, not turning.

She conducted him to a small room on the street side of the building. "In here, please, Mr. Tran," she said. She stood by the door until he went in, and then he heard the click of her heels again as she went away.

In front of him, his head bent over a pile of papers, sat a young man. The young man's hair was dark and neatly combed, with a part to one side, and he had on a white shirt and a dark tie. In his hand was a sharp pencil, and as Tran stood waiting, he saw the pencil make a small check-mark on top of the typewritten page. The young man finally looked up.

"Oh, yes," he said. "Mr. Drang." A smile flickered, and died, and a hand was motioned for Tran to sit in the chair directly opposite. Tran now saw that the young man's face was even younger than it had looked when the head was lowered. The features were sharp, the nose a little long but graceful, the mouth still curved in the posture of the fading smile. The young man had shaved very closely and had cut himself on the edge of the jaw.

"You have come to Saigon just recently? From where?"

"I have been with the Vietminh, as a physician," Tran said.

The young man inclined his head to one side, nodded once, and projected his lower lip. "So?" he said. "Were you a member of the Communist Party?"

"No," said Tran. "No, I did not belong."

He was surprised at the spurt of resentment the question produced. But he quickly recovered himself. It was, after all, a valid curiosity, a natural point of departure. Yet it was the difference between them, always: a matter of timing, beyond politeness. There were exceptions: the dark face of the Vietnamese inquisitor, the round and hairless head, came briefly back. . . . "It is why I am here," he said.

"Have you been in Saigon long?"

"Five days."

"What will you do now?"

Tran looked out the window, beyond the young man framed in it. The figures moving in the building across the street were like shadows on a sun-covered wall.

"That will depend," he said.

"Are there many casualties with the Vietminh? Much suffering?"

"There is a great suffering."

The young man nodded and wrote something on a small pad beside him. The shadows across the way flickered, and a woman's face looked out. The space between narrowed. A bird shot by outside, seeming by a freak of perspective scarcely to avoid the young man's head.

"They need medicines, don't they?"

"Yes," Tran said. "That is true. There is a great lack of medicines."

"What prompted you specifically to leave?"

"I did not wish to belong to the new party, the Laodang. Those such as myself, the men of professions and the intellectuals, as you call them"—he did not suppress the smile—"are being made to join, if they wish to remain. It was not this way before."

"How much time did you spend with the Vietminh?" The young man's expression was intense.

"Four years."

"Do you know Ho Chi Minh?"

"I have met him. I do not know him well."

"Is he ill?"

"He has trouble with his lungs. But he endures."

The hand ran over the pad again.

"The younger leaders have become powerful, have they not?" came the next question. "Do you know Truong Chinh?"

"Yes, I know him. He is an important man."

"The most important?" The young man gave Tran a probing glance.

"He is quite important, yes."

"Yes, yes, I know. But is he the most important?"

"Perhaps he is." Once more, the pad. Tran fixed his eyes on it until they blurred and the young man's pencil was a yellow stain.

"Is he the head of the new party?"

"I believe he is the general secretary."

"Do you know about his background, where he came from?"

Tran sighed. "I believe he was in China, and it is said he studied in Moscow." Mr. Goodenough himself had become a blur, with a toneless voice, speaking from a distance infinitely farther than the desk, closer to the shadows across the way, where there was emptiness now, a dark hole in the curtain of light. Tran twisted in the chair, shifting his focus. Mr. Goodenough loomed again, as from the side of a cliff. He seemed to lean over.

"Are there many new cadres, Mr. Drang?"

"Dang. Tran Phan Dang," Tran said.

"Oh, I am sorry," Goodenough said. He wrote the name correctly on the pad. "Well, then, Mr. Dang, are there many new cadres, recently?"

"Yes, there are many cadres. Many younger men, and many new political officers as well."

"From the north?"

"Yes."

"Chinese?"

"Yes, there are some Chinese. But they are advisers, principally of a military variety. There are some political men with them."

"How many Chinese?"

"I have not counted."

"Have you seen them yourself?"

"Yes, I have seen them."

"Both the military officers and the commissars?"

"They are not called commissars."

"Are they in the villages?"

"Yes, in the villages, and with the soldiers as well."

Mr. Goodenough stopped for a moment and wiped his mouth with the back of a hand. "Well, Mr. Dang, you have corroborated much of what we hear. I am sure there are some additional questions you will be able to answer. Are you staying in a hotel here?"

Tran nodded.

"Would you mind telling me where? It will be kept highly confidential." Mr. Goodenough's mouth had resumed the peculiar shape it had when Tran first came in.

"It would be better—" Tran began.

Goodenough raised a hand. "I understand, of course," he said. "There is no necessity." He waited a moment. "You'll be willing to return, however?"

"Mr. Goodenough," Tran said, "there is a matter about which I would like to speak at once." It was a wrench, painful but necessary, away from the dismay that was about to overwhelm him.

"Yes?" The tautness came back, and the serious look, touched with youthfulness.

"I have come a long distance," Tran said. He laid his left arm on the table, stretching the fingers flat. It was difficult to search for words. "There are many things I have seen. There is suffering in many places, not only where I have come from, but"—he gestured— "everywhere in my country."

Goodenough peered at him, curiously.

"There are many things being done, it is true, by the French, by the Vietnamese, and by the Americans as well. It is always temporary, you see." Almost abjectly, he added: "The people do not understand . . ."

Goodenough lifted his head. "We are doing a great deal to extend assistance, Mr. Dang," he said. His tone was one of injured formality. "Our program is being constantly expanded. Each month there are now more ships—"

"No," Tran said. "It is not a question of ships." He gave a half-completed wave of his hand. "It is not—it is not how these things are done solely. It is where they are done, and how frequently. It is not enough, you see, to come into the country to make—a gift."

A look of annoyance crept through the bewilderment on Mr. Goodenough's face. He spoke impatiently. "Mr. Dang," he said, "the Americans are always criticized, no matter what we try to do.

We could offer the moon and still you would not be satisfied. What is it, then, you want?"

Tran sighed. "I do not know," he said softly. "For myself, I do not know. But for others I am more certain. It is only that I wish to point out there is not belief. Not"—the word came out before he could stop it—"love."

"Love?" Goodenough said. He seemed embarrassed by the sound of it.

"What is given is in the way of tribute."

"Mr. Dang, you expect too much. We must do what we can," Goodenough interjected. "We can't be intimate with everyone," he added, clippedly.

Tran said nothing.

"It's only in the last few months we've been able to get these programs into operation. There are many arrangements, various levels."

"The war has lasted four years. It is a long time."

Both men grew silent. The room was airless. Goodenough looked down at the desk, tapping with his pencil, avoiding Tran's eyes.

"The people of my country are of many different needs," Tran said, at length. He might as well, he thought, continue speaking. "Among the Annamites themselves, among my own people, there are many variances. It is a country of many parts, and many moods."

"We are aware of that, Mr. Dang," Goodenough said, still not looking up. "I assure you, the question has been given some study."

"Neither the giving nor the receiving can be the same for all the regions," Tran persisted. "Perhaps that is why it is not right."

"In an emergency, the needs are always the same," Goodenough replied, expertly. "For drugs, for food, for plows, for wells . . ."

"The people in the country do not think, however, with the people in the towns. It is not the needs alone, or what the war has done. It is not even Ho Chi Minh or His Majesty. It is many other things first."

"Other things?"

Again Tran sighed. "It is fear, or ignorance, which is perhaps only the absence of fear, or what exists before fear comes," he said. "It is knowledge, which will vary, of what was done in the past to hurt and sometimes to help, but less often. It is remembering what was promised after the end of the great war, by the Americans as well as by the French—" Tran paused. Goodenough was watching him now intently. "It is also what the Vietminh does," Tran went on. "The propaganda of the Vietminh, you see, is very strong, Mr. Goodenough. It goes to many places, sometimes by radio, but more often it is brought by those who walk with it across the mountains and through the forests, in the manner in which I myself have come here. There are cadres in the villages which are left by the Vietminh, after the soldiers have gone."

Goodenough made another note.

Tran stared at the piece of paper in front of Mr. Goodenough and continued. "It is true that the Vietminh forces the people to believe, but this question of believing is extremely important, as I have said. It is what creates the activity that follows, like a motor. There is a formula, you see, but the consequences are great, an activity that covers all. It is an evil trick, as with the alphabet that everyone must learn. The old women cannot go to the market unless they have learned it. It is something to watch, this learning."

"What else?" Goodenough asked, sharply.

"There is always the matter of food, as you have indicated. The rice is brought on the backs of the villagers, from one village to another, while the Vietminh watches. There has been famine, but with little starvation."

Goodenough was jotting furiously.

"The Vietminh is very clever. There is hate in the villages where the treatment for malaria and trachoma has not been given by the Americans. The Vietminh will come and will say: 'Ah, you see, the Americans are capitalists, as we have told you. They will help only the people in the cities. They will not help you.'"

"We can't go everywhere at once," Goodenough said.

"That is true. However, the villages are impatient, and the impatience is made into anger. It is an anger that not only the Vietminh creates. The American planes come, with the bombs of gasoline and gelatin. And then they will come back again, I have seen them come the very next day, with the propaganda that falls the way the bombs fall. Since the planes are the same, the peasants will be angry. And the Vietminh will say that Bao Dai is no longer a French puppet—but an American puppet instead."

"That's ridiculous."

Tran smiled. "It is what they say, however. The people do not know either the truth or the lack of truth. But they see the planes with the real bombs, and the planes with those of paper. Since the Vietminh has no planes, there is no comparison possible."

"The planes are American, that is true, but the pilots are French," Goodenough said.

"It is difficult to distinguish from the sky," Tran said. "Either death or life."

Goodenough was staring at him, and then he looked away.

"It is enough that white men do the killing. The machine and the man in it are one," Tran added.

Goodenough coughed. "It is very unfortunate, of course. But do you wish the war stopped because of this? The Communists will walk in . . ."

"The Vietminh is still popular," Tran said, "yet not so popular as before. It remains true, above all, however, that the Emperor is not like Ho Chi Minh. The people do not have the opportunity to see him, and they do not forget the many times he has jumped, backwards and forwards. The Emperor has many pasts, with the French, with the Japanese, then with Ho himself. Now again he is with the French."

"And the Americans?" Goodenough laughed harshly.

"And the Americans," Tran said, smiling.

Goodenough stood up. "Would you mind waiting a moment, Mr.

Dang?" he said. Tran bowed from the waist in the chair, and Goodenough went out.

Listening to the soft rubber padding of Goodenough's shoes until they grew muffled amid the noise of the typewriters, Tran remained motionless in the chair. Outside, a bird flew by again, like an arrow. The small square of the window, the larger square of the room, empty except for the simple desk and the two chairs, reminded him sharply of that other square room he had been in yesterday. The waiting now, on top of what he had said, and the sense of futility he felt as a result of the odd response it had seemed to provoke in this odd young man, were worse than that other waiting had been, after the inspector and the Frenchman had gone out and left him on the bench by the wall. He had been resigned then to anything, to be left indefinitely in that void, alone with his fatigue and his hunger; but this was different: having re-roused himself, having been inspired by fright or by annoyance to a spurt of bravery, his fresh despair enveloped him almost indiscriminately and was echoed in Goodenough's footsteps in the corridor before they were subsumed by the typewriters' clack. The small, interior echo of his own proclaiming voice seemed still to rebound in his mind. The fear in his breast was like stone. . . .

At the other end of the hall Goodenough stopped at Nell Finch's desk. He bent over as he whispered: "Can I see him? It's something important."

"Couldn't Mr. Patch take care of it later?" she asked.

Goodenough pursed his lips. "I think the Minister would want to know directly," he said.

Nell went into the Minister's office, closing the door behind her. When she came out she told Goodenough, without looking at him, to go in.

The Minister had his sleeves rolled up and was working over some papers. "What is it, Robert?" he asked.

Goodenough gave a brief résumé of his conversation with Tran.

When he had finished, the Minister said: "Sounds interesting. I might want to see him myself." He picked up the phone and asked Miss Finch to get the Sûreté. The buzzer rang back in less than a minute. Goodenough stood by while the Minister talked. It was obviously someone with whom Smythe was accustomed to speak.

"Do you know one of them named Tran—" the Minister began, and then he looked up questioningly.

"Phan Dang," Goodenough said.

"Tran Phan Dang?" the Minister said into the phone. "Supposed to have arrived a few days ago. A doctor. From up north. Non-party member, he says. Caught in the squeeze." Smythe punctuated this with a short laugh.

Goodenough could hear the reply in rapid French. The Minister's French was excellent and Smythe nodded his head nervously as the voice kept talking.

"Yes, yes, I think you're quite right," the Minister said finally. "Thank you very much. Yes, we'll be in touch." He hung up.

"The advice is for caution," he said, lifting his eyes to Goodenough. "The man may be perfectly all right, of course, but he may also be a plant. It's a new maneuver, but a smart one on their part." Goodenough waited as the Minister appeared to debate. "Write a summary as a matter of routine," Smythe added. "Let me have a copy, and tell your man to come back. I'll try to fit him in later. What did you say he wants to do?"

Goodenough wrinkled his brow. "It's not very clear," he replied. "He seems chiefly to want to complain about all the things we're doing badly."

"Does he want work?" the Minister asked.

"I suppose," Goodenough said.

Smythe paused again. "Send him over to ECA for a preliminary clearance," he said. "Maybe he can fit into their health program. They could use some native wisdom. If the French want to question him, they can have him later."

Goodenough said, "Yes, sir," and went out. Back in his office, he wrote the name of the assistant ECA personnel director on a pad and handed the square of paper to Tran. From the window he pointed where to go. "Tell them you came and talked to us," he said. Tran took the paper from one hand to the other and deposited it in his jacket pocket. "Yes, thank you . . ." he murmured.

"Thank you for coming in," Goodenough said, formally. "It was most interesting. It's entirely likely the Minister will want to see you, in a few days, perhaps. Please come back here Monday."

Tran bowed and went out. He walked quickly down the hall and down the stairs. The sergeant was still at the desk, but scarcely noticed as Tran went past. The piece of paper Mr. Goodenough had given him was clenched in his fist—he had absently taken it out of his pocket again. He started to fold it and refold it until it was an inch square, and his fingers kept fumbling.

The sun was a stroke of fire. The cathedral chimes sounded like gongs as he crossed the square and he turned suddenly. He thought he had heard steps coming closer; but there was no one. He hurried on to the opposite side of the square, berating himself for his foolishness in crossing over so openly.

Panting, he stood on the sidewalk and stared through the filmy haze. A terrible urge to urinate came over him; glancing around, he saw no one and walked behind a tree. A fresh roll of perspiration, out of embarrassment, went down his neck as a *cyclo* boy rode past and laughed, looked back and laughed once more.

The foliaged street led past the palace gardens, which were empty now. Beyond he could see the yellow oblong shape of the Cercle Sportif. Slowly Tran walked toward it. Now he remembered what the sergeant had said. This, too, was the direction in which the Consul had gone when he had swung around in the square.

Thirty feet from the club's entrance, Tran stopped again. He sat down in the grass, letting the piece of paper that was still in his hand drop out. From his trousers he took a small piece of chocolate folded into tin-foil. It had melted, lumpily, but he unwrapped it and brought it to his mouth. He had scarcely swallowed it before his eyes closed and for a time he lost all sense of where he was. There was a ball of yellow fire burning out of the blackness, and then his eyes flung open again and he gasped. The image of the political officer, the pock-marked face in awful clarity, had vanished, emblazoned, and there were only the green of the grass and the pale surrounding stucco.

. . . A half block away, his stomach rumbling, his mouth bitter, the coolie in the black suit had watched with annoyance. He had waited in the sun outside the Legation and now there had been more waiting, and he was tired of it.

Chapter X

THE old woman crouched on the sidewalk and let the colored pieces of cloth go slowly through her fingers. She had no teeth to speak of, and her jaw bobbed back and forth as she sucked at the sides of her loose mouth. But the skin of her cheeks was like the bark of a young tree, cut in tiny creases, drawn tight and fine against her bones. She swayed to and fro among her squares of cloth as if borne by some inner tide, moved by the sun and not the moon.

She continued to sway, more gently now, as she extolled her cloth in muffled singsong and lifted the various pieces toward the two men who were suddenly standing in front of her. She did not look at their faces, but she had seen them coming, and when the one with the blemish bent down to feel the cloth with his fingers, she opened her hand like a claw and he took the message. For another moment the two men lingered, and then they wandered away. The old woman swayed on, not turning, and presently she closed her eyes, and her lips moved soundlessly.

It was not until they had reached the front of a café three blocks away that Cau came to a stop. Neither he nor the political officer had spoken, but now Cau unfolded the paper, and when he had read it he tore it methodically into tiny pieces and put the pieces in the pocket of his jacket.

"It is all right," he said. "We can go at once, this morning."

The political officer merely nodded. He felt sleepy. "I would like a *filtre* first," he said. They sat at a table and he called for the boy, standing barefoot and sullen in the dust.

The political officer felt strange in the city. He felt a detachment to the point of disembodiment. It scarcely seemed himself that moved about, that sat in a café, that saw the Frenchmen and the French-women drift among the Annamese. The white skins were like the skins of pantomimists, whom he only watched but did not hear, and their laughter was like the laughter of forest birds, nearby yet un-attached. He was always surprised that the city provoked no hatred in him. There was an atrophy of emotion, as if he were anesthetized, as if he held a jungle potion in his brain that kept him, for the time he was here, inviolable and invulnerable to hate, and he had neither fear nor contempt nor pity, but only resolution and the calm of intent.

The man he was with, Cau Minh Thien, was one of the new ones he did not know well. They had met only once before, some eight months ago, when the political officer had previously come to Saigon. He knew that Cau had become one of the leaders in the *Tu Ve*, the assassination suicide squad, but beyond that he had not had time to discover anything. He was curious about the man's background. There was something puzzling about him, something difficult to define, because it was a lack, a negative quality, unshared. The political officer did not invite an exchange of confidences. To him, this would be weakness, not strength. What he meant was conviction that need not be expressed, the certitude of fellowship. It was what a man carried in his body, on his face; it was in a man's voice; and in Cau Minh Thien, the political officer thought, it was missing. Waiting for the *filtre*, he dissected the feeling further. It was a solitude that Cau imposed, almost sadistically, an exclusion of the spirit, a loneliness that was like a germ. It sprang, he thought, from the old fester of independence, and within limits, perhaps, it might be condoned as a hangover from the earlier days of separatism, of Cochin-China Trotskyism, which went back to the fall of Saigon to the British, who took it for the importunate French after the war and then handed it over to them as if on the end of a spit. The city could not, under any circumstances, have been held by the revolutionary troops; but there were those who had wanted to maintain even then the steady pressure of attack, who had wanted to begin at once to reorganize the battalions and concentrate on underground activity within Saigon and Cholon at the expense of the countryside. Here, in the new revolutionary south, the opposition leaders had by now been purged; but there remained this mood these men in the ranks imparted. In Cau's case, it amounted to a sulk. It was something that would have to be met, and it was one of the reasons the political officer had wanted to come back here.

"The old woman," he said now, after the *filtre* had been set down, "is she always there, in the market?"

"She is the mother of one of the boatmen," Cau said. "She comes regularly each morning to sell cloth."

The political officer was silent, and Cau looked closely at him. "She is entirely to be trusted," he said, as if he were repeating an announcement. "The son and I were together before."

"Before?" the political officer said.

"During the time of the Japanese. In the villages, and also, for a time, on the river."

"What were you doing then?" the political officer asked blandly.

Cau seemed surprised. "What were all of us doing?" he replied. There was a note of sarcasm.

The political officer grunted. "As it happened, I was in China," he said.

Cau stared at him again, almost insolently. "You are part Chinese?"

It was a question the man had no right to ask. The political officer was scarcely known by him, but was at least to be regarded as a superior, not to be inquired of in personal fashion. He gave no answer; but then the political officer realized that he had affirmed the suspicion by silence.

"Come," he said, gruffly. "It is getting late. We had better go."

They walked back along the edge of the market, in the path of the sun. The political officer took in the faces that swarmed about him and made an effort to identify himself with the crowd and to escape the constraint of his companion. He caught a glimpse that startled him, but when he turned there was nothing familiar. If there had been, he could not have acted for the moment anyway. Undoubtedly he had been searching subconsciously, not only for the face of the doctor but for the others too. How many deserters, he wondered, would dare at once to come to Saigon? The increase of those who had fled had recently become alarming. From a dozen or so every six months, the total had jumped to thirty in the last three months alone, through all six regions. The amount of counterrevolutionary activity was hard to gauge. There remained the question of how much damage a renegade could do under the circumstances of what he was able to turn to, and to whom. There were those in the party who were still opposed to a campaign of terror and to trials, who still favored keeping the doors open. But only a few weeks ago, to the political officer's satisfaction, the matter had been brought up for review in connection with the new directive requiring strict party membership for all officials, including those who had been permitted to remain "independent" before. The political officer had been among the first to recommend a tightening of the security system. The question had been left unresolved, but he was determined to pursue it. If he could somehow manage to bring back an account of what a few of these scoundrels were doing, he would prove his point. A tightening of security would result; a new machinery of surveillance would be instituted, and someone would have to take charge of it.

As to Tran Phan Dang, in certain respects he considered the doctor to be the most important of those who had departed from the jungle, not only because of his status as one of Ho Chi Minh's earliest non-party supporters but also as a result of the special role he had played in securing non-military supplies. Moving in and out of the cities as much as he had, the doctor had come to know more than any of them about the secret traffic conducted through the manifold merchant channels, from which the Vietminh had always profited at least as much as the French. It was a dangerous knowledge, under the circumstances, and was reason enough in itself for tracking the doctor down, the political officer reflected. This should not be difficult. Tran had always been vague and undisciplined, inclined to be careless in his movements. If he was here, so much the better; and if not, he would doubtless be in Hanoi, where the political officer intended to go next. A man's character guided his behavior, and to act quickly had never been one of the doctor's attributes. At heart he was a thoroughgoing cosmopolitan; it had been the source of the political officer's contempt, and he could now expect to turn it to his own purpose.

They had passed through the market, he and Cau Minh Thien, and were approaching the boulevard de la Somme. But instead of continuing toward the Quai de Myre de Vilers, the main portion of the waterfront, Cau led the way across the first bridge of the *arroyo Chinois* and then back up along the parallel bank until they reapproached the river along the less-populated Quai de l'Yser. For a mile or more they went slowly along the unpaved road. The sun, in the absence of trees, was hot, and they walked in sweaty silence. In the river the cluster of sampans scarcely stirred. The water was quieter here, away from the ships and the port's bustle above, and it was still brown and muddy, even more so than by the wharves. Cau lifted a finger and pointed downstream to where the Saigon River swung in a huge curve toward its confluence with the Dong Nai.

"There is where we will go," he said. "A boat will take us."

The political officer nodded. He knew about the various places that were used for the transfer of matériel. Some were on the mainland and others were islands scattered throughout the forty-mile delta of the three rivers. From time to time the legionnaires invaded one or another of these hiding-places, but the Vietminh had always been able to return.

Cau halted, and leaned against the mud-brick wall of an abandoned warehouse to light a cigarette. His dark figure against the bright backdrop focused falsely in front of the political officer, who had crouched down to rest, and seemed farther off than it was. Fatigue had suddenly made everything seem small. The political officer was accustomed to walking in the jungle, but not here, not on a road, and his calves were aching. He rubbed them softly with the balls of his fingers, and balanced himself back and forth, teetering and holding his ankles.

There was no one in sight. After he had taken several puffs, Cau threw the butt into the dust. "The boat is over there," he said, pointing to the right. The political officer stood up and they walked twenty yards to the side of a small wooden pier that had broken down and sagged into the stream. Tied to a half-submerged bush was a sampan, and in it was an old man who lay on his back, his face barely in the shade beneath the canvas covering. He made no immediate response as the two men approached, but then he half-raised himself and spat into the water. "You are extremely

◇◇

late," he said. "Do you think I have nothing to do all day but tie myself to a bush and be bitten by flies?"

"You are always complaining," Cau said. "Be quiet and let us go."

The old man continued to mutter as he undid the rope and pushed the boat gently into the stream. The political officer glanced up at him as he skillfully, almost disdainfully, swung the boat about and began guiding it downriver. His body was thin and had the agility of youth, though his face was old and full of lines that were more than weather-carved. There was a withdrawn look about him, and also something dedicated, as if pain had been numbed and scarred over and had left a single tissue of purpose. The face of the old man, the political officer thought, had what the face of Cau Minh Thien lacked; it was belief, embodied in a kind of loving toughness. . . .

Overhead the gulls were shrieking, and then a pair swept close by and the political officer watched the skimming of their muscular wings, their long bodies soaring like dying bullets over the water's surface. The second one dove into the murky river for a fish, silver and small, incongruously gleaming in the brief moment between its life and death. The gull gulped it away and flew off with a fierce blue flapping. The political officer allowed himself to smile. There was a fresh peace out here on the water. Two hours with Cau Minh Thien had driven him too far into himself, had given him a sour feeling. He had been fatigued by more than the walk in the sun; there was an enervation from the strain of his companion. Now the old man, bending above them in the boat with his proud face, became a symbol, and the expansive river, the expanding sky, and the land that lay free ahead became part of an extraordinary calm that freed the political officer from the constriction of the city.

But he was also curious, and broke the silence as he turned and looked back at the old man. "Do you go out far, into the mouth of the river?" he asked.

◇◇◇

Without shifting his concentration or regarding his questioner, the old man said: "That will depend. It is not wise in the time of the monsoon. But it becomes necessary."

"And at such times?"

The old man spat into the water again. "For us, the revolution does not follow the monsoon," he said. "The soldiers fight in the dry weather, but when it is wet the weapons that have been lost in the season of dryness are replaced. It becomes necessary, therefore, to go to the mouth of the river." He moved his head slightly at the ocean beyond, as if there were a ship there now he was steering at.

The political officer acknowledged the reply. It was hard to believe that, in its different ways, so much had been endured for so many years, and that it might go on for so many more. He had lost his sense of time, forgetting his own age. One could see how those around one had grown, boys into men, and men older. There was a single calendar now to live by, the calendar of battle, and all the seasons turned with it.

"Do you have any family, old man?" he inquired. "Is there rice enough for them?"

He heard the old man grunt. "There are fish enough for myself in the water," he replied.

He had pushed the sampan far downstream, broaching the current, and they had begun to swing about toward the northern side and shore. It was very hot.

Cau Minh Thien sneezed and blew his nose out, leaning over the side. His mucus shone on top of the current. When he had sat himself straight, he said: "Come on, hurry, old man. We are being baked out here."

The boatman did not answer, but suddenly let his oar come still. There was a dot on the river ahead of them that was growing quickly larger, and then they heard the sound of an engine.

"We will wait," the old man announced.

In another few minutes the patrol boat swept by, and they saw clearly the French sailors in their red caps and blue suits gathered on the foredeck and leaning against the guns. A boy among them waved, but none of the three men in the boat responded. The sampan soon bobbed in the wake.

When they finally reached the shore, the old man let them drift onto a spit of land that stretched into the tide where the bottom was soft and clear. Cau stepped out first and the political officer followed, and they stood for a moment on a strip of beach. The marches beyond glittered in the sunlight, and the river curving away was a brown band sparkling. The old man stayed and looked past them into the undergrowth that came almost to the water's edge and was like a thick green fur.

The two men, Cau in front, followed a trail through the bushes and presently were in a forest that seemed as dense as any jungle. Overhead the trees were a canopy that obliterated the light, except for occasional rays that were refracted through and brought soft rainbow patterns to the pervasive green floor. There was an animal scurry, and the sudden droppings of a bird into the narrow space between them. Suddenly it became lighter and they heard voices. The trail emerged into a prepared clearing, where some twenty men and a few women were standing in groups of two or three, except for six youths, bare to the waist, who were working in a circle among wooden boxes piled in a three-layer square. The boxes were being opened and the contents separated in heaps on the ground, and the political officer knew without having to look that this was ammunition being sorted. It was a propitious moment, he thought to himself.

Cau walked to the center of the clearing and spoke with a large man who wore a European white shirt over dark, discolored, nondescript trousers. In the half-light his face seemed composed entirely of seams and furrows, into which the unallayed growth of beard had etched uneven patches and whiskery shadows.

◇◇

"I have brought the one who wishes to speak with you," Cau said.

The other looked squarely at the political officer, who had remained on the clearing's edge, and who met the stare in the eerie glow that seeped in from above. The eyes of both men shone with the game of looking at each other.

"You are from the north?" the question finally came.

The political officer was slow to reply. "I am from the headquarters at B—," he said. "There exists a condition of emergency, and I have a request to seek some ammunition, and if possible some guns as well, to a suitable point on the central coast. The material can be replaced later, since we are in the midst of an offensive—"

The man opposite, who had now come close, interrupted with a low rumble that was nearly but not quite laughter. It emerged from yellow teeth and a mouth that was thin and blue, and there was something in the manner and expression that led the political officer to wonder if there was not French blood in his companion.

"That is all very well," was the reply. "It is a simple thing for those of you in the north, who are accustomed to a wealth of guns and bullets, to determine what we shall do here with ours. We have not enough for ourselves, and of this you are aware."

"There is never enough," the political officer said bluntly. "There is not enough for any of us. I do not need you to point this out. It is a matter of necessity and circumstance that brings me here."

The heavy man smiled, as if he enjoyed the thrust and riposte. "Precisely so," he said. "It should not be required at all, such an explanation. And what has occurred to drive the rich begging to the poor?"

"There are matters, in the north as well, that should not require an explanation," the political officer said, with sarcasm. "You are aware, of course, that in the recent weeks the enemy has cut the northern routes. Our supplies have been curtailed temporarily, yet we must continue to attack."

"And we here?" the other broke in sharply. "We are in the midst of nothing? We are enjoying a well-deserved rest?"

The political officer coughed. It had begun badly, and while he had anticipated reluctance, he had not expected contempt. It was not, however, altogether surprising. He was dealing, he now realized, with another such as Cau Minh Thien, which was probably why the interview had been so promptly arranged. In a sense, the political officer felt vindicated. There was here again the telltale streak, the remnant air of injury and pride, the attitude, if not the act, of dissidence. He glanced across at Cau, who had also come closer, so that he stood directly between the political officer and the scowling man in the white shirt. The latter appeared abstracted, even bored. Cau seemed about to speak, but remained silent, with a look that was intense, exacerbated by the forest shadows, and the scar on his cheek seemed like a blight on the bark of a tree.

The voice suddenly resumed, but as though it had an existence apart from its owner, seeming to come from out of the ground. "The fact remains," it said, "that there are operations for which much material is required, more than we can possibly obtain, or than is due to arrive. It is true that there have been ships, but they have not brought enough for the needs of the day."

"Or of the night?" the political officer interposed, softly.

The eyes snapped back. The comment had reached home. It was the old difference about the division of effort. In the opinion of the political officer, and others, the nighttime terror and isolated attacks on recalcitrant peasants in the south, while they served a purpose, were a luxury in the light of the main effort: the interdiction of the rice routes and the destruction of as many of the enemy in force as possible.

"Yes, and of the night as well. . . ." Now less than a foot away, the man's smile was like a sulphurous glow. The bustle in the clearing had ceased and its members coalesced, until now they were gathered around the three men in the center, an amorphous group that whispered without knowledge of what was being deliberated, but with a sense that the stranger among them was not to be approved.

"The *Tu Ve*, as our friend here can tell you," the heavy man said as he indicated Cau with a nod of his head, "is deeply in need of rifles and grenades." The voice had seemed to thicken, and the clearing had suddenly grown darker, as if what little light there was had been dispersed from the roof of the rain-forest. Someone had started a small fire in the background, and the faces were illumined and burnished. "There are other needs that are great, in view of the increase of activity in the cities, the Chinese as well as the French. The forces at the *Cap* are equally needful. . . ."

The political officer sucked his gums and picked at his teeth with a thumbnail. "You will understand," he said, his tone now matter-of-fact, "that by disregarding what is a request, but is of course a suggestion as well, you are risking displeasure. It is your own good that is involved."

The other's eyes shone in anger through the gloom. "I cannot do anything," came the modulated answer. "What we bring in from the ships is not distributed at my will. Go to him who truly determines these affairs."

The political officer smiled at the small retreat. He knew who was meant. It was the Chinese, Li Kwan-sen, who by the free use of his own resources had lifted the siege of the guerillas in the south in the spring, and who had even managed since, in what way the political officer did not know, to revive the old supply line from the west, through the Siamese corridor. In the past year the route had been abandoned, until, mysteriously, and despite the presence of pro-French and independent tribesmen, Li had arranged for several shipments of arms at a time when they were most needed. Undoubtedly the Chinese would be even more difficult to deal with; he had a reputation not only for stubbornness but for almost fearless contempt, and his wealth stood in front of him like a battlement. What he obtained he regarded as his right to allot. He was peculiarly suited to his role as procurer provider. Outwardly Li maintained the emblems of loyalty to the movement. He had even, it was said, visited Ho Chi Minh in the jungle. There was nothing specific the political officer knew that could cast doubt on him, though he remained a source of private suspicion. What the political officer did know, standing immobile now in the island clearing, his two companions having moved away to condemn the fire that had begun to blaze, was that it might require more than himself and an oral demand to convince K. S. Li, as the Chinese liked to call himself for the benefit of the European community he served, to grant any favors. The political officer ground his foot into the soft island soil. He should have come better prepared, he told himself. The sector of battle he represented was tactically under a separate command. He should have followed the line to the top and obtained a written order from General Giap's headquarters. It was too late now. At best he could try to persuade Li Kwan-sen, and perhaps by the time he returned, the trails from the north would be open again and the labor battalions would be moving across the mountains. The danger lay in the effect his failure to persuade would have on other aspects of his journey. He was far more intent on exploring this intransigence and the matter of the renegades than in dealing with guns. Guns were not his affair, to begin with. However, to visit Li Kwan-sen under these conditions had its advantages; to come armed, as it were, with an empty rice-bowl. . . .

The thickset man had moved back from the smoldering fire, and the political officer stepped forward to meet him. "I will follow your suggestion," he said. "I will go visit Mr. Li."

The attitude of unconcern again infuriated him. "Yes, yes, that is best," his host said at length, as if the matter had long since been settled. "Perhaps Mr. Li will be able to help you. He is a sensible man. We can do nothing more, you see, with what we have here" —a wave designated the rows of boxes—"after the distribution is made." The yellow smile spread once more like a stain across the darkly furrowed face. "The nights are longer now. . . ."

The political officer turned about. "Is the boat waiting?" he inquired.

"Surely it is, and the old man with it, who never sleeps," came the reply, with a note of last-minute congeniality. "There are those who believe he is a water-demon. . . ." A youth, summoned from the circle, stepped up to act as a guide. Cau Minh Thien had vanished.

"I will keep our friend with us," came the explanation. "You will not require him further?"

The political officer had begun to move toward the path that led to the water. "No," he said. "No, thank you."

There was no additional response. The undergrowth thickened, encompassing him from both sides, and all he could see was the thin, stubby legs of the boy in front. The light scarcely penetrated now, until they emerged suddenly into the sun at the sandspit. The young guide murmured and was gone, and alone in the brilliance the political officer was left momentarily blinded.

The boat, when he saw it, lay half out of the water, on its side, and the old man sat in the sand. There was a cigarette in his mouth, and a faint curl of smoke. His eyes were closed and he seemed to be sleeping. His face, against the sun, looked like an earthen pot set out to dry. Presently the eyes opened and the old man grunted.

"Where is the other one?" he said. "The impolite one?"

"He is staying," the political officer said.

There was a second grunt and the old man got to his feet with the sudden agility he so well masked. Together they pushed the boat off. Neither of them spoke again until they were far out on the water. The political officer sat as he had before, with the old man hunched above him and guiding the boat into the current's sweep. The water seemed clearer now, and when they turned and pointed toward the city, the political officer saw, almost at the surface, a bright school of tiny fish. He followed their silvery track for some distance. There were no gulls, and he was glad.

"Do you know him well—him whom you call the impolite one?" the political officer, after some time, asked.

The old man said nothing at once, and then he spat and replied: "Well enough. He is the second son of my brother who is a half-brother."

"He spoke with a lack of respect for your venerable years," the political officer said.

"He is accustomed to being familiar," the old man replied. "He is a lonely one, without manners. It was always so."

"Nevertheless, he is a hard worker," the political officer said. "It would appear that he is very active." He paused. "I imagine he does many things . . ."

The old man went through the routine of spitting. But instead of picking up the remark, as the political officer had hoped, all he said was: "You appear to have arrived from a different part of the country?"

The political officer sighed. "That is so," he said. What he admired in this old man could be equally exasperating.

"Then you are closer to the heart of the struggle." There was an unexpected note of vehemence in the husky old voice. "That is the trouble with too many of the men here, with the younger men in particular. They are too much with themselves, and they are left to discover their own ways."

The political officer smiled at having his surmise, even to this degree, proved. He grew discursive, twisting about in the bottom of the boat. "The revolution cannot move with the same speed throughout the nation," he explained. "You are right, of course, but we must be patient. It is a difficulty of mountains and valleys, of time and of space, as well as of men. Ultimately there will be a single area, a single command, a unified nation. But it will take time." He waited again, and added: "Is this true, then, of your youthful relative—that he is among the independent ones?'

"Such things do not concern me," the old man answered promptly. "I have no interest in these matters of behavior. I understand the river only."

"There is more than that you understand," the political officer said politely, disappointed for the second time. "You have not lived all these years for the river alone." Once more he paused, to gain his effect. "They are jealous, these young men of the south," he continued. "I have noticed it, too. It is true that they are left to their own devices, and this is not altogether bad. But if the jealousy becomes too strong, and if there is pride that goes with it, there is a danger by itself. There is a mixing of revolutionary aims."

"You are extremely confusing," the old man said.

The political officer laughed. "I do not mean to be," he said. He admired this old man's canniness. As much to himself as to his companion, he concluded: "It is a serious matter, this spirit of independence, if it is allowed to go far. It is especially so when there is a widening of the front, and when we accept the help of our Chinese friends. It is important to be clear and undivided."

The old man said nothing, but only spat. They were nearing the shore now, and the political officer could see the sun-white wall of the warehouse against which Cau Minh Thien had leaned.

"Do you wish to return there, to the same place?" the old man asked, nodding at the point on the shore.

"If you would be so kind," the political officer said. "I shall continue then by foot."

The old man concentrated on guiding the boat past the last shoal. Gracefully he maneuvered toward the abandoned pier.

"When he returns, you may tell him I would wish to speak with him again," the political officer said. "He will know how to find me."

The old man muttered his having heard as he swung the sampan alongside the bush. "Well, then," the political officer said as he disembarked, "I thank you for your courtesy, and I wish you good luck with your boat and the river in the time of the monsoon."

"I thank you in return," the old man said. "I am glad you have honored my boat." He was being very formal now.

The political officer stepped onto the pier. At the far end, before he went out on the road, he turned, but the old man had vanished, presumably under the sampan cover. The matter of sleeping was not so difficult, the political officer thought, for an old man especially.

The road was still hot, and the dust was like brown powder on it. The bridge lay a mile ahead, and he would have to walk far, he knew, before he found a *cyclo*. He had not accomplished much, though the morning had not been wasted. The pieces had begun to fit. Perhaps Li Kwan-sen would prove a centerpiece. . . .

Chapter XI

AFTER leaving Remy, Genevieve had walked quickly, wanting to get away, to avoid his following her. Three blocks from the Hotel Continental she had stood in front of a silk-shop and looked at the bolts of cloth and the unfolded skirts and also at the reflections of the passers-by in the window. She had known she would go on to the club, but she was indulging first in a mild debate with herself, the result of her pique. She would go because she had planned to, because the Consul would be there; but Remy's oblique remarks and his air of patronage had prompted a prior pretense of indecision.

Their game of exaggerated courtesy was no longer a game. She had found him, for the first time, quite difficult. He had begun to prod, no longer cajoling. And after the long night of sleeplessness and her talk with Cau Minh Thien, she had felt particularly unreceptive.

She had stared at her image in the broad window and a lightheadedness had swept over her. Noon had seemed unreal behind, as if the pouring light, the hum of voices, had been separated from her by another sheet of glass. The quality of tension had left her unaffected and apart, with an easefulness and a new immunity. It was the potion Cau had given. She had thought of him again, in yesterday's sun, of his shadow gliding, the white figure in front of the café, and she had suddenly known what he had meant when he had said he could not constantly live in the dark. The night made one furtive and suspicious. It was true, one could hide in the mass and the glare sometimes. To be, like Cau, dedicated, provided a kind of underground *savoir-faire*.

Turning, she had started to walk again, in the direction of the club. There was a scuffle of feet ahead of her as a bicycle in the gutter had come to a skidding stop. A policeman, stepping from the sidewalk, had pulled the boy cyclist down. The face of the boy had been expressionless. It had remained so as his pockets were turned out and his shirt yanked out of his trouser-tops. There had been nothing: no grenades, no knives.

The policeman had grunted and the cyclist had remounted and ridden off. Neither of them had spoken a word. Genevieve had walked on without stopping as the crowd had broken apart. A wail of sirens had sounded, a tonal spray ascending the rooftops and then softly dying; a stillness, even of footsteps, had thereupon fallen.

Walking faster, she had passed the cathedral and skirted it. A sense of the Consul had begun to come to her as she approached the entrance of the club. The game now would be between herself and him. She would play it guardedly, for her own amusement as much as to satisfy others. There would be nothing beyond that. . . . But an excitement had possessed her, and with a small penultimate shiver, feeling strangely visible again, she had gone up the steps.

2

THE club was crowded with *fonctionnaires*, with their wives and their mistresses. The voices rose over the veranda as the Tonkinese bartender ran back and forth with glasses and fresh ice. Again Adam sat with Genevieve on the far side. He had emerged, black-and-wet-haired, at the pool's steep edge, as he had the day before, and now he sought the attention of the Tonkinese through the shimmer of sun.

Genevieve was wearing a different suit, a yellow one that matched her cap and made her look more pert and, if anything, Adam had decided, even prettier. There was a gentle breeze from the river to the north. The waiter came at last.

"The affairs of state," she said, with her white smile after he had ordered drinks, "do they move tranquilly?"

"Nothing is tranquil," Adam said. "We all jump on strings."

"Here we are all puppets," she agreed, laughing. "It is a stage in many ways, yes. The palaces are part of it, the shops with the goods no one can afford to buy, and the cafés, where only time is spent. This, too, the pool."

"Yet the war goes on, Genevieve. And Frenchmen are killed."

"Yes," she said. "I know. It is a pity. . . ."

He looked at her queerly.

"There is a special cruelty to puppetry," he said. "The flogging, the screams, the wooden anguish . . ."

She threw her head back. "You are amused, as I am, by the sense of theater." She reflected a moment. "If we were to give this up, you see, we would lose our stage to dramatize. It is something the French require for themselves."

"Because of defeat?"

"Yes," she said, "I imagine because of defeat."

"But is it fair to the local players?"

"They are about to be subsidized. A repertory for native dramatics, run by the Americans."

"The owner of the theater remains French," Adam said.

"You will take his theater from him. Soon perhaps," she said.

"You're very bitter this morning," Adam said.

There were cries and laughter from the other side of the veranda as the body of a girl hurtled through the air, in a tight white suit, and plummeted into the pool. The spray rose and seemed to hang. It was like a musical comedy, Adam thought, and he half expected cymbals and trumpets.

"They have thrown her in before," Genevieve observed.

"Who is she?"

"A general's daughter," she replied.

"She falls well, like a bullet," he said.

"The *fonctionnaires* are gay."

"There's been a victory in the north," Adam said. "It was announced this morning. The recapture of some forts."

"It is a turning-point, you see. The effect of the new High Commissioner's anger."

"He's frightened them all, the colonels especially."

"It was necessary."

"Yes," Adam said, "but it will take more than that, more than some colonels' heads."

Genevieve nodded, without replying. The pool was its own area of battle, but still only an extension of what went on elsewhere, behind the stucco palace walls. Those real headquarters were like sheltering sea-caves, she thought, where the sallow men in their darkly fanned rooms of deliberation struggled for fresh devices to gain time for those whose true cause lay here, in the warmth of the sun on the tiles. The pool was also a splendid anachronism. She responded to it without guilt, but she suddenly wondered if, in his American self-righteousness, he had ever regarded his coming here as something other than the therapy he claimed.

He had stood up and was smiling down at her.

"You're daydreaming," he said.

"When one sleeps badly at night, one must do one's dreaming by day."

"Let's go in, then we'll leave," he said, with just enough added meaning in his tone.

"You begin," she replied.

He dived in and swam the length of the pool twice. Genevieve enjoyed watching him. Once he brought his hand up and waved to her and shouted something she couldn't hear. His dark hair seemed to shake through the water, she could see his eyes flash against the green spray, and the sweep and ripple of his muscles. In the pool the Consul was as attractive as he was out. His body flowed in full unison of its parts.

She wanted to be swimming with him now, on the pool's crest, and she leaped up and dived in, flatly. The water seemed indecently warm at first. Genevieve felt his hand take hers and she returned the affection of his fingers.

When they came up together at the stone steps of the ladder, they saw, ahead and above, like a pale gargoyle, M. Remy in a wicker chair. He was smiling, but the smile looked as if it hurt him at the corners of his mouth.

"Two emerging dolphins," Remy said softly.

Adam introduced her, and Remy tried to smile again. "Yes, mademoiselle, I have seen you here before, of course—only yesterday, if I remember, with Monsieur Patch. He is an excellent swimmer, don't you agree?"

"Oh, yes," Genevieve said.

It was unlike him, she thought, to act so precipitously. To follow her was one thing, but to endanger his own position by engaging her in this fashion was something else. With a start she asked herself what if, after all, he suspected?

"And you also, mademoiselle," his voice continued, unctuously. "Together you are very beautiful in the water."

Adam had begun to move away, and without looking back Genevieve started after him. Remy was saying across her shoulder: "Perhaps you would join me. I cannot drink, you see, but it would be an honor. . . ."

Adam turned. "I'm afraid it's rather late," he said abruptly. "But thank you very much."

"Ah, the Americans, they are always so busy," Remy said. "It is a lesson we should learn, mademoiselle, if we wish to stay in the race."

Adam stopped at the edge of the tiles and gazed abstractedly across the pool. "Perhaps the horse is already gone," he said.

"The horse—gone?" The Frenchman was puzzled.

"It's an old American proverb," Adam said.

Remy was mystified and Adam let him be a moment more. "Concerning the closing of the barn after the disappearance of the horse," he explained.

Remy brightened. "Ah, but I see, of course," he said. He was laughing now as he addressed himself once more to Genevieve. "Monsieur Patch and myself, we are always joking. Even when I do not understand, it is a mark of friendship."

"And esteem," Adam said, taking Genevieve's arm.

Remy bowed as they went around the veranda and down the steps to the dressing-rooms. He kept watching them, and along the edge of the pool there were others who, glancing up, regarded with proprietary pride of old membership the good-looking couple and saw briefly the pale man left behind, who had sat down at length and asked the boy for a citronade while he wiped his spotted brow.

◇◇

Fifteen minutes later, beaded with perspiration, Remy opened his eyes. He had dozed off in the chair, his head back, the citronade warm on the concrete ledge where the boy had set it. Now standing, he held onto the rail until the blackness was dispersed and the outlines of the pool returned; the voices resumed shape and substance. He strolled under the pavilion and brought a cigarette from his shirt. The sulphurous match made him sneeze as he lit it too close to his nose. He walked to the outer edge, where a stone wall abutted the steps, and, leaning on his elbows, looked out across the expansive lawn. Just beyond the level of the hedge he saw the Consul and Genevieve moving down the street.

. . . Fifty yards farther back, Tran had risen from his patch of grass. He had seen the Consul, in his soft white suit, emerge from the club's entrance with his companion, glide out of the gate, and turn along the vacant street, and he had waited until they had almost reached the corner before starting to follow them. His dizziness had ebbed. He had got nearly to the hedgerow before he remembered that he had left the square of paper Mr. Goodenough had given him lying in the grass. It seemed unimportant, and there was no thought of returning. The coolie, in fact, had already found it and had put it away in his shiny black trousers. . . .

Along the sequestered, siesta-struck street the small procession moved, unknowing, unaware. A hundred feet or more separated its three component parts. Up on the parapet of the club, M. Remy blew the cigarette smoke out and flicked the butt away. It was like witnessing a play, he thought, or perhaps, more precisely, a vignette, perfectly spaced. He flexed his fingers pleasurably, his knuckles cracking, and thought for a moment of walking after them; but it would be as absurd as it was unnecessary. The report would be on his desk in the morning, containing, perhaps, more than he had hoped for. He turned back to the veranda and fetched the warm citronade. He felt surprisingly undyspeptic. In another month, he thought, the dullness might be gone.

3

ADAM was amused to see Genevieve impressed. It had taken him two months to find the house, and at the last moment he had almost lost it to a *fonctionnaire* who came armed from Paris with a letter from a cousin, purporting to be the agent. Adam had been forced to threaten the High Commissioner's intervention. A small additional fee was paid, and the *fonctionnaire* had been appeased. Now, when they met in the cafés, they bowed.

There was a screened porch and a spacious, L-shaped living-room downstairs, and two bedrooms, dark and deep and cool, with the kitchen in the rear. Upstairs were another three rooms. He had been accustomed to large houses and had hated the times between, here as in prior posts, when he had had to live in hotels. Most of all he relished a private garden. This one reached around.

"But it is all so large," she said. "Far too much for one person."

She sat on the double-length couch and curled up her legs. "The Americans must have the largest houses," she said. "Why is that?"

Adam frowned, without answering.

"I remember this house," Genevieve continued. "It was owned, during the war, by someone the Japanese did not molest. At the end a Japanese general lived here."

"One of my servants worked for him," Adam said. "My cook. He still makes good sukiyaki."

The house was silent. Genevieve looked around.

"The servants are in the market," Adam explained. "I forgot I told them I wouldn't be home for lunch."

"I am an excellent cook," she said.

"We'll go foraging," he said.

He went first to the bar in the corner and mixed a pair of gin and bitters. He handed hers down and stood above her as she sipped it. She turned her face up to him and he leaned over and touched his lips to her forehead. "Welcome," he said. "Just the right touch for the living-room."

"The Americans are very adept, at mixing drinks and serving them," Genevieve said, lowering her eyes.

"You still make us sound like a race from another planet."

"But you are," she cried, laughing.

"It's become fashionable to say so."

"It is more than fashion. It is a matter of behavior, of which the renting of large houses is a part. Because you are afraid of being by yourself, you escape in space."

"Come, now," Adam said. "It's not so simple as that. The French are equally spoiled."

"For us, the acquiring of wealth is a matter of position," she said. "For you, it is a game, like riding on a wheel. It is the difference between appreciating leisure and insisting upon luxury."

"And we are the luxurious?"

"You divide life between luxury and necessity. We distinguish between what is possible and what is not. So we become satisfied with less, and enjoy more."

"Chauvinism."

"Perhaps," she said. "But I do not think so. Nevertheless, it is an excellent house."

"I'm glad you like it, at least," Adam said.

Genevieve looked at him and laughed merrily. "You are hurt," she said. "Now you are hurt and uncomfortable, like a small boy with a peppermint stick among beggars."

"You're very perceptive," he replied. He got up and poured himself more gin. When he came back to the couch he sat down next to her. "You're a strange girl," he murmured.

"I would like to know many things," she said. "But first I will prepare the lunch."

She got up and walked to the kitchen, and Adam went after

her. Her arms folded, she stood in front of the new icebox, with an expression of mock rapture.

"A shining white horse," she said. "For the American knight."

He set his glass down on the top and took her in his arms and kissed her, holding her against him with both his arms, feeling her compactness and the tautness that gave way gradually until she was willing to cling to him, her head against his breast. Then she moved him off, gently.

"In some ways the planets are alike," she said. "The sense of gravity is the same."

She opened the icebox and peered in. Together they made a salad, washing it carefully with permanganate, and brought it back inside. He opened a bottle of white wine and drew the shutters closer to preserve the shade. He let her serve him then and waited until she had served herself.

"It's an excellent salad," he said, tasting it and pouring some of the wine.

"The wine is excellent as well," she said.

Adam felt strangely abashed. For a moment it seemed he was in someone else's house, himself a guest. It was the first time in as long as he could remember, in dealing with a woman, that he had felt himself under such peculiar scrutiny, one that assumed priority over his own. She made him feel meek. He saw her grinning at him, looking more Vietnamese than French.

"You are easily offended," she said. "Now I shall know how to make you kiss me."

"You're charming and you're exasperating," he said, meaning it.

"I am not so certain we will be lovers," she said, blandly.

Adam put his plate down and reached for more wine. Behind him he heard her ask: "Do you believe, actually, in love? Or do you pretend to?"

"It makes the monsoon bearable," he said, with some desperation.

"Like everything else, love is a habit with the Americans. You are affectionate, and sometimes lonely, but I do not think you believe in what you do about it."

"A kind word is all we want," Adam said.

"Where there is both pride and fear, love is difficult to buy," she said. "It cannot, always, be bought."

Adam sighed. "I wasn't speaking of it in that sense," he said. He reached for her hand, but she moved it away, almost angrily.

"No," she said. "You do not understand. You are willing to take us seriously, but only up to a point—if we will act like proper children and be grateful, for your love as well as for your assistance, if we repay you by telling you how fortunate you are to be able to extend such kindnesses. But you are the true beggars. It is a form of usury you offer."

"An old Oriental custom," he said, not liking himself.

"You are impatient," she said. "With nations as well as with women." She smiled again as she took back his hand.

"They are sometimes equally stubborn," he murmured. The wine was making him sleepy.

Genevieve remained undaunted. "The French have understood these matters. It is true that they are often selfish, but they understand the quality and the purpose of love. Perhaps that is why there is gallantry left, both real and false."

"You were sounding awhile ago more Annamese," he said. "Now you've changed again."

A solemn expression came across her face. "There are times, as I have told you, when I do not know."

She had put her head on his shoulder. He felt a longing for her now, more than desire; it was a kind of immolation he sought.

She surprised him by suddenly jumping up. "I must leave," she said.

Adam was astonished. There was a limit to such unpredictability.

◇◇◇

"There is the whole afternoon . . ."

Genevieve's smile hovered. "I must visit my friends," she said.

He knew she was lying. "I think you are running," he said.

"Perhaps," she said. "Perhaps I am running. One can run in various directions."

"Will I see you later—tonight?"

"No, not tonight," she declared. "I—I am busy."

"Tomorrow, then."

"I will come to the pool," she said, "like a mermaid."

"I'll drive you home. The car will be here in a moment."

"Oh, no," she said. "I will take a *cyclo*."

Adam gave up.

He went with her to the entrance of the garden. A *cyclo* happened by at once and she ran to it. With a half-gestured wave, she was gone.

Adam walked slowly along the garden path, his hands in his pockets. When he had reached a point halfway between the gate and the house, he stopped and turned to look up the street. The wonder on his face was boyish. He remained standing for several moments, until a voice seemed to come from the heart of a bush in back of him.

"Excuse me . . ." it said.

Chapter XII

Y ES?" Adam whirled about. "Oh, the doctor. . . ."
Tran stepped forward. He had come into the garden at the side, over the low fence, and had moved behind the bushes when he saw the American and the Eurasian girl emerge. Now the white man's blue eyes regarded him with queer but soft surprise, as if, focusing, they did not quite recognize. Like juxtaposed statues, the two men stood a few feet apart in the grass.

"Excuse me," Tran repeated. "I only wished—"

"Please—come in," Adam said, and he started for the house.

Tran walked behind him. "It is very impolite of me," he murmured. The American said something about the sun and the heat of the day, and his voice seemed to hang in the air ahead, thickly, the way Tran remembered it on the square. When he reached the porch, his left hand extended, Adam held the screen door open.

Beyond the threshold Tran stood transfixed. The polished floor spread out before him and brought on a reflex of hesitation, as if entering required an appraisal of his final weapons. He took another step. Again he murmured: "I have not introduced myself. . . ."

From a porcelain cup across the way the American was proffering a cigarette. "But we have already met," he said. "So it does not matter, except as a formality."

With a slight motion of his hand, the doctor declined. "My name is Tran Phan Dang," he announced.

"Dr. Dang, then," Adam said. He motioned to a chair, and, picking up two empty glasses from a low Chinese table, deposited them atop a cabinet in the corner. With his back still turned, he added: "I am the American Consul. Adam Patch . . ."

Tran's head lifted sharply as Adam crossed to the couch in the center of the room. "I did not know—" he started to say.

The Consul smiled. "I didn't mention it before," he said. "There was no reason." He thought of the doctor walking silently alongside, and of the whiteness of the square, and for a moment none of it had meaning or reality, his being where he was, the Annamite now in the house, the girl gone.

The doctor was still immobilized on a rattan mat, looking stranded as on an atoll. "Won't you sit down?" Adam repeated.

"Thank you." Veering to the nearest chair, Tran misgauged his distance and fell into it heavily. A feeling of abashment overcame him. "It is the first time," he started to explain, "in many years, that I have been in such a house."

"Some tea, perhaps?"

"No, thank you, it is not necessary."

There was an awkward silence. On the couch, Adam had crossed his legs. The doctor's presence was puzzling, though he could assume a purpose. But he had the odd feeling that the two of them might sit here endlessly, while the fan kept spinning. It was the vacuum again, the sense of stoppage, of all halt and dead air.

A shutter had come loose, severing the light so that the doctor's face was cast half in shadow. It gave him an unreal look, as if only part of him were present. Adam let the shutter be.

"Yesterday," the doctor said, from the side of him that was light, "after the explosion in the café, I did not tell the truth."

Now Adam got up and adjusted the shutter, out of politeness.

"Then you are not a doctor?" he said as he came back.

"No, it is not that."

"But there was not much else." Adam smiled. The spell of inertia was broken.

Tran reflected. "Perhaps it was not a matter of untruth," he said. He was trying to recall the conversation in more detail. There is something else—" he began once more, and again he hesitated. "This morning, at the American Legation, when I saw you—"

"Saw me?" Adam said. He tried to remember.

"You were leaving," the doctor explained. "Not long ago. Perhaps only an hour."

Adam recollected. "But of course—at the desk, in front," he said. He reached for a fresh cigarette. "You were speaking with the sergeant?"

"Yes, yes," Tran replied. There was an eager note in his voice. "Afterward I spoke with—Mr. Goodenough." He said the name slowly.

"Oh, indeed," Adam said, almost formally. Then the thought struck him, and the earlier episode projected itself. He glanced sharply at the doctor. "But—you—?"

Tran nodded, aware of the awareness. "I was going to explain. Today, in front of the club, I thought it likely—"

"You've been here, in Saigon, how long?" Adam broke in.

"Since four days."

"From where?"

"From Hué. Before that from the north."

"You were in the jungle?"

"Yes."

"How long with the Vietminh?"

"Since 1946, following the defeat in Hanoi."

"And why did you leave?" What Remy had said at the pool about the renegades suddenly impinged on the question. The doctor, Adam felt, with intuitive certainty, was not one of those to whom the Frenchman's suggestion would apply. But, at the same time, one could not afford to be rash. He heard the engine of his car come close and die out in the driveway.

The doctor, for his part, was thinking of the police station, and of the conversation he had had with Mr. Goodenough. The Consul's questions, while not unlike those of the others, were not inquisitorial. The difference was one of tone, or, since there was no reason yet to hope, perhaps purely of coincidence. Tran breathed deeply. "It was no longer possible to remain," he said. "But there are also other reasons . . ."

Adam walked toward the kitchen and, turning briefly, said: "Anyway, we'll have some tea." He re-emerged with the pot, holding the two small cups in his other palm, and set them down on the low table. Then he drew a chair closer to Tran's.

"Did you tell all this to Mr. Goodenough?" he asked.

"We established it," the doctor replied. "There were many questions asked, for which I could not provide the answers, out of ignorance."

Adam smiled, imagining Goodenough seated at his desk, probing. "I am glad you've come," he said, with still a trace of effort. His curiosity was further aroused. "I suppose you followed me?"

Tran grew abashed again. "Yes," he said, "from the club. In the beginning, I was afraid."

"Afraid? Afraid of what?"

The doctor laughed, without replying, and Adam's heart leaped, but then he realized he had misconstrued. "The city is difficult, of course," he said more gently. "After the jungle, one doesn't always know what to do with it."

"They are not altogether dissimilar, except for the variety in the animals."

The remark, and their joint laughter, relaxed them both, and after a moment Adam inquired: "But why did you travel all the way to Saigon? Hanoi was much closer."

Tran took a long swallow of tea. "It was necessary, and more advised as to safety, despite the length of the journey."

"But you are a northerner—?"

"There is another reason," Tran replied. "It is why I am here, I imagine, in the house of the Consul."

Adam refilled the cups, avoiding the doctor's glance. "But there are Americans in Hanoi too. . . ."

◇◇

"It is many months since I have been there," Tran murmured. "There are many changes, I imagine, of which the increase of Americans is but one. I suppose it is the same everywhere. . . ."

"We are more accessible," Adam said. "In some ways."

"Also, it is not always a matter of seeking, but of being sought," Tran said carefully.

Now Adam looked up. "So soon?" he asked, his voice rising. Then his brow lifted. "Who—the Communists or the French?"

Tran told what had happened after his walk to the piers. He described the questioning in the police station, and his peremptory release. Then he spoke of having seen the Consul on the veranda above the flower-market.

"I would have recognized you, I'm sure," Adam said, "except that when one looks down into the night, the faces below are far away."

"To expect it was foolish on my part—" Tran said, letting the sentence drift. He had not spoken of the tall girl by the balustrade, or of the scar-cheeked stranger.

"Perhaps you should have announced your presence in the city sooner," Adam said. The doctor said nothing.

Adam jerked his head up quickly. The possibility had suddenly suggested itself. "The Frenchman," he said, "at the interrogation— what did he look like?"

Tran described M. Remy so precisely, referring especially to the tightness and the color of the Frenchman's skin, that Adam knew at once. When he mentioned Remy's name, the doctor remembered. "Yes," he said. "It was the name that was used . . ."

"At what time did the interview take place? How long after you were apprehended?"

The doctor pondered. "An hour, or a little more," he said. "For a time—you will think it strange—I fell into a sleep."

Adam pictured Remy at the pool, hovering awhile longer in the sun, going directly thereafter to the dark little room in the police station and sitting, he imagined, astride a wooden chair, his legs spread and his shoes pointed outward, tapping the chair-top with a pallid finger and asking random questions while allowing the Vietnamese to conduct the inquiry. And he thought of the look on Remy's face when he had stepped from the jeep what must have been only a short time later, flustered, then sly, the politeness quickly replacing the consternation. How long, he wondered, had the doctor been pursued, across how many sunlit squares?

"And when you left, what did they tell you?"

"Nothing," Tran replied. "Except to declare my address."

"Which you did?"

Tran nodded. "Also, that they would wish to speak with me again."

Adam went to the window. The garden was still empty. "You have not since been followed?" he asked, coming back into the center of the room.

Tran shrugged. "It is possible," he said. "There is nothing I have noticed." He seemed undisturbed at the thought.

Adam had sat down again. Two flies, caught in the fan's breeze, whirled wildly. All else was motionless, the two men across from each other, the air outside, the atmosphere in the room that seemed contained, like that of a Chinese box within a box.

At length Adam asked the question Tran had been expecting. "And now, since you've come, what will you do?"

Another minute passed. Confronted with the problem directly, Tran found himself without speech, his mind not blank, but unfunctioning and scattered, as if the thoughts he had fastened down earlier had been devilishly unmoored. Adam's eye roved from the face of the doctor to the wall beyond, where the sun etched a yellow block against the gray plaster. Across it a shadow loomed, elongated and flat, as of a passing torso. Adam turned, but saw only the green garden through the window, and the sky, pale and empty, except for an isolated, elliptical cloud that hung down at the earth like a plumb. The doctor, at an angle, had not noticed the shadow; but he raised his head as he saw the Consul's motion, and when Adam veered back toward the garden, the doctor replied, stimulated by the image of the Consul leaving, as if across another square: "Perhaps, if it could be arranged, I would wish to return."

A foot or so from the window Adam stopped. He looked back to the doctor, noting the smile that hung, almost foolishly, off-balance, on the doctor's face. There was something nearly ludicrous in the little man's expression, at once old and childlike. But then the corners of the doctor's mouth moved, and a look almost of pain passed across. His smile vanished, and when he spoke again, he stared beyond Adam to the farthest wall, where a demon with disembodied eyes glared out of an angry tapestry. Like a medium intoning a dream, the doctor started to speak, softly: "In the valleys of the mountains, there are many villages where the fighting has come and gone," he said, "or where there has been no fighting yet. Here there are soldiers seldom seen. When the Vietminh comes, it is one or two men from the north, who do not stay, except to arrange for the transport of the food and for the selection of the partisans."

The sun-patch on the wall had faded, but the doctor's head remained adumbrated, like a tiny bas-relief, against it. "There are no Frenchmen there," he continued, with measured slowness; he might have been reciting at dictation speed for an unseen audience. "And no Americans. It is the indefinite country."

He ruminated a moment . . . "Except there are the American planes, which fly extremely high, but descend on occasion to the tops of the villages and to the trees on the edge of the jungle to drop paper, like a rain of color."

Adam coughed, but waited.

"At such a rain, I have seen the people rub their heads and laugh," the doctor continued. "What is written is both Annamese and French, but it is like a foreign tongue, or a dialect which is not comprehended. The name of the Emperor has no importance. In the villages of this country, it is Ho Chi Minh who is remembered, and many yet call him Nguyen Ai Quoc."

Now Adam murmured, half-audibly: "One has to combat a legend."

"It is more complicated that that," the doctor replied. He had not yet confronted the Consul, who sat with his chin in his hands and his elbows on his knees and seemed to have forgotten the window.

"There is sorrow still everywhere, yet the condition improves," Tran went on. "The hunger grows less because where the famine comes there is a sharing of rice among the farmers, and among the villages themselves." The doctor's smile returned. "The Vietminh can also purchase the medicines of the West, in the European cities," he added, and paused. . . . "Something else endures, which is of equal importance."

Adam interrupted. "I know," he said. "There is *dynamisme*, Communist style."

The doctor's smile flickered, as if again it hurt him. "It is unfortunate, but it is true," he said, "since it is the Vietminh's promise of independence that is still believed. It is true especially in the indefinite country, since there is less to be complained of. Yet the war continues, and the fighting spreads slowly, but moves like a great stain, with sureness. There are more promises required, new drugs to cure the malady of doubt."

"There's no doubt of that," Adam said. He stood up and moved to the wall, where he stood leaning against the Chinese cabinet. "There is the question of time. Time itself can become an illness, like a sleeping sickness."

The doctor shook his head. "It is not merely time," he said, "although in some respects the Vietminh grows constantly stronger."

"So do the French," Adam said, "but only in some respects."

The doctor swung around and regarded the Consul squarely at last. "And the Americans?" he asked. There was a silence, broken by the sudden ticking of the fan, of a large fly being struck by the slow, brown blades.

Adam returned to the couch. For a moment, where the doctor sat, he saw the bespectacled face of the Minister, with its cold and separate certitude.

"Yes, it is unfortunate," he said at length. "It's like the presence on the one hand and the absence on the other of the *dynamisme*. We are part of the lack."

"Between the French and the Americans, the circumstances are not equal."

"That is also true," Adam replied. "Yet an equality has come to exist. At least—" He stopped.

Again Tran's voice grew subdued. "In the valleys and on the slopes of the mountains where I have traveled," he said, "there are many untruths spoken. If there remains knowledge of the Americans, it is a knowledge that is turned false, because it is what the Vietminh has taught."

"And what has the Vietminh declared to be the truth?" Adam asked.

"Most recently, that the Emperor is the Emperor of the Americans as well as of the French."

Adam smiled wryly. "Perhaps it's not so much an untruth," he said, "as a half-truth, or a half-untruth."

"In itself it would not matter," Tran said, "if there was otherwise activity in behalf of the truth."

The doctor paused, as if to gather his innermost thoughts. "There are many things involved," he resumed. "To begin with, geography. There is a man who lies ill in one village, and another who is ill nearby, in a village perhaps only twenty miles away. It matters little where death stops to acquire a first corpse. But in a time of troubles it is the second man, deeper in a hostile land, who must be succored."

"A law of increasing returns, in the increase of the jungle," Adam

✧✧✧

said. "You may be right, Dr. Dang, but of course one must be careful."

"It is more than serum and men's bodies, more than death or life alone," Tran said. "It is the willingness to share a peril and a suffering. Perhaps by now, in such a time of fear, it is the risk alone that matters."

"Our risks are tarnished," Adam murmured.

The doctor scarcely heard. "In the indefinite countries, where there is greater ignorance than knowledge, there is also greater pride that accompanies the loneliness of men," he declared. "And where there is pride, there is bound to be fear, but with it a greater respect for bravery as well. There is time for the generous to be daring, and if there is also patience there can be greater love. . . ."

The doctor looked up and noted that the Consul's eyes had acquired a luminosity that made them darker, like the color, he thought, of a lake he had dreamed of. For a moment he was transported back into the dream, and then he met the Consul's gaze. The room seemed suddenly surfeited with light. "You were saying—?" the Consul asked.

It was easier now, Tran thought. "It is not the promises, or the activity of the Vietminh that alone succeeds," he said. "There is something in men's souls that grows violent, that is made to despise because it has been despised. It is like a chain reaction in chemistry. When it bursts, there are words used in the West to describe it, such as 'nationalism.' But it is that which occurs after the bursting that is most important."

"The hunters approach, from opposite ends of the forest," Adam said.

Tran smiled. "I prefer the analogy of my own profession," he said. "The condition is like an organism that requires treatment, that cannot, in the forest, be left to fester. The French are slow doctors."

"They have their own prescriptions, and their own pride," Adam said. "Which is why the reaction gets delayed."

◇◇◇

"That brings on surgeons, who operate in haste."

"There is danger in parables, yet a certain truth," Adam said. Another childlike smile suffused the doctor's face. "There are various antidotes," he declared, "and the manner of their administration can determine the recovery of the patient. A long convalescence is required, with a practical nurse."

"And a painless needle." The doctor, for some reason, engendered self-mockery.

"It is possible, and there is a way," the doctor said. "A cure." Adam recalled the cryptic comment in the square, and now it suddenly seemed to him that he had known the doctor a long time.

"It is not guns, therefore, that are required in the indefinite country, or leaflets, or beautiful machinery," Tran said softly. "These are all necessary, in time, but in the beginning what is most required is the effort it will take to reach there, through the trails of the jungle, and the ability when one has arrived to speak with a common tongue."

Adam sighed. "We can't all be missionaries," he said, but he knew what the doctor meant.

"It is a new irony," Tran said, "that it has become necessary to be so, for reasons that are not religious."

There was another silence. Tran waited for the Consul's question, as he had before. When it came, he was better prepared. "What do you want to do about it?"

The reply was prompt. "I would like to return, into the indefinite country."

"But not alone?"

"I would like to go with—some Americans. I will know where to go, you see, also where not to go. If there is uncertainty, I can proceed alone, for the purposes of exploration."

"To do what?"

Tran hesitated. "In order that one may travel quickly, without difficulty, in the jungle, it will be impossible, in the beginning, to

◇◇◇

carry many things. There are medicines needed, and some food. But it is chiefly important to bring ourselves into the places where only the Vietminh has been, where it has been the Vietminh that has come and has gone, unmolested, except for the planes that destroy and that do more harm than good."

"But you are one man," Adam said. "What you wish to do would require many men such as yourself."

"There would be such men," Tran said. "They would multiply."

Adam thought about it. "Yes," he said, "I suppose they might."

"It need not be everywhere," the doctor said. "If there were a few such expeditions sent farther into the jungle than the soldiers have gone, on the edge of the fighting or beyond it, the knowledge would travel quickly. It is such knowledge that will provide the cure to the malady of doubt."

Adam's fascination with the doctor grew. He thought of those who had dropped into Yugoslavia, who had been coast-watchers on Pacific islands, of the handful who had, for that matter, helped Ho Chi Minh himself during the earlier war.

"And the French?" he asked. "What of them?"

"The assurances of the French are no longer desired," the doctor said bluntly. "It is partly the reason that the war goes on, and it is why Ho Chi Minh and not the Emperor is remembered, in spite of what the Communists have done, and in spite of what the French concede. There are reasons for the presence of belief, or for the lack of it, that are beyond the kindness or the cruelty of men, beyond historical fact and truth itself. It belongs, this belief, to memory and also to hope, which is sometimes like a sickness that itself endures, and which grows into madness. . . ."

The doctor took a handkerchief from his pocket and wiped his face, which had become shiny with perspiration. He stared up at the fan, circling like a hawk. Adam walked back and forth through the middle of the room, and the doctor now lowered his head and watched him. He no longer felt a nervous vacancy or the shuttlecock of fear. He leaned over to pour himself more tea, though the pot was scarcely warm. The Consul was still pacing, like a disturbed priest, Tran thought, to whom a burden has been passed on. It was only temporary; it would be passed back again, he knew, as rightfully his own; but he was momentarily thankful to be rid of it.

The Consul came to a halt on the mat and looked directly at the doctor. "Your idea is not altogether new," he said. "It's something that's been mentioned." He paused, as if considering what he had said. "At least—it's been thought about," he added. "Perhaps, after all, it hasn't been discussed."

A clear image of the Minister came suddenly to mind, and Adam saw him at his desk, surrounded by the others, himself included. He even heard the buzz of voices.

The doctor sat in an oblong patch of sun, receding. Adam looked at him once more. "The working parties were projected," he said, half to himself. "That is"—he used a ridiculous word, and smiled—"under the ægis of the economic staff. You've heard of the ECA, of course?"

The doctor nodded, thinking of the piece of paper he had forgotten in the grass. He preferred not to speak of it.

"Supervision, that is—" Adam said. He felt suddenly foolish, and shook his head. "However," he said, "since you've come all this way, we'll see—"

Tran regarded him queerly. "If it is possible, I will wait," he said.

"Yes," the Consul murmured. "Yes, it would be better." He glanced at his watch.

"I have kept you too long," the doctor was saying, behind him. It was like the square again.

"No, it's not that," Adam said. He almost asked: "Have you ever felt—?" but restrained himself.

Instead, after a moment, buttoning his jacket, he inquired: "Where are you staying, in the city?"

"On the edge of it, in Cholon," Tran replied.

The Consul examined his watch again. "Come," he said. "I'll take you. Anyway, I have to go there."

They went out, leaving the door open. In the sunlight, near the driveway, one of the houseboys stood conversing with the chauffeur.

Adam beckoned Tran to get in first, and, climbing in behind him, closed the door before the driver could get to it. The dust swirled as the car backed out, and left a chaos of motes in the entrance. Adam pointed toward the Chinese city.

"There are others I will talk with," he said. "Tomorrow, perhaps, or the day following."

Tran obeyed an instinct. "I did not mention it," he said, "but Mr. Goodenough suggested I go to the offices of—"

"Of the ECA?" Adam said.

"Yes."

"Did he telephone?"

"He gave me a message."

"Oh? To whom?"

Tran hesitated. "I do not know," he said. "I—I have lost it. In the grass, in front of the Cercle Sportif."

"Lost it? How, then, do you know where?"

Tran laughed, shyly again, and said: "Perhaps it was unavoidable."

"Never mind," Adam said. "I will talk to them myself." He sensed the doctor's confusion. "I'll explain later," he added.

The car had come to the vague line that divided Saigon from Cholon and was gathering speed. Adam told the driver to slow down.

"Where is the hotel?" he asked.

Tran pointed. "At the turning, by the gambling parlor."

When the car had rolled to a stop, Adam held the door. "You must be careful," he said as the doctor disembarked. "I should advise you remain here. I'll send for you."

Tran realized he had not even mentioned the incident in the market. There was no point to it now. "Yes," he said. "I will wait."

Adam extended his hand, and the doctor went into the hotel. The car hurled forward and he told the driver to go around the block and come back to the farthest entrance of the casino. By the time he got there, the black-suit coolie was debarking from a *cyclo* and had the good fortune to observe the Consul at the same time that he took up his station in the teashop diagonally across from the hotel. It was half past four, and the coolie quickly ate some cakes, holding them in one hand and the tea in the other as he stood in the entrance of the shop and squinted up at the hotel window. When he saw the doctor's head framed briefly, before the shade was pulled, he turned and sighed, and stretched out across the wooden bench in the dank rear.

The shopkeeper grumbled. "Why don't you sleep at home?" he said. The coolie made no response. Inert, in a heap, he was let alone. The tea-man threw the dregs of the pot into the dust in front and watched the liquid globules roll into the curb. Across the way he saw the black European car shining in the sun, and the driver, in his white jacket, reclining across the wheel. There was no reason, after all, he decided, why he should not permit a poor man sleep. . . .

Chapter XIII

BEYOND a barren space that stretched from the back of the gambling parlor was a small, unweeded garden. A gray, weather-ravaged fence surrounded it, and what remained of a path led through the center from one wooden gate to another, which opened upon a shed that abutted on an old frame house. The main part of the house was a teashop that fronted the narrow street beyond. Pye-dogs and goats roamed the area in back and fought for the primacy of a high, flat dump that was shared by flies grown green and fat from scavenging.

The sun that had burned the grass and the weeds bore down pitilessly at two o'clock when a scuffed white door at the back of the gambling casino opened and two men came out. One of them was Li Kwan-sen, the Chinese owner, and the other was his chief assistant, a tall, thin man whose name was Kuo and who had a northern Chinese face that was long and full of mournful bones. The two men walked through the garden and entered the small house through a rusty, corrugated-metal door that hung tenuously at the edge of the shed.

The room they found themselves in was only a hollow space into which a table and three wooden chairs seemed to have been thrown. Li sat down, while Kuo walked to the front and rapped several times with his knuckles against the wall. Another door, cut into the wall at the side and scarcely noticeable, opened and was quickly closed again by an old coolie who peered in and who, after a few minutes, during which Kuo took another of the chairs across from his master and sat in silence, reopened it and carried in, now wearing a dirty gray apron over his baggy trousers, a pot of tea and several chipped, stained cups. He set these down and bowed as if a tired spring inside him had been stirred, and then he went back into the teashop. The sound of voices from the front was barely audible.

Kuo poured some tea into his employer's cup, and some for himself. The two men drank without speaking, bringing the warm cups to their mouths with both hands and taking in the tea in loud, soughing sips. The room was windowless except for a single long but shallow slit high on the wall in the rear. The faces of the men grew moist; almost simultaneously, they belched.

A quarter of an hour passed, and then the door that led to the teashop opened for a third time and a man wearing a white shirt and light-colored trousers and a broad sun-hat that cast a shadow across his face, which was younger than those of the other two men in the room, entered. His features were flat and his skin was pocked, and while the racial resemblance to the others was apparent, it was peculiarly modified. His bones were smaller and his skin a trifle darker. An immobility that seemed controlled furnished his only expression. He was the first to speak.

"Well, then, I am glad to see you, Comrade Li," the political officer said. His lips had scarcely moved and his tone and look implied a contradiction of the salutation. The mottled face was a stage across which the words stalked like actors.

Li nodded perfunctorily. He appeared to have caught some of the newcomer's constraint. The tiny room was suddenly in the atmosphere of play-acting.

"My coming was urgent," the political officer announced. "I assure you, I do not enjoy climbing over the tops of mountains."

Li poured tea for the visitor and more for himself.

"The shortage of ammunition is acute," the political officer continued, declaratively. "Also of medicines. The routes from the north have been temporarily cut and there is a delay in supplies from Kunming and Canton. At the moment, again, Hainan is vital."

He drank his tea and took a crushed pack of American cigarettes from his shirt pocket, passing them on to the others. It was his first relaxing gesture, but even this seemed mannered.

Li accepted the lighted match, inhaled, and then, having blown the smoke toward the roof, spoke harshly in Cantonese. "What about the production in the field?"

Slowly the political officer moved his head up and down, three times, as if he had expected the question and held it entirely reasonable. He drew a piece of paper from his pocket and read off a list of figures that told, in considerable detail, the amount of bullets that had been manufactured by the Vietminh workers in the last six months and how they had been distributed and expended, region by region and regiment by regiment. When he had finished, he carefully refolded the paper in a tight square and replaced it, took another long swallow of tea, and looked directly at the two Chinese. He said nothing more.

"There is a need here too," Li said. He said it matter-of-factly, but his tone was defensive. "The campaigns to the south and to the east have become more significant. And there is a need for weapons within Saigon itself."

The political officer smiled. "Of course," he replied. "Nevertheless, there is an official request, which I have been authorized to execute." The note of formality amounted to snobbery.

"There has been trouble with the shipments," Li went on, pretending to ignore, though he had clearly heard, what the political officer had said. "The weather has been bad. The boatmen have become frightened."

The political officer kept silent. He had expected Li Kwan-sen to speak like this. Whatever the Chinese might think, however, he would be aware of the circumstances. He would have to recognize the authority of those who were still determining the conduct of the campaign. The island of Hainan, in the early days, had been a chief source of guns; in fact, except for the remnant Japanese arsenals and what irregularly came in through the Siamese corridor, the only source. When the Chinese Communists had reached the Indo-Chinese frontier, the new lines of communication had been quickly established; but now, as a result of the *esprit* created by the new High Commissioner, the colonial troops had managed to seal off some channels of communication at the same time that they had withdrawn from the frontier redoubts. Even though the situation would soon be remedied, the political officer was freshly annoyed at having the emergency forced upon him.

Li Kwan-sen was as puzzling as he had anticipated. What the political officer knew, and what he had begun to suspect, were two different things, and he had learned long ago to be careful when there was doubt about such matters. He knew that Li, through his various activities, was as instrumental to the revolution as anyone in Cholon, which had by far the largest concentration of Chinese in the country and, in view of the growing liaison with Peking, was bound to become a center of action in its own right. The more he had thought about it in the last twenty-four hours, the more he had begun to suspect that Li was something else than what he seemed. The Chinese, the political officer had already told himself, must be involved in something larger than the financing and ferrying of guns from Hainan into the Saigon River. There was no point to guessing; the political officer preferred to suppose, and to suppose the most, so he supposed that Li's realm of influence extended at least as far as Singapore, if not to Jakarta, and that he was one of the permanent links in the chain of command that now ran from Peking through Hong Kong, Saigon, and Bangkok into Malaya and Indonesia. The pieces were constantly being altered; a new link was put in here, another removed there. But the chain was fastened by certain key men, and it was in this category that the political officer now chose to put Li Kwan-sen. If he was mistaken, it would be better to have acted on the assumption, especially in view of the ambiguous quality of Li's character, which, in the political officer's eyes, cast apparent doubt on the validity of the man's commitment. Had he been called upon to sit in judgment (which he was always willing to do), the political officer would have been of the opinion that the Chinese evinced a careless affectation of manner. While he recognized the nature of Li's camouflage, he could not but wonder if Li did not prefer, for so long as it proved both convenient and plausible, to maintain the *status quo* that so readily enabled him to amass a private fortune. At bottom, of course, was the final question—the length and degree of Li's service. This was what the political officer did not know. It was always difficult, when one dealt with the overseas Chinese, to distinguish between adherence and opportunism. It was particularly hard with such a man as Li, who clearly relished the undeclared strength of his independent position and derived such obvious pleasure from sheer bargaining suspense. All in all, the political officer felt he had gone about as far as he could in pressing his demand. Perhaps his strong point now was his own mixed blood.

"Is there a ship en route?" he asked.

"There is a ship next week," Li said after a pause. "But I do not know just what it will bring." He sounded, the political officer reflected, as if he were trading in hog bristles.

"If it is possible," the political officer suggested, "it would be advisable to meet this ship in the mouth of the river and divert a part of the cargo directly to the central coast. The routes to the liberated regions from the Annam shore remain open."

Li shook his head firmly. He wore an expression of distaste, as if he had swallowed a mouthful of bad food. "The sea is rough at this time of the year, and it is always dangerous to make new arrangements. The boatmen will not go. The ship must come in the usual manner."

There was another silence, which the political officer at length broke. "Will there be smaller boats available for a journey north?" Now he sought to be both casual and firm in his tone.

Li spat into a corner of the room, and, taking a fresh mouthful, swilled the tea and spat it out on the floor below the table. "We will consider the matter further," he said.

It was evident that he had no intention of committing himself. Yet the political officer felt he had succeeded. The Chinese was simply enjoying his role.

Reaching for the teapot, the political officer changed the subject. "You spoke of the increase of terror," he said. A trace of a smile appeared at the corners of his mouth. Here was an opportunity to discover more about Li Kwan-sen himself.

The Chinese turned to his subordinate. Throughout the conversation, Kuo had not moved except to replenish his cup from time to time. Li nodded at him and said: "He is in the city more than myself. My domain is more narrow."

The political officer shifted his glance. Kuo's bony face stayed sad and still. He guessed the man was from Hopei; the prospect of breaking a silence would not be considered lightly. Finally Kuo spoke. "The throwing of grenades has been more successfully organized." His voice, after Li's guttural speech, was surprisingly soft and ungrating. "The *Tu Ve* is being augmented. We received a fresh list of victims last week." He suddenly grinned, revealing teeth that were large and very white and that gave a new and somewhat humorous aspect to the boniness of his face. "There were five cafés attacked in the last month," he continued. "A total of seven killed, including three French soldiers. The anniversary of the revolutionary occupation of the city is near."

The political officer was interested in the list of those marked for assassination. Periodically, he knew, the names were sent out from headquarters, but the regional commands furnished suggestions. "Who is there, of prominence, on the list?" he asked.

Kuo glanced at Li, who interposed no objection. The political officer took silent offense at the questioning of his right to inquire. Kuo quickly named three French generals, two advisers to the High Commissioner, and three editors, two of them Vietnamese and the third French. The political officer recognized all but one of the names.

"And the others, previously designated?" he asked.

"There is no priority," Kuo said, his white teeth flashing again. "It is a matter of opportunity."

"Have you heard news of any deserters?" the political officer asked.

Neither Kuo nor Li responded, and a fresh silence fell. The political officer knew this was purely a Vietnamese affair. His inquiry about the assassinations had been made chiefly to satisfy his curiosity over how much the two Chinese knew or pretended to know. The answer of Kuo had been sufficiently glib, he thought, to render the suspicion that it had been composed solely for his benefit. By not replying at all to his second query, he suspected that the two Chinese were simply debating the wisdom of injecting themselves into such matters; also, perhaps, of carrying a game too far. For a moment, during which his face assumed the quality of a mask, the political officer thought about the doctor. He was certain he would find him. He was so sure of it that he found himself rehearsing the scene of confrontation. . . .

The room had grown stuffy, and what little air came through the high slit in the wall scarcely filtered beyond the pall of smoke. The political officer caught a whiff of the dump outside and sneezed. Li had become contemplative, and Kuo had dropped back into his mournful cast. They looked endlessly patient, the political officer thought. As of ancient ivory in a tableau, the three men sat at the table. Far from conspiratorial, they all seemed drugged.

The political officer was about to break the spell and get up when the door to the front part of the teashop opened and the old coolie reappeared.

"There is an American outside," he said. "He inquires for Mr. Kuo. It is the same American who has come before."

Once again Kuo looked to Li, who had stirred himself and was fitting a cigarette into his holder. After he had lit it, he looked up. "Go and talk with him," he said. "Like our friend from the north, he will want to know the news." He smiled. "Tell him we have had an important visitor—from the generalissimo, in Taipeh."

The political officer actually laughed. "Who is this American?" he asked.

"He is a curious but not a stupid man," Li replied. "Sometimes he comes to gamble. On occasion to converse. We are friends, you see."

Kuo prepared to go out, but Li motioned him to wait and told the coolie to return first and tell the American gentleman that Mr. Kuo would be fetched. Five minutes were allowed to pass before Li nodded and Kuo went into the teashop.

When the political officer walked through on his way to the street moments later, he glanced quickly at the two men already busily talking at a table in the corner. The American, he thought, looked much like the figures in the advertisements he had seen in the city— the white suit, the glistening hair, the odd mixture of intensity and repose.

2

LI WALKED slowly through the garden, his arms folded against the front of his gown. He stopped at the white casino door. The odor from the dump no longer reached him, and while what met his eye as he turned about was not particularly pleasing, he did not yet want to confront the tedious prospect of the month's accounts. A cater-wauling pierced the air, and was silenced by a pye-dog's snarl. Li heard the quick snap of the dog's teeth reaching for a fly.

The man was a zealot, Li reflected, an obvious extremist. It was a judgment of personality rather than of politics. There was a peculiarly pervasive tautness, essentially strained and pleasureless, hinting, in the final analysis, at self-destruction. As an effort at self-discipline, it was exaggerated and a failure. Instead of true be-lief, there seemed a cross to bear. Li was vaguely amused at the desire for vindication. They were like children, so many of them. It was hard to take their revolution seriously. Yet one had to.

He would not refuse the political officer. He would not even bother to communicate with Hainan. There was the question, simply, of how much matériel would arrive and what the require-ments were for the platoons here in the delta, where the difficulties were greater, in proportion, to those faced by the shock troops in the north. Two fresh battalions of legionnaires had been deployed by the French toward Cap Saint-Jacques. They were presently fanning out for a new offensive.

As for the boats, under ordinary circumstances they posed no problem. The boatmen's fears had now been aggravated, however, by the arrival of the new French cutter from Marseille. Still, Li felt, it would be wise to keep the little pockmarked man pacified. He considered Lacasse. The Corsican's influence extended downriver. He would know the men whose hunger outstretched their fear, who could be trusted. There remained, of course, the question of trusting Lacasse. It would be a step Li had not yet contemplated taking.

Slowly he withdrew the half-smoked cigarette from the ivory holder and stamped it out against the wall of the building. He rolled the butt back and forth between the balls of his fingers until the tobacco fell out and the soft paper disintegrated. When it dropped out of his hand, he opened the door and went into the darkened hall. The coolies were sweeping, the bartender was drying glasses. Li grunted at them as he moved toward the front. When he got to his office, he switched on the fluorescent light and lit a stick of incense. It was nearly four o'clock. He opened the croupiers' books and reached for his abacus.

3

A MAN could enjoy only so much tea, Kuo thought. He could feel the pressure mounting in his bladder, but rather than excuse himself and go out into the garden he decided he would wait a bit longer. The Consul was beginning to look wilted too. He had loosened his tie and undone his collar.

"What more have you heard about Truong Chinh?" Adam asked. "About his Chinese background, that is."

Kuo lowered his head, and voice. "We know nothing definite about this man," he said, "except that he has surely been to Moscow since the end of the war and that he is now the strongest of the leaders. Ho Chi Minh, in comparison, carries a bird-cage."

"Was he born in China, or in Indo-China—Truong?"

Kuo pondered the question. "There is one story that he is the illegitimate son of a Chinese Communist general," he said, measuredly.

"And his mother?"

"A daughter of the old imperial court at Hué." Kuo bent forward. "The liaison, however, was established in Hong Kong."

"It is an interesting bit of gossip," Adam said.

Kuo grinned. "One hears many such stories, of course," he said. "It is difficult to determine which of them are true. The truth becomes a matter of eliminating the greatest untruths."

"The survival of the fittest lie," Adam said. "But, anyway, one always ends by believing what one wants to believe."

"That is a Western rationalization," Kuo replied. "There is a difference. Among us, we accept the inevitable and develop belief out of it. When it is no longer of any benefit, or promotes a tyrant, a change is made."

"The mandate of heaven is withdrawn," Adam said. "There is a new truth discovered, and the old truth dies."

"The subject becomes unworthy of the mandate," Kuo interpolated. "But we are patient, perhaps more patient than most; so it does not happen often."

"Perhaps not often enough," Adam said. "However, we are getting away from our discussion."

"Yes," said Kuo. "There is no relation to gossip, although a point is reached where gossip becomes legend, on the path to belief. But Truong Chinh is too young for that." Both men laughed.

Adam picked up his subject. "The Communists adopt new forms and methods, but keep the old ways as well," he said. "In China they have allowed the secret societies still to exist. Here there is a contest for influence with the Kuomintang. I have heard the societies are at the center of it."

The Consul, Kuo thought, could be as indefatigable as ingenuous. "We are aware of such efforts by the Communists," he replied. "But there are other ways that are more important to them. Recently there has been an attempt to place young women workers in public places, such as this"—he tapped one of his long, tapered fingers on the table—"in restaurants, theaters, and gaming-halls, including the one behind us."

"Mr. Li, the owner—what about him?" Adam asked.

Kuo offered his broad smile. "Mr. Li is a very clever man," he said. "He has much money, I have been told. More than anyone in Cholon. He is wise and generous. An old friend, you know, of the Generalissimo."

"No," said Adam. "I didn't know."

"Yes. At the time of the Northern Expedition, Mr. Li's father helped, with money. The generalissimo does not forget such things."

"Mr. Li, then, is still a member of the Kuomintang?"

"I do not think he is active. However, he donates much money to the organizations here that have connections."

"I have spoken with him, once or twice," Adam said casually. "I had the impression he was anti-Western."

Kuo was taken by surprise. "Mr. Li is a strange man, as I have intimated," he replied slowly. "I do not know him well, but I have heard that he has occasionally expressed such an opinion. It is the result, I believe, of a sad personal experience. He had a sister, you see, who married an American, a sea captain. Afterward the captain deserted the girl. She died. Perhaps it is the source of Mr. Li's annoyance." He wanted to get off the subject. "These young women of whom I speak," he went on quickly, "they are being trained at a large school in Shanghai. There is a course of six months. Mostly they are the daughters of overseas families who have been kidnapped or who have run away to China. After the training, however, they are sent always to a different country, and they are never allowed to return to the place from where they have come. They live very poorly so as to arouse no suspicion, and often they pretend to be orphans. It is an effective system."

Kuo was impressed with his recitation, the more so as the Consul went through the unusual procedure, for him, of making a notation in a small black book.

"Thank you," Adam said as he snapped the book closed and put it back in his pocket. "It's worth looking into."

"However, I do not believe there is as much Communist activity here as before," Kuo continued. "There is trouble enough in China, in the south especially. It is too soon for a greater effort in Vietnam."

"The preparation goes on," Adam said. "The overseas elements can provide an excellent fifth column."

"It is an expensive matter," Kuo argued. "There is much money needed for dealing with the merchants, who do not believe in politics, and for creating organizations of the women and the youth."

Adam sat with lips pursed in doubt. Kuo wished he would go. In addition to the need to urinate, he was tired of the teahouse, and there were things to be done before dark. He rallied himself, hoping to provide a final tidbit, and looking back at the Consul said, evenly: "I have another piece of gossip for you. Something that will amuse you. There is information that among those the Communists would wish to eliminate are some Americans."

Adam smiled wryly. "Oh?" he said. "That's interesting. Who?"

Kuo shook his head. "We do not know. But I will try to discover." He paused, and added: "If it is possible, I will send a messenger to you. We can meet again."

"Maybe I'm one of them," Adam said. "They might get us both with one grenade."

"A double zero," Kuo said, laughing.

"That would close all the cafés," Adam said. "Perhaps it is unfair to risk, for the sake of the others."

He got up and extended his hand, which Kuo took and then bowed as before. "We'll keep in touch, even so," Adam said.

"There is a new Szechwanese restaurant in Cholon," Kuo replied. "I will have to take you." Adam waved his hand over his head as he went out. Kuo watched him walk up the muddy street.

The teashop was empty except for the old coolie and the owner, a scowling, bald man who was dozing in a chair behind the counter, and two men conversationally replaying a mah-jongg game they had just finished.

Kuo waited until the American would be safely in his car. Then he walked out the back. In the garden he finally relieved himself. A yellow mongrel, with sad, red eyes, stood watching a few feet away.

"You, dog," Kuo said, "you have it easier than I. You can eat and sleep and fornicate at will, and there is no one who intrudes, no foreign devils."

The dog sniffed. "On the other hand," Kuo said as he patted down his gown and started for the gambling parlor, "there are troubles for you too, I realize. The cats are your devils. One of them will scratch your eyes out some day." The dog was following him. When Kuo closed the white door in its face, it barked and ran back to the dump, where it daintily began to pick its way among the offal.

In Li's office the incense rose in a thinly curled smoke and drifted into vapor. Li sat behind his desk, clicking the abacus. Without looking up, he said: "You have completed your revelations?"

Kuo dropped into a soft leather chair and permitted himself a sigh. As Li said nothing else, he closed his eyes without answering. In the darkness, with the incense in his nose and throat, he felt a slow, immeasurable calm.

He awoke with Li shaking him.

"You have slept enough," Li said. When Kuo was fully roused, Li continued: "When you go into the city, go first to the Corsican, Lacasse. You will find him at his hotel or at one of his clubs. Tell him to come tonight."

It was growing gray out as Kuo left. The *cyclo* he hailed was old and bumpy and he was furious when he tore his gown on a nail.

Cursing, he upbraided the boy for neglect. The boy spat and said there was no money for nails or a new seat, and as the passenger continued to rant he grew angry and told Kuo he could walk if he wished. The street was deserted and Kuo became silent. It was not this way before, he thought. There were changes that made one wonder sometimes. . . .

Chapter XIV

THE Filipino band-leader rapped his bamboo baton lightly against the coconut shell by the potted palm. He turned and gave a small, sharp caper, and then his lithe frame slid into the rhythm he produced. His name was Carlos Porfiro, and he had been in Saigon nearly nine months, six of them at this Chinese club, and he was homesick for Manila and for the girl he was going to marry as soon as he had enough money, which was what kept him here—the dollars Li Kwan-sen paid him in place of pesos or piasters. It was one thing to say for the Chinese, that they made a bargain and stuck to it with a minimum of interference. Each Monday, Carlos got his envelope containing five twenty-dollar bills and another envelope with the money, in pesos, for the rest of the band. He had not exchanged more than an occasional word with Mr. Li. He doubted if the Chinese was even aware that four of his original musicians had quit and been replaced. It was a strange kind of club. At first Carlos had minded the fact that hardly anyone danced. The original band he had brought with him was the best he had ever assembled and he had been proud

◇◇

of it, yet it had been seldom that more than five couples had danced at a time. In the beginning this had worried him, but when he found out that Li Kwan-sen was also the owner of the gambling casino, he was able to rationalize his way out of hurt pride. It was natural enough, he told himself, that, after the tension of roulette, patrons would prefer to listen to music while they drank instead of cavorting heatedly across a dance-floor. The fact that they came to relax was, in its way, a compliment, Carlos had decided, and he had thereupon rearranged some of his numbers to make them softer and more languid, eventually adding his Hawaiian group, which would be useful when he returned to Manila.

The casino crowd was a mixed one, he had observed, and there had been few nights when the tables had not included representatives of six or seven nations. He had gradually come to enjoy a new sense of worldliness. Back in the Philippines, he remembered having experienced vicariously the adventures of his friends who had been to America. Now, although it was a far different mainland, he was finding out for himself.

It had also become more and more apparent to Carlos that Li Kwan-sen was someone important. Almost every night the Chinese was bound to have company at his private table in the rear, in front of which stood a screen that was frequently folded outward. Often, for an hour or more, he would be engaged behind it. Carlos had at first suspected a vast black-market ring. Then he had decided that Li's business was undoubtedly financial, that he trafficked in money, all kinds of which must naturally flow into his gambling concession. He had conjured up an image of Li's mind in which multicolored coins and bills jangled and hovered, the powerful dollar sign, with its bold parallel lines, a symbolic barrier at the wide brow's front.

Carlos brought his baton down as the music stopped. He listened, still facing the band, to the polite applause. Then he turned and smiled again. It was only eleven o'clock but the club was already half-filled. Over behind the screen that tonight partially obscured

◇◇◇

the table he saw Li Kwan-sen with a small man, an Annamite whom Carlos could not completely distinguish. There was a strange shadow on the man's face that must come from the Chinese lantern, he thought.

2

CAU MINH THIEN was doing something that he rarely did: he was drinking. It was only his second drink but he felt lightheaded, and now he resolved to stop. The tension of the last twenty-four hours had been unusual. He was used to going without sleep, but a variety of things had happened simultaneously, were in fact still happening; for the third night in a row, Cau doubted he would be able to return to the village where by morning he would probably be expected.

The grenading had been planned well in advance this time. That itself had been no problem. The French response, as usual, had been unpredictable. On one occasion they might turn every house in town upside down with searching and interrogate five thousand individuals; on another they might take it into their heads to concentrate on *cyclo* boys, or on market vendors. What they were trying to do, naturally, was impossible. For every culprit they caught, or every innocent, there were ten to take his place. The mere method and manner of the hunt increased the ratio. Ordinarily Cau preferred a long and intensive investigation. It made things more immediately difficult for himself, but the ultimate compensation was great. Only today, on top of other events, running and hiding had been harder.

It would have been unwise for him to postpone the matter of Genevieve, for example. There had been too much time devoted to squander the moment which, Cau knew, might not, out of sheer feminine perversity, present itself again for an indeterminate period. Properly and carefully encouraged, Genevieve could do what no one else could. Who else could sit across a table, at a given hour in a particular café, with an American consul; who else had such easy

◇◇

access to the Cercle Sportif; who else, because of her anomalous position and background, had acquaintances instead of friends (a specific advantage in this instance) among the *fonctionnaires* and their wives, among the military and among those who, like herself, remained the true *attentistes*, the waiting ones? It was a term far more than political, which should not be confined, Cau thought, to those Vietnamese who had not yet committed themselves to Ho or to the Emperor. It was a state of mind, *attentisme*, that affected everyone, the French and the Americans as well; even the conundrum Indians. All of them were waiting, except that they waited for different things. It was always a question, too, of how one waited, whether one let others determine the course of events three thousand miles away or took steps in one's own behalf. . . .

To add to his running, there had been the visitor from the north, the political officer, with his northern airs. Cau was pleased with the way this had been handled. It had taken more time to make the trip to the island, but in arranging for the political officer to be taken down a peg, he had kept himself out of it; whatever was now decided, the political officer would know he would have to do more than act self-important. Cau had liked him less as the morning had worn on; it was not only the imperiousness, but a kind of permeating air of mistrust he had imparted. Cau had no idea what his background was, but more than soldier and even more than commissar, the political officer was a policeman. Cau recognized the need for clandestine ways, the practicality of poison, the occasional advantage of a knife at the throat; but he preferred a grenade's roar, or the immaculate whine of a bullet. The political officer seemed to come out of the muffled ground, carrying a hangman's noose in his pocket.

Cau was still convinced that those who had taken part in the occupation and the battle of Saigon in 1945 had the right to consider themselves experienced in a way of warfare that was more hazardous, more nerve-racking, enervating even, than jungle slogging and ambush. Here in the south, where the whole psychological and emotional atmosphere was, in the worst sense, colonial, creating cross-patterns of wealth and responsibility among the Cochin-Chinese and their French protectors, affecting the independent sects that always gravitated, in the last analysis, toward the less violent change, here lay the ultimate battle, no matter what victories were first won in the north. It was not a matter of who had been right or who had been wrong when the Saigon defeat had occurred and the French had ridden into their palaces on the coattails of the British, shooting the revolutionary soldiers from the rooftops with their long American rifles. It was simply that those who had remained to fight had by now established prerogatives of their own that went beyond politics. Cau thought of a friend of his, one of the Trotskyists the Vietminh had murdered, and of another who had called himself a Socialist and had fled to Bangkok. It seemed so long ago, and scarcely should matter. Yet that it still mattered to the political officer was apparent.

As for the guns, there was a fine irony in that request. What was involved, the political officer surely having exaggerated, was no more than one salient on one front. Cau felt certain, too, that the political officer had overemphasized the interdiction of supplies. Nevertheless, that was not the point. The fact was that he was here formally to obtain weapons, here perhaps for something else as well (which Cau now suspected), and that, from a purely selfish sense, leaving all else aside, the response of the supply commander, the actual contempt with which he had treated the political officer, had been gratifying.

Now Cau was curious about Li Kwan-sen.

He did not quite know how to broach the subject, avoiding a direct question, so he said, taking a small sip of his drink to wet his lips: "We have had a visitor lately, one of the men from the central regions, the fourth, I think."

Li did not move his head nor change his expression. He held the cup of tea in his two hands. The music had begun again, a Hawaiian

◇◇

tune that Cau listened to unsympathetically. Finally Li replied, tersely: "I have spoken with him."

"Oh," Cau said, as noncommittally as he could. He waited a moment, but Li said nothing else. "He is a true northerner, that one," he added. "He comes from another world."

Li's shoulders seemed to hunch in the gentlest intimation of a shrug. "An interesting fellow," he said. "He has some Chinese blood."

"I did not know that he had come from China," Cau said.

"I do not know it either. We did not discuss it," Li replied.

"Have you known him from some time before?"

"I have heard of him. Perhaps we have met. I do not remember."

It was a strange answer, and it set Cau off. The political officer suddenly loomed alongside Li Kwan-sen as a related figure, with a shared, mysterious past. Cau realized once more how little he knew, how little any of them knew, about Li.

He wondered how he might mention the guns specifically without seeming to be too inquisitive, and he decided to allude to his own needs. For the length of a dance number he remained silent in order to create the attitude of a normal change of topics. When the band stopped, he said: "I have heard there will be some weapons on the new ship. It is a good thing. There is a need for rifles, for grenades as well."

Perfunctorily, Li said: "There is a need for everything, everywhere. It is always the same story."

Cau paused. He had the feeling that Li already knew, that somewhere in his pockets he already had a complete list of what was coming, and another list showing how it would be distributed. But as the Chinese offered no further clue, Cau said: "We have waited a long time to be replenished."

"There will be more waiting to come," Li said. "Even after victory, there is waiting—for the counteroffensive or for the new attack to begin."

Cau was not in the mood for Li's philosophy of struggle. "I am aware of that," he said shortly. "It is a reason for not spreading oneself too thin."

For the first time Li smiled, and Cau, turning his head so the Chinese would not see him, smiled in the opposite direction.

"It is hard to satisfy everyone, especially during a war," Li said softly.

"One must decide firmly," Cau declared, "whose needs are greater."

"Firmness is also a variable," Li said. "It must be used with discretion, like flattery."

Cau knew he would get no further. If anything, he sensed that the political officer had won his case, not because of logistic persuasion but simply because it was Li's way—to compromise, to avoid making an enemy, in this instance not merely of the political officer but of those with whom the political officer stood, to whom a repudiation would be more than rejection: an affront, a challenge. The significance would lie in how much Li decided to allow them, and, depending on the nature of the matériel, what. Cau's mind began foolishly to calculate ahead.

He was still calculating, like a merchant, when the figure of another man, a European, hovered before them, a large man, jowly, his face, even in the semidarkness, unhealthily white and streamed with the uneven effects of constant perspiring. He was a Frenchman and he had all the boorishness of his kind as he leaned over and grabbed Li's right hand, which was of an almost porcelain thinness, Cau noticed, especially in the other's flabby grip.

"Good evening, Mr. Li," Lacasse said, breathing audibly. "I came—"

Li interrupted him. "Ah, yes—how have you been, monsieur?"

Lacasse was at once abashed. He stood awkwardly and looked at Cau, as if he belatedly realized his carelessness, if not his rudeness.

◇◇

"This is my cousin," Li said blandly. He turned to Cau and asked: "Do you know Monsieur Lacasse, our leading hotelier?"

Cau acknowledged the introduction. He had of course seen the Corsican, many times. He had not immediately placed him.

He stood up and nodded at Li. "I will return later, then," he said. "There is a call I must pay, after which I have an engagement back here." He simulated an air of self-consciousness. "With a young lady," he added.

Li obliged by laughing and shaking a finger. "You will give my club a bad name by bringing a different woman with you every time," he said.

Cau's brief glance acknowledged Lacasse as he turned and walked toward the entrance.

Outside, in the neon reflection, he studied his watch. It was past midnight. He had time still to enjoy the cool night air before meeting Genevieve. The two men he had summoned had been reluctant to come at first, but he had convinced them. "You are known in the city, you are seen constantly," he had told them. "There is no need for hiding. On the contrary . . ." It was one thing he had learned, that it was always better to move normally. Far more than they, who lived and worked here, it was himself, whose comings and goings were perforce more irregular, who should be afraid to be seen in a public night club. It had been partly from watching the conduct of Li Kwan-sen that Cau had acquired this new confidence. There was a way of imagining oneself unseen, of ridding oneself of fear. It became almost mystic, a kind of underground Buddhism based on self-denial. There were times when Cau Minh Thien, walking through the city, felt a transmogrification that made his skin tingle. He could be a panther stalking the forest, and he could be a wandering divine.

He crossed the street and debated looking in at the gambling parlor; but that would be foolhardy, he decided, in view of the constant surveillance by both the French and the Vietnamese police.

Instead he walked toward the heart of Cholon, listening to the increase of the mah-jongg sounds in the restaurants. The smell of food made him hungry; invariably Cau had to be reminded, by smells or the sight of others eating, of his obligation to his stomach. It was not the only part of his body which, through sublimation, had been subject to neglect; but now he felt a stirring in his salivary glands, and he stopped and had a bowl of soup and another one of noodles.

When he started back, he was suddenly very tired. The political officer was still on his mind. He did not, actually, want to see the man again, despite the message given him on the river. At any rate, nothing had to be done at once. This time the political officer could come and do the searching.

The club and the casino loomed and Cau quickened his step. He recognized the large, far-apart lights of an American car coming up the street and watched them draw closer. The engine slowed and then stopped in front of a Chinese hotel across from the gambling parlor. The Vietnamese chauffeur went in and emerged, in a few moments, with another Vietnamese, a smallish man with glasses who wore a mussed, dark suit. From ten yards away Cau studied the stranger, who climbed into the rear of the car. It was not until the car had disappeared that Cau knew. He walked slowly toward the hotel door, re-creating, as well as he could, the conversation below the apartment veranda, the sense he had received of the aimless little man, the mixture of curiosity and of something else that had not been jealousy but rather a kind of self-indulgent frustration, a desire not only to be with the white figures along the balustrade but somewhere beyond them.

The manager was behind the desk, examining his books.

"Excuse me," Cau said, as the Chinese looked up. "You have a guest here, someone who has just come from the north, I believe. He has a letter from my relatives, you see. But I have foolishly forgotten his name—it was told me some weeks ago."

The face of the Chinese was blank as it regarded Cau. Then the small, black eyes rolled and a smile followed. "Perhaps it is the small man. He has only one suit. Yes, he is a northerner. Tran Phan Dang he is called. He has come from Hanoi, I believe." The smile dropped away and the manager looked unhappy. "But he has gone out," he added. "Just a few minutes ago. Perhaps he will not return tonight, since it is so late."

Cau created a sigh. "Ah, well," he said. "I will come back, then, in the morning. It is my bad luck to have missed him."

The manager waited a moment and said: "I can give you a room if you wish—at half the price, since the night is so far gone."

Cau shook his head. "No, thank you," he said. "I have some friends nearby."

"Is there a message you wish to leave?"

Cau shook his head again and stepped outside. It was five minutes to one as he walked diagonally across the avenue to the night club.

3

GENEVIEVE stood at the doorway inside, searching the unreal darkness. She saw no one she recognized until, half-turning, she felt her arm being taken and looked up into the expressionless face of Cau. "This way," he whispered, and guided her to one of the far tables, where two men were sitting. They stood up and permitted her to sit with Cau along the wall, after which they took the two chairs opposite. The music started and Genevieve watched the Filipino orchestra leader cut his caper and flash his white smile.

It had been a long time since she had been inside such a place. The aquarium sense now came back to her, the feeling of swimming through a velvet tank. The music grew loud in her ears and then quiet again as a man's voice began to sing. He sang a Hawaiian song, and Genevieve enjoyed it, forgetting, momentarily, where she was; but then the voice of Cau alongside her was saying: "The scheme of communication must be carefully arranged. . . ." His words, as usual, were without inflection. Like wooden chips cut by the slow, even blow of an ax, they simply tumbled into air.

The two Vietnamese across the table nodded. Genevieve now regarded them more closely. They were Cau's age, she thought, in their late thirties, and they wore the same aspect of seriousness, a fixed look that was more noticeable around the mouth than the eyes, a kind of lower-face compression. If she were Paul Remy, Genevieve thought, she would search the faces of the city for this look.

The two were identified by Cau as tradesmen. He told her where their shops were located, but warned her: "Go only when it is necessary, only when there is a reason for going. What would a woman be doing with tobacco or with rope?"

Genevieve now found herself listening to the modulated talk of the three men against the backdrop of more music, their phrases creating a percussion accompaniment to the keening of the saxophones and the piano's melodious bite. From time to time she glanced about. The room was crowded, with Europeans mostly, but there were some Chinese and Vietnamese too and a table of laughing Siamese across the way. It seemed a world removed, apart from the cold attrition of an endless war. The voices alone spoiled the illusion.

One of the shopkeepers was speaking. "There is talk of what the Emperor is doing, of his new persistence with the French," he was saying.

"It will amount to nothing," Cau said. "Even the concessions that are made will be untranslated into action."

"Nevertheless, it becomes more difficult to obtain information," the ropeman said. "Since the mood of waiting is upon a greater number."

"Then there is a greater reason to stress our victories," Cau replied. "It is wise always to combat the indecision of others with something positive. In a war as long as this one, periods of indecision are only natural."

"It is easy for you to say so," said the tobacconist, somewhat

◇◇

testily. "Except that you are not always in the city, and therefore you cannot comprehend the changes that take place. They are like changes in the weather, and they affect men's spirits as they affect the tobacco in my store. There are times, therefore, when it is better to keep silent."

The ropeman nodded and Genevieve saw the muscles of Cau's face grow tense in the half-glow. "You are wrong," he said in a whisper. "I will tell you that you are wrong. It is simply that one can never compromise."

The tobacconist shrugged. "You have only yourself to worry about, as I have said," he declared. "Your legs carry you away from trouble. You do not have things hidden on your shelves for which you can be shot without the asking of questions."

"It is a reason for care, but not for a lack of activity."

"I said nothing of a lack of activity," the tobacconist replied. He was more annoyed now, Genevieve saw, and he looked angrily at Cau. "That is your affair. I spoke only of restraining one's tongue when there are circumstances that make propaganda hazardous and when one cannot run to a friendly village if the Sûreté comes."

Cau ended the discussion by bringing Genevieve back into it. He smiled crookedly and inclined his head toward her in a brief gesture of designation. "Madame Brouillard will make your task easier," he said quietly. "Since she is not confined to a shop, she will be able to act as a thermometer of your weather. She will test the temperature in various places."

Genevieve felt herself far away. For the moment at least, she could not imagine herself entering the tobacconist's shop at all, whispering whatever it was she was supposed to whisper, the knowledge of somebody's whereabouts, a plane's arrival. She knew what Cau expected, in ways more exacting than Remy had ever pretended despite his protestations over her lack of American friends. Nor was it that Cau wanted too much; but she, too, minded this new didactic air of his. His manner was completely different from what it had been with her alone, when his persuasion had sprung from solicitude.

Genevieve addressed the two men across the table. "Perhaps, after all, you will not see me so soon," she said.

Cau gave her a sharp glance.

"The atmosphere of the city truly changes," she added. "There must be various readings."

The tobacconist smiled, a brief but unconcealed smile of triumph. The taciturn ropeman again shook his head.

"However," Genevieve said, "I will come. Before the fullness of the monsoon, something will perhaps warrant it."

4

LACASSE was more than pleased. The barriers were finally down; it had not taken as long as it might have. Li had not been explicit, he realized, but in his own mind he had no doubt what was involved. If not guns, then what else was worth the trouble and the expense to which the Chinese was willing to go?

Lacasse had carefully refrained from asking. Li's affirmation or denial would have been meaningless anyway. Guns, assuming it was guns, could be for anyone—for the defense of the secret patriots of Cholon, for the Cao Daists, for the Binh Xuyen or any of the private armies that often depended on men like Li Kwan-sen for weapons. Lacasse preferred his own silent assumptions. He had promised to supervise the job himself. "That will not be necessary," Li had said. But Lacasse had insisted. The Chinese had not replied.

It had all been arranged with a minimum of haggling. Lacasse already carried in his wallet half his price, a quarter of it in dollars and the rest in piasters.

Now he was enjoying, at Li's insistence, a bottle of champagne. It was wonderfully dry, and he felt an almost palpable release of loneliness. Perhaps he should start to drink again, moderately at any rate. There was a time when he had drunk a lot, cognac mostly; he had stopped more for professional reasons than for the sake of his liver. It had been one of the few deliberate decisions based upon self-control that Lacasse had ever made.

He stared out from his corner across the night club's expanse. The music had stopped, and with the dance-floor empty the room looked larger than before, larger than Lacasse had remembered it. The oval shape seemed to enhance its size, and at the same time, with the lighting and the arrangement of the tables, the Chinese had managed to retain an intimate atmosphere. A prick of jealousy probed, but Lacasse's general sense of well-being neutralized it. His eyes resumed roving the tables and concentrated on the one of four persons, three men and a girl, a few yards to the right of the bandstand along the wall.

"Isn't that your cousin?" he asked. "The one over there?" And Lacasse pointed.

Li glanced up. "Yes," he said.

"I didn't notice him come back," Lacasse said. "Who are his friends?"

Li examined the table casually. "My cousin has many friends," he replied. "He is very popular. It is hard to keep up with them."

Lacasse mused. "The girl is extremely pretty," he said. "From here she seems Eurasian."

Li was silent, and Lacasse moved the bottom of his glass in slow rotation on the surface of the table.

"Your cousin, does he live here in Cholon?" he asked.

"He lives near Dalat," Li said. "But he comes here often."

"He looks like a pure Annamite," Lacasse observed.

"His mother was half-Chinese," Li said. "The cousin of my father."

Lacasse said: "Ah," prolonging it, and then he added: "It is strange, the way the races blend sometimes. One cannot predict the generations."

Li murmured his agreement, though he seemed to Lacasse scarcely to have heard.

◇◇◇

"The girl looks somewhat familiar," Lacasse persisted. As Li failed to reply, he added: "Perhaps I have seen her on Catinat."

"It is likely," Li said.

"You know her, then?"

"No," Li said, "but such things are entirely logical."

Lacasse felt their new intimacy slipping away, so he finished his champagne and sighed. "I must go," he said. "You are an excellent host. But now you must visit me."

Li stood up and moved the table back, then adjusted the screen into a semi-folding position. "Not until you have roulette at least, Jacques," he said, and laughed. "I have told you before—it will double your profits."

"Perhaps there is not enough time," Lacasse said.

"You are a poor gambler," Li said. "Even though you win pennies from me."

Lacasse sniggered, and thought of what the American Consul had said. "I have learned to protect my bets," he declared. "It is the technique of the diplomats."

Li looked up sharply and then turned his back. When he swung around once more, he had his hand extended.

"It is worth learning," he said, "but if one carries it too far, one gains nothing."

Lacasse grinned. "It is a method, surely, that cannot be applied equally to all things," he said. He let Li's hand drop and watched it move delicately away from his own excess of flesh. "I will see that the arrangements are completed," he said.

"Thank you for coming with such promptness," Li said.

Lacasse murmured, unable to avoid brushing the wallet with the back of his hand, that the pleasure had been his. He started for the door and then, confronted by a chair, altered his course and went along the far side of the room. As he approached the table where Cau and the girl sat with the two other men, he stared broadly. Lacasse was certain now that he had seen the girl before. He nodded at Cau, who looked up but made no sign of recognition. His face, Lacasse noted, was thoroughly Annamese.

When he was outside, Lacasse stood beneath the doorway as he regarded the stars. It was cool, with the monsoon still riding a breeze. He lit a cigarette and walked slowly back and forth. He sensed a stirring within him, the feeling that he was on the verge of something. Desire mingled with curiosity, and the combination was doubly titillating. He threw the half-finished cigarette away and lit another one. He was having difficulty re-sorting his thoughts. The champagne was only partly responsible. It was important, he told himself, not to act too deliberately. One should always find out as much as one could before taking steps. He had made good progress with Li Kwan-sen. He would not push his luck. He would also restrain himself about the girl. But one could begin to find out. . . .

His car was parked thirty yards away on the grass, and he walked over to it and found the driver asleep, as usual, at the wheel. Lacasse shook him.

"Here," he said, handing the man some piasters. "Take a *cyclo* home. I will be here for some time."

The Vietnamese looked numbly at him out of his sudden waking and then took the money and walked off. Lacasse watched him turn once and glance back, and then wave to a *cyclo*-driver sitting on the curb opposite.

When the chauffeur had disappeared, Lacasse climbed into his car and sat behind the wheel. The champagne had worn off and he felt a lassitude enveloping him, and the beginning of depression. He was almost prepared to give up when she came out, with the Annamite "cousin," who put her in a *cyclo* after an exchange of a few words. Lacasse waited until the *cyclo* was halfway up the block before he started the car. Taking care to remain a full block behind, he managed to reach the front of her house just as she was completing the payment of her fare. He watched her go through the

◇◇◇

garden to her doorway. As he drove on by, it was too dark to see the number on the gate, but Lacasse knew that he would not forget the house, and, shifting his weight in the seat, holding the wheel with one hand, he began lightly to touch himself.

Chapter XV

TRAN sat back in the soft seat of the car as it sped through the quiet part of the city, along the shuttered streets where the headlights illuminated the rows of trees like flashes of lightning moving along the walls of the jungle. At nine o'clock he had found the Consul's message underneath his door and he had remained in his room ever since, not daring to go out for fear of missing the driver, even though the message had said he would not be called for until midnight. Tran had supposed that he would be taken to the Consul's house; but now the ride seemed longer. He started to ask, but thought better of it and let the question become a cough.

At last the car swung into a driveway. The driver got out first and led the way to a side entrance of a house that bulked large and pale in the moon's brief cloud-free glow. He left Tran there, and simultaneously the Consul appeared at the top of a step, standing inside the dark hollow of the doorway. They shook hands and the Consul led him to the front of the house, where two other men sat on a couch, with a bottle of whisky on a small table below them and a bowl of melting ice. All three Americans were wearing shorts and loose white shirts. One of the two who was seated, a broad-shouldered and broad-hipped man with hairy, firm-muscled legs, was smoking a pipe. The other was younger, dark-haired, and almost sleek, with a boy's soft face. As the Consul introduced them they stood up, with the drinks in their hands, and the Consul said, "These are two gentlemen from the ECA, the origanization of which we spoke." He smiled at Tran, as if he intended to keep between them the secret of the lost slip of paper in the grass. "They have asked to talk to you."

"Want a drink, doctor?" Lockman asked.

Tran declined politely.

"We call it jungle juice," Kelly said. "It's as bad as it was during the war."

"I've told them something about our conversation," Adam said. "I've explained where you've been, of course." He motioned Tran to a chair and sat down himself on the floor in front of the couch.

"It's a helluva good idea," Lockman said. "I thought we might kick it around a bit."

Tran turned to Adam with his puzzlement.

Adam laughed. "Discuss it some more," he said. "Monsieur Lockman has his own way of speaking."

"He's an American," Kelly said.

Lockman kicked at Kelly's shins and they both laughed. Then he suddenly became serious. "We should have done it long ago," he said. "As a matter of fact, we even had a name—economic commandos."

"That was a good idea too," Adam said. "I read the memorandum."

Lockman grinned and said: "Thanks." Then he added: "The commandos went back to Washington."

"For the battle of the Potomac," Kelly said.

"That's not the order of business," Adam said.

"No," said Lockman. "I guess it's not."

"Second things second," Kelly said. "All the way down the line."

Lockman cleared his throat. "As you know, Dr. Dang, we're trying to get as much stuff as we can into the delta. For trachoma and malaria; then food, of course. Down here it's mostly irrigation wells. It doesn't always work out the way we want, but it's better than nothing."

Tran looked back at Adam as if waiting for a cue.

"Tell them what you think," Adam said.

"The amount is only a part of it," Tran said. "Also the substance. It is of course important where the distribution is made." He shrugged. "In the case of the delta, I do not know what there is to be done. It is so much a military problem as well as political. It is like a tide that comes and goes. The Vietnamese who bring assistance to the villages do not remain. The effect vanishes with themselves. The Vietminh emerges in their place."

"It's simple enough," Lockman said. "The lads with us are afraid. Can't say I blame them. I wouldn't want to stay in there either."

"It is not a condition of cowardice," Tran said. "But the need to stay, nevertheless, is important."

"The partisans, doctor, are all on the other side," Lockman said. "Ours work daytimes only. Nobody wants that time and a half after dark."

"It is a matter for the Vietnamese themselves to determine," Tran said. "However, there is a way of encouragement."

"We can all stay," Lockman suggested. "With food and guns. Dig in. Four amphibious divisions. Pandemonium in the paddies. Only instead of rice, it's French chestnuts we pull out."

Tran didn't understand, but this time Adam made no attempt to explain.

"Pardon," Lockman said. "I don't mean to sound bitter. There's only so much we can do." He took a long swallow of whisky.

It was what Mr. Goodenough had said also, Tran remembered. Only Mr. Lockman had said it differently.

"The delta is a special case," Tran resumed. He spoke more

◇◇◇

quietly now and seemed almost to be whispering. "In time—it will depend on many things, such as the politics of the north in relation to the politics of the south—the situation may improve. The partisans will perhaps grow bolder." He waited a moment and the others waited with him. "The country of which I would speak lies farther south. Soon there will be fighting there too, but it is still the indefinite country."

There was a long pause, and then Lockman said: "Let's not be too indefinite." His large, square head, the brow furrowed, swung slowly around. "Got a map, Adam?"

Tran watched as the Consul stood up and went into the bedroom. He came back in a moment with a folded rectangular packet, which he spread on the floor. Lockman peered down through the pipe smoke and brought out a pair of horn-rimmed glasses as Kelly looked over his shoulder. Tran leaned across and waited.

"Now, Dr. Dang, just where do you say we ought to be spreading our germs?" Lockman asked.

Tran moved his chair up so that he sat alongside the South China Sea. He extended a finger and pointed to Hué. "I came here from the north," he said, "but I did not continue south along the Annam shore since the Vietminh is in control beyond Qui Nhon. Therefore I went inland to avoid difficulty. The people in the hills and in the valleys were friendly. They helped me as I traveled by the edge of the Moi plateau. There were Mois I met, and then Annamese again in the valleys below."

Tran ran his finger farther south on the map, which had three red check-marks on it to denote the passes in the Annamitic Range where the Vietminh, each season of the war, sought to cross. The Franco-Vietnamese forces kept a few troops in each defile.

"I did not go far into the jungle of the plateau," Tran said, pointing again. "When I reached the area of Dalat, I continued to Saigon."

"And there were no Vietminh?" Lockman asked.

Tran shook his head. "I did not see them," he said, "although it is true that from time to time the Vietminh comes to seek both men and rice. Except for the time of battles, however, when the Vietminh approaches from the coast, the people in these villages are not molested. It will not always be so. Each season the Vietminh grows stronger. It is something that one senses"—he smiled —"if one does not already know it."

"And we?" Lockman asked.

Tran's smile hung. "The influence of the Americans is like the miracles one hears in the forest," he said. "There are stories told of metal birds that drop from the sky with vials of healing. But the miracles grow dim from too much telling. There is an envy in the valleys where such birds have not descended."

"What we need," Kelly said, "is some guided missiles. Or maybe some missiled guides. Armor-vested missiled guides, with built-in medical pouches."

Lockman paid no attention this time to Kelly. He was looking hard at Tran through his glasses and then he went back to the map. "We've been in there, of course," he said, slowly. "As a matter of fact, it's been one of the few places where we didn't run into trouble."

"Trouble?" Tran repeated.

Now Lockman smiled and so did the Consul. "Not Communists, not the Vietminh," Lockman said. "It's a long story, Doctor, but the French don't always like the idea of our being angels of mercy. It depends on the territory we're selling. This one happens to include some real estate they're especially fond of. And since the Emperor likes it himself for hunting, it's been a bit cozier than some other parties we've tried to crash."

Mr. Lockman's way of explaining things left something to be desired, Tran thought. But he had heard of these jealousies. One

◇◇

had them in the jungle too. For one abstracted moment the image of the political officer returned, with his pockmarked face and his bitter ambitions.

The Consul had moved closer to the map, and now he spread his right palm across the area Tran had designated.

"No bigger than a man's hand," he said, "yet it could be the size of tomorrow. An airlift or two, Irving, means next to nothing. We just prove a point to ourselves. What the doctor talks about is something else."

Lockman nodded. "The grand cure. No week-end waters."

"We did it during the war—went into places and stayed, for weeks, for months. Sometimes we couldn't get out again so soon. Or there were rendezvous. It can still be done." Adam was looking at the wall.

"You really do want to play Rover Boy," Lockman said a little hollowly.

Adam laughed. "The grass is always greener."

"I can see the Minister now. A posse for the Consul," Lockman said.

"Ten years in chains," Kelly added. "Reading and filing tea-leaves in the jungle."

Lockman was thoughtful again. "We could try it once and see." He turned to Tran. "You'd be willing to go and stay, is that it?"

"But of course," Tran said. "As long as it would remain possible."

"Supplies can be dropped, if we know where you are," Lockman said. "How big a party?"

Tran considered this. "I am not an authority on such matters," he said. "It is something to be decided by others."

"How many villages could you cover, say, in a month?"

Again Tran paused. "It will depend upon the villagers themselves, on the amount of suspicion in the beginning, and on the presence of the Vietminh."

"Suppose you get shot at?" Lockman asked. "Then what?"

"You shoot back," Kelly answered. "Or maybe, as they say, you melt into the jungle."

"Who provides the guns?" Lockman asked. "That much commando we're not supposed to be."

"The manly art of self-defense," Kelly said, grinning, "is still legal."

"Sure," Lockman said. "The incident at the bridge, or how to start a war within a war."

"I always wanted to be an incident," Kelly said.

Lockman gave Kelly another elbow nudge. "You're an accident," he said. They were like children together, Tran thought.

"How many sturdy commandos then?" Lockman asked again.

"Five or six, I'd say," Adam suggested. "The guide doubles as doctor. Two men for food, an engineer, and—what else?" He paused.

"A commissar," Lockman said. "We might as well go whole hog and have a commissar."

"The doctor has some ideas about that, too," Adam said. "Less stress on the cosmic issues. More on the ward problems."

Lockman nodded. "I've begun to discover that myself."

"How do you say 'I love you' in Moi?" Kelly asked.

"You don't," Lockman said. "Not the way you mean it."

"On the plateau I'm platonic," Kelly sang out.

"You'll bring up the rear," Lockman said. "We'll be the points."

"Make them," Adam said. "You don't have to be them."

"What we need is a couple of dozen like the doctor," Lockman said. "Divide the territory. Paddie-pushers, Inc."

"You'll get them," said Adam.

Lockman glanced up with a strange sort of stare. "When?" he asked. "After the refugee camps are full up?"

It was after one o'clock. The bottle on the low table in front of Kelly and Lockman was almost empty. The Consul, Tran realized, had not been drinking.

"It'll take a bit of figuring," Lockman said, turning back to Tran. "Then we'll talk again. I'll send Mr. Kelly to fetch you."

"Thank you," Tran said, standing up.

Lockman looked at Kelly, and then they both looked at Adam.

"It's early," Lockman said. "We might as well." He was grinning again.

"Oh, my God," Adam said. "Don't you ever get tired?"

"I always lose. It helps me atone for my sins," Lockman said.

"All right," Adam said. "But it's a mistake."

They went out into the night, which had grown warmer and somehow still more silent. The moon had emerged, hanging yellowly in its own haze, like an egg in a bowl of soup. The stillness was uncomfortable, more ominous than any jungle's, less identifiable. Tran stood alone for a moment in the pit of the driveway. Then the only sound was the crunching of footsteps on the gravel, and the Consul beckoned for him to get into the car. All three Americans had put on white jackets. With their shorts half-hidden, they looked like odd tropic birds, Tran thought. Adam took the wheel himself and Lockman and Kelly followed in another car.

Tran felt a return of embarrassment in being alone again with the Consul. He gazed fixedly out the window as they swung through the streets, turning left and right at alternate blocks. His recollection was being jarred—it was the same pattern, of course, the progressive right angles through the paddies when he had come out of the jungle. The lights of Cholon glimmered ahead as the dirt road into Hué had emerged above the serried plots of grass and water.

"You are very kind to have arranged such a meeting," Tran said.

"On the contrary," Adam said. "We are grateful for your help."

Tran hesitated and then asked: "If the arrangements are completed satisfactorily, you will come with us?"

"Perhaps," Adam said. "I'd like to."

"It would be better," Tran said. "Better if you come."

"I am not sure of the possibility, or the wisdom," Adam said. "Perhaps one of us is enough."

"Monsieur Lockman?"

Adam nodded. "It's his job," he said. "And an engineer's."

They were in Cholon now, and ahead of them the lights were banked against the sky. "It's the best thing you could have done," Adam said. "The best for you."

Now Tran nodded. The air carried into the flowing car. It was a thicker air, with the odors of the Chinese city on it. He took them in, with a sense of his own invigorated being.

"I would like to do something for you as well," he said, not turning his head.

"That's not necessary," Adam said.

Tran was silent a moment. "There are some things to tell," he added, softly. "I did not tell them to Mr. Goodenough."

Adam looked sharply at him, but Tran's eyes still averted his. "What sort of things?" Adam asked.

"I will explain," Tran said. "I will come to your house, and I will explain."

The Chinese hotel loomed, and the white wall of the gambling parlor beyond it. Adam slowed down and stopped at the hotel entrance.

Tran extended his hand. "Good night," he said.

"Come whenever you can," Adam said. "You'll be welcome." He held back a moment and added: "If there's something you need, some money perhaps—?"

"I have money," Tran said at the window of the car. "Thank you." He moved away and Adam drove toward the casino parking-lot.

In the teashop opposite the hotel, the black-suit coolie lay asleep on the bench where the owner, an hour earlier, had left him after an argument settled by a threat.

2

Adam turned the ignition off and sat for several moments. He had parked at the extreme end of the lot, and he had the odd sense of being on the edge of a cliff. He closed his eyes and heard, as from far off in a canyon below, the faint lifting of voices. The casino became a white hotel on the rim of a northern lake, where he had come alone in autumn. It was after he had returned from Tangier. He had not expected to see her again. But she had found out where he was and had come up that week-end without telling him, so that, appearing at breakfast on Saturday, he had suddenly found her, at a veranda table.

He had written to her from abroad only once after receiving her letter, having waited for her first to say what they both had known, that they had waited too long. But when the letter came and he had read it, propping it up against the sugar-bowl and the Mediterranean sky, he had known he had let something slip away that might not soon be replaced. He had torn up three attempts before he finally answered her, stiffly by then, more hurt-between-the-lines than he had had a right to be, giving himself away when it came to expressing approval of the "experiment" she was making with the naval officer she had known for almost as long as she had known him, only never, since the first time it had been at issue, with an intimation even of intimacy. He had waited for the engagement announcement to follow; but there had been only silence. Once back, he had put off calling her, a final but valid procrastination. And then, that Saturday, she had been simply there.

He remembered exactly how he had walked over to her, at precisely what point she had lifted her head and smiled in the path of the sun. And what she had said: "You see, I did learn something in OSS," and how he had sat down and replied: "I'll revise my estimate."

The "week-end" had been an extended one. They had taken

◇◇◇◇◇◇◇◇◇◇◇◇◇◇◇◇◇◇◇◇◇◇◇◇◇◇◇◇◇◇◇◇◇◇◇◇◇◇◇

long walks through canyons, eaten ravenously and drunk ridiculously expensive wine, and finally, on the third day, having waited foolishly some more, made love into the fourth. He had been like an incarnation of an earlier image, of what he might have become. Time, the mere passage of it, was not an explanation. There was something else, something of the war and the wild grapeshot of its ways. The several days had been an abstraction and a gift. He had wondered what she had thought in the moments between, but he hadn't asked. Her experiment, he knew, had failed, but they had jointly avoided the nibble of analysis. Probably she had been trying to help him find a belated answer, on which might have depended hers; his own suspended self had obtruded. Walking up the canyon on the last spent day, she had held his hand and said: "The split, splendiferous Americans. . . . Now I know why the world's become a proving ground for men like you."

She had not been wrong. The state of suspension had lasted. The layers of his life had mounted, year upon year, leaving him, at the center, still impermanent. How many times, without conviction, had he told himself he would be ready at forty?

He wondered what had brought on this sense of past, feeling suddenly uncomfortable in it. Like an apparition, a pye-hound rose atop a dump and howled into the moonlight. It was when Adam snorted, jerking his head, that the lateness drove in upon him, in a continuum. The image of the dog was like the mockery of a hero, astride an embattled hill. He climbed out of the car and walked quickly toward the shining casino entrance. Lockman was there, looking for him.

"Christ," Lockman said, "where the hell have you been? The wheel's a hot-rod."

Adam nodded and followed him in. In the next twenty minutes, without speaking, he won more than he had ever won before. He did not lift his head from the board until he heard Lockman say, over the cold drop of chips on a white square: "This one's for the little doctor." Adam felt the skin of his face tighten. He stared at Lockman. "Don't," he said, but the wheel was already spinning.

3

LI KWAN-SEN came into the casino when it was still crowded, and it was several moments before he saw the Americans. He stood near the entrance and watched, then called an assistant to his side and ordered the boy to find out from the croupier if the Consul was winning. The boy returned and repeated the croupier's nod, and Li Kwan-sen went into his office. He lit an incense stick and carefully embedded it in a pot of sand on the window. Then he sat down behind the desk and closed his eyes. His large, round head was motionless below the fan. He might not have been breathing, his whole body was so still. Then suddenly his eyes emerged again, like a pair of turtle heads from underneath their shells, and he reached down and pressed a button. A young boy entered and stood by as Li wrote on a white card: "Please do me the honor of joining me in a cup of tea." He signed his name in English and placed the card in an envelope, then gave it to the boy with instructions for it to be handed to the Consul.

When Adam read it, he showed it to Lockman. He was still far ahead, and he cashed his chips in, leaving Lockman and Kelly playing. Then he followed the boy across the floor of the casino. Li met him with a broad, enduring smile. "Ah, the Consul," he said. "You are kind to forsake your winnings."

"No wonder you end up rich," Adam replied, laughing.

"It is a matter of self-defense, you see," Li said. "Otherwise I would not disturb you."

Li waited until Adam had sat down in the only leather chair. "You would like something to drink, or some tea?" he asked.

"I'll take you up on the tea," Adam said.

Li pressed the buzzer twice and ordered tea and cakes. Then he proffered a cigar, which Adam declined.

◇◇◇

"There is a personal matter I should like to ask your advice about," he said, after a lengthy pause. "It is a very small thing with which to trouble you."

"Not at all," Adam said.

"I have a nephew, you see," Li began. He had outlined it all in his mind, down to selecting the boy he would use, if he had to. "He has just arrived from China," Li continued. "That is to say, he is in Hong Kong." He shook his head slowly, back and forth, and glanced down. "It is extremely sad," he said, "the condition of my brothers and sisters."

"Are they all there?" Adam asked, curiously.

"Most of them," Li said. "They are mostly merchants, although one or two are middle peasants, since they own a little land as well. Perhaps two acres."

He waited while the attendant set the tray down and poured two cups of tea.

"The boy is the only one who has managed to escape," Li went on, after the attendant had gone. "He will come here. Very soon. I will take care of him."

"That'll be nice," Adam said.

Li waited once more, as if he were wary about reaching his point, and then he said, "He wishes very much to go to America. He would like to study at an American university." He smiled again and added: "Afterward he will become a guerilla."

"It's rather hard to arrange," Adam said. "The circumstances make it difficult."

"If it is possible—" Li resumed. "It is what I wanted to ask you."

"There are some exchange agreements, between Taiwan and Washington," Adam said. "But I'm not sure recent mainland refugees are eligible. Not that they oughtn't to be."

"I would appreciate it very much," Li murmured. With a note of caution, he added: "He is a very smart boy."

◇◇

"I'm sure he is," Adam said, swallowing his smile in his tea-cup. "I'll try to find out for you. But don't expect any quick answers."

"I will be lastingly grateful," Li repeated. "We will be patient, yes. Perhaps I will send the boy to friends in Taiwan, if it is wiser."

"We'll see," Adam said. "When is he coming?"

"I do not know exactly," Li said. "In a month perhaps."

"Let me know," Adam said. "I'd like to speak to him."

Li nodded. "Of course," he said.

Adam finished his tea and got up.

"You will win some more?" Li asked.

"I don't know," Adam replied. "It's pretty late."

"One must take advantage of one's luck," Li said.

He showed the Consul to the door and they exchanged several good-night nods and quarter-bows. When the Consul had gone, Li returned to the desk and sat down with his eyes shut, as before. It had been a painless little performance, he thought. Perhaps it would amount to nothing. But even before Kuo had told him of the Consul's reaction, he had chastised himself for being too outspoken in the night club. It was worth ameliorating. The American intrigued him, besides. In a week or so he would invite him and his friends to a banquet.

4

ADAM stared at the gambling floor through the smoke-haze. Far off, he could see Lockman's broad back still bending over the roulette table, and Kelly alongside. He turned and walked out into the night; he smoked a cigarette, leaning against a fender as he thought of Li Kwan-sen. There had been nothing strange about the request, except its aspect of purposefulness. The Chinese was a puzzling man. One of these days, Adam decided, he would have a longer talk with him. Perhaps the way to do it was to arrange a quiet dinner.

He threw the cigarette away. The evening had been full, yet

✦✦✦✦✦✦✦✦✦✦✦✦✦✦✦✦✦✦✦✦✦✦✦✦✦✦✦✦✦✦✦✦✦✦✦✦✦

he wasn't tired. He enjoyed the night crowded. His decision was already made and now he let the car out swiftly, feeling the burst of speed in his loins. By the time he reached the block of her house he was full of certitude, and he knew her lights would still be on behind the shutters. When he stopped, he had the sense of her expecting him with the motor's cease and the car door's slam.

"You're up very late," he said as she let him in.

"I seldom sleep early. Recently it has become more difficult," she said.

"How recently?" he asked.

"Not as recently as you would like to imagine." She laughed at him as he kissed her on the forehead.

"I've been to the casino." He felt intoxicated with Li Kwan-sen's tea. "And I've celebrated winning with a cup of jasmine."

"A harmless celebration," she said. "Would you like some cognac to provide more substance?"

"Sure," he said. "One."

They brought their glasses together and he kissed her fully with the taste of the cognac in their mouths.

"Will you tell the Sûreté this as well?" he asked.

"Not until there is a change of administrations," she replied, bringing his hand to her face.

"That could happen any time," Adam said.

"Well, then," she said, "not until the Americans depart."

"All the Americans?"

She laughed again. "Perhaps, after all, there will not always be Americans here."

"We shall return," Adam said.

"Asia today, tomorrow the world," Genevieve replied. Her expression was suddenly still, her face changing with that already familiar abruptness. "There will always be the last plane at the airport for the foreign diplomats to catch."

"The Consul and his entourage took refuge on a neutral planet," Adam intoned.

"We talk too much of doom," Genevieve said. "Everyone."

"It's the penalty of waiting, of being static." He turned his smile away.

"Why, then, if nothing moves, should we even console ourselves with love?" Genevieve asked. "To remove boredom?"

Adam's head swung back abruptly. He was more sure than ever, of various things. "Come," he said, taking her hand. "Let's set the clock back."

Genevieve permitted herself to be lifted. "It will be an illusion," she said softly. "Nevertheless, they are still required."

"When the illusions become reality, the clocks begin again."

"And we are where we started?"

"Clocks have their own half-truths, their own mechanism of illusion, like the rest of us."

She let him touch her, leaning against both him and the bed, half-standing before she gently slipped down. She had only the dress on, and when he began to remove his clothes alongside her, she raised herself into nakedness first and helped him, crouching with insistence, so that his excitement burgeoned while she hovered along the length of his body extended, which reached not therefore singly but in all its nerve-ends to grasp, discovering her and rediscovering her in the various ways of her elusiveness. She made the surrender sacrificial, serene at the beginning with the ritual of invasion, and then accomplishing in the forest of the night a sharing and a true surcease. She had astonished him, the more so as he found, in his first small after-motion, that her eyes were full of tears.

An hour later the light seeped through the shutters, and with it came the artillery reverberating across the river. They lay and listened, and it lasted longer than usual. When it was done, there was the awful stillness of far-away destruction.

Genevieve reached up and touched her lips to his brow.

"The clocks have moved again," she said.

Chapter XVI

LASHED by the sun's rays, the river, a chameleon, stretched away from the city toward the liquid jungle of the delta. Through the infinite haze, pieces of islands and the mainland joined in erratic horizons.

The political officer contemplated the scene happily. He felt at home in this gray-green infinitude. Even the dampness, except for the salt in it, seeped familiarly through his nostrils. He felt unseen, as in the forest; it was a feeling he relished, establishing control over nature. He had not expected this to work out so well, not so soon anyway. That he would get the co-operation of the Chinese he had surmised, but after the rejection of the idea of a transfer in the bay he had assumed that Li Kwan-sen would first hold him off. He had already accepted as unavoidable another meeting with the insolent supply commander, whose head he had resolved to have, but without demeaning himself. Li Kwan-sen's change of mind would make that easier too.

He glanced at his American watch. It was eleven o'clock. The old man and his boat should arrive at any moment. He heard the sound of what might be an oar on the water, but nothing emerged except a gull's wings beating whitely against white. He watched its pursuit and silently felicitated it on the capture of a fish.

Then the old man did come, laboring as if the thickness of the atmosphere retarded him. The political officer heard him breathe before he saw the oar's soft plash and the narrow silhouette of the sampan. The boat struck the ledge of sand and the old man took shape. A grunt formally announced his arrival.

◇◇

The political officer climbed in before he said "Good morning," and the old man regarded him with a minimum of interest. The political officer was amused. This old man was someone whose benign contempt he didn't mind, possibly because it adumbrated his own. "You are well, I trust?" he said when he had sat down.

"I am well enough," the old man said, guiding his oar as casually as he had replied. They were already enveloped in the white haze and the shore had faded away.

No return solicitude was extended, and after a pause, during which the political officer let a hand dangle in the water, he said, with equal casualness: "We are fortunate in the delay of the monsoon."

The old man spat as familiarly as he had grunted, both things belonging to him. "I will be satisfied to have it come," he said.

"How far is it to the ship?" the political officer inquired.

"Far enough to wear away my back," the old man answered. "As far again as the distance the time before, and perhaps greater."

"If you wish, I will help you," the political officer volunteered.

The old man laughed. "You are not created to deal with the river," he said. He kept laughing quietly to himself, and the political officer began to get annoyed.

"Very well, then," he said. "You are a proud old man, as well as a stubborn one."

"It was not an impertinence, my laughter," the old man said. He was not being penitent. "Only that no boatman of value will permit a stranger to conduct his boat. It will bring bad luck."

"Then bend your back," the political officer replied.

Now they remained silent for some time. The political officer had suddenly had enough of the old man's crustiness. He was sorry he had made the suggestion in the first place, which he had not meant with total seriousness.

"You have had your way with the guns," the old man said at length. He stated rather than asked it.

"It is not a question of having my way," the political officer

❖❖❖

replied, wondering what carelessness was responsible for the old man's knowing so much.

"Nevertheless, it is true."

The political officer said nothing, liking the old man less.

"I do not mean to offend you," the old man went on. "It is actually a compliment that I meant."

"Thank you," the political officer said. He wished they would get it over with and wondered where the other boats were.

"You will go north?" the old man asked.

"When I am ready," the political officer replied.

"The emergency of the weapons is foolish," the old man declared, "since the season of the fighting is at an end."

"It is fortunate for all of us that you are not running the war," the political officer said.

The old man was chuckling again. "There will be another war, among those who win this one."

"It is possible," the political officer said. "Such things occur."

"I will not wait to see it. I have seen enough as it is."

"How much further have we got?" the political officer asked.

"You are exceedingly impatient," the old man answered. "One cannot be impatient with the river."

The political officer ignored the reply. "And the other boats? Where are they?" he asked.

"Each comes by himself," the old man said. "It is safer." He was grinning down the sampan.

The political officer gave up and they rode in silence; the water became choppier and the haze thinner and brighter. He had a whiff of the ocean far off and no longer felt hidden in the weather. The sampan began to dip and bob. A large fish leaped high in the air alongside and startled him. Another quickly followed and they appeared to lunge at each other before they plummeted back.

"The fish have their wars as well," the old man muttered. "Only the river and the sea are better at containing them."

◇◇◇

The political officer simply nodded. Some time later, near the shore below, he saw the outline of a ship. They had come into the wider water where the rivers came together, and the ship looked smaller than he had expected and was like an ocean-going tug. It must have steamed up the Soirap at dawn, he thought, and dropped its anchor with the full light of day. The haze still surrounded it. It was, nevertheless, a danger to be there, the political officer said to himself, and he wondered again why Li Kwan-sen had changed his mind; had the decision been his, he would have taken a chance on the bay. Too much here depended on the whim of the mist.

As they approached, the political officer saw the other sampans scattered across the river. They could be fishing, he realized, and in themselves provoked no suspicion. The old man was pushing closer to the ship's side, and now he asked: "Do you wish to go aboard?"

"Yes," the political officer said.

He had some difficulty climbing up the short ladder of rope that dangled to the water's edge. When he reached the deck he was surprised to find no one there. The deck was about fifty feet long and curved like a gourd. He started to walk along it, toward the stern, when he was nearly thrown over by two men who suddenly emerged from a passageway. One of them was Li Kwan-sen's bony-faced assistant, Kuo, and the other was apparently the captain, who, having been taken by surprise himself, was reaching to his side where a leather strap that tied over the top of his bare shoulder indicated he carried either a gun or a knife.

Kuo's long face expanded with a grin. "A friend," he said, with what the political officer thought was a note of sarcasm. He had put a hand on the captain's arm, and now he looked over the captain's head as he added: "You are too accustomed to the jungle, therefore you come too quietly."

The political officer stood immobile. Against the backdrop of the fog he looked smaller than he was, but more indomitable. The

captain, who was also a Chinese, had a scowl on his face. In the
frame of grayness, the three men stood there, until Kuo finally
said: "The boats will come and take the allotment. They will proceed at once down the Dong Nai and along the coast to the area of
liberation."

The political officer nodded. He was waiting for what came
next. "I have the list," Kuo said. He reached beneath his gown
and brought forth a folded paper. Unfolding it, he handed it to the
political officer, who saw at a glance that Li Kwan-sen had given
him very little. He nodded now again, but said nothing as he handed
the paper back.

One by one the sampans floated out of the fog. The political
officer stood in the stern of the ship and watched the squat boxes
of ammunition being handed down, and a few rectangular ones of
guns. All the boxes were painted green, but their size and shape
told him they were American, the vestiges, the political officer knew,
of what had been smuggled from the Philippines. How many wars,
how many revolutions, how many counterrevolutions had such
boxes affected! Even now, over the regular routes from China, there
were still these recognizable shapes. The political officer was staring
so intently that the boats below became a blur and he was conscious
only of a singleness of movement between the side of the ship and
the murk of water. It was one of those rare moments when he experienced a sense of himself as a person, permitting himself to reflect
at random without being guided by an organic situation at hand.
Reflecting, looking back, meant no one; only places. There had
been only himself on the streets of Amoy and Canton. He did not
know his family name. He knew that his father had been an officer
in the Kuomintang and that his mother had been an Annamese merchant's daughter, and that he had been brought up in a Kuomintang
orphanage. The revolution had gathered him in when he was fifteen
in the Canton cigarette factories. Chiang Kai-shek's perfidy had occurred in the same year. It seemed impossible to him that he could

now be anything other than what he was. The anger in his breast had been branded there.

He had no wish to return to China. When this war was won, before he went elsewhere, he wanted one thing only: to go to Moscow. It was his sole "romantic" aspiration. All the rest had been sublimated. There had been no women, and only a few prostitutes. The political officer considered himself, almost literally, an instrument. It was why he detested weakness. Pleasure, even conceptually, was weakness, and religion was a form of it, since it fostered escape from reality. Reality to the political officer meant hardship, if not pain; an all-night march in the jungle was a proper kind of proving, and he enjoyed emerging at dawn, the metal in him reannealed, as someone else might emerge from a healing bath of steam. Unlike others around him, he felt no absolute need of violence. Violence was only part of the rest, and war itself was an eruption in which men killed and got killed and those left organized the future. There was no preordained selectivity; a degree of luck perhaps. If men were what they should be, it made little difference which of them survived. What was important chiefly was to eliminate the weak ones.

He felt someone's presence, and bringing a flash of the boats up with him, he swung his head away from the water. Kuo had come alongside and was standing at the rail. He wondered how long the Chinese had been there and felt the nearest thing he could feel to embarrassment for having been caught in a reverie.

"You will return with them, by the sea?" Kuo asked.

"No," the political officer said sharply.

"Ah," Kuo said, and he paused. "You will remain in the south, then?"

The political officer's annoyance edged toward resentment at being questioned. "For a short time," he said.

Kuo was shaking his long face up and down. "After the jungle, the city must appear tame," he said. "A relief, perhaps."

"On the contrary," the political officer replied. "I dislike it."

"Ah," Kuo murmured again. "It is truly difficult to dislike a whole city, as it is difficult to dislike all of a woman."

The political officer took a deep breath as he looked down at the boats again. The task was very nearly completed and there was only a pair still waiting to be loaded; the others had already begun to slip off through the fog. There was no point to anger, the political officer told himself. He realized that Kuo, in his cryptic way, with his old-fashioned airs, his caricature of the benevolent philosopher, was only pretending to play a part.

Coughing, the mist in his throat, the political officer said: "The city belongs to the colonials."

"We shall also have need of it," Kuo said.

"We will build a new one," the political officer replied. He started to move away, searching on the river-side for the old man's sampan. He heard Kuo walking softly behind him, and then simultaneously they stopped. There was no mistaking the sound: from up the river came the throb of the French gunboat. It seemed to carry above the fog and then drop through from overhead, like a flare of sound.

The captain, who had been below, came running to the deck. The two crewmen who had been loading the boxes stopped working, and the boatman alongside pushed off toward the reeds. The engines in the distance grew louder.

"He will go down the Dong Nai," Kuo said. The confluence of the rivers lay a quarter of a mile ahead, where the mist was white.

"And if he does not?" the political officer asked.

Kuo shrugged. "We will wave as he passes, as friends," he said, with a trace of a smile on his broad mouth.

The engines seemed almost on top of them. The political officer thought he could smell as well as hear them, and he thought he heard the high French voices of the young cadets. And then the engines seemed to hover on the water, settling down, and grew neither louder nor softer for several moments as the three men remained motionless at the rail. They had not seen the gunboat's lines. Finally the sound diminished.

"We can be grateful for the mist," the captain muttered.

"It would be unnatural without it," Kuo said.

"I do not like it on the river," the captain said.

"You are done. You can return to the sea," Kuo said.

The political officer gave a low whistle, which he had to repeat three times before the old man heard it. When the sampan had come alongside, the political officer climbed over the rail and let himself drop in. He glanced up from the bottom. Kuo was standing alone above him.

"You are in a hurry to return to the city after all," Kuo said. He was grinning again.

"I have other tasks," the political officer answered, shortly.

"It is good to be so busy," Kuo said.

The political officer did not reply, but beckoned to the old man to move off. He did not look up at Kuo again until they were some distance away, and then, when he did, he saw him still standing at the rail, a gray figure etched against gray. He imagined that he still saw the thin line of the smile like a last thin streak of light, which, when it finally dropped away, left only the vague oval of the ship for a moment more, and then evanescent gray emptiness.

They scarcely spoke on the way back, the old man and himself, and for some time the political officer closed his eyes. He felt a new easefulness now, a sense of liberation. It was not true satisfaction, but still a genuine relief. The weapons would arrive and his part would be quickly forgotten, which was what he wished. The situation, he could finally admit, was not so serious as had been pretended. The fighting for the season, as the old man had sensibly said, was almost done. There would be time at most for a last thrust across the Annamitic Range, to frighten the French in the passes before the monsoon shut them all in.

The river was quiet in its confluence and quiet toward the city, where it turned west. The political officer kept his eyes closed without trying to sleep; he no longer wanted the old man's talk. He would allow himself another three days, he had decided, before proceeding north. If he was at all successful, he could come back again. To discover the doctor now would be his quickest fortune.

2

LACASSE walked across the street from the hotel at three o'clock. The mist had started to lift and the heat reached down at his back as he stepped through the dust that was still settled by the dampness. He had awakened late, with the recollection of having been aware at an earlier hour of the mist's existence. He had fallen asleep again and had dreamed of home, of chalk cliffs and the blue Corsican sky.

He seldom allowed himself to do what he was doing now, to be seen on the docks; but he had decided this time to indulge his curiosity. The weather had been almost too good; not that he had any doubts about the boats, or about what, at this very moment probably, they were carrying through the mouth of the river. All he actually wanted to do was find out if the old man, whom he knew by sight, had returned. On the farthest floating wharf, Lacasse now saw him, tied loosely to his neighbor, which indicated he had only lately come alongside. He was grumbling to himself in the bottom of his boat. Lacasse stood safely away and saw another boatman, a younger one he knew, come up and speak briefly to the old man, who gave a grunt and a nod. It was all Lacasse had wanted. He turned and walked away.

An hour later, newly showered and wearing a fresh linen suit, he came out of the hotel and went three blocks along the waterfront in the opposite direction, to his club. He arranged with his German assistant, a middle-aged Jew he had imported from Shanghai three years before, to have a payment made to a representative of the waterfront association who would call for it that evening. Then he sat at his bar and had a *perrier* while he discussed the possibility of installing a half-dozen slot machines in an adjacent alcove. The German stroked his chin and murmured that he had a connection in Macao, that if Lacasse would arrange for transport from Hong Kong he could acquire any number of such machines at a low price. Lacasse said he would think about it. The German, he told himself, even if he had his private conduits of graft, was a most useful man, maintaining the neat balance between honesty and dishonesty that all Europeans who came to Asia seemed to acquire Orientally in time. It was the old economic philosophy of Shanghai, a kind of amoral code that had its special roots there. Without ever having been in China, Lacasse felt himself in the Shanghai mold; in its heyday he would, he was certain, have been a splendid entrepreneur. What was involved more than anything else, as the German demonstrated, was a sophisticated sense of restraint, a limited mobility; it grew out of awareness of one's capacities and one's limitations, of knowing instinctively, as the beasts know, which opponents not to cross. To be careful but not servile, almost but never an equal, was another qualification. Silently Lacasse congratulated himself on his good fortune; he had hired this man on the basis of a letter from a Corsican friend.

He drank the last bit of *perrier* in the bottle and got up to go. He had no inclination to return to the hotel. Instead he began strolling along rue Catinat. The after-siesta crowds were out, and while neither the sun nor the air was bright, it was pleasant enough, considering the fact that the rains should have arrived by now. Lacasse debated the evening's prospects. He did not feel like gambling. He could, of course, spend a full evening back at the club, which he hadn't done for a long time, but ever since the Americans had begun to take over the hotel, he had found it difficult to be their constant host, going from one place to the other. Furthermore, since the German ran the place with complete efficiency, there was no need to be there. Lacasse next considered the Cercle Sportif, which he had not visited for many weeks; he knew what he was driving at—if she was not there, he would have provided himself with the open alternative of going to her house. But for that he still needed a reason, an excuse. At that very moment Lacasse heard his name called from the sidewalk to his right, and, turning abruptly, saw Remy at a table. It took him a full moment more to realize who the girl at the table with Remy was.

He felt as if he had been caught naked. Slowly regaining his equilibrium, he walked over to them. The seat of his suit was stuck between his buttocks and he wiggled it free. He started to smile too soon, so that by the time he reached the table the smile was frozen. Remy moved a chair out for him.

"You look like a lost tourist," Remy said. "Sit down." He introduced Mme Brouillard.

"Ah," Lacasse murmured. "Of course, I have seen you." He felt his skin grow warm and shifted his position at the private thought of the night before.

Genevieve waited a moment and then said: "You must be extremely busy these days, with the Americans."

"It's the truth," Lacasse said, sagely, "that their demands are heavy. They are not yet accustomed to the tropics, our saviors."

Remy smiled. "They will mellow with the monsoon," he said.

"Their clothes will spoil, and they will only complain about the laundry," Lacasse said.

"One should be patient, especially in the hotel business," Remy suggested.

"It is no longer a business," Lacasse replied. "I might as well be in the Army."

Remy laughed. "You are too fat, Jacques," he said.

"I have seen many fat colonels," Lacasse said. "And many thin ones that are useless."

◇◇

"That is true," Remy acknowledged. "It is not simply the shape that counts."

"How many Americans are there now?" Genevieve asked.

Lacasse pursed his lips. "Twenty perhaps," he said. "There will be twenty more before the month is out. The hotel will soon have nothing but Americans, but I will keep a few rooms for myself."

"What will they all do?" Genevieve mused.

"Make the telephones work," Remy said. "The telephones and the sewers."

"There is no limit to their largesse," Lacasse said. "You have heard about the useless cement, of course?" He snorted. "For American highways."

"It will be good to build forts with," Remy said.

"I thought there were to be no more forts," said Genevieve.

"There will always be forts," Remy murmured. "Castles in the jungle."

"You are here permanently, madame?" Lacasse asked, turning to her.

"Permanently," Genevieve said. "I come with the city."

"It is her advantage of belonging both to East and West," Remy interposed.

"A lovely advantage," Lacasse murmured, smiling. His voice had a gurgling quality.

"There are disadvantages," Genevieve said.

"Nothing is perfect," Remy said. He stood up. "I must go," he added. Then he shook hands with both of them. "I will leave you with him," he said to Genevieve. "But be careful. He will try to find out too much at once."

Lacasse fidgeted. "An injustice," he muttered, trying to smile again. He turned to her and quickly added: "But you will stay and have a drink, madame?"

Genevieve, he thought, nodded.

◇◇

They watched Remy walk down the street, with his steps that no longer had a spring in them, as if it were broken.

"Have you known him long?" Lacasse asked.

"He has been here since the beginning," Genevieve said.

"And you?"

"Almost."

Lacasse waited a moment, after which, not looking at her, he said: "You must have many friends in Saigon, then."

"My life is quiet," Genevieve said.

"That is difficult here," Lacasse said, sniggering.

"I do not find it so difficult," she said.

"Ah," he said. "You are a lady of leisure. I am envious." He was deciding not to mention seeing her at the night club, not yet; it was both too late and too soon. What interested him more for the moment was her association with Remy.

"Monsieur Remy, like myself, has found it difficult, you see," he said. "It is harder for the men than the women, I think. In his case, his liver is extremely bad."

"He is a patriot," Genevieve said. "Patriots are stubborn."

"It is a matter of principles, I imagine," Lacasse said softly.

"They are easier to die by than to live with," Genevieve said.

"I am fortunate in not having them," Lacasse said.

"Were you born without them?" Genevieve inquired.

Lacasse sat back, licking the *apéritif* off his lips. "I imagine so," he said. "We are known, in Corsica, for our common sense."

"It is an attribute to be desired," Genevieve said. "In business especially."

"Not only then," Lacasse said, utilizing the opening. They watched the strollers without speaking, and then Lacasse observed: "It is a pity so attractive a man has never married. This Remy."

"He will marry later, when he comes to rest," Genevieve said.

"As for yourself?" Lacasse asked.

"I have tried it," she said. "I am not sure I am interested again."

"Ah," Lacasse mused. "Perhaps it is wiser. Yet one grows lonely."

"There are worse things than loneliness," Genevieve said.

Lacasse hesitated. "I am not so certain," he said.

Genevieve shrugged. "It is a matter of opinion."

"One must feel—have, something," Lacasse said.

"Not always," she said. "One does better sometimes without."

"Without?"

"Without feeling. So there is no regret."

"It is unusual for a woman to say such things."

Genevieve was silent. "Perhaps I do not mean them, finally," she said.

Lacasse realized that a moment was upon him.

"If you are not occupied, would you join me this evening?" he asked.

Genevieve did not answer and he wondered if she had heard. She had been looking directly at him, so it was doubtful that she hadn't, but now she was looking away.

"There is the gambling in Cholon," Lacasse murmured. "Or the various clubs . . ."

"Thank you," Genevieve said, at length. "But I am very tired, you see."

Lacasse pursed his lips as before. "Ah, that is a pity," he said. He looked down at his hands on the table, as if their folded pudginess contained some special fascination, and then looked up again, but beyond her. "It would be interesting to talk about—many things," he mused.

Genevieve was regarding him with a quizzical smile. Lacasse could not tell if she was actually laughing at him. He waited a moment for her to say something, but when she did not, he grew bolder, with a kind of foolish desperation. "I am curious about you," he blurted. "I am curious about anyone who lives alone in this place."

◇◇◇

"How do you know that I do live alone?" Genevieve asked, her eyes twinkling.

Lacasse felt better. "I do not know, of course," he said. "It is a surmise."

"I have a house," she said. "It is a small house, so there is only room for myself."

"So small as that?" Lacasse exaggerated his incredulousness, narrowing his eyes as he stared at her. "Where is this miniature?"

"Oh the rue Colombier," Genevieve said.

"Ah, yes—I passed there last night," Lacasse said. "There was a lonely light. It may have been yours."

"It is possible."

"As a matter of fact, I believe I saw you," Lacasse said, full of feigned surprise.

"I came home late," she said. "Actually, I was in Cholon."

Lacasse brightened further. "Ah, well, that is a coincidence," he said. "I was there myself, you see." He paused. "Of course, I am there often." Measuredly, he added: "I was at the Club Chinois. The owner is a friend of mine."

Genevieve waited what seemed to Lacasse an eternity before she replied. "I was also there."

He swallowed the last drops of the *apéritif*. "I saw you," he said softly.

"Why did you not mention it?" she asked.

"A man must also have his secrets," he said, laughing. "It was the reason for the increase of my curiosity."

"You are too secretive for a man," Genevieve said, "but you are not truly mysterious. That is the trouble."

She was still smiling at him, but Lacasse thought she was also annoyed. "I cannot help it," he said, almost sheepishly. "In my profession it is unavoidable."

Genevieve stood up. "I must go," she said, curtly.

"I shall drive you to your small house," Lacasse said. "My

car is only down the street." He was lying, but he knew where he could get one.

"Thank you, no," she said, and before Lacasse could reply she was gone.

He paid the bill and then decided to have another *apéritif*. It was almost dusk and the air was suddenly cleaner. He held the glass in his hand, sipping steadily and staring at the street with an empty expression. It had turned out well, in spite of her abrupt departure; the afternoon as a whole had been a success. He would let her alone for a day or two. It was entirely possible, he thought, that she was actually involved with both sides.

3

THE first rain fell in the evening, quietly, as if the monsoon, knowing it was late, had tried to reach the city undetected. Lacasse did go to his club, satisfied he could do nothing better, and, despite himself, got along famously with a group of American engineers who stood at the bar through two floor-shows. At midnight he was still engaged in a friendly but vociferous and thoroughly masculine debate about the variability of pulchritude and its interhemispheric attractions (the discussion had started after successive dances by an almost naked Japanese and a slightly more clad French girl Lacasse had imported from Casablanca). The conversation took Lacasse away from himself and made him feel less defensive, so that when he finally went to bed he slept soundly, with a new if tentative conception of his manhood. . . .

Genevieve, after she had left him in the café, had gone home and dined alone, simply and shortly, after which she did something she had not done for many weeks; she read a book, another new French novel about the Resistance. She found herself so engrossed that she neither thought about herself nor noticed the hour; it was two o'clock when she set the book down and went to bed. The several simultaneous choices she had made had left her, for the moment at least, detached, and, if anything, she felt freer than she had before, freer perhaps than at any time since her marriage. Tomorrow, she told herself, she would walk past the tobacconist's shop, if only to identify it. Her commitment, as she had expressed it to Cau Minh Thien, remained firm enough, representing a fresh anchor in her mind. But the Consul had opened a door, or kept one ajar. Remy could be dealt with under any circumstances. On the other hand, this Lacasse was someone to avoid. One had, however, to discount what one heard about the Corsicans, as one discounted what was said by women about other women. But she wondered briefly, as she turned over, whether he was actively homosexual. . . .

Early in the morning, when the rain had slackened and the dampness hung over the countryside, Cau Minh Thien reached his village. He could not remember when he had been more tired. He had left the city at eleven o'clock, but the rain, spurring darkness, had slowed him beyond the edge. As always when he stayed away so long, he had begun to lose track of time, even to forget the number of days and nights he had spent in the city, whether, the hours of dark and light meshing, he had been away from the village half or three quarters of a week. Cau rendered importance to minutes and to hours; the *Tu Ve* had its own calendar of life and death, thrust and flight, spelled out in the absence or the presence of men in cafés, by arrivals and departures of individuals rather than of seasons.

There were still things to be done that he had not got around to, Cau reminded himself. Were it not for the fact that he had been gone so long, he would have remained in the city, catching up with his sleep in some fashion, as an itinerant peddler or fortuneteller gives himself a short rest by a roadside. As it was, he would have to return at once.

He found his mattress occupied by one of the young runners. He gave the boy a short jab in the ribs with his heel, and the boy leaped up; his eyes were saturated with terror. Cau snorted. "Did you think it was the police?" he muttered. "Or were you dreaming of a

girl?" The boy laughed with sleepy relief and lay down in a corner
of the hut, where the mud was the least thick. Cau allowed himself
the luxury of a cigarette as he lay naked on his back, blowing the
smoke up at the roof. The rain had quickened again, creating a warm
hush.

He whispered to the boy: "What time is it?" but the boy was
asleep. Crushing the cigarette out on the hard floor, Cau rolled over
and closed his eyes. The mattress was his home, his sole possession;
but he had even forgotten where he had got it.

Chapter XVII

IN WHAT Adam called the catacomb, Nell Finch was preparing
breakfast. She felt the oppressiveness of the weather already in
her bones, a stiffness that made her whole body ponderous and
drowsy. The rain was falling steadily again. From her stone porch
Nell saw the city as through gauze; the familiar and ubiquitous
brown stucco looked darker and sickly, as if the water had penetrated in the quick way of a blight. There was a smell to the monsoon that was different from that of other rains. It was not of the
sea in itself, but it had brought an essence of the ocean across the
tops of mountains.

Nell forgot the coffee as it began to boil on the tiny range. She
felt the monsoon as a harbinger. Its grayness descended over all,
animate and inanimate. It would put an end to conversation, blanket-
ing the cafés, deadening the voices. Color would vanish from the

streets, the shop windows would be dulled; the silver in the trays would tarnish.

Stirring herself, she drank the burnt coffee and began to dress. She moved about the room absently, her hands clumsy, her touch fuzzy. Tonight she would fix the place; both she and the maid had grown careless.

She tried, when she was alone, not to think of Adam. Long ago, what at any rate seemed long ago, she had warned herself; even before the trip to Manila. It seemed to her, retrospectively, that she had known then what would happen, and how she might feel. During the war, when so much that in normal times had seemed wrong had acquired the quality of blind permissiveness, one had shut one's eyes in the face of greater if less graspable evils. Pride had entered into the ability to garner scattered moments, to rationalize them so that they became not only more impressive than they were in themselves but provings and affirmations of things that did not exist, except as bravado antitheses of death. With Adam, Nell had known how foolish she was being at the start, how temporary, in a permanent climate, would be her dispensation. It was when the lark was over that she had fallen in love with him, in part to be un-ashamed. It had become a penance and a cause.

In an atmosphere such as Saigon's, suspicion became epidemic, affecting the most ingenuous. Nell was not ingenuous; but as the Minister's secretary, she knew how careful she had to be, not only in relation to Adam but generally. It was not simply what happened here, but the whole mood of jitteriness back home as it had come to be reflected in the field. Those like herself, who had been in the service for a number of years, had watched this attitude extend, until all of them, where they had once joked about it, now sensed, self-consciously, that their lives were under a pervasive surveillance. It made little difference if it was official or unofficial, regular or irregular; it was felt ubiquitously, a kind of sixth sense that guided what they said or didn't say to each other and even what they thought, creating awkwardness where none had been before. On the level of the girls in the catacomb, Nell had seen the results in small but mounting ways, in the form of self-imposed restrictions which, in a lonely place, made loneliness worse. She had wondered if the catacomb, with its separate rooms for those even two grades lower than herself, had been built to spur privacy and uncommunication. The process of suspicion, feeding upon itself, grew worse when one reached the point, as during several alcoholic evenings she and some of the older girls had done, of open imaginings, bruitings of names of those they guessed might be called upon sometime to pass judgment on others. These intimate sessions, furtively balanced between the psychoanalyst's couch, the confessional, and the bare inquisitor's room, served at once as a kind of clandestine outlet, the empty beer cans piled crazily on the floor, and as an expression of fitful, feminine rebellion, bitter and subversive in its own right, against the coalition of men that had caused it. It was also a sort of joke they could play on themselves, wondering silently, while the game went on, who among them could conceivably become a traitoress. That there would be nothing except a state of mind to report made the proposition more destructive. Nell had even pictured herself engaged in final cathartic act, confessing in a gray monotone to crimes of gossip she had not committed.

Privately, and by a process of elimination, she had suspected Goodenough, believing him, by her own observation, to be the most logical of the men in the post for doubling in brass—as an assistant political and unofficial security officer. But until yesterday she had been willing to think that Goodenough was scarcely adept or daring enough to be dangerous. She had regarded him more as a symptom than as the disease, and she had watched his approaches to the Minister with amusement, the number of times a week he wandered around to Smythe's office on one pretext or another, or had telephoned from down the hall. When Goodenough's voice had responded to hers yesterday afternoon over the phone and, more

◇◇

hollowly than usual, had asked to speak to the Minister, Nell had done what she had known she would do sooner or later; she had held her receiver open just long enough to hear him tell the Minister that, by some peculiar coincidence, Mr. Patch had apparently also been in touch with the man they had spoken of previously, the little doctor who appeared to be so zealous a renegade. Did Mr. Smythe still want to see the man if he returned, Goodenough had inquired. The Minister had said he thought he did. The rest of the conversation Nell had cut off.

2

THE Minister sat drumming his fingers. A sunbeam, silted by motes, played over his balding head and onto the glass table-top, from where the reflection bounced back obliquely and caught the edge of his horn-rimmed reading-glasses. He had been talking to M. Remy, having returned a call made late yesterday afternoon. They had dealt with a variety of things before M. Remy had mentioned the matter. What he had said posed a problem the Minister had never had to deal with before, and he resented it.

As a career man for nearly twenty-five years, Smythe considered himself to have been fortunate in his posts. They had been normally scattered at first, except for Asia, and he had moved from Australia to Bolivia, back to New Zealand, and then to Europe, where he had remained. Recognition as an expert on Communism in the West had been accorded him, and an assistant secretaryship had loomed. It was still in the offing. He had not been anxious to come to the Far East, but the advisability of acquainting himself with Asia was evident, and there had been no doubt of the importance of the Saigon post; but for the first time Smythe had not felt at home in an assignment. He had surely benefited from observing at first hand the difference of attraction Communism had here and in Europe, the contrast between fixed power by tank and bayonet, ruthlessly maintained with the help of a rigid police system, and the subtler method

of capturing legitimate nationalist movements and subverting them
while at the same time inspiring them, often, to the too hasty intern-
ment of colonial empires. Smythe had been pondering the question
anew. He did not, the more he reflected about it, believe that he was
too deeply oriented in Europe, though it was obviously what Patch
and some of the others, too, had concluded. He was willing to grant
that there had been missed opportunities, and he also recognized the
simple truth that lower standards of living in Asia permitted the
Communists, in the first stages, to make quicker inroads here than
in Europe. Their appeals were on firmer ground in other respects
as well, on the land itself, perhaps; in the careful conduct of their
native troops, and in their attacks against illiteracy. It was what
happened afterward, when the carrots became sticks, that brought
on the great equalizer.

Smythe was even ready to admit that Patch might be justified in
posing a gamble, but it was purely theoretical. He could argue, that
is, to cut themselves off from the French was the best way, under
certain circumstances, to defeat the Communists in Indo-China. By
dealing directly with the Vietnamese, the base of the overly dependent local government could conceivably be broadened. But
what Patch refused to admit was the sustained priority of Europe;
what lay exposed west of the Elbe, like a central nerve, would
determine all their futures.

One could not, at the same time, regard a single situation without
considering its relationship to all of its parts. Smythe prided himself
on his understanding of the French. He spoke the language fluently
and he felt that he knew the French at all levels, in their selfish
devotion to property, their stubborn and now injured pride, and
their practical wisdom too. Nor had he seen any reason, despite the
sad succession of cabinet crises since the end of the war, to mistrust
their political experience over the longer stretch of time, compounded as it was of hardheaded logic and ever-recurrent flashes of
idealism. He did not feel either, as had on occasion been suggested,

that the French in Indo-China were a different breed, that those who had stayed here during the war and had been interned toward the close of it were fundamentally any different from their compatriots back home. Their holdings, their responsibilities, might be more particularly concerned, he could admit; but their character, their patriotism, and, in the final sense, their *raison d'être*, Smythe felt, were the same.

His fingers, still idly drumming, came to a stop. What Remy had confided was distressing. Smythe had no opinion, one way or the other, about the advisability or inadvisability of fraternization. Most often, in the places he had been, it had been impossible, anyway; and the quality of Balkan spies, out of his own knowledge, had surely deteriorated during the era of Muscovitization. The physical problem, he had found, usually settled itself in harmless enough ways, with the normal amount of bickering and perhaps a few protocol flurries. He had never pretended to be a disciplinarian. A man with Patch's experience should know how to handle himself, using his maturing judgment. Yet Remy's information was oddly in keeping with something else, with a general air of independence on Patch's part. Smythe remembered, as he pressed the button on his desk, what Goodenough had told him. For the moment he decided to say nothing about it.

"Miss Finch," he said shortly, as she opened the door, "will you get Mr. Patch to come in here, please."

3

WHEN Adam entered, he found the Minister casually turning the pages of a magazine and knew at once that something was wrong. He also knew Smythe well enough not to expect whatever it was to come up immediately. They discussed the continuing cabinet crisis in France, which by now, according to the names that were being mentioned, promised no drastic change in Indo-China policy after all, no matter which man took over as premier. The question of the

Dai Viet leaders and their friends in the north who had been mentioned for membership in the Vietnamese cabinet was brought up briefly. Under the circumstances, the Minister pointed out, any new pressure for readjustment would have to wait. Adam nodded; it had been waiting so long, another wait would scarcely make much difference, he noted. The Minister gave his thin grin, tilting his head forward like a beagle, and Adam kept his own expression fixed, his legs carelessly crossed as he allowed himself a slight chair-borne slouch. They had reached a point of pause and he let it hang, waiting for the Minister, but when Smythe volunteered nothing, he finally said: "I went to Cholon, as you suggested. There's been a step-up in Peking pressure. It's a general process, but they're still bending the way the wind blows."

The Minister nodded. "Naturally," he said. "It's a matter of gauging the velocity."

"Not only," Adam said. "The prevailing winds grow more various. Moscow, Peking, Paris, Washington, all puffing together. And Nehru—"

The Minister looked up, almost amiably. "Right you are," he said.

Adam stared at him, but let it drop. "You may be interested to know," he said, with a quick, small smile, "that we've made the honors list."

"The honors list?" Smythe repeated.

"The *Tu Ve* has us down, some of us, for possible elimination."

"I don't believe it," the Minister said, evenly.

Adam shrugged. "It's pretty difficult to prove or disprove, except in one way," he said. "Accidents can happen."

The Minister gave him another grin, even thinner than the last. "How many sides do you want to be killed by?" he asked.

"None, if possible," Adam said, laughing.

"You continue to place a high value on your head," said the Minister. He gazed across the desk. "And mine," he added.

"A consul is dispensable," Adam replied. "I'd be easy, you'd take more planning."

"You know," Smythe said, and he seemed almost pleased, "I never thought of it quite that way. Not even in Europe, where it was always worked out to the last detail."

"There's something to be said for casual killing," Adam said. "One of life's small surprises. . . ."

"One can guard against it," Smythe said.

"How?" Adam guessed what was coming.

"By not exposing oneself unnecessarily," the Minister said, softly. "If you're really serious, you, more than the rest of us—" there was a moment of hesitation—"get around."

"I'm not that serious, or that worried," Adam said. "But I've always felt it was one of my jobs."

"It's all our jobs, to a degree, of course," Smythe replied. "It's a question of how and why it's done."

It had been a Smythean retort, the rectitude couched, like an acorn, in the platitude. Once more Adam waited.

"Curiosity, of course, is always commendable," the Minister went on. He was looking out the window, having swung his chair, and was running a pencil through his fingers. "There's a difference, none the less, between exploration and adventure."

"Some of the greatest—" Adam began, and stopped. He already sensed the vacuum, and the room seemed to have gone bare. "Have we reached the point of non-exposure, of no contact, as part of policy, of tactics?" he asked.

"I didn't say that," the Minister said.

"Where's the magic line? Who draws it?"

"All of us can draw it," Smythe said, and then he added: "have to . . ."

"The process also works in reverse," Adam said. "The element of risk is more than physical. And alternatively, of non-risk."

Again the Minister smiled. "We can't all be martyrs," he said. "I guess it comes back to that."

"If we make our sorties conveniently, the way the French do from their towers, we might as well lock up shop," Adam said.

"I didn't suggest that either," Smythe replied.

"I was only speaking abstractly," Adam said. He paused and, having reached, he knew, an inevitable moment, took a deep breath. "We might as well face it," he continued, his voice now lower and the words spoken more slowly—"whatever differences, even healthy ones, that arise between any of us have become adumbrated by something else, the shadow cast by the hand of a man on a lad's head . . ."

"You put it quaintly," the Minister said.

"It's a simple allegory," Adam replied, "and you can extend it. Shadows lengthen on all sides. Since China's gone, we're Exhibit A in shadow-land. And now, when we ought to be most active, we're beset by the shadow from home."

The Minister permitted himself a sigh. "There's still the question of guarding oneself. And of avoiding indiscretions."

It was a word designating a woman, Adam thought, and the idea of Genevieve for the first time crossed his mind. He had been considering the conversation as a polite and non-objective ministerial sermon, engendered by his own random comments, prefatory still to something else. It was possible, too, of course, that the Minister had heard about the doctor. Adam recalled the flicker in the garden, the shadow across the window of his house. Yet he did not think this was what Smythe now meant.

The Minister was looking away once more. As if he were announcing the twelve-o'clock news, he went on: "There's an increase of agents here, I'm told. In Saigon, that is. At least"—and now he turned back slowly in his leather chair and confronted Adam—"that's what our French friends tell me." His eyes were motionless, but his facial muscles had stiffened.

Uncrossing his legs and then recrossing them again oppositely, Adam said, in a half-whisper: "They should know." Perhaps, after all, it was the doctor, he thought.

"It's possible they may be mistaken," the Minister went on. "But it would seem a good time to avoid any—unnecessary contact."

The choice of words brought ludicrously to mind the image of an Army prophylactic tent, the three-o'clock-in-the-morning lines of GI's underneath the pale-yellow bulbs. "Be Careful," the signs had said everywhere. Like "Think."

It was evident who the Minister's friends were, and Adam wondered how long it would take before it was brought out openly. Scarcely aware of the challenge he was throwing, allowing ideas to become words, he coughed and asked: "Was Monsieur Remy specific, sir?" The "sir" had slipped out a little foolishly, as an afterthought.

"Fairly," Smythe said. Now he was being stiff.

"Male or female?" Adam asked.

The Minister managed his smile. "You've a normal predilection," he said.

There was a moment of silence. The confirmation struck Adam queerly, almost dully. There was an abrupt change of levels, labyrinthian.

"She's a Sûreté agent," he said, measuredly. "That's what makes it rather odd."

The Minister's mouth was still etched in the shape of his last smile. "Maybe that's what they want her to think. Maybe that's part of it."

"I don't believe it," Adam said.

Smythe cleared his throat and picked up the pencil from the porcelain cup into which he had dropped it. "You've been around long enough," he said. "I'll leave it up to you."

Adam waited to see if the admonition would carry further, but

◇◇

Smythe seemed finished; also vaguely embarrassed. He was leaning slightly forward with his eyes lowered to the desk-top. Adam finally got up.

"Okay," he said. "I guess I better get back to work."

Behind him, as he went toward the door, he heard a rustle of papers and the Minister say: "Hmmn."

Nell stopped him. "Adam," she whispered. "I want to see you."

Oh, God, he thought, not that too. It was astonishing the things that shot through a man's mind.

He had gone a step past her desk and now he turned. The entreaty in her eyes was plain.

"Can we have lunch?" she asked. "Please—"

"I'll ring you at one," he said, and walked quickly to his own office across the hall. He closed the door with a snap. From the top drawer of his desk he took a fresh pack of cigarettes. The Cellophane crumpled in his fingers, and the tobacco, which smelled stale, tasted bitter and dry. He smoked quickly, to envelop himself.

It was all too ridiculous; "and, damn it," he thought, "it's none of his business." But obviously it was, and just as obviously there was more to it.

Two questions crossed: what had Remy actually said, how much had the Minister interpolated?

There was a third. Suppose, after all, she had done Remy's bidding? Even to the point of allowing herself to be used in decoy fashion. It was possible, he realized, simply because, as always, it was all possible here.

He reconstructed the moment at the pool when he had spoken to her, remembering watching her on the diving platform, and Remy's distracting voice. There had been no indication of a plan. Or had that been part of it too, that she might have time to join the two Frenchwomen on the tiles? The reappearance of Remy the next day took on a new dimension.

What was impossible to know, what he was most curious about, was the tenor rather than the substance of Remy's observation to the Minister. Had it been the Frenchman's spoken purpose, or had he, as was more likely, let fall the kernel of suspicion in the peculiar brand of his random talk? The Minister, almost certainly, could have had no other way of knowing. Something else: Remy's surmise, with concomitant logic, would have gauged the Minister's normal response; and since the Minister always acted normally, the response had already taken place. *Touché*, Remy. Which also meant that Remy had looked ahead, before telephoning the Minister, to the next time he would see Adam. He could already hear the light disclaimer at the pool's edge. "But, my dear Patch, it was a purely subjunctive reference, you understand, ha ha. That is, under the circumstances, in this fantastic atmosphere, such matters, such tactics, could conceivably affect all of us, even you. . . ." And the pale smile on the pallid face.

There remained, then, the question of whether it was principally Remy or the Minister who had thrown the gauntlet. Adam suddenly became aware of the possibility that it was both.

He leaned back, letting the cigarette drop onto the cement floor, and thought carefully of Genevieve, of the things she had said, of her manner and expressions and tone. The one fact that made the Minister's warning at all credible, in a weird through-the-looking-glass way, was the total irreconcilability of the projection with the actual image she presented. She pretended to be so completely and so naturally at home in her small tight world that, in a sense, it was perhaps almost too pat. There also remained the marriage; the bitterness and the double resentment, over being dependent and enjoying its hothouse fruits. Conceivably this could lead her to dabble in anything, black magic or one of the ridiculous potpourri religions. Or espionage. Genevieve still did not seem the type. But even if Remy was right, or if the Minister had simply interpreted wrongly, there had been no indiscretions. At least, not of the kind that the Minister meant. Smythe undoubtedly belonged to the old

◇◇◇

Balkan school that believed one unavoidably confessed one's innermost thoughts to a bedmate.

Adam reached for the phone and dialed Nell's extension. She waited for him below, where the car was parked. When they were riding, he asked: "Would a Chinese lunch sound good?"

"Can't we go to your place?" she asked. The entreaty was still there.

"There's not much to eat," he said.

"I'm not that hungry," she said. "I'd like a drink, and just a snack."

They drove in silence until Nell brought her left hand to his shoulder, where it hung gently before she let it fall over the top of the seat.

"I just wanted to talk to you," she said.

"You're not worried, are you?"

She smiled up at him and touched her long fingers briefly to the back of his head. "Yes, darling, I'm worried," she said, "but not the way you think."

It was his day, auspiciously, Adam murmured to himself, for being treated like a boy.

"It's you," she said.

"I thought—" he began.

"I know," she said. "Good men do. If I were worried about that, at this point, do you think I'd tell you?"

"We ought to be shot for taking chances," he said.

"I read somewhere that it's harder in the tropics. The State Department's girl guide."

"Luckier," he said. "I think luck is more involved. It's actually easier, because it happens more often."

"What does?"

He realized his mistake. "Conception," he said, meaning desire.

She smiled again and paused. "The figures are on your side," she said. "Anyway, I used to want six. Used to."

When they reached the house, Adam told the cook to do the best he could, and mixed Nell and himself some gin and bitters. He brought two glasses and the pitcher over and sat down next to her on the couch. "Okay," he said, "I've had a hard morning, now tell me."

"I knew about it," she said. "That's why I wanted to see you."

"You knew about it?" he repeated. "How? What did you know about?"

"About Goodenough," she said.

Adam set his glass down and shook his head. "Look," he said, "let's begin at the beginning. What's Goodenough got to do with it?"

"Wasn't that what he talked about—the Minister?" Nell asked.

Adam shook his head again. "No," he said.

Nell said: "Oh," and took a sip.

"It was just—the usual sort of thing," Adam said. "Some day we'll agree to disagree."

"I'm not so far off, then," Nell said.

"What about Goodenough?"

"I'm a silly girl, and sentimental," Nell said, "so would you kiss me first?"

Adam kissed her and she let her lips cling, more pleasantly than he had felt them; but she didn't put her arms around him. They reached simultaneously for their drinks, on a note of sadness.

"Darling, I hate myself for being so right about someone," she said. "But I've been right about him all along. Mr. G., that is. And I happened to hear a conversation yesterday afternoon."

"Happened to?"

"I listened," she said. "I had to. Maybe I knew."

"Knew what?"

"Not what he would say, specifically, but that it might be about you."

"And he said what?"

She swallowed the rest of the drink. "That—and he made it full of by-the-ways—you had seen someone, a Vietnamese, a doctor, someone he had seen earlier." She paused. "He made it sound kind of indecent."

Still looking straight ahead, Adam said: "And what else?"

"There wasn't much else," she said. "Maybe I'm even more foolish than I think. It was simply—the whole tone of his voice, and of the Minister's, more briefly. He asked if Mr. Smythe would want to see this person, this doctor, when he came again. Or maybe it was if. Anyway, the Minister said yes. That was all."

"And what do you think it proves?" Adam asked.

Nell looked at him. The skin around her mouth had grown tight and the small veins above her eyes were trembling.

"I love you," she said. "Let's not play games about this."

"I'm sorry," he said.

He sat for a moment more, the empty glass in his hand, and as he turned it over he thought of the Minister's pencil turning. The idea of a wind tunnel came oddly to him, a whistle mounting to a roar. But why had Smythe held back?

"Will you excuse me a moment?" he said, getting up.

"Don't you see?" she said.

"Yes, I see," Adam replied.

He went into the bedroom and, after two misconnections, managed to get Lockman's house. The boy who answered said master was asleep.

"Wake him up," Adam said.

The boy stammered. "I know," Adam said. "Knock on door."

After what seemed at least five but was only three minutes, Lockman's voice came across the already bad connection. "Christ," he said, "can't a man—"

"A man can, but not now," Adam said. "This is important."

"It's always important," Lockman said. "Siestas are important."

"What happened about Dr. Dang?"

"What do you mean what happened?"

"How did Bob Goodenough find out?"

There was a pause, and then Lockman said: "Jesus—he did, didn't he? Wait a minute. Let me reconstruct."

"Yes," Adam said. "Let's reconstruct."

"Kelly called him, yesterday morning."

"In God's name why?" Adam asked.

"To get the report on the doctor."

"Why didn't he call me?"

"Goodenough interviewed him. Goodenough, with the Minister's blessing it seems, had sent him to us—officially, so Dang told Kelly. It seemed the best way to do it. Channels."

"It wasn't," Adam said shortly. "Not by a long shot. When did Kelly start all this?"

"He saw Dang the next morning, yesterday, after our session. We wanted to get a few facts down, on our stationery. Dang told him about Goodenough. Kelly called."

"There has to be more than that," Adam said. "When did I come in?"

Lockman paused. "Look," he said, "I'll call you back. I'll get hold of Kelly."

Adam put the receiver down and returned to Nell. She had mixed a second small pitcher of drinks and had just begun to sample the tray the boy had brought in. "Well?" she asked.

"I don't know," Adam said. "It'll take a few moments, but the developer is working." He went to the sideboard and refilled his glass and leaned against the wall.

"Aren't you going to tell me?" Nell asked.

"Irving's calling back. But you're already right."

The phone rang, interrupting their looking at each other, and Adam ran to answer it.

"Not very smart, I'm afraid," Lockman said. The pixy had gone gone altogether out of his voice.

◇◇◇

"No," Adam said. "It doesn't sound like it. What was it?"

"Kelly asked Little Lord Fauntleroy for the report. Said it might help, could we have it? Normal enough. Goodenough said no. His usual stuffy. Maybe he never wrote one. Kelly had that feeling. Maybe he learned in college not to write letters."

"Then what?" Adam asked.

Lockman sighed audibly, and across the phone it sounded like a rasp. "Our boy was a bit anxious," he said. "His heart but not his head was cooking."

"He got mad," Adam said. "He told Goodenough what he could—"

"Not quite," Lockman said, "but that's the general idea."

"Oh, Christ," Adam said softly.

"Yeah," said Lockman. "Anyway, Goodenough can drive a man to say such things. All that Kelly actually said was we'd find our way of getting it."

"You'd rifle the files?" Adam said, mockingly.

"Hmmn," said Lockman. "Or other friends would tell us."

Adam took a deep breath. "Kelly should never have left that newspaper," he said.

Lockman permitted himself a snort. "Helluva police reporter," he said. "The voice of the press, I'll admit, isn't always diplomatically rendered."

"Scarcely," Adam said. He had the strong and sudden feeling that Lockman didn't fully comprehend, either. Outside, in the front room, he thought he heard voices.

Lockman seemed to be hovering. "Look," he said, "if you can come over here later, I think we better talk about it. Or I'll come to you."

"I'll call you," Adam said.

Lockman grunted and hung up.

Adam started for the front room. After two steps he stopped short. The sound of women's voices came clearly through the bamboo drop. He had the feeling that, had he wanted to, he couldn't move. The second voice belonged to Genevieve Brouillard.

"I don't know how long he'll be busy," Nell was saying. "Perhaps you'd prefer to return?"

There was a silence that seemed to Adam an eternity, and then Genevieve said: "I will wait a few moments, if it is satisfactory."

Nell said: "Perfectly," and Adam heard the sharp sound of a match being struck.

There was a stirring, of the boy removing plates, and Adam pictured Genevieve's expression.

"You are Mr. Patch's friend?" she asked.

"I am a friend of Mr. Patch's," Nell said.

"You are at the Legation, of course?"

"Of course," Nell said.

"May I ask—what you do?"

"You may ask," Nell said.

"Ah—so?"

"I clean the place," Nell said. "I'm a char."

"I do not understand," Genevieve said.

"No, you don't, do you?"

There was another terrible silence, and, retreating, Adam sat down on the side of the bed.

"Why do you want to see him?" Nell finally asked. "Maybe I can give him the message."

"Oh, no, I do not think so," Genevieve replied. "But perhaps it is not so important."

"Then what are you waiting for?" Nell said.

Adam gripped the edge of the mattress.

"He is a very nice man, Mr. Patch, isn't he?" Genevieve said.

"Look," Nell said. "It may be none of my business, but why don't you see Mr. Patch at his office?"

"Perhaps it is not," Genevieve said.

"Not what?"

"Of—interest to you. It is such an American word—business."

"Excuse me," Nell said. "I'll see if Mr. Patch is nearly finished."

She came through the drop as Adam stood up abruptly. He could see the anger in the depth of her eyes as she came across the room.

"There's a dame—a Eurasian—" she began.

"I know," Adam said. "I just heard."

"You're not very discreet, darling," Nell said.

He started to say "Neither are you," but stopped himself. "What does she want?" he asked.

"You, obviously," Nell said. "She looks like she's from the girl-of-the-week club. I never thought it existed, but maybe it does."

"Hmmn," Adam said. "I've never been solicited."

"Tsk," Nell said.

"I wish everybody would be nicer," he said. "Maybe I'd better go out."

"I'd better go with you," she said. "Wherever she's from, I'll bet my next check she's *grata* at the Sûreté. I think I've seen her before."

"Where?" Adam asked.

Nell shrugged. "In a variety of places, darling. Constantinople, Belgrade, Mexico City."

"Do me a favor," Adam said. "Wait here."

Nell said nothing as she walked into the bathroom. Adam went quickly outside. Genevieve was not there. He ran to the porch and then into the garden, but she had disappeared.

He re-entered the living-room slowly as Nell came back.

"Well," she said, "did you settle your accounts?"

"All settled," Adam said.

"Who was she?"

Adam hesitated. "She's the secretary of Paul Remy," he said. "It was a last-minute invitation—to a session with a group of released prisoners."

"See, I was right," Nell said. "Sûreté to the mixed marrow of her lovely little bones."

Adam laughed. "You're jealous because you're one-blooded," he said.

"I'm just jealous," she said.

It was not until they were in the car and out of the driveway that Nell calmed down. "I'm sorry, as usual," she said, leaning her head against his shoulder. "It was just that the moment she walked in, I could have sworn you had slept with her."

"You've been prescient enough for one day."

"What did Lockman say?"

"It was Kelly, all right," Adam said. "I guess I can't really blame him. The old technique: 'We've got the story anyway, Mac, you might as well tell us.' "

"Goodenough must have loved that."

Adam exhaled audibly, through his nose.

"Am I forgiven, darling?" she asked.

"Sure you're forgiven," he said.

"I don't mean for being a jealous bitch," she said. "I mean for eavesdropping."

"Oh, that," he said.

"I'd be a good spy," she said.

"For whom?"

"You," she said. "You need one. You're too easy."

"Easy? Easy what?"

"Easy-going. Adam, the good American. All the birds and beasts love him."

"I thought we'd done with that," he said, twisting the car past a *cyclo*.

"Maybe we're compound-ridden, like you say," she went on. "But we stay out of trouble."

"You're not making sense," he said. "One thing's got nothing to do with the other."

◇◇

"Fraternize me no fraternizations," she said. "Or do I sound like my boss?"

"You could," he said. "At any rate, I'm glad you told me. I'm glad you did listen. But don't do it again."

"Yes, sir," Nell said. "I mean no, sir."

They drove the rest of the short way in silence. When they drew to a stop, Adam beckoned to her to go first. She stood at the car door a moment and her face grew clouded.

"Don't," he said. "I'll try to talk to you tonight, if I can."

Nell's smile flickered. "Darling," she said. "Be careful. . . ."

He watched her long legs walk out of the driver's mirror above his head. His stomach ached and he suddenly realized that he had had no lunch.

Chapter XVIII

FROM his hotel window Tran watched the rain begin again. The room had grown quickly damp and the water dripped down the edge of the rotting sill and was seeping through. The streets were empty except for the *cyclo* boys with their broad rain-hats and their coats that came to their knees and made them look otherworldly, as if they had emerged from the recesses of the jungle to forage in the monsoon. He felt imprisoned here, the more so in the rain's confining, which underlined his own. The day and a half gone by seemed as long again as the rest of his time in the city. Except for Mr. Kelly's brief visit yesterday morning, he had spoken to no one since Mr. Patch had driven him back to the hotel, leaving him with his queer sense of dissatisfaction in the night, not yet a foreboding, but a new breath of skepticism. To find the Americans also puzzled and unsure desolated him anew. He had not expected dedication, the certainty of the forest; but he had hoped for purpose, to which he could attach the quality and sense of direction. Direction without purpose, like its opposite, was only more blind faith.

The rain fell harder, assaulting the trembling pane, and even the *cyclos* scurried for cover below. In the entrance of the teashop across the street Tran saw two men, one of them a shivering coolie in the doorway. They had cups in their hands which they held tightly, and Tran envied them their communication and their warmth. A roll of thunder rode across the shining roofs, and the old frame of the hotel shook in its path and wake. Tran felt a pressure of tears.

An hour later the rain receded and the sky was a wrung cloth. Tran got off the bed where, his body immobile but his eyes open, he had been lying, and went downstairs. He had had enough of his solitude. If they came to look for him, he would be in their midst. . . .

The sergeant at the desk of the Legation told him where the ECA entrance was. The sergeant did not appear to have recognized him, and Tran felt that he was back at a beginning, in the vestibule for the first time. Outside again, he stood for several moments on the sidewalk. The street, during the pause of rain, had come quickly to life. In and out of the bank opposite, Frenchmen scurried with small satchels Tran knew were filled with money for telegraphing to Paris at the officially swollen rate. Through the flick of a signature, millions of cheap piasters were turned into francs and delivered nightly into mother-country pockets. The simple vignette denied all the protestations of a "dead" colonialism. Tran half-closed his eyes. He saw the men in their white suits as slivers of light moving across the sheen of rainwater pools. The shouts of the *cyclo* boys urging each other out of the way were like forest sounds after a storm. He heard a sudden whir and splashing and found himself soaked to the knees by the wheels of a car. The immaculately combed head of a Vietnamese was framed in the car's rear window.

Stamping, sadly regarding the spreading stains, Tran walked the short distance to the two-pillared entrance along the arroyo. Now he saw the small ECA placards. It was dark inside, the single bulb extinguished above the desk where a young Vietnamese girl sat, motionless. He explained that he wished to see Mr. Kelly and gave his name, and after a few moments he was allowed to go up.

Kelly was waiting at the top of the stairs. "Hello, doc, I was just thinking about you," he said, and he extended one hand to shake as he put the other on Tran's back.

"Perhaps I should not have come," Tran said.

"That's okay," Kelly said. "We're having lots of fun."

"Fun?" Tran repeated.

"In a manner of speaking," Kelly said.

He led the way down the hall to his office. As they passed one of the open doors, Tran saw Mr. Lockman with his tie undone and his shirt-sleeves rolled up, dictating to two serious-looking Vietnamese clerks.

When they were seated, Kelly offered him a cigarette, which Tran declined; it was a ritual with the Americans. Kelly leaned back with his hands clasped behind his neck and the cigarette hanging from one corner of his mouth.

"Well, doc," he said, "I guess we're having a little trouble."

"It will not be possible to go?" Tran asked.

"Maybe, maybe not," Kelly said. "Maybe it won't be as bad as that."

Tran sat with his hands folded on his knees. His premonitions were being confirmed. Mr. Kelly was not Mr. Goodenough, but the effect of what Mr. Kelly was saying was the same.

"What——?" Tran began, and then he simply said: "It will be a pity, if one cannot go."

"Snafu," Kelly said. "Situation normal, all frenched up. It could just be a few crossed wires. One thing, though, it'll take time. That much, doc, for sure."

"Do they offer objection?" Tran asked.

"That's SOP," Kelly said. "Automatic. Only way to beat it is by a solid all-American front." He brought his fist down mockingly on the desk. Then he added, more quietly: "We haven't got together yet on the arrangements. I guess that's it."

"I see," said Tran, though Mr. Kelly's explanations, like Mr. Lockman's, were not altogether satisfactory. "It is a difficult thing to arrange," he suggested.

"It oughtn't to be," Kelly said, "but it is."

"The Americans have a reputation among everyone for efficiency," Tran said.

"Sometimes," Kelly said, "sometimes, doc, I think there are almost too many Americans."

Tran smiled. "It is the reverse of the customary opinion," he said. "That there are too many of us."

"Maybe both are true," Kelly said, and he lit another cigarette from the one he had been smoking. Above his head, through the window, Tran watched the top of a barge move down the canal.

"I shall have to wait, then," Tran said. "Do you wish that I should remain in the hotel, or shall I come back tomorrow?"

"Better wait there," Kelly said. "I think it might be better."

Tran nodded without enthusiasm. He stood up and stepped toward the door.

"Don't be worried," Kelly said, still seated. "There'll be something to do."

"In Saigon?" Tran asked, half-turning.

"Here, anywhere," Kelly said, with a shrug and a grin. "It doesn't have to be the jungle, doc. The whole damn place is sick."

Tran responded to the wave of Mr. Kelly's hand with a flicker of fingers. He walked down the long corridor without looking to either side, and down the four flights of broken stairs, where the shrapnel scars from the Japanese bombs were concrete cancers on the walls. In the ground-floor vestibule the Vietnamese girl in her pale Western dress sat with her hands still folded in front of her. She took no notice of Tran's departure.

. . . The black-suit coolie drifted out of the crowd around the bank entrance and strolled along the sidewalk. He had been told to report at three o'clock, but there was ample time yet. The last two days and nights had been the easiest, except that by now he would be grateful for the comfort of his own floor and pad. He wondered why M. Remy chose to wait further when it was obvious what the man was up to—had been obvious, in fact, since the incident on the docks. One did not require verbal proof to establish such things. The pattern of movement was sufficient in itself.

He was an interesting fellow, at that. Out of his field. Apparently it never crossed his mind that he might be under observation. Were they so certain of themselves in the jungle, so guarded by nature, that they presumed a protective coloration in the city too? The coolie spat, and looked back across the street.

His quarry was indecisive, the way he had been when set free at the police station. Now look at him, the coolie thought, just standing. Actually, it made pursuit more difficult. How could one pursue a standing object? It called for the best of one's talents, to circle idly, to daydream, to stare in a shop window if the reflection was clear enough and one could keep the object in focus.

Something about the doctor, in his gray isolation, made the coolie suddenly wonder if he had a family. It was not a matter of curiosity. He was a revolutionary waif. There would be more of them.

The doctor had begun to walk again, aimlessly. The coolie let him go ahead, halfway down the block. He had the feeling that a long morning would develop, and then a longer afternoon perhaps, if he had to hunt for the doctor again. The teashop across from the Chinese hotel had become a second home, and the coolie now found himself longing for a cup of hot tea. The owner had been generous since their one brief altercation.

The streets had become busier and it became necessary to close the gap between himself and the doctor. Lolling his head back and forth like an addict, the coolie started to whistle tunelessly as he quickened his pace. The doctor seemed more determined, with a fresh objective in mind. The atmosphere had grown darker and it was apparent the rain would soon begin again.

Then, abruptly, the doctor stopped. He stood for a moment in his tracks before he turned and started back in the opposite direction. He did not run as he had done once before, below the market, but he was as close to running as he could be and still be walking. The coolie glanced at him and then looked back to where they had been. Something in the manner of the action indicated that neither forgetfulness nor sudden inspiration had prompted the change of mind and movement. There had been something seen. The coolie looked carefully at the two cafés on the parallel corners of the street. The curbs were lined with empty *cyclos*. A few peddlers moved their carts along, and some Annamite girls strolled by. There were no Europeans, either on the sidewalks or in the cafés. The tables were populated mostly by young men, students, the coolie surmised, who sat in threes and fours, though there were some pairs, such as the two older men on the far side who looked like merchants settling a transaction. One of the two had a blemish on his face. It was worth remembering. Such things were always worth remembering, the coolie told himself, except that they cluttered the mind. One feature of one face, nevertheless, was all one needed. With a last embracing look, the coolie swung around and hurried after the doctor, whose brown suit he could still glimpse ahead. The rain, in a half-horizontal mist, had resumed.

2

Cau Minh Thien had come back into the city in midmorning. He had drifted through the market on his way to the waterfront and had found the political officer near the cloth-vendors. Not that he had been looking for the political officer—on the contrary, he had hoped not to see him—but he had considered it a point of proper caution to extend this much of an effort. The political officer had immediately insisted they have a *filtre*. "It is a luxury for me," he had said, grinning. "I will tell my friends in the forest that I have been subverted by bourgeois habits."

Cau had taken him out of the area of the market to the café he knew was relatively safe, where the students of the military school gathered. The political officer seemed in a happy frame of mind— considerably more so at least than when Cau had seen him before— and Cau had taken advantage of the condition to remark that apparently there had been success in arranging matters with the Chinese, Li Kwan-sen. The political officer actually smiled.

"It was accomplished," he said. "I did not anticipate any further difficulty." He had emphasized the word "further."

"And what did you think of our Chinese friend?" Cau asked.

The political officer considered the question. "He is a shrewd man," he replied. "I imagine he has been extremely helpful in his various capacities."

"And what are they?" Cau persisted, blandly. He was enjoying himself.

The political officer looked queerly across the table, then smiled again. "That is something for you to have comprehended by now," he said.

"You are closer to the north and to the Chinese question, and you are accustomed to dealing with politics," Cau said. "I am only an instrument of action."

The political officer accepted the compliment. "He is a hard man

◇◇

to judge," he said. "It is likely, of course, that he is more than he seems."

"When one builds a bridge, there are many who would use it," Cau said.

The political officer said nothing for a moment and then declared, "There is a time for consolidation, after one has strengthened one's own position. Now there is a solid front from the north to the south, from Peking to Saigon." He was purposely testing Cau's reaction, and Cau was aware of it.

"One must still conduct one's own affairs," he replied. "In spite of all that has occurred, the Chinese remain Chinese."

The face of the political officer tightened visibly. He nodded, as if he were accepting a confession rather than agreeing. "It is good that we can get the help of friends when it is given so that we may meet the greatest enemy at equal strength," he said. "It is the Americans who have forced such decisions upon us."

"One must still be careful," Cau said, "or the identity of those who have conducted the long struggle will grow dimmer."

The political officer fingered the pewter *filtre*-holder. What Cau Minh Thien was saying clearly proved the point: he and those like him were an extremity of the revolutionary body, belonging to the whole but always separated from the central system.

He changed the subject.

"I have some other tasks," he began, "involving matters of security." He waited, but Cau's face remained expressionless. "There is concern over the traitors, particularly over those who have fled recently from the liberated areas."

Cau said nothing.

"It is natural that some of them would run for Saigon, since it remains the citadel of the enemy," the political officer continued, with a smirk. "There are certain of these scoundrels I am anxious to find."

"Your duties are manifold," Cau murmured.

<><><><><><><><><><><><><><><><><><><><><><><><><><><><><><><><><><><><>

The political officer pursed his lips. "This is also a political question," he said. "Not one of terror."

"What will you do when you find them?" Cau asked.

"That must be carefully considered, not only in the light of what they are doing, but with respect to what they can do and with the possibilities of reclamation and re-education also in mind," the political officer said. He stopped and looked directly at Cau. "It is something that has not yet been fully determined."

"We have always settled these things here more simply," Cau said.

"When the revolution approaches its climax," the political officer responded sharply, "there are new complications. One cannot simply function with a grenade in one's hand."

"We all have our peculiar heritage," Cau said, flatly.

The political officer nodded again. "The matter of the deserters, however, is not merely one of obtaining revenge."

"If there is a danger, it is wise to act with promptness."

"Tactics and strategy are not always logically connected."

"I do not understand such logic," Cau said.

"At any rate," the political officer went on, "I have my job to do. Have you any information about the renegades?"

"I have no information," Cau said.

"Perhaps some of your people have."

"One does not keep such things a secret. I would be told."

The political officer considered Cau's reply carefully. "If there is knowledge," he said slowly, "I would ask to be told—and ask that you restrain your comrades."

Now Cau maintained his silence for at least half a minute. Gazing at the street, he thought of the man below the European veranda, whom he had mentioned to Genevieve, and then seen again outside the Chinese hotel. There would be reports coming in as soon as the object took steps to reidentify himself. It had happened before, in the same sequence of time, and Cau had estimated that between the point of arrival and identification, of alliance with the puppet government, something like a fortnight usually went by.

He turned back and confronted the political officer's frown. "It is still a local affair," he said, bluntly. "It is impossible for me to make such promises."

The pocks on the political officer's face seemed suddenly to stand out. "You would be unwise," he said quietly. "It is more than a request."

"Perhaps," Cau said. "But I have not been told."

The political officer appeared to debate with himself. "I admire your sense of discipline," he replied finally. "But you must take my word."

Cau stared at the table. "I will make inquiries with our cadres of the Committee of the South, who are in touch with the north," he said flatly.

"I had not forgotten that either," the political officer said, and he no longer made any attempt to hide his anger. "But they will not yet know what I am telling you now."

"At any rate, it is worth discovering," Cau said.

The students had started to disperse and the tables nearby were left unoccupied.

"We had better go," Cau added.

He placed some piasters beneath the sugar-bowl and sauntered out behind the political officer. They shook hands formally on the sidewalk and, without further words, went off briskly in opposite directions through the warm, diagonal rain.

Chapter XIX

Iᴛ ᴡᴀs half past two when Adam drove into the Cercle Sportif. He scarcely expected to find Genevieve there, mixing casually over coffee and cognac on a rainy afternoon, but it was not until he actually saw him that he realized he was searching for M. Remy as much as for her.

Remy having spotted him first, Adam was at once aware that he had acted according to plan: Remy's. The Frenchman looked almost benign as he walked over. Against the gray sky and the dark, rain-soaked stucco, the yellow smile seemed less periolous than usual.

"You are waiting for someone, *Monsieur le Consul?*" he asked.

"Perhaps," Adam said.

"I have not seen her, unfortunately," Remy said.

Now Adam smiled. "It's hard to keep track of everyone," he replied. "Even for a man with many eyes."

Remy was staring at the pool, bluer than it had been and fragmented by ripples. "You will not swim today? I am told the Americans swim when it rains." He was being his blandest.

"Another wild rumor," Adam murmured, gazing about.

Remy shrugged. "About the Americans," he said, "one still wishes to believe anything. It is as poor a day, at any rate, for sitting in offices as for swimming. Come, we shall have a *filtre*."

They found a table, and Remy summoned the Tonkinese. Adam ordered a sandwich as well. For some time both men were silent, and then Remy said, "She is an attractive girl, that one."

Adam took the bait lightly. "Which one?" he said, lifting his head.

"No, no—Madame—Brouillard is it?"

Adam laughed. "Come, you've certainly got her dossiered."

Remy squeezed his chin reflectively, maintaining a grimace. "One cannot be too careful at present," he mused.

"When one accuses—"

With no show of embarrassment, Remy said: "It is always best to be preventive."

"Where does the suspicion start? Because she's Eurasian?"

Again Remy shrugged. "It remains a possibility. The quality of deprivation, a confusion of purpose."

"A natural catalogue," Adam said. "Anyone's prescription."

"Perhaps there are other reasons to suspect."

Adam cleared his throat. "If there are, why not speak directly, instead of—?"

Remy picked it up at once. "The reference was purely oblique," he replied. "A simple projection."

"Syllogistic, I'm sure," Adam said. He munched the sandwich, staring into the water. The explanation had been expected. He was more certain than ever of his surmise, that she was Remy's conscious weapon, but he would keep that to himself.

"It is an example of what we are confronted with," Remy continued. "You will admit the opportunity that lies on their side?"

"As you say, she's attractive," Adam said, agreeably. "Ergo, all attractive girls are spies. Tell me, what do you think she could discover from me? That is, as compared to what I might find out from her?"

"It is unwise to place oneself against a woman in such matters," Remy said, dryly.

Adam again laughed. "That's a nice way of putting it."

Remy was blowing smoke out over the pool. "Many battles are lost in bistros and in beds," he said.

Adam did not reply. Remy's motives had become clear enough, but his tactics remained puzzling. Unless he had more knowledge

◇◇◇

than was likely of Adam's relations with the Minister, the risk of using Genevieve so bluntly would seem obvious. Once more Adam thought of the doctor. Remy's silence was worth probing.

"How about the others, the males?" he asked. "How does it go with the renegades?"

The Frenchman snorted. "The female is more subtle. The male of the species is a dreamer. He meanders. Sooner or later, foolishly, he gives himself away."

"You have pinned them all down, then?"

"Not altogether, but there will be no difficulty."

"And they are all spies, you are convinced of it?"

"I am convinced of nothing," Remy said. "I am never convinced until the logic of events permits no other conclusion. My *logique* combines patience with skepticism."

"*Logique*," Adam repeated. "It is a word with a greater French meaning. System, scope, purpose, more than a mere mathematics of ideas. With a *logique*, one can do anything, one is irresistible."

Remy coughed lightly. "You have your money, we have our *logique*," he said.

"It's not exactly the same, but there's a basis for comparison," Adam replied. He waited a moment and asked: "Have you arrested any of them yet?"

"It is actually a Vietnamese affair," Remy said. "I have not yet looked at the latest lists." He was being impish.

"I won't detain you," Adam said, rising. "I've got to get back myself. Thank you."

Remy stood up and shook Adam's hand. "It is always a pleasure."

"I'll keep you posted," Adam said.

He walked quickly down the steps, knowing Remy's eyes were on him. At the outside gate he turned and saw the Frenchmen at the stone balustrade, gazing out on the lawn and the street. Adam was aware of the ludicrousness of what he was doing, but he waved. And, even more ludicrously, Paul Remy waved back.

◇◇

2

AT THE Sûreté the Vietnamese inspector was waiting impatiently. It was typical of them, he thought, a good example of the fact that, even with the administrative turnover, the old attitude remained, an imperious contempt for local time.

The coolie lay on his back on the wooden bench by the window, his eyes closed. The inspector had given him permission. He was the most reliable man the inspector had and entitled to small favors. Besides, one had to sympathize because of the nature of the assignment. If the inspector had had his way, had he been able to act, that is, as independently as he was theoretically entitled to act, he would not have set the doctor free to begin with. Certainly not at once. But M. Remy's motives were always ulterior, and sufficient unto themselves.

Now he was finally arriving. The inspector heard his step in the hall. Remy opened the door and entered briskly. He said nothing about being late. "Well, then?" he asked. "Where is he?"

The inspector pointed to where the coolie was stretched out. Lifting himself like an automaton, the coolie sat up stiffly and yawned, after which he stared impassively across the room. From a trouser pocket he took out two small, dirty slips of paper. He walked over and handed one to M. Remy, then went back to the ledge with the other in his hand.

"Go ahead," Remy said, and he sat down on the edge of the inspector's desk, a leg swung over the corner.

The coolie recited the movements of the doctor as if he were rendering an incantation, referring only now and then to his grimy memorandum. Remy and the inspector listened thoughtfully, and when the account was finished Remy pursed his lips and moved his suspended leg back and forth in a slow dangle. He asked the coolie to repeat the episode in the Consul's garden.

◇◇

"You are quite certain you were not seen yourself?" he asked. The coolie ignored the question.

"He is the best of them," the inspector said, from the back of the desk.

There was a silence and then the inspector asked: "There is enough information, then—no need to continue?" He made it sound only partly like a question.

"On the contrary," Remy said. "We will maintain the surveillance." He examined the folded piece of paper the coolie had given him.

The inspector grunted. "What is the purpose?" he inquired. "He has made no effort to establish himself. He does not accept the Emperor's authority. It is dangerous to allow him to wander this way indefinitely."

"I did not suggest it would be indefinite," Remy replied, without turning.

"If he is not a spy, he is a meddler," the inspector said. "It is as bad."

Remy smiled thinly. "To determine the way of the meddling is also a purpose."

The inspector made no further response. The coolie was still motionless on the window-bank. Now Remy spoke to him.

"Tomorrow I will require another report. Perhaps then we shall stop," he said.

He turned back at last to look at the inspector. "That will be acceptable?"

The inspector sat stonily. Without moving his head and not meeting the Frenchman's eye, he said one word only: "Yes."

Remy stood up. "Until tomorrow, then." He thrust out his hand, which the inspector took, and walked out.

The coolie gathered himself up and went soundlessly toward the door. His silk suit hung loosely on his lithe frame, and the sheen of it was like dark glass. At the door he paused and, with a hand resting on the knob, turned, with remarkable gracefulness, toward the room. The inspector nodded once, his bullet-shaped head moving in the way of a hinge, and the coolie slid out.

3

FROM three thirty, when he returned to the Legation, until after five o'clock, Adam sat at his desk without working. There were reports from Hanoi and from Vientiane and a large sheaf of general routine business, but he let all of it stay in separate piles in front of him. He looked outside. There was a sulphurous hue in the sky, as if a gas had been let loose on the city.

He spoke to no one, not even to his secretary. Nell Finch did not come to see him. The phone did not ring. The fact that the Minister did not call did not surprise him. If the subject of the doctor came up, it would only be in larger context, a part to be fitted into the whole, depending on far more than his having acted informally in the doctor's behalf. Yet a pattern was becoming discernible.

At five thirty Adam left and drove to Genevieve's house. Under the circumstances, on top of Remy's superciliousness, he had to test her further. Between the Minister's oddly couched admonition and the unreal, even surrealistic experience of listening to her conversation with Nell from behind the bamboo screen of his own bedroom, he had already formed a new and filmy conception of her. It was as if she were being returned to him in small, separate, and distorted doses, sifted through others' eyes, almost autopsied. . . . There were living things he had to rediscover for himself.

She greeted him with coolness, extending her hand fendingly. When he sat on the couch, she took a chair opposite.

"I went looking for you this afternoon," he said. "I'm sorry I missed you before."

"I was unable to wait. Also, you were occupied."

"Only in a fashion," he replied.

"You have a good secretary for protection."

"She is not my secretary."

Genevieve smiled. "She is still your protector," she said. "Are American girls always jealous?"

"Frequently. There is a greater possessiveness."

"That is a mistake."

"Usually." He paused. "What made you come by?"

"I was on my way here."

Adam hesitated. He would make the test a proper one, and not necessarily unpleasant. He had not given the Minister any promises, nor had the Minister asked for any. If Remy's bluff had to be called, it would better be done on home ground. The Frenchman's response could be gauged by the Minister's in the morning.

"Shall we drive back?" he asked.

He thought that her eyelids fluttered a little unusually. "If you like," she said, and promptly got up. He was no longer surprised at the shifts of her mood. She remained predictably unpredictable.

"I went to the pool afterward," he said, when they were in the car, "thinking you might be there."

"I am a worshipper only of the sun."

"All I found was our friend Monsieur Remy."

Genevieve did not pick this up.

"He seemed to assume I was hunting for you," Adam went on.

"He is a man of many assumptions," she murmured.

"I did not realize you comprehended him so well," he said.

"It is a quality that is not difficult to discern."

"Then you really have met him before?"

She was staring ahead. "He has been in Saigon a long time, you know."

"Since the end of the war, yes."

"The city is not so large. One meets many people casually, but without importance."

"Monsieur Remy is not one of the casual ones."

Genevieve waited, but only for a few seconds. "He is an important man, of course," she said. "But, in our case, we have met unimportantly."

He let another moment pass. Then, with a broad grin, he said measuredly: "I had thought perhaps you were reporting to him directly."

She countered quickly. "Oh, no, he is too important for that, for the likes of me." Her laughter, for the first time, sounded strained to Adam.

"I have the feeling, nevertheless, that he has a high opinion of you."

"I am pleased to hear it."

"You will be promoted."

Adam parked the car at the front of his driveway and helped her across a row of puddles. The mood of playfulness had passed and there was a look on her face that was at once abstracted and pained. He caught a reflection of her figure in one of the pools, the false shape of her wavering among the shimmering branches of the trees. The distorted image resembled an old woman pulling her hair in a black night. He hurried across, stepping on islands of mud.

The electricity was off and the boy had put candles out. Adam lit them and distributed them around the room so they exuded an even white glow that was like the suffused pallor in a Chinese rainscape. Genevieve sat pensively on the couch.

"What are you dreaming about?" he asked, bringing the familiar small pitcher to the low table.

"The chronic malady," she said. "Oneself."

"We manufacture loneliness," he said. "We generate it, and sustain it in self-pity." He reached for her hand. "Enuring and enduring, it's all a matter of adjustment."

Whatever her purpose, she was indulging her third self, he thought, the part that willfully hovered. Her hand lay limply in his.

"One must continue the struggle to identify," she said. "You were right about that."

Adam remembered, disquietingly, Remy's comment at the pool. "You've managed yours so far," he said. Her fingers were suddenly more pliant, and she offered him one of her mystifying smiles, half childlike, half oracular.

"Not yet," she said. "Time will run out."

"You're the one, this afternoon, professing doom."

"One grows more possessed with self, but perhaps not self-possessed."

He wondered why she was dramatizing herself. If, in Remy's interests, she had all along been seeking this greater confidence, their love-making had been premature.

"We've got to know ourselves first," Adam said. "All the philosophers agree."

Genevieve murmured something that sounded Annamese.

"Have you ever thought of seeking this identity—elsewhere?" He had managed the question spontaneously and now he followed it up at once: "That is, under the circumstances of rebellion?"

She laughed, gaily once more. "Perhaps I shall end by joining the Catholic sects. Monsieur Remy must also be curious about the bishoprics of the delta."

"You should always strive to please," Adam said, flatly.

"Do you think they would accept me?"

"A natural candidate for sainthood."

"I shall consider it, then," she said. "I would not be the first convert."

"The first in Indo-China perhaps, under such circumstances."

"It is a small salient, this."

"There are no salients that are small in the eyes of Rome." He waited only a moment. "What about the Vietminh?"

He watched her carefully at the same time that he reached down for the pitcher.

Her glance had shifted to the window. "The Vietminh is death." Her voice was in her throat. "There is no salvation there."

◇◇◇

Gently, Adam drew her to him. Her head rested on his shoulder, but now, in a gesture of unexpected boldness, she raised herself and placed her arms around him. They stayed where they were, in quiet half-embrace. The rain was falling faster, but as an overwhelming mist. Adam felt himself restrained, as if, by advancing, he would lose a certain supremacy. It was not caution that held him back, but a new and sudden fear he could not define, in which he recognized intimations of both impotence and grief.

Their silence was sustained; a sense of contest encroached, and then at once receded. The servants were nowhere. A siren wailed on the river, and the sound of a far-away bell, as of an animal lost, floated across the air. Adam felt himself transported, an impression of himself only, inanimate as wax. Genevieve's breathing alone was close at hand. What a way to die, he thought, an easeful sinking from immobility into oblivion itself, a painless tapping of blood like sap released from a tree into the bottomless bucket of time. And then, quietly but becoming quickly louder until it seemed to fill not only his body but hers too, the beating of his heart mounted again and he could feel the blood surge back through its arterial branches. With it came a return of desire, flowing into his limbs.

He heard a sound of footsteps on the wet gravel, and the wild thought that it might be Paul Remy shot through his brain. It would be an intrusion on many levels, such as Remy was gloriously capable of making; but it could only be one of the boys moving toward the hut in the rear. Genevieve was smiling her customary smile, her mouth purple in the dimness of the dusk. The new energy he felt, and a new mastery of himself, allowed a tender burgeoning; he was about to enfold her when he heard, incontrovertibly, the single sound he least expected or wanted to hear, the doctor's voice.

It was outside in the garden. "Monsieur Patch—hello," it said, and then, somewhat closer, throbbing: "Monsieur Patch—may I speak with you?"

The candles had gone out. Adam hadn't noticed until he stood up and went to the door. The doctor was directly below. He was carrying an umbrella which he held high over his head. His suit was wrinkled and he had his trousers rolled up.

"Dr. Dang," Adam said softly.

Tran stepped into the house. He didn't see Genevieve for some seconds. When he did, he turned to Adam with his embarrassment. Adam took his arm and conducted him toward the couch.

"Madame Brouillard"—he hesitated only briefly—"a friend of mine from the north, Dr. Hinh."

"How do you do, doctor," Genevieve said.

"I am very sorry to intrude," Tran said. "It is very rude of me."

"It's quite all right," Adam said. "Please sit down."

"Perhaps for a few moments."

Adam looked at Genevieve and then again at Tran. He wondered if the doctor had recognized her from the time before, in the garden. "Has anything happened?" he asked.

Tran did not reply and seemed not to have heard the question. He was sitting on the far end of the couch, with Adam opposite, leaning forward from the straight-backed chair. Now Genevieve got up and went to relight the candles.

"That's a good idea," Adam said. Again he inclined himself toward the doctor. "What is it?" he asked.

Tran took an envelope from the inside pocket of his jacket and handed it to Adam. It was addressed to the Chinese hotel and had the ECA stamp in the upper left-hand corner.

"I spoke with Mr. Kelly this morning," Tran said. "This afternoon the letter came."

Adam opened the envelope, which he laid alongside the pitcher. He unfolded the typewritten sheet he had withdrawn.

Dear Doctor Dang [it said]:
Our plans have been delayed and I must tell you there is a probability that we will not be able to carry them out at the present time. It

◇◇

would be advisable, for all concerned but especially for yourself, if you did not come to this office again for the present. Unforeseen events have arisen which I cannot fully explain now. Please be assured, however, that I shall do my best to overcome these difficulties.

Yours very truly,
Irving Lockman

Adam read the letter through once more and then handed it back to the doctor. "I think I know what the trouble is," he said.

"I am sorry to disturb you some more," Tran said. "But, you see—"

"I know," Adam said. "You don't have to apologize."

Tran looked sharply at Adam and then at Genevieve, who had finished with the candles and was standing with her back to the room at the garden window.

"It's all right," Adam said.

Whatever she knew, whatever Remy might have told her, he was suddenly certain that the visit of the doctor would not go unreported. If the Frenchman's challenge was to be accepted, if the doctor had to be involved by having involved himself—the letter had surely altered the circumstances already—the results could still be firm, firmer, certainly, than had seemed possible when he had heard the doctor's voice, like a lost soul, in the garden. For reasons as various as they begged to be resolved, Adam now knew what he had to do.

Genevieve was slowly walking back toward the couch. The doctor's eyes were following her across the floor, and Adam watched him.

Gently he said: "There's still time, you know, in the indefinite country."

Tran smiled, and Adam smiled with him. "We'll see how serious this is right now," he added. He turned to Genevieve. "I've got a short call to make, but it won't take long," he said.

She betrayed no expression. Her glance went from the visitor back to Adam across the table.

"Consulting physician," he said, with a twinkle. "For internal disorders only."

"I have an errand I can do," she said. "I should have done it before."

"Where?"

"Near the center of the city. It is not far."

He held back a brief moment and then suggested: "Suppose I drop you, and then pick you up on the way back."

"Very well," she agreed, "but I will return alone, afterward."

"I won't be more than half an hour. . . ."

The three of them drove in silence to the cathedral square, where Genevieve asked to be let off. Adam saw her move in the direction of rue Catinat as he made a half-turn ahead to Lockman's.

"She is French?" Tran asked.

"By inclination, not always by temperament. Her mother was, and a husband."

"That is how it often is," Tran said. "There is a schizophrenia of the soul."

Adam laughed. "I didn't know you were a psychoanalyst also," he said.

"In the jungle," said the doctor, "one is everything. Priest and veterinary as well."

Chapter XX

A T THE top of rue Catinat, Genevieve hailed a *cyclo*. She motioned to the boy to swing about and told him to pedal quickly. In less than ten minutes, having waved him all the way, she ordered him to stop at an intersection. After he had disappeared she walked down the block and through the gate and garden of Adam's house.

She stood for a moment in the doorway. There was no sign of anyone, and no sound. The empty pitcher was still on the low table. The candles had gone out again (Genevieve reflected, with a house-keeper's odd awareness, that they should have put them out before leaving). She stepped toward the table and saw the envelope still lying there. Hurriedly, and without looking at the name, she folded it in half and slipped it into the pocket of her dress. But when she had sat down, with this done, she took it out again, as her own, and studied it. "Dr. Tran Phan Dang, Nienh-po Hotel, Cholon," the address read. The ECA stamp in the upper left-hand corner was partly blotted out by whisky.

Her feeling of unreality transcended her nervousness at being in the room alone. Pleased with herself for remembering the envelope, she had made a game and a test of the act of purloining. It would have been easier had she simply stayed and waited for the Consul, but part of the game, and of the unreality too, had driven her to create the fiction of the errand; so that, by leaving and returning, not only had she been able to render herself a clandestine fillip but, out of pride, she felt better as a woman also. It was a kind of rehearsal, except that she was not yet sure what she was rehearsing, beyond secrecy itself. She had scarcely considered the envelope as a rewarding object; but now she was struck by the fact that the name on it was not the one the Consul had used when he had introduced the doctor. Annoyed, she took it out for a second time and stared at it, almost sullenly, as if it had betrayed her. She had forgotten what the other name was. An image of Cau and Remy, shaking their heads in mutual dismay, made her burst out laughing. She remembered, at least, the sound of the name the Consul had spoken, and that it had been different. She considered him again, the stranger. There had been a shy quality she had liked, a sense of gentle loneliness; perhaps because, like herself, he had seemed to be searching for something. The Consul's also gentle response had heightened the impression; with his defenses down she had felt closer to him too, watching him and listening to him, closer in a way than she when he had held her, which remained an altogether separate challenge.

She had still to test both deprivation and desire against the finality of her decision. Its impetus, the manner of choice, the technique of Cau Minh Thien, all seemed part of a lesson learned in a long yesterday, to be suddenly applied now. In the Consul's house, awaiting his return, the envelope in her pocket was also aphrodisiac.

The phone rang and Genevieve jumped. She let it ring several times and then walked over to the sideboard and answered with her voice pitched unnaturally low. "Mr. Patch's residence—"

"Hello, I thought it might be you," he said.

Genevieve said nothing.

"Hello?" the Consul asked. "Genevieve?"

"I just—" she began, and stopped. "No one is here. The house is empty."

"Except you," he said. "Those damn boys." He waited, but she remained silent. "Look, I'll be back soon," he said. "Have a drink.

Take a nap. Don't run away—this time." His laugh was as boyish as when she had heard it for the first time, at the pool.

"All right," she said, with her own voice again. "If it is not too long."

"We're almost through operating." There was another laugh.

She hung up first.

For several moments she walked through the room. Her body felt unrelated to her thoughts, which were rebellious. She was angry, not at him, but at herself, for having put herself, by answering the phone, in the position of a mistress in his house. By calling, he had done no more, she knew, than fulfill the functions of the male, to arrange and importune. She was disturbed also because she had been caught coincidentally in her own dilemma. And now she saw the extent to which love was bound to be lost, remembering Cau's handclasp in the dark. . . .

She stopped walking and in the same instance knew someone was in the room with her. Slowly, she turned, and at the door of the kitchen saw the Chinese houseboy. He was a man of indeterminate age, forty perhaps, and his rather smoothly handsome face had the quality of inexpression that Westerners liked to call inscrutable. He was watching her, curiously, patiently.

"Master?" he asked.

"Master come back," she said, with intentional Western inflection. "Master go out, come back soon."

"Missy hungry?" He, too, was willing to play the game.

"No," she said. "No, thank you. I'll wait for him to come."

The boy bowed, and darted in to clear away the paraphernalia of drinking. She moved to the window, beyond the couch, to escape the completeness of his eyes. When he had disappeared into the kitchen she walked back into the center of the room, where there was a light breeze. She could hear the rain's surrounding hush and could smell the monsoon on the river, with its vague odor of turbulence and fish. The city seemed far off, the house an island in a separate estuary. Except for the sound of the rain there was nothing but the coming and going of her breath. She was suddenly very sleepy and, moving stiffly, almost primly, she went into the Consul's darkened bedroom and lay down.

She slept, or seemed to have slept, for she was roused by a ringing again. It was a different ringing, more muffled than before, but then she realized it came from the phone's extension next to the bed. How like the Consul, she thought, to have two of them! It rang four times, after which she heard the houseboy answering inside. She waited several seconds before she quietly lifted the receiver below her. At once she recognized the voice of the girl from the Legation.

"Where is he?" Nell was asking. "Didn't he say where he was going?" The voice had a curious metallic quality the old Japanese phone accentuated.

"Mr. Patch come back soon," the Chinese replied.

"It's very important, I've got to see him," Nell said.

"Master not here," the boy repeated.

Nell paused, and added, flatly: "I'll come and wait for him, then."

Genevieve buried the phone in the pillow to take a deeper breath. She lifted it in time to hear Nell's voice again: "You say you don't know if he's coming back? But you just said soon?"

The houseboy stammered. "Master not say for sure. Maybe come—dinnertime."

"You're no help," Nell exclaimed. "I'll come and take my chances."

She hung up before the houseboy could say anything else.

Genevieve replaced the receiver carefully. She lay on her back, with her eyes closed, until she knew the boy was in the doorway, staring at her. She turned and saw him sheepishly grinning.

"Master not come back. Come back later," he said.

"How do you know?"

"Master telephone. You hear ring?"

"I heard it," she said.

"If you want go, maybe come back later also, I tell master."

Genevieve let herself smile. His smile lingered, until his eyes moved to the phone on the floor and then swiftly back to her.

"Missy sleep?" he asked, anxiously.

"A little," she said.

"Rain stop."

"That's good."

He hovered another moment and then was gone. When she stood up and put her shoes on she heard him rummaging in the kitchen. She walked out into the living-room. The breeze through the middle had gone. It was growing darker, with a ubiquitous grayness, mist-soaked, advancing in visible layers to the fall of night. The rustling in the kitchen stopped and Genevieve knew he was waiting. She went slowly to the door, opened it, hesitated a final moment, and, letting it slam, ran through the garden and beyond the gate without looking back.

The street, at the end of it, was empty. She walked three more blocks before she found a *cyclo*. After telling the boy where to go, she sat with her face lifted to the mist. There was nothing worth thinking. She wanted only to act, and to act immediately, so that it would be done simultaneously with the Consul's return and his discovery, in her place, of the American. The *cyclo* swayed through the gray-green streets, and Genevieve let herself sway with it. The boy pedaling seemed carried away by the momentum, lending himself to her flight in a kind of rain-spun euphoria. Her head still back, Genevieve could see the edges of his hat flopping and could hear his heavy breathing and catch a glimpse of his chest glisten and heave beneath the open shirt. There was a smell of grease and sweat and old-canvas grime of the vehicle's hood behind her.

He slowed and stared at the row of dim shops. Then he

◇◇◇

climbed down and began to walk the *cyclo*. Finally he grunted.

"Is this the place?" she asked.

He grunted again, and when she paid him with a generous tip, he went away quickly, with only a brief stare at her standing there, his long wet legs pumping.

It was impossible to tell from the shutters that it was a tobacconist's shop, but when she knocked on the boarded door the face of the tobacconist himself peered out. He let her in at once and closed the door after her.

"You were seen?" he whispered.

"No."

"You came by *cyclo*?"

"Yes."

"And waited?"

"Yes."

He motioned to her to sit down and went behind the counter. In another moment, almost ritualistically, he brought forth a cup of steaming tea and moved it across the cracked counter-glass.

"Cum-sha?" She smiled.

"Cum-sha," he said. "In the monsoon, the cum-sha is hot."

He brought up a cup for himself and sat down on a stool, so that only the top of his head was showing. Genevieve felt as if she were consulting a fortune-teller. She gazed across the counter-top at him, and then down through the dark glass at the assortment of pipes, cigars, cigarettes, and silver cigarette-cases. In the glow of a candle set on a rear shelf, the tobacco glistened wetly.

"I did not expect to see you so soon," the tobacconist said. He was lighting a pipe.

Genevieve moved her head, studying the rest of the shop. There was a small door in the rear, but only more darkness beyond. She wondered if he slept here, alone, or if he had a family somewhere. The sweet pipe smell floated up at her and she let it penetrate.

"Will he come?" she asked.

The tobacconist puffed away. She could see the ember in the pipe-bowl drop and rise.

"When he is in the city, he comes at this hour," he said. "Perhaps a little later."

He looked up at her. "Is there something you have—something to give?"

Genevieve shook her head. "No, only that I wish to speak with him."

The tobacconist had lowered his face again. He sat with his legs straddling the backless stool, the pipe once more between his lips, sucking it and ruminating.

"He is destroying himself, with his constant coming and going," he said softly. "He is possessed with a particular demon."

Genevieve was surprised at the odd paternal tone. "He lives in one way only. He could not live in another," she said.

"He is the tiger who is held by the tail."

"And who holds him?"

"It is hard to tell. There are many demons now."

"Perhaps there is more than one that holds, more than one for all of us."

He had raised his face again and was looking at her with a curious expression. "And yourself, Madame Brouillard? How many to hold you?"

He was not being unmannerly. "It is better when there is one only, I imagine, held or holding," she replied. "But in Indo-China it is complicated." She did not pursue it.

The tobacconist nodded. "That is true," he said. "It is one of the troubles with Vietnam. That too many ride too many tigers, in various directions at once. It has always been so, but the men are worse than the women."

"It is not only tiger-riding," she said. "There are the *attentistes*. Myself, perhaps." She paused reflectively. "The Americans have a phrase to go with *attentisme*, with what you speak of," she went on.

"There is not only a condition of sitting upon a fence, in the middle, but of mending the fence as well, to make the best use that can be made of it."

"An encouragement for traitors."

"There are many opportunists also."

Again he nodded. "I have heard of those who trade on all sides, in the cities and in the forests as well now." He knocked the pipe on the floor to empty it, and the smell of ashes rose less sweetly toward her.

Genevieve found herself thinking about Lacasse. Surely his behavior was involved with his fear. Opportunism without bravery, without proper bravado at least, was cowardice purely. But also dangerous, in the way of a woman crossed. Lacasse, she realized, beyond sexuality, was womanish.

She was so comfortable where she was, feeling unexpectedly at home here, that her flight from the Consul's house seemed less shameful. What if she told this old man about it, this tobacco philosopher? Would he believe her?

"He is one of those truly dedicated, so one must give him his due," he murmured. "Yet he is filled with anger and impatience."

It took her a moment to return to Cau. She remembered the conversation in the night club.

"Will he come this late?" she asked abruptly.

The tobacconist pondered. "I have the feeling he will come," he replied.

"That is a dangerous activity, to feel, to divine," she said, and laughed down at him. "Counterrevolutionary. At any rate, I can wait no longer."

She wondered why she had said so, since she had nowhere to go. What she did want was time, however, even a little, and now her need for it was greater than when she had first come into the shop, still caught up in flight.

◇◇◇

"If you will tell him—" she began, and hesitated. "Tell him, if he comes, that I will be—in Cholon."

"No one, especially this one, can meet at such an hour. It is too early."

"Eleven then, or midnight."

"I will say eleven, if he arrives," the tobacconist said. He had refilled his pipe and was bringing a match to it.

Genevieve got down off her stool.

"It has been a pleasure, madame," he said, with formality. They found themselves in the sudden, geographic position of customer and owner.

"You have an excellent shop," she said. "I like it for the reason that the smells of it are good."

"I have been here thirty years," he said, simply again.

"You are at home in it, and make others so."

"Go quietly," he said, "in the manner that you came."

Before she was aware of it, he had opened the door and ushered her onto the street. She walked away, the mist once more seeming to carry her. The street was black, except for a single light at the curb a hundred yards ahead. And then again Genevieve found herself running.

2

ALL during the long afternoon, with its intermittent rain always catching him on the move, Cau Minh Thien had darted around the two cities on his multifarious errands. He had managed to visit all but three of the squads that were under his command, and for the first time in several weeks he felt a degree of satisfaction over the tightness of the organization and the discipline he had re-established. The stocks of grenades, in view of the general shortage and the inadequacy still of the local brand, were well up; the availability of cyclists was adequate, while the shock troops themselves, the out-posts of the *Tu Ve*, were no longer so undermanned. All in all, Cau considered it a propitious moment for the new assaults, which were to coincide with the general strike of utility workers. Now, at the end of the day, he was even ready to admit that he was tired.

He had stopped for some raw fish and tea at a small restaurant on the edge of Cholon, near the arroyo, and having let himself rest, smoking a cigarette with his eyes closed, the smoke acrid but pain-fully delicious in his nostrils, he felt the fatigue steal through his body; in ambush upon ambush, it captured his last resources, his own outposts of energy. He had still, he reminded himself, to go to the tobacco shop. There also remained, in the back of his mind, the annoying matter posed by the political officer. Even if he chose to regard what had been said as a bluff, it would be wise, none the less, to discuss it with one or two men of the liaison cadres. The political officer was no threat, as far as Cau was concerned. He created a tactical problem only, setting up fresh possibilities of response. Cau had always looked upon the deserters from the north as controllable elements. They had been so easily frightened, their spirits already broken, that only rarely had it been necessary to go beyond surveillance, which, in a number of cases, had offered its own rewards in point of patience. When harsher solutions had been re-quired, they had been simply and quickly applied. The victims in most cases had by then all but asked to be removed from limbo.

Cau glanced at his watch. It was past nine. He paid his bill and walked across the second arroyo bridge. It was only raining lightly for the moment and he scarcely noticed it against his thoroughly damp clothes. He walked the half mile to the tobacconist's, who greeted him with unusual effusiveness, without any of the customary grouches. When the cups of tea were served, Cau twitted him about his good humor.

"There is always a reason," the tobacconist said. "In this case, I have received a visitation."

Cau looked up. "Genevieve?" he said, and then, quickly, he added: "Madame Brouillard?"

The tobacconist twitted him back. "We are competitors," he said. "I will not give her to you without a contest."

"You are an old man, without use for women," Cau replied tersely, with only a trace of a smile. "Aside from that, you misinterpret."

The tobacconist laughed up at him from his counter stool. "There are cracks in your armor after all." He waited a proper moment. "We discussed you."

Cau stared at him. "And what did the two of you decide?" he asked. "That I am more machine than man?"

The tobacconist was only briefly set back. "On the contrary," he replied sagely. "That you have a forest of tigers for mistresses."

Cau snorted. His hand brushed his cheek. He did not reply.

The tobacconist picked up the thread. "Perhaps you will find time for women," he said, "when the tigers set you loose."

"What did she want?" Cau asked.

The tobacconist grinned at him. "To see you. In the same place, tonight."

Cau looked around the shop, at the shelves behind the counter, where the nondescript boxes were heaped up, and then toward the inner blackness.

"Where do you keep them?" he asked. "The grenades."

The tobacconist pointed toward the rear. "The younger leaves are excellent preservatives," he said.

Cau snorted again. "How many are left?"

The tobacconist calculated. "At least three dozen."

"I will see that you get three dozen more," Cau said. "You will need them."

He got ready to go. The tobacconist stayed seated.

"The time comes close," Cau said. He opened the door a crack and, peering up and down the deserted street, slid out. Behind him, in the darkness, he heard the old man chortling. . . .

An hour later, reinvigorated, Cau debarked from a *cyclo* at Li Kwan-sen's. A self-conscious anticipation held him in the shadow of the club's curtain, away from the blue overhead light. He did not discern her at once, but then, far in the rear, he saw her, at a table with Li Kwan-sen himself. Cau tensed and sprang forward across the expanse of the empty dance-floor. He arrived in the midst of their chatter. Li stood up perfunctorily, still talking, now laughing. The opening blast of Carlos Porfiro's music drowned conversation out, but Cau sat down. In a matter of moments, with the music blaring, Li Kwan-sen excused himself, motioning for them to stay where they were. . . .

3

THE blocklike figure of Lacasse was pushing its way through the curtain. Before he knew what was happening, Li Kwan-sen was ushering him across the avenue to the gambling casino.

"We'll have some jasmine," Li said. "Afterward you will win your customary pittance."

In the office, Li immediately lit the joss-sticks. Lacasse had hoped he wouldn't, but said nothing, only bringing his handkerchief out and blowing his nose ostentatiously. Unlocking the desk, Li handed him a sealed white envelope. Lacasse fingered its bulk and dropped it into his outer jacket pocket.

"Someone will steal it—be careful," Li said. "I do not insure my customers against pickpockets, nor does the Binh Xuyen insure me."

Lacasse had every intention of counting the money as soon as he could, alone, and then putting it in his wallet. He fidgeted over the admonition, which had spoiled his attempt at a graceful acceptance. Li still made him feel like a child.

"I'm sure it's all there," he finally said, compounding the awkwardness.

Li laughed. "You can count it now, Jacques, if you want," he said.

Lacasse reddened. "I'm glad it worked well," he said. He took the envelope out and put it, still sealed, into his inside pocket.

Li nodded idly. "Your sampans are reliable," he said.

Lacasse thought of the various hands through which this money had passed, and would still pass. The *mystique* of money fascinated him, its peregrinations, its dwelling-places. He thought of it as having a special life of its own; the faces on coins and on bills came alive, and, more than the faces themselves, the body of a coin, the shape of a bill. In Lacasse's image, they acquired the aspect of nimble centaurs.

Who was there, he wondered, beyond Li Kwan-sen, at the source of what bulked in his pocket? In time he would find out from the boatmen, but now he preferred to wait, to ride along on Li's satisfaction. Simultaneously, on an entirely different level, a level envisaged in the odd double vision of Lacasse's mind as surrounded by tall pickets of protection, where men like M. Remy stood twenty-four-hour guard, he was still convinced, because he wanted to be, that guns were involved, and that their destination had been north.

"How is your cousin?" he asked abruptly.

"My cousin?" Li repeated. "I have many cousins."

Lacasse enjoyed a rare moment of supremacy. He flickered his fingers through the air. "The Vietnamese," he said. "The half-caste one, that is," he added, with a small-mouth grin.

Li's blank stare floated back into place. "Oh, that one," he said. "He is at the club again. His blood runs thick for pleasure."

Lacasse crossed and then uncrossed his legs. He sniffed the incense around his head and felt a brief giddiness. "He has a good eye," he said. "The Eurasian, the girl he was with before, is a pretty creature." He waited only a moment. "You said that you knew her?"

He remembered exactly what the Chinese had said the last time, but now he found Li's pause peculiarly deliberate. There was more than forgetting behind it.

"I met her tonight," he replied, at length, "but very briefly."

Lacasse mused. "These people all live in the night. The day is nothing to them."

Li was shuffling the papers on the desk. "And you? You are a man of the sun and the day, then?" He laughed, somewhat absently.

"A girl like that, for example," Lacasse went on, undaunted. "What does she do with herself? Where does she belong? To whom?"

"I do not know why you concern yourself," Li said softly.

"You will admit her attractiveness," Lacasse said as he smiled across the room. He felt almost elfin.

"You are too old for such mixtures, Jacques," Li said, looking up. "They are exotic, too rich for your blood. You require something stabler, someone who will take care of you when you retire with your gold to Corsica."

Lacasse coughed, and then he sneezed. "All of us require diversion," he said hoarsely. Again Li was silent. Lacasse still felt he was making progress. "And your cousin does nothing either?" he persisted.

"He is a surveyor," Li answered, shortly. "The war has naturally interfered with his business."

"An interesting profession," Lacasse murmured. "One gets to know the country." He smiled from his perch again. Li was standing up, closing the desk drawers.

"Well," the Chinese said, "I will release you to the tables. There are accounts to go over." He looked suddenly dismayed. "I have forgotten the jasmine," he said. "Forgive me. We will celebrate later. At the end as well as the beginning of bargains, one should drink champagne, ha?"

Lacasse lumbered up and walked to the door. "Perhaps you will introduce me to the girl," he said. "She interests me."

Li laughed. "We shall see," he said. "Perhaps I do not trust your intentions, ha?" He put a hand on Lacasse's broad back and brought his mouth close to Lacasse's right ear. "I suggest the fan-tan," he whispered. "The cages will fly for you tonight."

Lacasse strolled toward the gambling floor. The tables were moderately crowded, with a mid-evening hum that indicated, by the quality more than the quantity of decibels, to which his comprehension was professionally attuned, a rising of the betting temperature, a ubiquitous titillation that would mount further until he would be able to smell as well as hear the spinning. He lingered at the first roulette game. The Chinese croupier grinned across the green-hooded light. Lacasse's particular fondness for roulette was due, more than anything else, to the manner of betting. He relished the sly placement of chips, the last-second shiftings among the cross-patterns of the lines and squares. More than other games, roulette was life itself, the way life seemed to him, at any rate, compartmented, altering, and, if one kept one's wits, to some extent, at least, alterable. The dancing ball was as uncontrollable as fate, in the larger sense; but the board below could be controlled, as men could be controlled by money, and destiny tampered with. When Lacasse played roulette, he felt as if he were pulling long strings.

But now he passed his favorite table by. Li Kwan-sen's advice was in his mind and he headed for the fan-tan, though he had no respect for dice, either swung in a bird-cage or rattled in a cup. He played several times and won once, which put him ahead. The hum had grown louder and Lacasse glanced around at the filling hall. Then suddenly there was a commotion at the front and he saw the uniformed men of the Binh Xuyen, the sect that controlled the city's gambling, pour through the revolving door.

Two shots sounded and the tables became deserted as the customers deployed toward the sides or dropped to the floor, as Lacasse did, hurting a hand as it bent under him. From where he lay, he had a view of the front and could see a young man in white, an

◇◇◇

Annamite, with a stain of red at his side, supported by five soldiers in their mustard-colored suits. The youth was quickly dragged off, and then, almost unbelievably, the gambling began again with the immediate reappearance of the croupiers in their seats. The customers rose and reclustered. Only the hum had to mount from the beginning.

Lacasse saw Li Kwan-sen at the door of his office. Ordinarily he would have rushed over, curious to find out who the young man had been, how many grenades he might have been carrying in the pockets of his white linen suit. But this time Lacasse restrained himself. When he saw Li, he cashed in his winnings, which were twice what he had started with, and left the casino by a side exit.

It was half past twelve. The rain was falling thinly again, but more in earnest than before. Lacasse went quickly to his car in the parking-lot. He was driving it himself, and he swung out into the avenue and around the concrete island until he came up alongside the night club from the Cholon side. He turned off the engine and the lights.

Fifteen minutes later Li Kwan-sen came across the avenue, wearing a raincoat. He was walking with his head down, stepping heavily but carefully around the puddles. Lacasse watched him go into the club, the shaft of light reaching wanly over the abandoned trolley tracks as the door opened and shut. The sheen on the rusted tracks seemed to linger in an afterglow.

Another quarter of an hour passed. Lacasse decided to wait ten more minutes. His earlier conviction was being dissipated, and he now found himself in the mood of a lonely challenger of his premonitory self, a part of himself that he regarded, with superstition, from afar, addressing it on occasion in the third person. He had been so certain tonight that, letting himself be tantalized, and also because he did not want to be seen in the club for the second time alone, even briefly, he had not gone in. Li Kwan-sen had told him enough.

He yawned, throwing his head back, and by the time he had

leveled his eyes again, out of their blink, he saw her. The "cousin" was walking with her. Lacasse was already toying with the alternative of offering both of them a ride, but then she summoned a *cyclo* from the huddled group in front of the casino. Before she had even climbed in, the impolite "cousin" was walking back up the path toward the club.

Lacasse waited until the *cyclo* was bobbing halfway down the block. Then he started the car and drove slowly after it. Near the corner he blew his horn and drew up alongside, repeating the blowing and at the same time forcing the *cyclo* boy closer to the curb. The boy finally stopped and began to shout Annamese imprecations. He was a middle-aged man, compact, with gnarled, bowed legs. Lacasse climbed awkwardly out of the car.

"I saw you, just as I was coming out of the casino," he said. "It is raining so hard. Please allow me."

He had already taken a roll of piasters from his pocket and was handing the *cycloist* more than three times what the fare would have been. Genevieve had said nothing, but now she let Lacasse help her with a hand across the soft mud that lay between her and the car door. He waited until she was safely in before he went around to the other side. After the car was moving, he asked: "Do you come often here by yourself?"

"No, not often," she said. She was sitting stiffly, and between them, despite his girth, there was room enough for a third person.

"Your cousin?" Lacasse said softly. "Do you come to see him?"

Genevieve looked away, through the darkness of the car window. Lacasse waited patiently. Finally he said: "He is your cousin, of course?"

"Who told you that?" she asked, still not looking at him.

Lacasse coughed. "Someone," he replied. "Perhaps it was Mr. Li." He waited a moment longer, and then he added: "It was undoubtedly Li Kwan-sen, since it could not have been our friend Remy."

Genevieve's head swung back. Only her eyes betrayed her. Lacasse let the car slow down, and now he looked straight ahead. "Then he is not your cousin?" he said. "Ah—it is one way, of course, to hide a liaison. One must be careful in such matters, and circumspect."

"I did not say he was not," Genevieve said. "You are also impudent."

"Forgive me," Lacasse said. "I was not thinking of it in the manner that you meant. There are various ways of liaison, and various reasons for maintaining them. Even the nature, the substance, of the romance varies."

"There is no question of romance," Genevieve said tartly. "You misunderstand."

Lacasse pretended to be fair. "I do not think so," he said. "I do not think so, after all."

They had passed the corner where he should have turned to her house and were moving toward the cathedral square and the top of rue Catinat.

"You have taken me too far," she said.

"It is still early," Lacasse said. "I thought we would stop at my club, perhaps. Or my hotel."

Genevieve shook her head decisively. "No," she said. "I must go home."

"To meet your cousin again?"

"You have made your point," she said. "There is nothing to gain by repeating it."

Lacasse breathed audibly. "There is a matter of reason involved."

The car was moving faster again and a great spray of water flew up at the windshield. "There is reason, at least, for discussing the possibilities in any situation."

Genevieve looked sharply at him once more, and this time he met her glance. Then he smiled and stared back at the road. "It is a time of compromise, my dear Madame Brouillard," he said softly. "Of *quid pro quo*. Everywhere. In different manifestations."

"If you do not wish to drive me home, allow me to find another *cyclo*."

Lacasse laughed in short bursts. "Come, Genevieve," he said, "we will drive a bargain. My demands are modest enough. Come with me tonight, to the club at any rate."

"I cannot," she said.

Lacasse waited a final moment. "It is a pity," he said. "When a man is rejected, he seeks the company of alcohol or of *confidantes*. Since I drink but little, I should be forced to the second solace. Monsieur Remy, for instance. An excellent listener, *sympathique*."

Genevieve sat more stiffly than ever against the back of the seat. He saw her fingers move across her purse, and the odd thought that she might be carrying a weapon struck him, and left him, even more strangely, unperturbed.

"It is even worse to be undone by a cousin," he said, with a note of melodrama. They had reached the north end of the square, and Lacasse suddenly stopped the car alongside a plot of grass. He slid bulkily toward her and extended an arm across the top of the seat.

"The solution is much simpler than it appears," he whispered. "It will not be so difficult. On the other hand, the alternatives present infinite complications." He sighed. "I am actually, you see, a lonely man." His hand had dropped against her shoulder and he felt her withdrawal. As she moved forward, his hand leaped after her, almost involuntarily, and he swung about with his other arm stretched out. She seemed to hold herself tensely, and then he felt the sting of her palm across his mouth. He gasped, but she was already gone, and the car door slammed shut. He saw, first, that she had forgotten her purse. There was no point in shouting after, or trying to follow her. She was actually running. Lacasse sat back and watched her disappear, like a youngster, he thought, running to get home in the rain. He sighed, and brushed his mouth with the back of a hand. It was bleeding a little, and he brought out a handkerchief and rubbed it lightly across his lips. He sat for some time,

<><><><><><><><><><><><><><><><><><><><><><><><><><><><><><><><><><><>

turning the handkerchief between his fingers and now and then
touching his mouth with it again. When he saw a Vietnamese policeman at the other end of the square slowly start walking in his direction, he turned on the ignition and drove down rue Catinat to the
hotel. By the time he got there, his anger had mounted. He stood in
the entrance and smoked a cigarette, intensely. He had forgotten
the purse himself, he realized, and he walked over to the car to
fetch it. When he went into the lobby, he saw the night clerk smile.
He brandished the purse, like a sword, and went upstairs to bed.

4

CAU MINH THIEN stood in the rain in front of the night club and
stared across the street to the Chinese hotel. It was dark, except for
a paleness around the entrance and a streak of light at the bottom
of a window on the second floor. His eyes fastened there, and he
noticed the light narrow and widen. The window was open at the
top, and the breeze was swinging the shade.

He crossed over to the opposite side of the avenue. The light upstairs went out and as the shade went up, a man's head became
dimly framed. It seemed to hang there, bodyless. Cau fell back
against the wall of the teashop. Presently the head moved away
and the shade came down, leaving only a square of blackness until
the light flicked on again, its sliver thinner than before.

Cau edged toward the teashop entrance. He glanced in and was
surprised to find it still open. At least the door was ajar and a kerosene lamp was on top of the counter. The owner sat in the rear,
smoking a long pipe of opium. Not until he had pushed the door
open and stepped in did Cau notice another figure in the corner
shadows. It was a coolie, dressed in the customary black silk slacks
and loose black shirt, both of which looked soiled. The youth's head
rolled as if he, too, had been smoking.

Cau sat down at a table in the other corner and asked for a cup of tea. From where he was he could see through the door and across to the hotel. He placed both his palms around the steaming cup set in front of him and brought it to his lips. Then he rubbed the warmth of his hands onto his face and, lifting the hot cup, moved its thick edge along his blood-mark, where there was a tenderness. He stopped when he saw the coolie staring at him. It was a strangely persuasive stare, but Cau set it down to the wearing off of the opium. When the coolie saw himself scrutinized, he looked away and, rising, went to the door and stuck his head out in the rain.

The tea in his throat and his stomach could be alive, the warmth of it was so embracing, Cau thought. He hadn't noticed the extent of the dampness, how bone-chilling it was. For the first time during the long day he grew conscious, in sheer physical terms, of how much walking about he had done. Genevieve's unexpected appearance had been a special reward. He had refrained from offering any response to the envelope she had, almost bashfully, shown him; in fact, he had made a point of accepting her performance as a simple exercise, though he had later asked her to describe the doctor. She had done so, and also had given him the substance of what the Consul had said. Reaching for her hand, holding it briefly, he had almost told her who the doctor was. He was glad he hadn't; if she saw him again, it would be better if she did not know.

Cau thought once more, as he had found himself doing at odd intervals all afternoon, of the political officer. He had not expected to have his options so rapidly presented. There must be something else about the doctor, he reflected, that made him such a prey.

The coolie had brought his head in from the rain and had closed the door to a crack. He seemed to glide rather than walk back across the floor. To neither one of them, the owner or the newcomer, but as if he were addressing a fourth, unseen person, he spoke the first words since Cau's murmured order for tea.

"Now it has come to stay, you see," he said. "The rain has grown steady."

The owner remained silent and motionless on his tall stool. The coolie sat on his haunches near the charcoal stove.

"Are you a stranger here?" he asked, looking over at Cau.

Cau nodded. There was something that disturbed him about the youth's conduct, something beyond addiction.

The coolie nodded in return. "I thought as much," he said.

Cau spat on the wooden floor.

"Why?" he asked. His voice caught and the word came out in a split whisper. "What matter is it to you?"

The coolie now smiled, his large teeth flaring. "A thousand pardons," he said. "There was no offense meant."

Cau's acceptance of the apology was confined to the gesture of taking another long swallow of tea, during which he allowed his eyes, across the top of the cup, to meet the coolie's quietly.

"The monsoon makes lonely wanderers," the coolie said, even more oddly. "One should stay with one's family, if one has one."

"And if one doesn't?" Cau asked.

The coolie seemed to consider this. "One should at least be in bed," he said. "With a woman, or with one's thoughts."

"And you," Cau asked, "why aren't you in one bed or the other, then, instead of chattering here?"

The coolie laughed. "I have insomnia," he said. "I cannot sleep before dawn."

"It is the same with myself," Cau said. "Those who are able to sleep are the fortunate ones of the earth."

The coolie shook his head up and down. "It is the blessing of the gods," he said sententiously. He seemed to have lapsed back into the apartness of his opium.

Cau finished the rest of the tea and put a piaster note on the counter. The owner muttered his thanks, more in sibilance than words.

Without looking at the coolie again, Cau went toward the door. "Good night," he said.

"May I hope sleep comes quickly to you?" the coolie said. "Perhaps the sound of the rain will help."

Cau did not reply. The lights of the hotel were out, the dim ones below as well as the one behind the shade on the second floor. He did not pause to look up, but walked rapidly into the blackness. At the corner, just before he swung around, however, he did glance back and saw what he had expected to see, the figure of the coolie in the teashop doorway. It was not until he had gone a block farther that he admitted his gratification at having confirmed his suspicion. The choice of action was no longer solely his. The thought, in relation to the political officer, was at least as amusing as it was serious.

Chapter XXI

WITH his elbows on his knees, smoking a cigarette, Adam sat in the dark house. The cook and the Chinese boy had gone to their corrugated hut in the rear of the garden. In the silence of the night, sound was the enemy lurking in the imminence of a grenade's roar or a rifle-shot. Adam felt that he and the larger silence were joined, that the silence within himself and the greater silence without would suddenly and simultaneously be shattered, if not by some explosive force, then surely by the telephone's cold, close ringing. Yet there was no one he expected. Nell was gone; he had sent her home in the car. Whatever it was that had made Genevieve run off earlier, she was not likely to call back and explain. After the accident of the doctor's arrival, Adam saw the futility of further pursuit, for the moment at least. As for Lockman, he had probably gone off to the casino. Adam had taken the doctor to his hotel and had suggested, quite firmly this time, that he remain there until the plane left, promising to take him to the airport. Smythe never telephoned after hours; yet Adam's eyes kept moving to the sideboard, ahead of his thoughts, which centered slowly, involuntarily, on the Minister, until, finally, having twice got up and moved toward the receiver and sat down again, he stood up a third time and picked it up himself to call Smythe's home number.

The Minister answered, his "hello" flat and ascending, as if he had been in the middle of a sentence. Adam paused before he responded with: "Good evening, sir."

"Oh, hello, Patch," Smythe replied. "How are you?"

"I wondered if I might stop in for a few moments? That is, if you're not busy?" Adam asked.

Smythe was hesitating, and Adam guessed that someone, other than Mrs. Smythe, was there with him. Now he coughed and said: "Why, yes. Is it something important?"

"Yes," Adam said. "Rather. But I don't like upsetting your evening."

"That's all right," the Minister replied. "Come on ahead."

"I'll leave now," Adam said, and hung up.

He put a tie and jacket on and went into the bathroom to douse cold water on his face, but the water was lukewarm and unsoothing. There were no stars outside and no indication of a moon behind the monsoonal clouds. He drove at even more than his usual nighttime speed, but then, realizing he ought to allow a proper quarter of an hour to elapse, he slowed down and took a detour of several blocks. He had scarcely considered what he was going to say. What Nell had told him, of the afternoon conference between the Minister and Goodenough, of the telephone call to Remy (to part of which, enough at least to recognize the name of the doctor repeated, Nell had listened), and, finally, of the call she had been asked to make to Lockman, which the Minister had then canceled, was proof enough of M. Remy's determination. It was again apparent that Remy had chosen his moment. The likelihood that Genevieve had simply been used to affect the Minister preliminarily, as a beach is softened by blows from the air before a sea assault, took on new significance. The only unknown factor was Goodenough, the degree to which, either fortuitously or consciously in Remy's behalf, he was concerned or had concerned himself. Perhaps Nell had all along been right.

He parked the car in the driveway behind Smythe's black sedan and rapped on the screen door. The Vietnamese houseboy—the Minister had only Vietnamese servants—let him in and pointed to the living-room. Adam heard two voices as he stepped forward. He recognized both of them, and stopped. If he could have left, he would have, but Smythe was already in the doorway. Despite himself, Adam smiled at the nicety of the Minister's extended hand. It was the only time since their first meeting, at the Legation, that he remembered having Symthe's hand in his. Goodenough clung to the opposite wall. The Minister quickly offered a drink, and it was the first time, too, Adam recollected, that he had ever heard Smythe himself make such a proffer, beyond the disassociated sponsorship of a tray. Adam saw Goodenough's half-empty glass and accepted.

"Robert and I have been talking over some report material," the Minister said. "A little nocturnal homework." The thin smile made its debut.

"I was about to leave," Goodenough said. He seemed transfixed.

Adam set his eye on one of the Minister's soft red chairs. Vintage Vienna, he thought, prewar Habsburg retread. "In the cool of the evening . . ." he murmured, letting himself drop into it. It was less uncomfortable than he had anticipated.

"What was that?" the Minister asked.

"Doggerel," Adam said. "Old country verse."

He wondered how long Goodenough had been here. It was hardly the case that he had come to catch up on office routine.

"Is your wife home?" Adam asked.

The Minister gave him a queer look that wavered between simple surprise at the solicitude and resentment over the invasion of privacy. "Bridge," he replied. "With the ladies of the realm."

Adam nodded. "Every day, in every way, we grow broader and broader and broader."

He had decided, at that moment, that Goodenough should stay. It was not something he would suggest first, but if Goodenough again announced his intentions of departure, Adam would let him know he was welcome to remain. Having been present at the earlier discussion in the Minister's office, there was no longer any reason why he should not be present now. Goodenough was involved in the settling of accounts.

"I suppose I better be going," he suddenly said, as if on cue.

The Minister looked ill at ease and muttered something that sounded like a possible demurrer.

Adam picked it up. "Why don't you stay?" he said, and added: "No secrets ahead."

A long moment of silence ensued, which only Adam enjoyed. He sat back and sipped his drink.

Goodenough's hovering had carried him halfway across the room. Now he turned. The Minister waited a moment more and said: "Why, certainly, Robert." Then, incongruously, he added: "It isn't often we get a chance to relax, is it?" He held it, and then, even more oddly, said: "any of us."

Goodenough sat down in the twin of Adam's chair. The Minister, looking somewhat lost in the whole of it, chose the center of the couch. "We'll have some coffee," he said. "That is, if anyone wants any."

Neither Adam nor Goodenough did.

"Well, then," Smythe said.

"If you don't mind, I'll sweeten the drink," Adam said.

"By all means," the Minister said. "Please help yourself."

With his back still turned, stirring the ice, his eyes concentrating on a Cambodian hunting print above the portable bar, Adam said: "I hear our French friends don't like the way we treat with deserters."

Halfway through the long pause he turned. Neither the Minister nor Goodenough had moved. Slowly, gazing at the floor, Adam walked back across the room. Now he saw Goodenough glance over at the Minister, then at his glass and back to Smythe. It was apparent, beyond what Nell had said, that the subject had already been discussed.

"Atrophy or death," Adam said. "Neither really seems a practical solution."

The Minister gave one of his preliminary coughs. "Hmmn," he said. "The case of this doctor is an odd one."

"What about him?" Adam asked.

"Apparently there's reason to doubt his identity."

Adam restrained himself. "Who said that?" he inquired, overingenuously.

The Minister cleared his throat some more. "After all," he replied, "in these respects, the French remain in a better position to render intelligence."

"Physically or morally?"

The Minister's face stiffened, and Adam detected one of Goodenough's gray, subcutaneous smiles.

"It comes down to the same thing," Smythe said. "The same fundamental thing we've discussed, you know. This isn't our arena." He was making a conscious effort to be conversational.

"We're only picadors, is that it? Goading and frightening the universal bull?"

"I don't know about picadors," the Minister said. "But I don't like metaphors."

Goodenough looked up. He opened his mouth, closed it, then opened it again. "The point, I think, is that the renegade, under any circumstances, whether he be disillusioned and broken or purely refugee, is a poor candidate for hasty reform or for new attachment. Now, take this doctor. I spoke—"

"Wait a minute," Adam said. He stared at Goodenough. The man belonged on a college lecture platform, not in the Asian ant-heap. "I know you saw him," he continued. "He told me. I gather it wasn't an overwhelmingly successful session."

"I sent him on to ECA on the Minister's recommendation," Goodenough said, curtly. "He should have been channeled through by now."

"Decontaminated," Adam said. "Tried and fitted for a proper non-sensitive post."

"What would you like to do with him?" Smythe asked.

Adam wondered if the Minister had spoken to Lockman at all. Irving would have telephoned if there had been any conversation after the call Nell had canceled. That reduced the possible time element almost to nothing.

"I'd let him be useful," Adam said. "Not tomorrow, or next month, or next year. The fight is now. In himself too." He let a moment go by, and added: "He had an idea. But, mostly, he wanted to help."

The Minister's gaze was fixed on the window. "You seem to know a great deal about the fellow," he said. "Why didn't you talk to me about him before?"

"He came to me by accident," Adam said. "As a result of one, that is. Actually, although I'd forgotten it, I'd met him before, on the street."

"On the street?" the Minister murmured, like a dowager.

"He walked next to me, the morning of the last grenading. Explosions have a way of bringing people together. And random death."

The Minister said "Hmmn" again, and then: "That's a strange way of putting it."

"Not strange," Adam said. "He simply wanted to talk. He was striking in the dark. He didn't know who I was, and I didn't tell him. Later, after being grilled"—he glanced at Goodenough, but the Minister didn't notice—"he found out and came to my house."

"And that didn't make you suspicious?" Smythe asked.

Adam hesitated. "Not the way it was done," he said.

The Minister smiled once more and Goodenough's mouth curved in customary adumbration. "Did you know the French and the Vietnamese police had, as you put it, 'grilled' him earlier, and have had him under observation?"

So Remy had seen to all of it. The shadow in the garden floated back, and Remy himself at the pool before that.

"I assumed he was being watched," Adam replied. "Probably by more than one side."

"And yet you spoke with him? You went out of your way to make yourself available?"

"Out of my way?" Adam repeated.

"You let him come into your house."

"Would you have thrown him out?"

The Minister stopped. He thought a moment, and replied: "I would have told him to come to my office," he said. "To the proper place of business."

Adam sighed. "What you call going out of the way," he said, "seems a necessary expedient sometimes. Being available can't always be on our terms, at our discretion."

"What you're talking about is pretty vague, you know, a little spiritual, isn't it?" the Minister said. "The fellowship of man, empathy and ambiance and all that. It's important, I know, in books and in heaven. But here we're dealing with something else. Being touchy, our position is bound to be anomalous. So we proceed with double caution. It's not just channels. It's whole avenues of responsibility, form and formality."

"Protocol before diplomacy," Adam said.

Symthe hesitated. "A kind of protocol, yes," he said. "It's not purely a matter of right and wrong, or of what we'd like to do. You know perfectly well what we're up against. Somebody has to take the rap, the rap of patience, at any rate."

"That time factor again," Adam said. "We keep coming back to it."

The Minister waited another moment. "What did you tell him, the doctor?"

Adam permitted himself a short laugh. "Mostly I listened to what he had to say. About the Vietminh, about the people in the indeterminate areas."

Goodenough broke in. "He didn't seem to me to have anything new to offer."

"Maybe you didn't ask him the right questions," Adam said. "Maybe your inspiration was low, or your pencil was moving too fast."

Goodenough flushed. The Minister saw it, but said nothing. He seemed to be waiting for Adam to continue.

"What was most important was what he had to say of the country between."

"Between what?"

"Here and there," Adam replied. "Where there's still some time."

For a moment no one spoke. Adam stood up and walked a few paces, then turned. "The fact is, we're bleeding hearts at bottom," he said. "Under conditions of emergency, our hearts go out. When someone cries in the night, or shoves a corpse under our nostrils, or a photographer from a slick magazine takes shocker pictures. We lie in wait to be moved, to generosity, to heroism, or to rectitude. But disaster's got to strike first."

◇◇◇

The Minister gave his low cough and went to the window, where he adjusted a shutter. "I think you're being somewhat dramatic," he said, with his back to the room. "There's still a limit to capability."

"I suppose I am—being dramatic," Adam said. "I think we have to be. Talk about crusades, for freedom or what have you, the right to eat, live, drink, and be merry, fornicate or fail. That small, undoctored gamble that can do more than all the dollar signs with zeros on strings placed behind them by senators running scared! What makes it so hard for us?"

"I think we've taken risks," the Minister said flatly. "A lot of them, in a lot of places."

"We still need proof, on one of the off-beat country tracks, that we can look ahead, and guess right. The melody of too little and too late is an old song, and it doesn't much linger. There won't be any revivals on the Asian boards."

"We can't be everything to everybody everywhere," the Minister said, and now his voice was cold.

"Naturally," Adam said. "We've got to decide, both where to be bold and how. It's something you and I haven't agreed about, let alone a few higher echelons. But it's not just place. We seem to have forgotten the companionship that comes from sharing a quick and early danger. We used to have it, in our own queer, backwoodsy, honest way."

"The doctor," Smythe said, softly—"what did he want to do?"

"It's too late," Adam said. "He's leaving tomorrow, for his ancestral home."

"Hanoi?" the Minister asked.

Adam hesitated only a matter of seconds. "Hanoi, yes," he said. "ECA needs doctors in the delta."

"That's important enough, isn't it?"

"Sure," Adam said. "It's important."

"What else could he have done that's better?"

"It doesn't matter any more," Adam said, dully.

The Minister turned and looked at him in such a way that Adam knew a further reply was expected. In a new and quiet voice that had gone slightly husky he said: "He wanted to go back where he came from, or near it. To stay, as long as possible."

"And take you with him?" the Minister asked, with his thin smile again.

Adam waited. He saw that Goodenough was staring at him harder than ever, his head lifted like a bird's. The Minister was also waiting.

"I'd have learned a lot," Adam said, at length. "But it didn't come to that. It was ECA's baby anyway."

"You were just acting as a middleman?" Smythe asked.

"In a manner of speaking."

"Over and above what had already been arranged?"

"You mean dispatching him to personnel?" Adam motioned through the air. "He would never have stirred from the city under the circumstances."

Smythe was snapping his fingers together. There was a further silence before he took a step toward Adam and then veered to the couch. Looking first down and then in the general direction of Goodenough, he said: "We're back where we started. Damn it, Patch, won't you admit this isn't our private back yard?"

"It's nobody's," Adam said. "It doesn't belong to the French anymore, either. Why do we have to attach ourselves to their illusions?"

The Minister dropped himself heavily onto the couch. "I'm not here to plead guilty to why we do or don't do something," he said. "For better or for worse, I carry out a program that's been determined back in Washington. I don't belong to the policy planning staff, and it's not my job to gauge the ultimate effect of our actions here on the rest of the world—not all of it, at any rate. I've got my own ideas, but until I'm asked to express them I'm the Minister, and I execute the verbal functions."

"In this corner of the world, policy has got to be played by ear, and by heart," Adam said.

"Finding things out and acting in a way that subverts a larger common purpose are still two different things," Smythe replied.

"And I'll still wager one thing—that if you put it to the people back home, they'd resent being anyone's salvational pawns," Adam said. "Why do you think the French don't want us here, prying around in the countryside? How many Frenchmen would admit their fear of American competition? None, to your face. But when you've been here long enough, and watched them long enough, it begins to soak in that the greatest illusion of all is their illusion of doing business through endless tomorrows, even with the Communists."

"Maybe that's none of our business," Goodenough said.

"And maybe it is," Adam shot back. "At least to the degree to which we've become underwriters."

The Minister was rubbing his face. "A little bit of chicanery takes place everywhere," he said.

Adam didn't answer for a long moment. "It's not only cynicism, or greed," he said. "The trouble is, we've become tied up to what the French are in fact fighting for, in spite of what they say, in spite of what we say. And, even more disastrously, we've allowed the Vietminh to represent us by default."

Now Smythe gave a small sigh. "We can't seed a jungle with alfalfa in a season," he said.

Adam felt that all of them had had enough. He set his glass on the bar and walked across the room to shake the Minister's hand.

"Thanks for letting me come," he said. He smiled at Goodenough, who offered a vague, two-fingered salute. "Can I give you a lift?" he added.

"My jeep's coming back," Goodenough said. "Much obliged."

The Minister walked to the door with Adam and held it open.

"There'll be other doctors," he said. "Other places." And he actually smiled with his lips apart.

In the car, after he had switched the headlights on, Adam laughed. He drove around for half an hour, past the casino, past Tran's hotel, and finally past the house of Genevieve Brouillard, which was dark. He felt drained of emotion, but the driving was restful, despite the vague sense he had that it was also dangerous. Unlike the other times, he had difficulty reconstructing what had been said, or even why he had felt it incumbent to go. Nevertheless, the relief spread through him. He no longer was outward bound. The point of no return had been identified.

Chapter XXII

THE sky was wet in the morning, hanging darkly down, holding back the rain for a sudden assault. Scudding lighter clouds moved across the lower portion like messengers with swollen pouches carrying the announcements of battle. The market was only half-filled, and even the vendors present were gingerly displaying their products.

The political officer emerged from the river end of the avenue, having come along the edge of the arroyo and the river itself, making it a point to pass in front of the American offices to see, if nothing else, the limp flags hanging. The placards screwed onto the stucco walls had fascinated him even more, the eagle heads with their blue-gold trimmings, their look of caparisoned and plated scavengers. There was something so largely neat about the Americans, he reflected; so panoplied, a quality that stared, plastically, across the world.

Now the market, gray and tentative, beckoned him farther. He had had a futile time of it. Since his conversation with Cau Minh Thien in the café, he had sipped countless cups of tea in various parts of the city. In the evening he had continued his wandering through the squares and around the hotels and then along the quieter parts between the cities. But he had seen no one, no face that he recognized, and especially not the doctor's. Yet he was more certain than ever that the doctor was here. The longer he searched, and the more certain he became, the angrier he grew over Cau's refusal to help him find the renegades. If Cau was not actually harboring Tran Phan Dang, he at least must have an idea where Tran could be, the political officer was convinced, and as he strolled through the market he found himself scarcely looking for the doctor any longer or for the others, but rather for an image of Cau Minh Thien himself again.

To his left, sitting cross-legged near the curb, he thought he recognized the old woman Cau had spoken to, who had handed up the folded message the morning they had gone down the river. He stood away and regarded her from three sides, and then he walked over and pretended to examine the few pieces of cheap cloth she had un-folded across the blanket. Her tarnished eyes gazed up at him in cloudy, mercantile supplication, then suddenly shifted, gaining not light but movement, and looked away. When they turned back up, the political officer was crouching and fondling a cotton sash. "Have you seen him, the one with whom I came before?" he whispered.

Her voice fell off into silent motion of lips. She shook her head instead, and then the political officer heard the few broken words, "He has not been here . . ." He debated with himself, keeping his crouch, and, nodding once, walked off slowly. It would do no good to tell her anything else. He would simply go on searching. There was one other possibility. If by dusk he had not found either Cau or the doctor, he would return to the teashop of Li Kwan-sen. There was a risk involved, but he could manage to mask it in courtesy. He recalculated the time, how long he had been here and how long it would take to return north. He could still afford another day, two perhaps. The city was not that big, he told himself; but he was aware that it was, actually, if one did not know where its bigness and its smallness lay. What was worse was this constant feeling that he was not the sole pursuer, that someone was also pursuing him, or watching him pursue and was therefore responsible for the failure of his own pursuit. There was something devilish about it, something inversely eerie in being so open and unlike the jungle. His resentment grew as he walked faster, crossing the square and following the picket fence around the gardens of the palace. Cau Minh Thien would suffer, he repeated silently. If nothing else, at least that much had been established, which in itself was something.

2

M. REMY rested on his elbows on the doctor's table. The small room smelled bad, of stale urine, or perhaps it was only a combination of sweat and wet leaves rotting in the old stone crevices of the ministerial garden below.

The doctor, a veteran civil servant attached to the political section, who had come out from Africa a year ago, was probing the liver with two fingers. Remy could feel the dull ache rise up toward the balls of the doctor's fingers and then, almost spitefully, fall away between them. The doctor put another palm on M. Remy's stomach and then moved it slowly, still probing, toward the groin.

"There is an enlargement still," he said, "but it feels better than it did." He spoke with a heavy accent, the result of years in Morocco.

"I'm glad you think so," Remy replied. "I don't think it favors being pushed about."

The doctor shrugged. "None of them do," he said. "That is not the point." He looked at Remy's face and pulled the lower lid of Remy's right eye down. "When did you last say you were going home?" he asked.

"I didn't say," Remy replied. "There are things that keep happening."

"You should go," the doctor said. "But, of course, I've told you that before."

"Yes," Remy said.

The doctor looked away, then walked to the sink in the corner and poured water over his hands. "You are being foolish," he said as he dried them. "It is not a matter of indispensability. There are—"

Remy interrupted, climbing off the table. "Let's not talk of it," he said. "I know what you think. I shall go when I can. Soon, perhaps. Perhaps even sooner than either one of us imagines."

"It's none of my business," the doctor continued. "But what makes it so hard? Don't you want to go back, for a vacation, at any rate? Don't you want to see Paris, or home, wherever that is?"

M. Remy smiled. "It's in the south," he said. "But that was before."

"You haven't been there since the war?" the doctor inquired.

Remy had finished dressing. "For a day," he said. "To visit the grave of my sister."

The doctor said: "Ah." He stirred about, now ill at ease.

"One of these times will be the last, I promise you," Remy said, finally.

The doctor nodded vaguely. Walking away, Remy saw him take off his stethoscope. "Poor devil," he thought, stepping down and through the garden; "how sick he must be of all the sick livers, of feeling them disintegrate, day by day, under the same two fingers of his helpless hand!"

He looked at the time. He was late, but not late enough to make him want to rush. They would wait for him. They had waited before and they would wait again, if he wished them to. That was part of the game and it was too soon to change it.

There was also Genevieve to think about. When Lacasse had told him this morning—the Corsican had been oddly abashed, then actually flustered—Remy had found himself at first pretending it was all a shadow-play. Then, forgetting Lacasse's presence, hardly hearing the words of embellishment Lacasse was offering, he had begun to consider not the idea of her but of himself, and of what he had, in fact, not only said to the Minister but had perhaps believed, without knowing it, subconsciously or even a little madly (as all of them were becoming madder), until, looking back at Lacasse, he had started quite suddenly and on the verge of uncontrol to laugh. Lacasse had thereupon stopped talking out of his own mounting embarrassment and had begun simply to blow sounds incoherently, his face red and the perspiration running down it, managing finally to add: "But I see you will not believe it. . . . Perhaps after all, I should not have come. . . ."

Now that he had had more time to think about it, Remy was torn between disbelieving Lacasse entirely and being further amused at the possibility that the Corsican was right. It raised the whole fascinating question of the futility of trust; of morality itself as a gauge of ordinary human behavior—not so much in relation to the ways of the heart as to the whole mechanism of self-imposed loneliness, to what motivated men and, even more unpredictably, women.

He wondered, assuming now that what Lacasse said was so, how long she had been dividing herself, how helplessly she had got herself involved on both levels at once. Or had it happened, as it sometimes did, almost accidentally, beginning as a kind of game from which she had kept thinking she could withdraw when the time came, simply by pulling down a curtain on one side of the split stage of herself?

There had been a point, but that had been before the sapping of his strength, when the prospect of getting to know her on a different plane had suggested itself; it had occurred to him the afternoon he had driven to her house for tea, with the declared pretext of finding out what she had discovered about the Vietnamese bookstore he had sent her to, and the undeclared one of wanting to discover where and how she lived and what the circumstances of her odd apartness were, of its almost compulsive expression. They had talked pleasantly enough, and he had left with the feeling that he had got to know her better, that they had reached an understanding based partly on a mutual sense of the ridiculous. But, as can also happen at such moments between a man and a woman, a premature joint frigidity sets in with earnest conversation, so that they become sexless in advance of even the touch of a hand.

Now his dispassion had left him unresentful; but also uncaring. The idea that he had, without telling her, already used her as an instrument was not a factor—not a conscious one, at any rate. Having told the Minister what he had, he was in a way relieved at having the possibility of its truth thrown belatedly, if ludicrously, up to him. Aside from precluding the further possibility of any guilt he might feel (which was unlikely, since he had promised at the outset to protect her), the fact that she may for some time have been what he had just pretended she was could now conceivably bring on a more satisfactory resolution.

Remy turned at the side alley of police headquarters and walked through the parking yard to a flight of narrow wooden stairs that led to a veranda running halfway around the second story. He went briskly along it and then seemed to pop through one of the curtains that concealed an inner door. Inside were the black-suit coolie and the inspector.

◇◇◇

"Good afternoon," Remy said. He thought a moment, and added, gratuitously: "A busy day."

Both the inspector and the coolie awaited his further pleasure. He had sat down and folded his legs.

"Do you have a French cigarette?" he asked. He was not supposed to, he knew, but it seemed a proper compensation for having had his liver prodded.

The inspector started to move a silver case across the desk-top; then, seeing that M. Remy would not be able to reach it without getting up, he stood up and brought it over. Remy lit the cigarette with the proffered match.

In the center of the room, on his haunches, the coolie had barely moved. Now Remy looked down at him. He was almost too inscrutable; as if, beyond pretending that he was an addict, he was in fact one, or at any rate had got himself to the point of believing in his role. How many of these "loyal" informants too, Remy wondered, had dealt or were dealing with the Vietminh; or, if not with the Vietminh, then with the Binh Xuyen or the Cao Daists, either one of which would willingly pay something for the same or portions of the same information gathered for the Sûreté?

"What more have you found out?" he asked.

The coolie kept his posture. He looked at Remy with the question, but then, as if the Vietnamese inspector were a necessary translator, shifted his glance to the top of the desk. Remy found himself engaged in the geometric calculation of determining whether, from where he was squatting, the coolie could actually see the inspector's face. The idea that only the top of the inspector's head was visible in the coolie's odd field of vision added piquancy to M. Remy's restored mood. The depression of the doctor's office was gone.

"He has stayed in the hotel," the coolie replied. "Last night, however—it was really this morning—there was an occurrence in the teashop."

"The teashop?" Remy repeated. "Where? What sort of an oc-currence?"

Speaking rapidly, his words seeming to leap up from the floor, the coolie related the episode with Cau Minh Thien. When he had finished, Remy asked for a description of the man. What the coolie told him, including a mention of the scarred cheek, had no special meaning.

"What sort of scar?" he asked.

The coolie barely altered his hunch. "A wound perhaps," he said. "It could not be seen very well in the small light of the lamp."

"And why did you consider the appearance of this stranger of importance?"

"The hour was a late one, the teashop is small," the coolie re-plied. "We were also curious of each other."

"Nothing else?"

The coolie hesitated. "I had seen him before as well," he said at length. "In a café."

"And what does that signify?"

"It is true that one imagines things," the coolie said.

"You are not being paid for your imagination," Remy snapped.

The inspector, silent throughout, coughed, and Remy turned to him impatiently.

"What was it?" the inspector asked. "You must tell Monsieur Remy everything. Only do not make inventions." He gave the Frenchman an almost beatific smile.

The coolie rocked and adjusted his feet by moving an inch or two forward. His expression had not changed.

"It was a matter of even more curiosity," he said.

"What kind of curiosity?" Remy asked. He was becoming an-noyed.

"There was a curiosity concerning the hotel," the coolie said.

"On the stranger's part?"

The coolie's silence was an implied affirmation.

"What proof is that of anything? There are many guests in such hotels," Remy snapped.

The coolie stayed silent for a longer moment. The inspector stood up and walked back and forth as if he were about to declaim, but all he finally said was: "Still, Monsieur Remy, you will admit the possibilities?"

Remy had already admitted them to himself. The stranger could well have been what the coolie intimated. By now, the *Tu Ve*, especially, should have found some trace of the doctor. He had been aware of that all along, as the inspector had too, of course; ever since the doctor had been set free. What the inspector cared little or nothing about, however, was the position of the Americans. If he was conscious of it at all, his thoughts would be altogether removed from the basis of French thinking, and especially from the extension of such thinking that, by necessity, was Remy's own.

It was part of their colossal naïveté, he reminded himself, that the Vietnamese in the new government, and for that matter throughout the country, still believed what the Americans said: not only about themselves, but about the French. Naïveté was no excuse. It was easy enough to think ill of the French and well of the Americans, but were it not for French endurance, the inspector himself and the rest of the Emperor's men would not be sitting, even now, in any parts of the palaces. It was the Americans who were responsible for the inspiration of pride, for the fact that all of them, the inspector included, thought themselves far readier than they were to carry on the functions of government. The Americans, wide-eyed, harping on the shibboleths of their own distant revolution, were at least as difficult if not as implacable an enemy as the Communists themselves. In fact, Remy had concluded, since one had to deal on a daily bureaucratic level with the Americans, they presented a far more serious problem. It became exacerbated when their peculiar romantic mixture of blandishment and infantile enthusiasm was regarded as a kind of clarion call.

The question of the moment was still the doctor. It was one of time; whether, in view of what the coolie had disclosed, it was advisable to act at once, or wait for him to make another pilgrimage to the Consul's house. The risks of waiting were apparent. On the other hand, Remy reminded himself, there was also the intriguing matter of Genevieve; that, too, was worth some risk pursuing.

He rubbed the perspiration off his hands, using the front of his blouse, and then ran his still-moist fingers across his brow. The inspector and the coolie seemed to be drifting away.

"Very well, then," he said with an effort. The coolie shifted his feet again and glanced up. "Undoubtedly, the doctor will be returning this afternoon, or this evening, to the home of the American." He nodded at the coolie. "You will inform me at once."

He paused and breathed deeply, feeling the recurrence of pain. "There is one thing more," he said. "The woman, the Eurasian who was with the Consul earlier. If she comes to see him, you will also report it immediately."

He wrote three telephone numbers on a square of paper. "I will be at one of these," he added.

The coolie seemed to unwind as he stood up. He stared vacantly at the inspector, who gave his cutomary small nod, and then the black suit appeared to glide through the door, which closed soundlessly.

Remy also rose. The inspector watched him.

"You are sure you are not waiting too long?" he asked.

"I am sure," Remy said. "By himself, the doctor is not important, either in life or in death. Other things are more so."

The inspector shrugged.

"Thank you," Remy said. The two men endured a moment of nearly hostile silence, and then Remy went out. Neither he nor the inspector had bothered to say good-by.

The rain was still holding back. It was siesta time, but he went directly to the political-section building. There was an old army cot in the rear of his office, a product of American lend-lease he had commandeered. He lay down on it, using a khaki-colored towel for a pillow, and closed his eyes.

Chapter XXIII

NOT since Paris, when it had been a matter of delaying as long as possible each day the sight of German soldiers on the streets, had Genevieve remembered staying in bed until ten o'clock. Nor had she slept, but only lain with her eyes open, staring at the increase of light across the floor and then, when it had reached the wall, at the mottled sky beyond and the rain waiting in it. She could smell the fullness of the monsoon now, or imagined she could, the traveled mixture of sea and mountain freshness that was also fish and fowl and flood-tide.

A small throb of an ache at the base of her skull was like a spar between herself and the pillow. The floor, when she reached underneath the mosquito net, felt far away and softer than it should have been. She brushed her fingers across it and then, with a sudden effort, swung her nude body forward and sat there, behind the gauze, her legs spread thinly. A momentary coolness touched her breasts and, lifting her right hand, she wriggled the sleep-numbness out of her fingers. She had thought of Lacasse when she had first awakened, but now the total recollection of her slap returned, and with it the sense she had of him, abject and pitiful, to which her self-deprecation, by her physical response, was attached. She must have satisfied him perversely. The likelihood that he had gone directly to Remy, or to anyone, seemed less strong now; not that pride would have kept him from it, but he would savor his flagellation.

The soles of her feet had quickly clung to the floor. The morning's actuality drove in at her, and with it the earlier events of the evening re-emerged, the conversation with Cau, his odd disinterest when she had mentioned the doctor's name. Each of the last two times he had been apart, like a lover abstracted in the after-mood of possession.

She slid under the net and stood in front of the long mirror. Her face was thin and her body looked like someone else's. She felt removed from it. Lacasse had something, but not everything, to do with the sensation of withdrawal. The Corsican and his ridiculous blackmail were only coincidental results of her having involved herself, of her prior act of commitment. But when he had announced his threat, she had been made suddenly aware of her betrayal of the doctor.

She stared at the mirror again. A vague image of Lacasse loomed above her. She shivered. The inconsequential slap had run a current through her, which was worse than his touching her, than any intercourse, would have been.

Genevieve showered and dressed hurriedly. Fifteen minutes later she was on her way to the tobacco shop.

2

TRAN found it impossible any longer to remain on the bed. Ever since he had awakened before dawn, he had got up and lain down so many times that he felt not only caged but chained. He had sat in the dining-room at breakfast until the questions of the Chinese manager had driven him back upstairs. What the manager had told him of the visitor in mid-evening had left no doubt about who the stranger had been. He felt not so much afraid as impatient to be

◇◇

gone, to be as isolated as he had been before. There was no question any more of waiting. He was beyond any *attentisme*. What he wanted was simply to talk to his wife, to tell her what had happened, from the first months in the jungle to the nocturnal conversations with the political officer that had become part of his subsequent life in the forest. What had occurred here, in the city, he would speak about less.

He stopped a few feet from the window and peered down. There was nothing but the car-tracks, the gray avenue, and the dust in repose. The door of the teashop was still ajar, and through it Tran perceived the continuing movement of figures. They were like darkly turning shadows, whose circular flow brought to mind the fountain in the village of the indefinite country, where the women had bathed the festering children. It seemed long ago that he had been there.

He stepped back and, involuntarily, sat down on the edge of the bed. The Americans, he now knew, were also shadow-folk, no longer white men in white walking swiftly. Like everyone else, they, too, were obscurely driven. Perhaps he had expected too much. The fault might be in themselves, the Vietnamese, for having erected the pedestals in the public squares. It was true that promises had been made at the end of the great war; but had that not always been the case? The fact remained: no more than evil was conflict eradicable. What made the Communists so successful was the cold reality of the struggle they pursued. Their idealism was a whipping-post. Words were unsheathed as flatly as swords.

So long as evil, pretending to be good, found fallow ground in ignorance and want, what could grace and generosity accomplish? In all of the indefinite country, would it ever be enough, Tran wondered, to alleviate pain, to improve the land, to teach men how to read and write? Could dignity be acquired like a vaccine, to immunize against bitterness and pride, or to substitute for the drug of dogma?

◇◇◇

The Communists had perfected their formula—a perpetual marginal existence for the sake of an unreachable goal, shared deprivation for the glorification of the whole. It was like a Great Wall on which all shadows were simultaneously projected; a universal togetherness of the faceless, never fear through loneliness but only through disobedience. Had the alternatives become flight and self-imprisonment? Even if one wished to escape, Tran reminded himself, one could not escape into a vacuum. Where else, then, could he go except to Hanoi? He could do what was asked of him; he would inoculate against time and disease, and guard against more promises, including the Americans'.

He stood up and moved about aimlessly. The Consul had said the plane left late in the afternoon, when the winds died down. Tran went to the closet and took his jacket out and, carrying it on his arm, walked downstairs. In front of the hotel he hesitated. Then he took the turn that led to the Consul's house. There would be no time to talk on the way to the airport, to tell the things he had not yet told. Because they had not concerned himself and his purpose, he had not mentioned them before. He had not come as a purveyor of information. Nor had he wished, even before his arrest near the docks, to involve himself with the French. The fact that he had come to know the channels through which the underground trade was being conducted had been only a by-product of his foraging for medicines and drugs. The number of shopkeepers, Vietnamese and Chinese, and their French sponsors, including those in the Army, who were dealing surreptitiously with the Vietminh, in guns and piasters as well as in supplies, had of course steadily increased. Tran was aware that such activity was common enough in time of war, especially in such a war as this, both fluid and fratricidal. He had, however, regretted acquiring his knowledge; which was another reason he had harbored it. Now he wanted to be done with that too.

The Consul, when he understood, would forgive him this dis-

◇◇◇

obedience. A sense of the confessional came over him and reminded him of the nuns floating through the cathedral square. He began to walk faster. The street was so quiet that it seemed he was back in the forest. The houses appeared to recede, and the trees to form both a curtain and a canopy. There was no one in front of him. Had he turned, he would not have seen the black-suit coolie, who had just disappeared. Out of ear-shot, a block and a half away, a jeep in which three men in indeterminate khaki sat immobile crawled along.

3

GENEVIEVE could tell at once that the tobacconist did not welcome her. He held the door at a narrow crack for an unduly long time before he let her enter and then he vanished into the back room, from where she heard the sound of several voices. Presently three youths emerged, each with a package the same size; they went out quietly, without glancing at her. She stood gazing at the boxes of tobacco above the counter, reflecting how careless of him it was to allow the shelves to look so undisturbed, when she heard him behind her, saying: "To come twice in two days is unwise."

She turned. He was watching her from the inner doorway.

"There is special activity, that is apparent," she said.

He ignored the comment. "You should know now that he does not come until long after dark."

"It is important that I find him," she replied.

The tobacconist shook his head as much in continued disapprobation as disclaimer. "I do not know the various places he goes," he said. "There is no reason for me to know."

Another knock at the front door sounded and Genevieve saw his expression tighten. Two more youths slid in and he motioned them immediately to the rear. The pair scarcely comprehended her though the second boy, who did not look to be more than fifteen, grinned shyly. The old man followed them, and when they came out they had their twin packages overwrapped in burlap.

This time the tobacconist stepped behind the counter. "He will not come tonight, anyway. I tell you that," he said. He began to rummage among the boxes below.

"Do you know the village to which he goes?" she asked.

The old man said nothing for a moment, and then, without lifting his head, he muttered: "He will not be there either."

"Perhaps tomorrow he will return directly," Genevieve suggested.

She heard more footsteps and the tobacconist brought his face up sharply. He stared at her in brief bewilderment. "Please," he said. "It grows less safe."

As the knock came, he stepped toward the door, then looked back at her. "It is the village of An-chi," he said. "Beyond the canal, on the west."

She waited until he had let three more youths in and had joined them in back. Then she let herself out and darted away.

The gray air was electric. The rain still hung precariously along the edge of the sky. The people in the streets kept looking up at it with a quality of supplication, as if they were tired of outrushing the quirks of the monsoon and wished the rain would fall. There was something else, a breath of violence, like a chemical irritant.

The importance of Cau momentarily receded. If she found him now, he would treat her like a child anyway, laugh at her anxiety or chide her some more about her foolish romanticism. She remembered the conversation they had had about the Consul. For the first time she became completely aware of the impossibility of partial commitment. Only the Lacasses of the world could get away with it. Perhaps this was what Cau had been trying to tell her.

Subconsciously, she told herself, she may have come not so much to seek Cau as his location. It was not something he would readily have disclosed. Her value to him lay here, in the city, but there would be little after the fact he could do about it. By this final barter with her conscience, she would also reaffirm her choice. Had she had to explain to Cau first, it would have been more difficult; whether the doctor was important to him or not, he would, by rejecting her, have prolonged her indecision.

The possibility that the Consul might not be home or that someone might be with him had not even suggested itself. She already had come close enough to see his limousine in the driveway, parked crookedly, indicating he had driven it and got out hurriedly, and might soon be off again. Whatever pause she might have had was dispelled, and she went through the garden and up onto the porch.

When he opened the door, he stared at her.

"Genevieve," he finally said. "You come as unexpectedly as you depart."

"But I am really going," she said. "So I have come to say good-by." The cliché sounded more formidable than she had meant it, and she saw him smile.

"It is not really so dramatic," she said, laughing with him. "Only that I am going to Paris."

She had sunk into the couch and he sat in the chair across from her. "Paris," he repeated. "What for?"

"My father is ill," she replied, vaguely surprised at herself. "I do not think it is serious, but he sent me an Air France ticket."

"Round trip?"

Genevieve laughed again. "No," she said. "Westward only."

"Do you think you will come back?"

She hesitated only a moment. "Yes, I will come back," she said.

"The retired civil servant," Adam said. "Your father arranges things with alacrity and dispatch." He waited, and added: "I hope the sight of you will improve him."

Genevieve nodded. "Thank you," she said. Quite formally, she asked: "And you? You will remain here?"

Adam looked quizzically at her. "Why not? I should think so."

"But the Americans come and go without notice."

He laughed, forcedly, and unfolded his arms. "How about a *bon voyage* drink?"

The small pitcher of gin and bitters, cool and pink, was mixed and set on the low table, and after he had filled their glasses he leaned forward to touch hers with his. "For a long road!" he said.

It seemed to Genevieve that she had met him in another year, in another place, and that they were politely catching up with what each of them had done in the interval. The thought that she had only lately lain in his arms seemed unlikely, but she felt an almost anachronistic tenderness.

As if he might have read her mind, he asked: "Why did you run off again?"

She shrugged and turned her head away. "I do not like to be alone in the home of a busy man," she said.

"I'm sorry about the doctor," he replied. "It was a matter of urgency."

The silence that followed seemed muted by their separate, nearly spoken thoughts. Genevieve came closer than she had believed possible to putting herself in a man's position. The American girl faded away. The blind totality of unfulfillment, desire and recoil, burgeoned into a shared sadness.

"You're a runaway child," he said. "It's something way inside."

She would not mention the girl. Instead, she said: "The doctor is another reason for my coming."

He looked at her with puzzlement. "The doctor?" he repeated. "Why should the doctor concern you?"

"Tell him," she replied, almost whispering, "to go home. At once."

"What do you mean?" Adam asked.

"You must not show astonishment," she said. "After all, you have suspected. Here is your proof."

Adam said nothing. He stood in the center of the floor, holding his empty glass. Then he walked part of the way to the window and looked out at the garden. With his back turned, he inquired: "Why have you come to tell me this?"

She took a long breath. "He is a good man. One can see that."

"Aren't you taking matters into your own hands?"

He walked slowly back and sat alongside her.

"Or did someone tell you to come?"

She glanced angrily at him. "There is nothing more. Only what I have told you. It is important that you do it."

Adam's gaze was fixed ahead and he was frowning. Genevieve kept her own eyes on the open window in front and on the top of the tree beyond it, across the street. It was extraordinarily still, a kind of cosmic quiet that held all things locked. The sound she heard first was the beating of her heart, another awakening of flesh. When he reached for her hand, she withdrew it, but then allowed her fingers to stretch back. They touched and intertwined with his, fleetingly, and then again she removed them. It was the closest she would allow herself to a farewell.

"He is already going," Adam said softly. "It's against his wishes, but he will go."

Now he looked at her. "What will Monsieur Remy say? Whom will he blame?" There was a mild taunt in his voice.

"It does not matter," she said.

"Of course, one can be arrested anywhere," Adam went on. "All policemen here are ubiquitous."

They fell silent again. Genevieve was ready to go, yet she was overwhelmed by lethargy. It would be an effort to get up, to speak again, to say good-by. . . .

Outside, thirty yards from the house, Tran increased his step. Behind him, on the opposite side, the black-suit coolie had reappeared and had come to a stop alongside a broad tree-trunk. He saw the jeep shoot by and knew what it was, instinctively, even before he noted the blurred temporary license-plate. There was nothing he could do any longer, so he simply stepped forward and waited. It was only a matter of seconds. As the doctor opened the gate, the shots sounded with a peculiar dullness that was nearly wooden and that scarcely carried, and his figure seemed to leap and then drop down into the Consul's garden. The jeep was sputtering far down the block as the Consul and the girl rushed from the house. The coolie watched them bend over the body, and then the Consul went back inside. He came out holding a white sheet, but the girl had already vanished. The coolie had seen her run and had only waited a moment longer before he padded swiftly away in the opposite direction.

At a booth in the next block he telephoned the inspector and then M. Remy. M. Remy said nothing when he was told what had happened, which the coolie thought odd, and all he finally did say, after being told about the Eurasian girl, was: "That will be all, then. You may go now." Whereupon he hung up.

When the coolie came out of the booth, the first few drops of rain were at last falling. He stood for a moment, with his face to the sky, and then started to walk slowly back toward the Consul's house. A sense of frustration came over him and he felt a little foolish and lonely. He went no further than the same tree he had stood behind before. The doctor's body had been moved from in front of the gate onto the garden grass. Only half a dozen persons stood on the sidewalk looking at it. The stillness seemed scarcely to have been disturbed. The Consul was standing on the porch of the house, and the coolie noticed that, for some reason, he had put his jacket on. Presently the police wagon arrived to pick up the dead man, and the coolie waited until this was accomplished. A police officer had gone up to the porch and had questioned the Consul, shaking his head as he wrote in his pad. When the police had driven away, the Consul went into the house again. The rain was falling more heavily, and the coolie felt his blouse beginning to cling to his skin. He walked off rapidly, thinking he might as well go home and get some sleep now.

4

GENEVIEVE felt herself crying as she ran, and the drops of rain were as warm as her tears. When she reached her house she was surprised to discover that it was only one o'clock. With a sense of deliberate avoidance of herself, she dried her hair and carefully pinned it up. The operation took fifteen minutes. Then she reheated the tea that had been on the stove since morning and drank several cups of it. The doctor's image still hovered in front of her, like a supine figure in a Gauguin painting. He had been smiling the smile of a man caught dreaming.

All that she remembered the Consul saying was: "He's already dead." The Consul would not come searching for her again, nor could her escaping have any longer astonished him. But he would think of what she had told him.

She had done Cau's bidding after all. But it had been nothing she had expected. There had been no further lunches arranged, no rendezvous of any sort. His pretended indifference when she had spoken of the doctor had made it seem humdrum, and herself feel foolish. Or had he known from the start that this was the way it would happen, the way she might prove herself? She thought of all the long months of nocturnal visits, the slow process of persuasion and dependence. How guardedly he had come to her; how she had gone to him, ultimately, out of petulance and pique. Pierre and the Consul were both accessories to her guilt; but finally there had only been herself. She remembered what Cau had said about the "lost ones" alone, and she thought of the odd look on the Consul's face when the shots had sounded, as if, before the sound had died, he had known who was being murdered. Perhaps, in time, he would know more. But never all of it.

And Remy . . .

The teacup froze in her hands.

The conversation she had had with him on the hotel veranda catapulted through her mind. He had spoken of the Consul in such specific terms. Down to the last bit of bizarre timing, it could have been his way, too. He might have arranged it himself, or through the Binh Xuyen.

The Consul's garden became a burial ground. . . .

She jumped up and paced the room. The spontaneous falsehood she had told, about going to Paris, became something she wished were suddenly true, which a day ago, even a few moments ago, could not have been imaginable. It was too late for that, as for other things. Yet she could think of it, and it would do her good to think of it, so that in the monasticism of the villages it would bolster her. Even retrospectively, another alternative to her old inertia might be worth cherishing.

The rain had begun to fall monotonously. She had to get ready. The idea startled her. She had not considered mechanics. What did one take with one? The proposition of going upstairs to select clothes was ludicrous. The Consul's phrase, "a runaway child," came back to her. What was *comme il faut* for a runaway?

With an odd sense of embarrassment, she went into the bedroom and began opening the drawers in her bureau. What of the rest of it? Was it simply to stay here, indefinitely, as the monthly checks gathered, until Pierre's father delegated someone to dissolve it all in the manner of a deceased's estate? One by one she took the drawers and placed them on the unmade bed. She stood contemplating the whole of it, and it gave her a strange spur of courage because it all seemed, at that moment, worth surrendering. Then quickly she reached out and underneath the mass of clothing, the skirts and odd blouses that were neatly piled in the drawer on the far side, found and felt what she knew she had to find, the single, ridiculous memento of Pierre Brouillard she had kept, simply because he had forgotten it, a Luger revolver. . . .

The two jeeps had sputtered from the courtyard in perfect unison, the twin puffs of exhaust floating thinly away into the wet air. Each of the two Vietnamese drivers had his gun slung over his shoulder, and the other pair of Vietnamese and the two French sergeants, divided evenly, sat on the ledges inside with the seats below vacant. Down rue Catinat they roared, and hardly anyone seemed to notice. It was a common enough sight. At the corner below the square the two cars swerved and raced across the city, keeping the same distance apart, like a pair of well-trained hunters. When they reached rue Colombier, they slowed down, the sergeant in the forward jeep putting his hand out like a semaphore to the one behind. As they arrived in front of the house, the first thing they noticed was that everything was open—the windows, the door, and the garden gate. Together, as if this too had been rehearsed, the two Vietnamese soldiers ran up the pathway, and the sergeants walked slowly after them.

"She lives well," the first sergeant said. "I wouldn't mind such a house."

The second sergeant nodded. "A good place to keep a mistress," he said. "Far enough from the center of things."

They stepped onto the porch to take themselves and their guns out of the interminable rain while they waited. . . .

Chapter XXIV

THE terror in the twin cities lasted two days and two nights. The number of individual assassinations mounted to twelve, while indiscriminate grenadings killed fifty persons in public places and wounded many more. On the third day the activity abruptly ended. The Vietminh had proved its point. At the expense of some fresh antagonism, it had made itself reckoned with as never before in the south, and a vast, conglomerate suspicion spread like a poison gas, so that each man eyed his neighbor more carefully, and spoke less. In the markets one could sense this best, in the whispering, re-emergent clusters that broke apart quickly at the sight of a uniform or the sound of an onrushing car.

The dampness lay heavily in the newly plastered rooms and corridors of the Legation. On the afternoon of the third day Adam was summoned by the Minister, who had so far requested only a brief account of the assassination in the garden. When Nell Finch came to fetch him, Adam was finishing a summary of the disturbances for transmission to the Department. He brought the report with him into Smythe's office.

The Minister did not look up from his desk until after Adam was seated, and when he did he glanced away and swung himself around toward the window. He waited a moment more, and then he said: "I might as well tell you first. You've been recalled to Washington."

Adam heard the announcement, in Smythe's thin monotone, repeating itself in his ears. He said nothing for a full minute, during which the Minister did not move. Then he asked: "Under what circumstances?"

"My recommendation," Smythe said.

"Only yours?" Adam asked.

Smythe turned the chair around and their eyes met. "I didn't say anything about it before," he replied, "but the French broached it informally some time back. I didn't report it, on my own responsibility, until three days ago, after I received a call from the High Commissioner. The confirmation arrived this morning."

"Was there anything else that prompted it?" Adam persisted.

Smythe cleared his throat. He seemed perturbed by what he was about to say. "The French news agency and some of the Paris papers filed considerable copy on the assassination. The doctor is described as a probable Vietminh spy masquerading as a renegade and seeking to befriend certain Americans into a trap."

"That's ridiculous," Adam said.

"I wouldn't know," Smythe said. "I suppose I can take your word for it. Naturally, the stories were reprinted in the states."

"And a senator or two, or three or four, have commented," Adam added.

Symthe said: "Yes."

'They'll want me to explain what the hell is going on over here?"

"That's possible," the Minister said.

"I'll be asked to account for myself, and even after I convince enough people that Tran Phan Dang was no more a Communist than I am, or you are, the question will remain of propriety, of why I should have taken any chances and seen him at all?"

"You're jumping to conclusions," the Minister said.

"No," Adam said. "I'm not. There's no point to either of us being naïve."

"I'm sorry," Smythe said. "There was nothing any longer I could do about it. My own feeling that you've been here long enough didn't enter into it. I certainly would have picked a quieter time."

"Who do the French think killed him, according to their theory?" Adam asked.

"Local terrorists who were either unaware of his mission and function, or who mistrusted him," Smythe replied.

"That's even more preposterous," Adam said. "Do you for a moment believe it?"

"It's simply their projection. I've heard you say yourself that anything here is possible. The accounts given in Paris included details of his being questioned, and then followed in the city over several days, to your house and elsewhere. Apparently there's something about a conversation overheard on the docks between himself and some Vietminh boatmen."

Adam lit a cigarette. The Minister tilted the chair back to one side.

"Have you thought of the possibility that the French themselves might have arranged it?"

"That suggested itself to me," Smythe said evenly, with a hand across his mouth. "It's a little overelaborate, isn't it?"

"But the other isn't?"

"The other remains a theory," the Minister said. "Assuming the Communists did kill the doctor, because he was a traitor to them, what possible purpose would the French have in fostering a fabrication? They'd be satisfied enough to settle for murder, outright."

"On the other hand," Adam said, "suppose the French really believe Tran Phan Dang was what they say he was. What could be more logical than killing him, or having him killed, or for that matter letting him be killed on someone else's schedule, if they had got wind of it, and then blaming anyone they liked for it, or anything specifically—a party feud, simple anarchy, a mistake?" He hesitated, and then, speaking more deliberately, asked: "Did you know that Madame Brouillard was at my house when the shots were fired? She came to tell me that the doctor's life was in danger."

"Why should she have done that?" Smythe asked. He seemed genuinely surprised.

✧◇✧

Adam nodded. "I asked myself the same question. I suspected a trap on Remy's part, an effort to make me culpable, let's say, for another flight of the doctor. In Remy's image. But then I decided she meant it. My guess is she somehow found out what might happen and was suddenly dismayed."

"On a personal level?" Smythe smiled.

"To a degree," Adam said. "But only to a degree. I hadn't expected to see her again. She also came to tell me she was leaving. I didn't wholly believe that."

The Minister began to say something, stopped, and then started once more. "Remy informed me she had been seen at your place, and that she ran off after the shooting. Apparently she was also being watched, in line with what I warned you about."

"What she said to me would seem to indicate some sort of attachment to the Sûreté, though, wouldn't it? No matter what else she may have got herself involved in, or how she had come by her information. First-hand or second-hand."

"Even so," the Minister said, "she was already about to be arrested."

"Remy was undoubtedly suspicious of her relationship with me, even though I'm sure it was his own idea. There had developed quite a contest between us, her and myself, and him and myself. Furthermore, if she was not what Remy now claims, I think it would have been necessary, under the circumstances, for Remy to have invented her."

"Nothing was known about her warning to you," Smythe replied tersely. "The one has nothing to do with the other. She was being apprehended on suspicion of espionage."

Adam blew smoke out thickly. "Do you believe they've found her?"

The Minister shrugged. "I don't know. Remy implies it. What do you think?"

Adam let a moment go by. It was something he preferred not to conjecture about, even though he had asked the question. Whether it had happened already or would soon be happening, the seed of destruction had long since been sown.

"I think he may have," he said at length. "In any event, he'll move heaven and earth to get her. If she's with the Vietminh, she won't last either. I'm not sure which is worse."

"It's the penalty of confusion," the Minister said. "What makes you think she wouldn't last?"

"She should have left long ago," Adam said. "For somewhere else—Paris, anywhere. Her mixture is outdated, an exotic hangover of a happier colonial time. Take it as a symbol, if you will, of retrogression. Even if there was no excuse for her, someone should have pitied her sooner."

The Minister smiled. "Yourself perhaps?"

Adam no longer minded. He smiled back at Smythe. "I imagine it was Monsieur Remy who made the representations against me you spoke of?"

"Not just in his own behalf," the Minister said.

"He did it well," Adam said softly. "That much, anyway. Heads I win, tails you lose."

"You're exaggerating," Smythe said. "That's where the over-elaboration begins. Logically, of course, you'd grant a desire on the part of the Communists to kill the doctor, assuming the French theory is only a theory, and that he was a bona fide renegade?"

"Of course I would, and I do," Adam answered. "It's just that one good theory deserves another. Certain sad truths also remain. Tran Phan Dang represented everything not only the Communists but the French opposed. It isn't the first time that's happened, here or elsewhere, and it'll go on happening. If you think I've dramatized it, even in point of my own safety, I'll say we're still the common enemy—the doctor and myself. In the eyes of Paul Remy, I represent as much of a threat in one sense as the Vietminh does in another, and it's not strange that the Communists should feel the same way. The doctor and I are partners in crime, if you will. The fact that we'll never prove who did the actual killing isn't unusual. But there isn't much doubt about me, is there?"

Smythe was drumming his fingers on the desk-top. "I'll do what I can—" he began.

"Don't you consider it odd that, under any circumstances, the murder should have conveniently taken place where it did?"

The Minister looked up. "Conveniently?" he repeated. "It simply shows once more, and finally, that you had no right to let him come there in the first place."

"You're agreeing prematurely with the senators," Adam said. "The era of no risk. See no evil, speak no evil, hear no evil."

"Perhaps," Smythe answered. "But only as a matter of wisdom and—"

"And not of loyalty, is that it?"

The Minister paused. "Yes, that's it," he said. "And not of loyalty."

"Suppose it does go further," Adam suggested. "Suppose you're called upon to testify, to give your professional opinion. What are you going to say?"

"You're jumping the gun again," Smythe said. "I hadn't even thought of it."

"But you would have to say that you admonished me about seeing such individuals as Dr. Tran Phan Dang, privately?"

Once more the Minister waited. "I suppose I'd have to," he said. "But it would be a matter of context."

"Whose?"

"What do you mean whose?"

"Yours—ours, or the senators'?"

"Look," Smythe said, "really, you get much too far ahead of yourself. You've been recalled. Just that, and no more."

"To the accompaniment of French trumpets."

"You've enough conviction, enough rectitude, to take care of that."

Adam laughed. "Thanks for the compliment," he said. "I hope you're right." He stood up. "When do I go?" he asked.

"Forthwith," Smythe said.

"Forthwith then," Adam said. "I'll start getting ready right now."

He went toward the door and then remembered the report he still held in his hands. Turning, he came back to the desk.

"Here's the defendant's case," he said. "The first brief, with citations."

The Minister glanced down at the summary. "Oh, good," he said. "I want to get that off immediately."

Adam stared at the balding top of Smythe's head as the Minister glanced over the first page. Then he swung around, and as he walked to the door for the second time, he heard Smythe saying: "I can see you've done your usual excellent job."

Without going back to his own office, Adam went down the long corridor. He walked downstairs and out of the building, and turned left along the canal. In a few minutes he had reached its confluence with the river, and he stepped across the street to the outdoor café that looked out over the whole expanse of water and sky, boats and ships, and indefinite land beyond. Here everything came together in a kind of permanent but ordered chaos, as if this might be a place where the war could best be understood; or, if not the war itself, then the lack of peace that preceded and would come after it.

He asked for a glass of local beer and sipped it slowly, staring. It was the first time he could recall feeling actually numb. It was a numbness that was not deadness, but simply the refusal of his thoughts to join together; of sentences, the pieces of which drifted through his mind, to collect themselves into proper appraisals.

A group of sampans came floating past and hugged the inner pierline. Adam watched the men in them, already shouting to those on shore, and he felt the impossible thrust of tears. What was it about these people, the time and place, the smells and sounds—an odd quintessence of something tragic and magnificent that was almost, but never quite, expressable—that fascinated and perplexed one, and that made a man care more than he had ever cared before?

Adam did not know: except that part of it was that he himself had grown older here; that, retrospectively, he could count the months in years, and the years in some other abstract unit of both memory and time, one that he could only identify, now and finally, by watching the sampans nuzzle the shore, and the small boy selling peanuts, to whom he had scarcely but knowingly nodded, smile up at the white man's sadness. . . .

2

REMY twisted on the cot in his office. This weather made him feel worse, sinking into his bones the way it sank into the old stucco of the political-section annex. The room was full of dampness and the smell of dampness, wet walls, and wet clothes. He finally wished he were done with it.

He turned on his back, his hands folded behind his head, and managed, nevertheless, to smile. The Communists' terror had been less extensive than he had anticipated. He had been prepared for it, at least, and damage to French property had been slight. The next task would be to take the fullest possible advantage of the public disillusion over the Vietminh tactics. The *attentistes* were the ones, above all, to be re-evaluated.

The success in the affair with the Consul was a further satisfaction. The High Commissioner had informed him this morning that M. Patch would shortly be leaving. Nothing specific had been added, but the expression on the High Commissioner's face had afforded M. Remy all the reward he had either expected or needed. It had been worthy of note that he had not been asked to explain the peculiar circumstances surrounding the assassination in the Consul's garden. Obviously the High Commissioner preferred to be uninformed. Remy was now thankful it had happened as it did.

The Consul's imminent departure, in another sense, an entirely personal one, was partly responsible for his malaise, Remy admitted. He had grown strangely fond of him. In point of fact, of course, he was worth a dozen of the others, from the Minister down through the callow men now coming out in a tourist stream. That had nothing to do with it, but one could still regret the elimination of a proper adversary. Remy was a little astonished at himself for the admission, for his *pour le sport* attitude. "I am getting old," he told himself. "I'm ready, at that, for the pastures of Paris."

He sat up and put his shoes on, noting with distaste the color and odor of his socks. It was almost five o'clock. The rain had slackened. Some unencumbered air would do him good, he thought, away from this plaster incubation. He went along the annex porch and down the narrow stairs at the far end, which constituted a back entrance, and headed for the waterfront. The rain had washed the leaves off the trees and they clotted the dark gutters. Here and there he spied the empty core of a grenade. The fronts of three cafés he passed were shattered and bolted.

The docks were idle. Two destroyers lay side by side, and an empty transport was anchored in the river beyond them. Fewer sampans than usual were clustered together, and except for a dozen or so men and women moving listlessly along them there was no activity anywhere. The flags on the ships hung like wet rags in the windless atmosphere. Remy was depressed by the scene, and he turned back toward the hotel doorway. He needed something warm to drink, a cup of chocolate.

As he entered, he saw Lacasse lumbering down the circular stairway. The Corsican looked as if he had been asleep with his clothes on. His heavy-lidded eyes were cast down so that he didn't see across the new marble lobby until he had reached the bottom step. The usual broad smile thereupon creased his mouth.

"Monsieur Remy!" he cried, and he shook his visitor's hand with an unexpectedly strong grip. "I thought perhaps you were being held as a hostage."

Remy did not appreciate the joke, but offered his yellow smile. "It wasn't as bad as all that, Jacques," he said. "I'm surprised they didn't go after your beautiful new hotel."

"You might not believe it," Lacasse said, "but I formed my private army. We established a twenty-four-hour guard."

"Splendid," Remy said. "We should turn the protection of the city over to you and your room-boys. Are you sure they're all on one side?"

Lacasse snorted. "I have my own Sûreté too, you see."

He took Remy up to the almost completed restaurant and went to the kitchen himself to see that the pot of chocolate was properly prepared. When he brought it out, he poured two cups.

"Well, then," he said, when they were both seated, "do you think it's all over?"

"For the time being," Remy replied. "It can begin again any time; tonight, tomorrow, at the next full moon."

Lacasse became thoughtful and a frown passed across his face. "Perhaps I should not have mentioned what I did about Madame Brouillard. I understand she has—disappeared."

Remy took another sip from his cup. The sweet, creamy warmth felt wonderfully soothing inside his chilled body. "I am obliged for your warning," he said.

Lacasse shook his head, to himself. "Will she be executed?"

There was a considerable pause. "Eventually," Remy said.

Lacasse repeated his gesture. "What I told you might have been—premature," he began. "Perhaps I should have waited."

"But why?" Remy feigned surprise. He enjoyed seeing the Corsican flustered. "It was a matter of duty, naturally."

"Even so—well, she was—" He searched for new words.

"A woman, yes. In that sense, it was unfortunate. And an attractive one, with considerable charm. A little too uncertain for the climate. At any rate, Jacques, there will be others."

Lacasse reddened and began to cough, averting Remy's gaze.

"I haven't asked you how you reached your suspicion," Remy said blandly. "Whether it was osmosis or a divining-rod."

For once Lacasse was ready. "I have my sources, as you know," he said. "It would not be wise to mention them too soon."

"Never mind, then," Remy said. "I can understand. A man such as yourself occupies an unusual, even a difficult, situation. In a way, too, you are a private army, like the other sects."

"I?" Lacasse now pretended to be astonished.

"The Corsicans," Remy said. "All of you. You have a way of enduring, at an everlasting rate of profit, and you have your private sources of strength. You're all blessed with prescience." He saw Lacasse swallowing his anger and stood up and put a hand on the manager's back. "Never mind, Jacques," he said. "It's only the weather that corrupts my temper. You will come have dinner with me one of these nights, yes? The chocolate was splendid."

He slapped the broad, pudgy back once more and was off down the steps before Lacasse could even ponder a reply.

He went briskly along rue Catinat toward police headquarters. The avenue was still half-deserted, though a few of the cafés had gingerly slid their iron gates a quarter way and relit some of their lights. The air presaged more rain. The *cyclo* boys sat impassively along the curbs. A squad of Vietnamese soldiers marched across the square up ahead and the rest of the street was so quiet that the click of their heels sounded down to the docks.

In front of the Hotel Continental, Remy came to a stop. Most of the shutters in the rooms were closed. Only a few figures, hallboys and sweepers, stirred in the lobby. Outside, on the veranda and in the dining-room beyond, there was a pretense of activity, protected by four military policemen on the sidewalk. At one of the tables on the outer rail of the bar, Remy was surprised to see M. Goodenough. The young American sat alone in a wicker chair with a drink set in front of him.

Remy made it a point to pass directly by and, smiling across the balustrade, commented: "We can relax again, eh?"

"I suppose you'd call it that," Goodenough replied.

"You're wise to compromise with the hotel instead of a café," Remy said. "The difference, perhaps, between a regimental and a company command post."

Goodenough laughed mirthlessly. "It's quite safe, I think. Would you join me for an *apéritif?*"

Remy declined. "I have an appointment, thank you. Perhaps I'll come back. We'll have a talk."

He smiled again and was off, loping down the block. Goodenough followed the Frenchman's figure until it passed the last of the sidewalk tables. The evening chill bore in from the ocean and brought on a shiver. He didn't suppose that Remy would return, but he admitted the need for another drink. In fact, he realized, he was now likely to have several.

3

THE night dropped quickly over grayness. The rain held off again, but the air grew cold. Cau Minh Thien was sick of the city. He had stopped at enough teahouses between Cholon and Saigon to get a thorough idea of what the populace was saying, and what he heard was encouraging. There was some growling and even some open denunciation of the Vietminh, but he sensed a general attitude of satisfaction over the French tail having been newly twisted. Now he was anxious to leave.

When it was dark, he went to the tobacconist's shop. The old man seemed startled as he opened the door. Cau chided him. "Do you think it's the police?" he asked. "You know they would not come this far so fast."

"On the other hand, I did not think you would return so soon," the tobacconist grumbled. He was smoking a pipe and in the rear he had a small charcoal stove burning.

"You are having your supper, I can see," Cau said.

"A little soup and some rice. I can offer you some."

"A bowl perhaps," Cau agreed. "Thank you. It is uncomfortable tonight."

The old man fetched a second bowl from the top shelf and poured them each a portion from the steaming pot on the stove-top. Then he rummaged around underneath and came up with another pair of chopsticks.

"It went well, without a mishap, then?" Cau asked.

The tobacconist nodded as he pushed rice into his mouth and drank some of the soup.

"How many were there?"

"Fourteen."

"That was the number I gave you?"

"Yes."

Not until he had finished and set the bowl down did Cau ask any further questions. Then, wiping his mouth with the back of a hand, he said: "Was there anyone else who came the first day?"

"She came," the old man said. He was still eating.

"When?"

"Early. It would have been shortly before noon."

"What did she want?"

"It was important that she find you, she said."

"And you told her that was impossible?"

"She was very anxious. Her nervousness provoked mine. I did not want her to remain, with the others coming and going. In order to have her leave, I gave her the name of the village."

Cau's eyes bolted from the counter-top and he regarded the old man sharply. "You did that?" he repeated. "That was in error." His voice was no longer conversational.

"I am sorry," the old man apologized. "I realized it afterward myself, but it was important that she not stay."

Cau was already considering the consequences. As soon as he went back tonight, they would have to move.

"Did you think she really intended to come to An-chi?" he asked at length.

The tobacconist reflected a moment. "I think she intended that," he said, "although I indicated you would not be there."

Cau stroked his face. "She will not be welcome," he said. "It will be a mistake if she comes."

"It was a mistake to begin with," the tobacconist said.

"What was a mistake?"

"To have her come here. To deal with her at all."

"That's none of your affair," Cau snapped.

Cau continued to drink his soup in silence. It was a good thing, at any rate, that he had not gone to her house during the period of action. He had thought of it, the second night. Why had she so anxiously sought him? There were two possibilities—the Sûreté and the Consul. Either one would make her an unsafe companion. Nor were there many like Genevieve in the villages. He sighed as he put his bowl down. What entered his mind was not pleasant.

"I am thankful the attacks are over," the old man was saying.

"You can sell your tobacco in peace," Cau said, more gently. He reached up to a shelf for a pack of cigarettes and some matches. Dropping them in his pocket, he stood and stretched.

"I will let you know the name of the new village," he said. "It will be a few days before I come back."

The tobacconist unbolted the door and Cau saw that it was raining again. There was no point to remaining here. The others by now would all be back in the various villages, and it was more important to have his own location moved.

He arrived quickly at the side of the city and crossed the swollen canal by the bridge that seemed on the verge of being washed out. The night was blacker than he ever remembered having to walk through it along the crisscrossing paths of the paddies that would bring him eventually to a point near his own hut. It was four miles in all, but in spite of the rain he did not try to hurry. The matter of Genevieve weighed more heavily upon him. The political officer had left his legacy. Had it not been for his threat, and notwithstanding the experience in the teashop across from the Chinese hotel, Cau would have preferred to wait. On the other hand, there had been the unique opportunity of the Consul's garden. . . .

Chapter XXV

L I KWAN-SEN emerged from his office and gazed through the moted smoke that hung over the casino floor. Considering the fact that the disturbances had ended only forty-eight hours ago, the attendance was more than satisfactory. He had kept the place closed an extra day, despite the private assurances he had received, and what the Binh Xuyen had also told him—that there would be an end to it. If he had opened at once, no one would have come anyway, but tonight the hall was more than half-filled. He looked for the Americans and saw a pair of them, the two Economic men, the tall one and the short one, playing roulette at their customary station. There was no sign of the Consul. Undoubtedly, Li thought, with a tired smile, the Consul had chosen a woman instead of a wheel to help celebrate the restoration of peace.

The "terror" had amused Li Kwan-sen. There was something ridiculously ritualistic, on a minor scale, about boys on bicycles tossing grenades and shooting guns from careening autos. In a superficial sense, it was rather like an American Wild West show, a way of letting off steam. Not that it lacked purpose in frightening the French, and, to a lesser extent, the native population. But when one compared it with the larger manifestations of popular rebellion, with whole warlord armies, for example, splendidly battling each other across entire provinces, breaching village gates and walls and pillaging with a kind of barbaric éclat, then this sort of eruption, in spite of all the fuss, was laughable. Still, Li was prepared to admit that it was a necessary demonstration of intent. Whenever the French in Saigon felt too secure, they had to be jolted back to reality. It was only a matter of time. Half of the north was gone, and now the delta lay ready to be plucked from the vine. The rest would soon wither away.

Li turned back into the office and closed the door. The sight of even that many people annoyed him. He lit a fresh stick of incense and carefully set it on the windowsill. Then he reclined in his soft chair and shut his eyes. The prospect of a visit to Kowloon and Hong Kong was beginning to intrigue him more than he had expected. He had not been there for two years. It was a place that invariably refreshed him, perhaps because of the sharp contrasts: deep free water and peaks; cleanliness and filth; wealth and poverty. It was the kind of place one ought to conspire in, preferably in one of the old English houses on the hills. He would be there a week, according to what he had been told. A possibility existed of going on to Canton, which he hoped to avoid.

There was a rap on the door. He recognized it immediately. This evening, along with the others, the Corsican was bound to emerge. "Come in," he said, and, grinning slyly, a little guiltily, as if he had run away and was penitently returning home, Lacasse bulked into the room.

"You have come out of your nest, up on the roof, ha?" Li said. "This will be the last battle when it is safer to be high than low."

"Good evening," Lacasse said. "You are intact, I see."

"Only in part," Li replied. "My tables have been paralyzed."

"They show a quick recovery," Lacasse said.

He plumped heavily into the second easy chair and tucked his chin in. "It wasn't so bad after all," he went on. "Not as bad as I had anticipated."

Li looked over, bemusedly. "You anticipated?" he repeated. "How and what did you anticipate, Jacques?"

Lacasse flushed. "It was generally expected, of course," he said. "There were the usual warnings. I had my own protection established at the hotel."

"There will be time for the hotel later," Li said. "Furthermore, it is not yet finished."

"Almost," Lacasse said. "It will be a pity if it is destroyed so soon."

Li laughed. "Hotels have a way of enduring, even when injured, ha? They are always useful."

"Like gambling casinos," Lacasse suggested.

"On the contrary," Li said. "They will all be closed."

"It will make a good auditorium," Lacasse said. "This one."

Li was smiling the Puckish smile Lacasse had long ago recognized as preceding a barb. "You and your associates will be reduced to janitors," he said.

"I will depend on you again for rescue," Lacasse countered.

◇◇

"A little suffering first will do you good, ha? Some forced labor."

Both men became suddenly, a little awkwardly, silent. Li felt the incense drift penetrate his nostrils. It gave him a slightly heady sensation, time-spanning, space-destroying. He had gone further with Lacasse, beginning with the matter of the boats, than he had meant to, and now the Corsican was presuming. It was one thing for him to make his transitional arrangements, but Li found the projection, which he himself had perhaps foolishly stimulated, distasteful. At the same time he remained aware of the need for discretion.

"When are you going home, Jacques?" he asked suddenly.

Lacasse looked at him with surprise. "Home?" he echoed. "I had thought of taking a short trip, yes. It would depend, of course, on the military situation. But it would be only a visit, in any event."

Li confronted him without a trace of expression. After a purposeful pause he said: "You should make some preparations, ha. You have spread yourself thin, with your clubs and your hotel and your coteries of boatmen."

It was enough. Lacasse was taken aback. He offered no reply, but sat flexing his fingers, and then the incense mercifully allowed him to sneeze. He brought out a handkerchief and blew his nose. Li waited, shifting a few papers on his desk. Finally Lacasse rose. He had prepared his answer.

"I suppose I must liquidate or be liquidated," he said, managing to laugh. "But there is still some time."

Li kept his face lowered. He may have spoken too soon; as with the hotel itself, there would be opportunity enough. The Corsican was like a swollen mosquito. Out of fright alone, he would guard his tongue. Yet it had been worth while to see him chastened; even if he went on imagining that this would remain the best of all possible worlds.

2

ALL morning, and part of the afternoon, the plane had flown through rain, swaying across the immaculate-appearing jungle. There had been a storm over Burma, with a rolling of thunder and lightning jagging across the black tropic sky. Then the great ship had plummeted and lifted again, its four engines straining for balance and thrust, the propellers' pale spin clearer in the whirl and catapult of wind and water. Once more Adam had wondered, watching the warping of the wings, how any of it was possible, non-breakage and flight, man's courage and gall. It was then he had begun the conversation with the Vietnamese in the white linen suit next to him. Earlier they had exchanged the conventional remarks of departure and arrival; in Bangkok they had smoked a cigarette together, and again in Rangoon, speaking of schedules and the weather and the characteristics of the tea the Burmese girl had served up to them under the protective gaze of the French hostess. They met the storm soon after they took off, the captain striving to climb quickly, the motors pulsing; but they had to refasten their belts as they rode into a cloud that was like a roiling sea-cave. The Vietnamese sat stiffly, his head thrown back and his legs thrust out, the way the ailerons extended in the wild wind oppositely. Finally he turned to Adam, the perspiration running on his face, and, smiling bravely, said: "A bad storm."

"We'll soon be out of it," Adam reassured him. "Sometimes you get caught in the middle and can't make any headway at all."

Except for the fact that it was a moment of danger, the Vietnamese might not have responded as openly as he did. Even at that, he could have been speaking to himself as much as to the man alongside. "It is like the war in Vietnam," he remarked, staring straight again.

Adam laughed, a release of his own tension. "You have been involved?" he asked.

"Which of us has not?"

"You are a northerner?"

"Hanoi, yes."

Adam waited a polite moment. "You are a man of politics?" It was a blunt but already a proper question.

The Vietnamese did not answer at once. He smiled, but not as before, and then he said: "I have been concerned with politics, that is true, but I am going to Paris, you see."

The plane broke out of the encompassing cloud into a scudding haze. Below lay the Bay of Bengal. The gray-green water seemed immobile, thin sprigs of white interspersed.

The Vietnamese peered down. "We have survived," he said.

"To all intents and purposes."

"You are an American, of course?"

"Of course."

"A businessman?"

"No, I myself have been somewhat concerned with politics."

The Vietnamese regarded him differently, with a quality of reverence. "You are going to Paris on leave?" he thereupon asked. It was the first thought that had obviously come to him.

"No," Adam said. "I'm going home to Washington."

"For consultation," the Vietnamese suggested.

Adam once more laughed. "I suppose so," he said. "But I don't think I'll be coming back."

His companion considered this. "Do you regret your departure?"

"Yes," Adam said.

The Vietnamese seemed pleased.

"And you?"

The man's brow contracted. "I have my family in Hanoi," he replied. "I do not know if I will be able to bring them to Paris."

"You will be there some time, then?"

"Indefinitely."

Adam was certain, without asking. The one word had confirmed it.

"You are a member of the Dai Viet?" He thought quickly of the long, futile fight that had been made for representation in the Emperor's cabinet.

"I have been affiliated," the Vietnamese said. "However, I consider myself an independent."

"Are you retiring, then, from politics?"

The reply was immediate. "I have no plans but to teach. Later, if there is a fresh opportunity—" He let the sentence complete itself.

"You will miss your country," Adam said. "Even in its time of troubles. Or perhaps especially."

"The principle of exile is ancient," the Vietnamese answered. "Sometimes it is as necessary as it becomes unavoidable. It is better to act first, since it can remain a matter for reflection, and perhaps afterward of philosophy as well."

Adam smiled. The concept was a tested Asian one, with proper overtones of devotion, if not of religion. One went into the wilderness of the West. Ho Chi Minh had done it when he had traveled to Paris in his youth and had found his Marxist *logique*. Even the Emperor, after his brief tenure as Ho's Supreme Councilor at the end of the war, had retired to reflect in Hong Kong and then on the Riviera, though he had shortly turned to pleasure.

"Unhappily, the troubles increase," Adam said.

The Vietnamese nodded. He was silent for a few moments, and then, softly, he said: "If you will forgive my suggesting it, the good intentions of your country, you see, have not been enough."

"No," Adam said. "They haven't been."

"You have ridden two tigers at once. It should have been one or none."

"It would have been wiser," Adam agreed.

"There is no way of compromise with freedom," the Vietnamese continued. "To grant it slowly and to grant it reluctantly are also two different things. Perhaps the French could not help themselves. But you are not affected by guilt or by pride."

"Oh," Adam said, "you are mistaken. We have our share of each."

The Vietnamese seemed genuinely astonished. "In Indo-China you have no source of guilt," he repeated. "You are not to blame for what occurred before."

"It might have been better if we were," Adam said. "Sometimes it's easier to be a repentant sinner than a well-meaning friend."

"Particularly if one is a friend of both the sinner and the sinned against?" the Vietnamese said, rhetorically.

"The two tigers again," Adam replied, laughing. "There is a guilt that derives from too much friendship as well as from too much good fortune."

"One is apt to lose both, although I do not think it will happen with the Americans."

"It's unfortunate," Adam said, "that one cannot be a better leveler. To be tied to one hemisphere by necessity, by blood and by tradition, and to believe at the same time in the other, becomes a source of confusion."

"Perhaps you will have to make a fresh choice?"

"It may be made for us," Adam replied. "The neutrality of procrastination brings on the tyrant. We may save half the world and lose the other. And we'll have lost the better one."

"A gambler cannot look back. . . . You are still gamblers for men's souls. The tyrant captures them."

"I think," Adam said, "that we have ten years left for gambling, you and I. It will be the greatest gamble in the history of man."

"The largest, or the greatest?" the Vietnamese inquired.

"The last one," Adam said, "and therefore both."

The plane had conquered the clouds and now flew in the first blue sky they had seen. Underneath them lay a universe of white, a vast, unending panoply that seemed to stretch as far as the planets could fall. In the cabin the passengers took heart, and the weather within corresponded with what seemed to lie without, a moment in time, separate and inviolate, compounded of energy and hope. Wearied with talking over the motors' drone, Adam and the Vietnamese fell blissfully asleep, and when they awoke, refreshed, the Indian sun was upon them, and the pilot had turned toward the subcontinental shore. The huge plane scarcely quivered as it sank down into the soft limbo of white and at the earth again, and the day of man below.

A NOTE ON THE TYPE

The text of this book was set on the Monotype in JAN-SON, a recutting made direct from the type cast from matrices made by Anton Janson. Whether or not Janson was of Dutch ancestry is not known, but it is known that he purchased a foundry and was a practicing type-founder in Leipzig during the years 1600 to 1687. Janson's first specimen sheet was issued in 1675. His successor issued a specimen sheet showing all of the Janson types in 1689.

His type is an excellent example of the influential and sturdy Dutch types that prevailed in England prior to the development by William Caslon of his own incomparable designs, which he evolved from these Dutch faces. The Dutch in their turn had been influenced by Garamond in France. The general tone of Janson, however, is darker than Garamond and has a sturdiness and substance quite different from its predecessors. It is a highly legible type, and its individual letters have a pleasing variety of design. Its heavy and light strokes make it sharp and clear, and the full-page effect is characterful and harmonious.

This book was composed, printed, and bound by KINGSPORT PRESS, INC., Kingsport, Tennessee. Paper manufactured by P. H. GLATFELTER COMPANY, Spring Grove, Pennsylvania. Typography and binding based on designs by WARREN CHAPPELL.